A Forest for Calum

Frank Macdonald

Cape Breton University Press
Sydney, Nova Scotia

© Frank Macdonald, 2005

Cape Breton University Press recognizes the support of both the Province of Nova Scotia, through the Department of Communities, Culture and Heritage, and the Canada Council for the Arts Block Grants Program for our publishing program. We are pleased to work in partnership with these funding bodies to develop and promote our cultural resources.

NOVA SCOTIA

Canada Council   Conseil des Arts
for the Arts   du Canada

Cover Design: Cathy MacLean Design, Pleasant Bay, NS
Layout: Gail Jones, Sydney, NS
First printed in Canada under isbn 978-1-897009-05-5

Library and Archives Canada Cataloguing in Publication

Macdonald, Frank, 1945-
    A forest for Calum / Frank Macdonald. -- New ed.

Originally publ.: 2005.
ISBN 978-1-897009-63-5

    I. Title.

PS8575.D6305F67 2011   C813'.54   C2011-901570-6

Cape Breton University Press
PO Box 5300
Sydney, Nova Scotia
Canada B1P 6L2   www.cbupress.ca

For

Jack D. Macdonald
1881-1963

Wesley Ferguson
1946-1982

1

T hey're in!"
Word of the smelt run, like news of death, was everywhere at once. It was Duncan MacFarlane who brought word to me, galloping up Culloden Street, one hand slapping his rear end, trying to coax more speed from his imaginary steed. In his other hand he waved a fishing rod.

"They're in!"

We were in the sun porch, me sitting on the old car seat that had been fashioned into a bench, Calum asleep on the couch, hands folded coffin-like across his chest, the glasses still on him. So was the salt-and-pepper cap, covering a cloud of white hair. He was wearing his usual uniform: bib overalls and wine coat-sweater, shoes a splattered palette of workshop paints. I shook his foot and my grandfather's lids raised slow as a movie curtain.

"They're in!" I shouted loud enough to leap the hurdle of his turned-off hearing aid. He nodded as the lids slid down again, and I shot from the sun porch toward Calum's workshop. When I came out carrying my own rod, Duncan was turning circles on the street in front of the house, trying to control his energetic mount. Then he charged away, taking a head start. I leapt the gate and chased after him, knowing he didn't stand a chance because this was one thing I could do better than Duncan every time out. Soon we were running neck and neck for the river.

Every spring, men with nothing to do, and there were plenty of those since the last coal mine closed, walked along the banks of the Big River, smoking, daydreaming, watching. Some afternoon in early June one of them, lost in whatever world his imagination was wandering, would grow gradually conscious of a shadow gliding across the surface of the river, then a second, a third. Checking the clear sky for clouds, his gaze would plunge back to the river as he crouched on the bank, his attention riveted on the water. They were not cloud shadows sweeping across the river's surface, he would realize, but schools of smelts gliding under it, one school following another, swimming against the clear cold current of newly melted snow flowing down from the highlands.

He would squat there breathless, suspending the moment, holding onto it for as long as he dared, risking with each passing second the chance that someone else would claim the discovery. Then he would rise and run along the shortest path through the woods toward town, his steps hurried by the burst of words aching in his throat. Through the evergreens and the hardwoods onto the blueberry barrens he would run until there was somebody, anybody, to whom he could yell,

"They're in!"

It was like hollering into a ditch pipe. The words just kept repeating themselves, house to house, yard to yard, street to street, until everyone in town knew.

By the time Duncan and I reached the barrens, more than a dozen men and boys were already running across it with rods and baskets and burlap bags, laughing and calling to each other. I pulled ahead of Duncan then, racing over the low bushes until we joined the river of people pouring down the narrow path through the woods, one behind the other, panting, pushing, until the forest opened onto a clearing.

In the field across the river stood the town's power plant. From its windows the men on shift watched the fishermen jostle and push each other for a place to stand while the air sparkled with flying jig hooks and the silvery flash of jigged fish being jerked from the water. Wedging our way into a spot on the bank, we claimed a piece of the shoulder-to-shoulder territory. Duncan pulled a burlap bag from his back pocket and threw it on the ground beside him.

I stepped away to cut the crotch of a branch for a gad to carry my catch. Calum wouldn't allow me to bring home any more than one feed for the two of us, a dozen, two if I stretched it. While I was shaving the bark, someone called my name.

"Hey, you, kid! What's your name? Roddie, right? Go below and scare them up before you start," Angus John Rory ordered, then turned back to the river. Picking up a couple of hefty rocks I hurried down to the end of the lined-up fishermen.

In a clear run up the river, enough smelts would be jigged to feed anyone's appetite, but it was not a clear run up the Big River. At the power plant the returning smelts thickened in growing numbers at the foot of a small dam, milling there in confusion until the water was a churning mass of small frantic fish. From the river banks, a hundred fishermen cast strings of jig hooks, soldered into four-flanged grapples.

Below the action at the dam I hesitated, watching the river. Smelts by the hundreds, by the thousands, swirled in eddies as though resting, as though preparing for a rush back to the sea, away from the confusion of the dam, only to be met by their own instincts still arriving, school after school, in an irreversible urge to spawn. The two directions milled there in a cusp of panic.

Heaving the first boulder as far down-river as I could, it exploded in the water behind the smelts, and they shot back toward the dam like a single startled creature. I watched the water clear below me, then threw the second stone for good measure and raced back to elbow my way into my spot, kicked away dirt until I had exposed a large stone, and tossed my line into the web of other ones reaching into the river. Before the rusty washer that served as a sinker could carry my hooks down to the tangle of roots and rocks, I yanked it back, breaking the surface of the river with one wriggling smelt flashing on a jig. Swinging the line toward me, I could see the nearly disemboweled smelt oozing guts and blood down the metal hook. Ripping it from the hook, I snapped its head against the exposed stone, leaving a dark stain, then worked one side of my forked branch through the smelt's gill and out its mouth, pushing it down to the "V" of the gad. I threw my line back in and pulled out a pair of smelts, one caught through its white belly, the other through an eye.

The smelts did not stop coming, and from the banks we pulled them out with a flick-of-the-wrist rhythm while the river kept replenishing the spot with an inexhaustible supply of fish. Long after many of us had used up the means to carry home all we had caught, the trance-like jigging went on. At my feet lay many more smelts than Calum would ever allow me to bring home. They were basted in dust and drying in the sun, an occasional one of them still weakly flicking its dying tail, mouthing the dry air. I picked up the still- living and snapped their heads once more against the now gory stone.

Like limiting the number of smelts I could catch, the stone was one of the fishing conditions Calum imposed upon me: kill them quick. It was an order that made Duncan laugh, but then everything about my grandfather made Duncan laugh. All along the bank, Duncan pointed out, 100-pound oat bags quivered. "The longer they stay alive the fresher they'll be when we fry them," he reasoned.

Reluctantly, I began gathering my extra smelts to put in Duncan's oat bag when my foot slipped on the slime-slick stone and my arms wind-milled in an effort to regain my balance. Too late Duncan saw and reached as I was falling away from the brush of his fingers, and I made what seemed a slow-motion plunge to the river. For a moment, I floated on the surface, looking up at the row of fishermen facing me, most of them oblivious to my fall from their midst. Then the river closed over me, and the people on the bank turned watery and unreal through my liquid vision. Sinking into the cold current, trying to find my feet quickly, I felt the sudden terror of ten thousand smelts under me, around me, over me, squirting away from the new horror that had descended among them. Small, chilly bodies brushed my face, swam away from my flailing arms and bumped into my ribs. I opened my mouth to scream and the river rushed in.

Struggling to my feet, coughing and gagging and slipping on the slimy moss-covered rocks of the river bed, I surfaced to the slapstick laughter of the fishermen. I tried to make light of my embarrassment by taking an awkward bow in the water when the river suddenly wrenched me back into itself, my hands surging through the smelts to grab this new terror. I struggled to the surface again, breaking it with a scream only half completed before the river's grip drew me back again, this time with a pain deeper than the numbing cold of the water. Twice more I surfaced, and twice more I was dragged under, my hands grabbing at my leg, trying to free myself from the river. Surfacing once more, Duncan's hand flashed out, caught my jacket collar and with the help of another fisherman dragged me on to the bank. My screams didn't diminish with my safe landing.

I continued flipping and twisting and screeching every time the fisherman, who still believed his jigs were caught on the river bottom, tried to tear them free, embedding them deeper into my calf. When Duncan saw the line leading to my leg he pulled out his pocket knife and cut it. The pain changed from its ripping agony to a steady throb. While I buried my face in the crook of my arm to hide my tears, someone slit my pant leg. The other fishermen gathered around me to discuss the situation.

The hooks in my leg reminded someone of the time Charlie MacDonnell lost his left eye to a jig hook, which brought up the scar on Archie Burns' cheek, leading to the river's all-time favourite story, the day Runt MacKenzie snagged his own arse while casting a string of jigs. He didn't even know they were his own hooks. He kept casting and screaming, casting and screaming. All this was to let me know I got off easy.

"Guess we know who was the first one in swimming this year," Angus John Rory said, noting a feat that had been lost on me. "Better check your pockets there, boy," he said, squirting tobacco juice down his unshaven chin. "Might be full of smelts. I think that's illegal. Same thing as using scoop net. Next thing you know, they'll be calling you Roddie Smelt." A small chuckle rippled through his audience, and I just knew....

The general consensus among those most informed about jig hook wounds was that I had better have the doctor remove mine. There were offers to carry me home, but I refused. It was bad enough to be smeared with tears without getting carried home like a woman who fainted in High Mass. Duncan left his burlap bag of smelts on the riverbank, and with one hand supporting me and one hand carrying my gad of smelts, we hobbled home along the path.

"It's a good thing those jigs didn't stick in your pecker, Roddie," he said. "I'd be carrying that home on the gad, too."

2

The pain woke me in the middle of the night and I lay in bed feeling the throb and listening to the silence of the house, broken only by a wheezy snore rising from Piper, asleep somewhere at the foot of the bed. I sat up, turned on the light and examined the bandage, stained brown with iodine and dried blood. Cupping the sore calf in my hand I rubbed it gingerly, remembering Calum's prediction that there would be a scar. I hoped he was right. Duncan had more scars than Christ, but I always seemed to heal over from everything.

Calum never called the doctor. When Duncan helped me up the front steps my grandfather came out of the sun porch and examined me. Calum, who didn't use many words, talking mostly with nods of the head, grimaces, glares and Gaelic grunts, gave Duncan a directional nod that instructed him to help me into the house. Putting some newspapers on the couch beside the kitchen stove, he told me to lie face down and place my wounded leg on the papers. What happened next, to hear Duncan tell it, was the bloodiest butchering of one human being by another since the massacre at Culloden, and he added it to his growing accumulation of evidence that Calum was crazy. He never tired of telling it.

"The old bastard puts Roddie on the couch, and then he goes and stokes the coals in the stove. And then he puts on the kettle! I say, 'Jesus, Roddie, he's making a cup of tea.' But it wasn't tea he was making. When the water's boiling, he pours it into the potato pot and puts this big butcher knife in it and leaves it there and comes over to Roddie with rags and bottles and he clamps Roddie's leg between his knees and begins looking at the hooks, tugging them this way and that way. Old Roddie, boy, was screaming Holy Hell with a pillow stuffed in his mouth and feathers coming out his nose.

"Then crazy old Calum goes over to the stove and comes back with ... THE KNIFE! He clamps Roddie's leg again and pulls on the hooks some more, studying them through the glasses on the end of his nose. Then he begins slashing away like he's skinning a rabbit, blood everywhere. I could hardly keep watching. 'Be careful, Roddie,' I warned him, 'he's taking the leg off.'

"For a while there, I thought I was witnessing a murder, and just when I thought it was all over what comes along but the worst part of all. 'Look out, Roddie!' I scream, but it was too late. The old bastard has a grip on Roddie's leg again and starts putting the iodine to it, pouring it on like it was water. Roddie comes straight up off the couch screaming like one of those opera women. I thought the windows were going to go. And then the old frigger takes Roddie's leg again and wraps it up in a strip of torn sheet and safety pins it to the leg. Have to give the old guy credit there, though. I never saw John Alex bandage one of his horse's legs any neater than that."

From where I experienced it, it felt every bit as bloody as Duncan described, but I knew it wasn't a butcher knife that Calum used, it was his own pocket knife, which he kept so sharp that if I held a loose scribbler page in one hand I could slice it in two with Calum's knife. And when it was all over there was no blood on the ceiling or anything like that. The neat bandage was a point in Calum's favour. Duncan practically lived in John Alex Rankin's barn, and anything that reminded him of race horses was alright with him. Seeing Calum bandage my calf like a professional horse-man put some sanity in Duncan's perception of Calum's craziness.

Piper blinked, stretched and yawned, then crossed the bed to rub against my sore leg with a touch so soft I could barely feel it. I stroked her calico fur, tracing the shocks of white hair that had grown over her own healed scars.

Four summers earlier, when we were ten, Duncan and I were walking through the Company Rows on our way to John Alex's barn when we heard the screeching.

"A cat fight!" Duncan said, but before the words were out of his mouth I was already running toward it. When I rounded the corner to the back yard where the screams were coming from I stopped dead in my tracks. I knew what I was looking at but had never seen it before.

If you rub turpentine on a dog's arse, anyone will tell you, it will run like sixty trying to get away from the burning. Or if you tie two cats together and rub turpentine on their holes and hang them over a clothesline they'll tear each other's guts out. Two cats were hanging on a clothesline, ripping each other apart.

It was like watching a storm, the cats hissing and screeching, whirling on the clothesline, blood and clumps of fur spraying from them, the fur flying out wildly beyond the fight, then floating peaceful as a dove to ground. Archie Ack-Ack and some of his friends were laughing themselves silly watching the fight.

Duncan never stopped at all. He came around the corner, saw the cats on the clothes line and ran right up to the fight, his right hand poking into the middle of the cats. He kept having to pull it back and shake the scratches out of it, then drive his hand between them again, cursing louder than the cats. At last he managed to fling the cats from the line and they landed on the ground. One of them broke loose and was running as fast as any turpentined dog, its agonizing noises diminishing in the distance.

Ack-Ack walked over to Duncan and glared at him. He was a lot older than us. When he turned sixteen during his fourth year in grade seven, the nuns told him that if he would quit school they would hire him to be the janitor, meaning he got to light fires in twelve potbelly stoves every morning all winter. He also got to bully any boys who came to school early enough to be caught in the same room with him, because he liked to fight. Angus John Rory, the same man who stuck me with the name Smelt at the river, had been away in the war, and when he saw Archie fighting with another kid, he said Archie used his fists like a pair of ack-acks, big anti-aircraft guns. The name stuck.

"What do you think you're doing, runt?" Ack-Ack asked, pushing Duncan on the chest.

"See how you like it," Duncan said, hauling off and kicking Ack-Ack on the shin so hard I could hear the sharp crack of Duncan's shoe on the bone. Ack-Ack went down with saucer-wide eyes and a yell, rolling around on the ground, holding his leg. After a minute, with all of us standing around waiting to see what was going to happen, Ack-Ack got to his feet, but he could barely stand. There was something close to tears in his eyes.

"I'm going to get you, MacFarlane," he threatened, displaying a closed fist for further effect, and then, with the help of his friends, he hobbled away.

"He's going to kill me now," Duncan said as he walked over to the cat that was lying on the ground. He was right, and it didn't do my stomach much good to know I would probably be with Duncan when that time came. "We're going to have to drown her," Duncan observed, licking blood from the cat scratches on the back of his hand. The cat was gasping. Blood oozed from gouges in her flesh. "I'll get a feed bag from John Alex's barn," and with that Duncan was off and running.

Duncan and I had drowned kittens for lots of people. For fifty cents we would tie them in a burlap feed bag with a bunch of rocks and take them to the old mine reservoir and throw them in. They would drown before they ever reached the bottom of that watery pit because everybody knew that the mine reservoir had no bottom. The kittens just sank forever.

The calico's sides were heaving and she was breathing in short gasps. I put my hand out to touch her and she tried to pull away, but she was too wounded to do anything but cringe. My hand grazed the edges of her fur, not touching her, really, but just feeling the tip of the fur like a tingle. She seemed to stop worrying about me because her eyes just glazed over as if she didn't care what I did.

"I'm keeping her," I told Duncan when he got back, the oat bag rolled up under his arm. I took it from him and began wrapping the cat in it.

"She's a goner, Roddie. Let's drown her and get it over with. Calum will kill her anyway," Duncan argued.

I thought about that as I lifted the cat. Calum hated cats. He wouldn't even allow them in the yard. The only time I ever saw Calum looking silly was when he was chasing cats out of his garden or away from the birdbath. He would even run after them, and for Calum, who walked like a funeral, that was quite a sight to see. But it didn't seem so funny to me as Duncan and I walked through the gate with the injured cat. Calum left his flower garden to examine the cat in my arms.

"She's dying. Get rid of her."

"I told you," Duncan whispered behind me.

"No!" I said to Calum, as surprised by my refusal as Calum and Duncan were. Calum, who had been turning away, turned back sharply, his mouth set firm against my defiance, and stared at me. He never said anything, just stared hard. I held tighter to the cat; then he walked away toward the house.

"So long, it's been nice to know you," Duncan sang, then said, "I'll bet he's going to get a hammer and crack her head open. And then yours."

I didn't know what to do. I was trying to find the courage to just walk into the house past Calum and fix the cat when, with the back screen door slamming behind him, Calum walked out of the house toward us, stopped in front of me, and into my already full arms he dropped some strips of ripped rags and ointment.

"You're wasting your time," he said. "Keep it in your room. If I see it, I'll bury it."

Duncan was curious for days, following me up to my room just to look at her and laugh. I had never bandaged a cat before. Duncan said the cat looked like the cartoons that doodled out of me all the time.

It was Duncan who accidentally named her. Recalling the fight on the clothesline, he remarked that the two fighting cats had sounded like bagpipes. That was when I decided to call her Piper. I liked the name, and besides, my father was a piper when he was killed in the war. Piper lay in a cardboard box in my room for days, drinking a little water from a saucer while lying on her side. I kept changing her bandages, rewrapping her like a mummy and trying to talk her into living.

Calum woke me for school the same way every morning. Standing in the doorway of my room, he would make a guttural Gaelic sound, a sound that, whenever I tried to spell it, came out all consonants. Inflections of that same sound could mean a lot of different things coming from Calum, and when he was standing in the bedroom doorway in the morning it meant "Get up!" Before I even opened my eyes, he would be walking down the hall, his slow steps scuffing along the floor. He had never woken me from downstairs before, but I woke to the same guttural sound, angrily inflected, loud and foreboding. I could hear Calum stamp his foot after each Gaelic grunt, and then there was a sudden clattering of pans in the kitchen.

A moment later, Piper, tail flared with fear and bandages flapping, tore into the bedroom on uncertain but desperate legs and disappeared under the bed. While I tried to coax her out from under there my delight in her miraculous recovery suddenly vanished at the slow, deliberate sound of Calum mounting the stairs.

The empty porridge pot in Calum's hand was trembling, and it wasn't because of his age.

"Your breakfast is on the kitchen floor whenever you're ready for it," he said, showing me the empty pot. A lot of things like that went on over the next few weeks, Calum doing his cat dance to the sound of Piper's claws clicking across the linoleum as she escaped from another close call with curiosity. To listen to them, I told Duncan, you'd think I was living with a cat and a dog. Even after Piper had figured out that whatever room Calum was in was a good room to be absent from, they didn't get along very well, but Calum never once mentioned getting rid of her.

The ache in my leg wouldn't let me sleep. I tested it on the floor, then limped down the hall past Calum's closed door and downstairs to the kitchen, Piper trailing me. I poured milk for the two of us, and, leaving Piper to lap from her saucer, I grabbed a handful of store-boughten cookies and went out on the front step. The June air at that hour was crisp but filled with a sense of the coming summer. I turned the white porcelain knob of the sun porch door and went inside.

The sun porch still held some of the day's heat, and, lit by a streetlight, plant shadows made jungle shapes on the walls. I left the light off and sat down on the car seat which was the visitor's seat. The couch was all Calum's, and he liked to stretch across it head to toe. It had been a verandah first, but when Calum retired he closed in the long narrow space with a door and a wall of windows, adding a wide, red sill running the length of it holding the houseplants. The plants spent the winter inside the house, but on the fifteenth of May Calum took a bucket, mop and broom and, turning the key in the lock, cleared out the cobwebs, cleaned the windows, and put the plants on the sill. Then he walked to Bartholomew Fraser's store, got his paper, came home and stretched out and read while the windows filtered the chill out of the spring sun. On the fifteenth of October he moved the plants back inside and turned the key the opposite way in the lock. Calum's dates had nothing to do with the weather. He might have to shovel his way into the sun porch some Mays, or close the door on a beautiful October afternoon, but Calum had his own calendar. I learned to live around it.

Our little family had been whittled down to just the two of us, if you didn't count Aunt Evelyn, and I didn't. My father had been killed during the war even before he knew I was on my way into the world. When my mother came to Canada from Scotland, she was a war widow on a ship filled with war brides. After I was born, my mother got sick, and Calum and Belle, my grandmother, took in the two of us. When my mother died, leaving me just a few vague memories, I was three. Calum and Belle kept me.

When I was six, Calum's friend, Bartholomew Fraser, came to the school and took me home in his panel truck. The house was filled with people, women carrying trays of food and the men whispering. My grandmother was in the parlour, the same place I had last seen my mother. It was dark and cool and filled with the good furniture used only for visiting priests, ministers and wakes, and it was my grandmother's wake that Bartholomew took me home to. Her bad heart finally gave out, I heard people telling each other.

The house changed like a light going out after my grand-mother's funeral. All the singing and the stories in it came from her. Calum was never much fun, but that never stopped Belle from enjoying herself, Mrs. MacFarlane said. What was left after she was gone was Calum's silence. I grew used to it, but a lot of women in Shean couldn't get over the fact that I was being raised by my Presbyterian grandfather, and they liked to check that he was raising me as a proper Catholic. I frequently got called in off the street for milk and homemade cookies by women who told me stories about my father and mother, and about Calum and Belle. They knew that Calum could cook a square meal, but he didn't have a sweet tooth in his head. It was Duncan who said I was do-ing all right for an orphan.

In the house after Belle died, rules were set without penal-ties ever being clearly defined, probably because Calum never expected his rules to be broken. His rules were about school, church, chores and homework, stuff to stop a kid from getting lazy. With just the two of us, a 70-year-old man and a six-year-old kid, conversations were pretty scarce, most of our time over the following years filled with habits and patterns.

Often after Calum went to bed, I sat in the sun porch, sometimes with the lights on, drawing pictures, sometimes with them off, trying to piece the world together from the stories I had been told. After I had outgrown Calum's nine o'clock bed curfew, I was left to shut down the house before I went to bed at ten o'clock on school nights and eleven o'clock on weekends or holidays. Duncan, who was forever slipping out a window or back door of his own home after being sent to bed, couldn't believe my luck, or how little use I made of it.

3

In the morning, Calum's hand shook me awake. I had fallen asleep in the sun porch, pulling the quilt Calum used as a couch cover over me.

"Go to bed," he ordered, even though it was a school day. Yawning, I hobbled groggily up the stairs, glancing at the clock as I went. Six a.m. I slipped back into my own bed and woke when the sun found my window sometime near noon.

They were in the sun porch, the three of them, all gazing into different worlds, no conversation. Calum was scanning the headlines. Bartholomew was staring into some problem he took with him from his store. Smoke from Taurus MacLeod's roll-your-own curled around him while he hummed thoughtfully.

Calum and Bartholomew had been friends since Calum first came to Shean more than fifty years before, when it was booming, when carpenters were as much in demand as miners. Calum came from outside Sydney, way over on the other side of Cape Breton Island, to work on the construction of a church, and it was from the roof of that church that he fell, nearly busting his back. Shean had no doctor back then, so somebody ran to get Bartholomew Fraser who owned the patent medicine store, as close to a doctor as the town had at the time.

Bartholomew examined my grandfather. He knew enough about broken bones to know that Calum's back wasn't broken, but there was damage, lots of it. The pain in Calum's back was barely visible through the grim determination on his face, Bartholomew told Taurus MacLeod years later. "There was nothing I could do for him, but that didn't matter because I could see that the man was going to heal himself," he said. "Some people are like that." Several men carried my grandfather down to his boarding house, and it was there that he fell into the clutches of Belle Stewart, the 17-year-old daughter of Calum's landlord. He never had a chance, according to Taurus MacLeod.

His only visitor was Bartholomew Fraser who stopped by one day to see how Calum was healing. Calum began to close the book he was reading when Bartholomew started quoting from it in the Gaelic. They fused as friends in that moment, self-taught scholars of the language of their hearts. They studied it with a grammatically precise arrogance that made them contemptuous and even intolerant of most of Shean's substantial but illiterate Gaelic-speaking population. They formed a club of two that day, and as Bartholomew was leaving Calum's room, he reverted back to English for the first time to tell his friend that his fall from the roof was just punishment for his sins. "It's what an Orangeman deserves for building a Catholic church," Bartholomew quipped. That, Taurus MacLeod told me, was as much humour as ever passed between them.

As for the rest of his recovery, it was like Taurus said, Calum never had a chance. Belle nursed him all the way to the altar. Not the altar, exactly, but the vestry of the church. Mixed marriages couldn't be carried out in the proper part of the church, only around back. If they wanted a regular Catholic wedding with candles, incense and gold-gilded robes, Calum would have to convert. He had traded a lot to marry this woman: a Catholic church wedding and an oath to raise any children in Belle's church, not his. He wasn't allowed to keep even one little Protestant for himself. Maybe they were getting his children, but the papists weren't getting him. He even made the priest tolerate an Orange best man, Bartholomew Fraser. A year later, the two of them were back in the same vestry with their roles reversed, Bartholomew making the same promises to the Catholic Church, this time in order to marry his wife, Sarah. Protestant women must have been pretty scarce at the time, Taurus observed.

It was Taurus's presence in the sun porch that people couldn't figure out. Taurus was everything Calum and Bartholomew thought was wrong with the world: too loud, too drunk, too brutal and too Catholic. Taurus was so famous all over the county that he didn't even need his last name anymore. "Taurus" was enough. It drew its own pictures in people's heads of a short man with a chest like a team of horses, only stronger. He was a coal miner until the mines closed, but the coal dust was there for life in the laugh lines around his eyes and the broken knuckles of his hands. He had a hefty, purple nose that was broken a few times, but not by anybody who had beaten him. It was just hard to miss in a fight, and he had had lots of those, sometimes two or three a weekend out behind the tavern or in a bootlegger's backyard, and he never lost one. That's what he was best known for, the fighting, but people respected Taurus for lots of other reasons, too.

Nobody could drink like Taurus MacLeod. Moonshine that blinded other men never kicked Taurus any harder than a crying jag. People said that nobody ever drank more than Taurus, who never had to be carried home once in his life. That was quite a compliment coming from the men who drank in John Alex's barn, men who were tighter than nuns at giving out good marks for a job well done.

The men who worked with Taurus MacLeod had their own stories. Duncan's father told Duncan and me that when he worked with Taurus in the mine it was the hardest he ever worked. Taurus worked the way he drank and the way he fought, Mister MacFarlane said, as if his salvation depended on it. Sometimes, Duncan's father told us, his own waist would be rubbed raw, even bleeding from straining against his pit-belt, just trying to keep up with Taurus MacLeod, and he was a lot younger than Taurus, who was ten years younger than Calum and Bartholomew.

There was something else about Taurus that people knew, but compared to his other accomplishments, it was small talk. Taurus MacLeod was a poet. He composed songs that he sometimes sang at the summer concerts or when he was drunk in somebody's kitchen or barn. Like most people, I didn't know enough Gaelic to understand them, but the airs sent chills up my spine. Most of them made me lonely. Some of the others, though, according to people who understood them, were really, really funny, just what you would expect from Taurus.

I was there in Calum's sun porch the first time Taurus ever sang his most famous song, "*Cumha nam Méinneadairean*," which means Lament for the Miners." That was just after the last mine shut down, and the song was about Shean's coal mines. In it, Taurus sang the name of every miner who had been killed underground. There were more than fifty of them. It was a long song, but I never stopped listening, even though I didn't understand it until Calum explained it to me. All of the names were in Gaelic, including the first name, *Domhnall*, who was Taurus's own brother Donald and the first man to die down there. It was that song everybody in town knew the chorus to, and at least a couple of verses, especially the verses about their own relatives killed in the mines, and sometimes you would hear people humming it for no reason at all.

When Taurus finished singing "*Cumha nam Méinneadairean*" that day, Calum and Bartholomew never said a word. They just kept looking out the sun porch window long after the song had ended. I thought we should applaud or something myself, but they just sat there as if they never heard a word. Then Taurus took out his makings to roll a cigarette and pulled out a roughly folded sheet of paper along with it. It was covered with scribbles.

"I wrote it down so I wouldn't forget it," he said, passing the paper to Calum who glanced at it, refolded it neatly and put it in the top pocket of his bib overalls. Taurus rolled his cigarette with nervous hands like he really needed it, then began puffing fast.

That night, Calum sat at his heavy Underwood typewriter, copying the words Taurus had written. When he finished, he took the song and put it in the same folder where he kept Taurus's other songs, with dates and notes written on them. He even paid Miss Margaret, the organist in his church, to write out the music to Taurus's songs.

That was why Taurus was in the sun porch so much when he was sober, because of his songs. Calum and Bartholomew believed that Taurus MacLeod was one of the last bards of the language they loved, not because his songs were so beautiful but because they were so perfect. He was born with a gift for the language they had spent their lives trying to master. They forgave him a lot because of it.

"Ciamar a tha thu?" Taurus asked when I walked into the sun porch.

"Glé mhath. Agus sibh fhèin?" I replied, telling him I was fine, and asking after himself. I sat beside him on the car seat while he continued speaking to me, and, although I could understand a few more words, I couldn't follow him. It amazed Taurus that Calum had never spoken a word of Gaelic to me, although it didn't bother me at all. If Calum had taught me, I'd be the only kid in school who could speak it and that would have been awful.

My father, Taurus often told me, had beautiful Gaelic. It was the language of the house when he and my aunt were growing up, and the language of the front yard was the skirl of the bagpipes, my father marching across it from boyhood, playing for the love of it. "A shame what happened to your father, but you gave Calum a second chance and he never took it," he said with a shake of his head.

Taurus was waiting for me to respond to his Gaelic spiel. I shrugged my incomprehension.

"I was saying that someone told me you got jigged at the river yesterday."

I pulled up the leg of my pants, showing the bandage on my calf. Neither Calum nor Bartholomew were paying any attention to us, still staring into their own half-deaf worlds. I told Taurus what happened, and how much it hurt when the jigs were in my leg.

"Think if you had swallowed them," Taurus observed, ending forever my fondness for fishing.

"Calum says there'll be a scar. He took the hooks out himself in the kitchen," I added casually.

"So which was worse, the jigs or Calum?"

"The doctor would have froze it."

"Maybe. I'd have given you a good belt of rum myself, but I don't suppose Calum thought of that," he said smiling at the thought of rum in Calum's house. "He wouldn't have done it if he didn't know what he was doing, and I'll say this for Calum, he always knows what he's doing. If he worked on you as smooth as he works on wood, you probably wouldn't even be able to see a scar, boy," Taurus said. Calling me "boy" signalled that he had forgotten my name again. Taurus sometimes had trouble remembering my name, but unlike Calum and Bartholomew, he never forgot that I was there.

Calum folded his newspaper, coughed and tugged the watch from its pocket just as the bells of Holy Family Church began singing the Angelus. Noon.

"Would anybody like tea?" I asked on cue, already leaving for the kitchen.

I shook the grates down to a bed of hot coals and added another shovel of coal from the scuttle, moving the kettle over the heat. Calum cooked all the meals in the house, but noon tea was my job. He made us porridge for breakfast, which I coated with brown sugar and milk, and he cooked meat and potatoes for supper, fish on Fridays, although I would have preferred if he forgot that I was Catholic once in a while. Calum barely ate anything at noon except a cup of tea and buttered biscuits. Waiting for his kettle to boil, I would make myself a sandwich or open a can of soup for lunch.

Duncan came in the back door while I was putting water on to boil. We heated a can of soup, split it into two bowls and crumbled crackers into it until it was a soggy red bog, then laid a carpet of salt across the top. I had been the story in school all morning, Duncan said. I hadn't been there to tell it myself, so that meant that Duncan's version, including Calum's operation, had a pretty good head start. The best part, though, Duncan said, was that while everybody who was at the river was describing how funny I looked flipping around on the ground like a jigged smelt, making everybody else laugh, Mary Scotland didn't think it was one bit funny.

"She was telling us to stop laughing and asking, 'Is Roddie all right?' and stuff like that. I'm telling you, Roddie, she likes you. Why else would she stand up for you? If I fell in the river she'd be in stitches."

That news made what happened worthwhile. I stood and walked to the stove where the kettle was roiling. With my back to Duncan I nonchalantly asked, "What exactly did she say?"

"What exactly did she say?" Duncan mimicked. "She said, 'Did my darling loving Roddie get hurt? Give him all my love when you see him, and tell him that if he promises to get better I'll let him feel me up.'"

"No, what did she really say?"

"She said what I said she said, 'Is Roddie all right?' That's all, but that's more than you knew yesterday. Yesterday you were just wishing Mary Scotland knew you were alive. Today she's worrying about you.

"But that's not the very best part," Duncan said while I poured boiling water over the handful of leaves I had thrown into the teapot. "You know the way people, when they have bad news, always say, 'I'm sorry to tell you this but...'?"

"Yeah," I replied, placing the teapot to steep at the back of the stove.

"Well not me, boy. I'm going to love telling you this one...," he said, pausing for effect, then "... Smelt."

"Shit," I said, knowing that this was more serious than some of the nuns' persistent use of Roderick. Almost everybody in Shean had two baptisms, one for your Christian name, and one for your nickname. Smelt! That's what they called the worst racehorses at the track, smelts. I knew this wasn't going to go away. At least it wasn't as bad as Farter, whose real name was Farquhar MacRory.

He never had a chance since he nicknamed himself when he was just learning to talk. "What's your name?" people asked him, just to hear him say "Farter," him not even knowing the difference until it was far too late. But that was Farter's problem. I had my own. At the moment I learned that Mary Scotland knew my name, it had been changed to Smelt. If that didn't make her forget me again, nothing would.

Putting buttered biscuits on each of the three saucers, I poured the tea and asked Duncan for a hand carrying them to the sun porch. He grumbled about "silly old fools" until I told him that the cup he was carrying was for Taurus. I knew Taurus from the sun porch; Duncan knew him from John Alex's barn.

"Mister MacFarlane," Taurus said with a nod of acknowledgment to Duncan as he took the cup from him.

"Time for you to be on your way back to school," Calum told Duncan, taking out his pocket watch.

Duncan cupped his hand over his ear and said "What?" like he was deaf. Calum just snorted as Duncan started out of the sun porch.

"See you after school – Smelt!" Duncan called over his shoulder. No one heard but Taurus.

"Didn't take long to fashion you, did they, boy?" he said, putting the saucer on the window ledge and pulling out his tobacco.

"The first guy who says that to my face is getting this," I replied, punching an angry fist into an open palm.

"That's one way, I suppose," Taurus said, "but you'll need a lot more meat on your bones than you have right now, because once they see they're getting to you, you'll be scrapping every day. The other way's to take their fun away, don't give them the satisfaction of reacting."

"They'll have fun with it, all right," I answered.

"A nickname's a fact of life around here. Only way to tell John MacDonald from John MacDonald ... I wasn't baptized Taurus, you know," he said, sweeping his tongue along the paper and seal-ing his cigarette. You could always tell when Taurus was getting ready to tell a story. He stuck the making in his mouth and searched his pockets for a match. He scraped it across the bottom of the window sill, and the wooden stick exploded in flame. Touching it to the cigarette, the flame transferred itself for a brief moment onto the paper before settling to its red glow. Taurus waved the match out and puffed and inhaled without taking the smoke from his mouth. Finally he pulled it away from his lips and studied the swirl of smoke rising from it.

"Some years back, this young fellow came to the mine for a summer. College kid. I'd get his name if I thought about it. They put him to work with me, a sort of joke some of the miners liked to play on people who were playing at being miners, especially college kids. The kid stuck with it though, although he said working with me was like being yoked to a bull. So he started calling me Taurus. Cocky kid, you know.

"Well the first time he used that name on me it was damned near the last word he ever uttered. 'What the hell does that mean?' I said, grabbing him up against the wall. His whole face disappeared behind a pair of eyes. I haven't seen anybody that scared since my wife on our wedding night. 'Bull,' he squeaks. 'It's Latin for bull.' By this time, of course, every other miner on the mine face had heard Billy – Billy, that was his name – had heard Billy use it behind my back and it caught on. I was saddled with it whether I liked it or not. Fortunately, I didn't mind very much. One dead language's as good as another, the way I see it."

"Smelt's different than Taurus, though," I said, thinking that Mary Scotland probably wouldn't mind if I had a Latin nickname, but Smelt....

"What's your real name?" I asked Taurus.

Puffing hard on his cigarette, he looked bewildered for a moment before answering. "Archie," he said uncertainly, then more confidently, "Yes, John Archibald MacLeod, that's who I am."

4

On the last day of school, Duncan pushed a wheelbarrow across the lawn, leaving tire marks along the edge of the front flowerbed, knowing it would drive Calum crazy when he saw it. Piled on the wheelbarrow was a wobbly avalanche of old boards quilled with rusty nails that Duncan juggled by shifting its weight from handle to handle, bringing it to rest at the kitchen door.

"John Alex's putting new stalls in the barn, so I took the old boards," he told me, as if the wood, half of it horse-gnawed and the rest urine-soaked, didn't speak for its own origins. "We gotta finish the shack today."

The shack was located in the back yard behind Calum's raspberry bushes. There had been other choices. Duncan's yard was where we built our shack the previous summer, but Duncan lived in the Company Rows with their small scraps of backyard. The night we finished the shack we tried to sleep in it, but made ourselves so scared telling ghost stories that we were asleep inside Duncan's house before midnight. Good thing, too, because our shack was raided during the night by guys from River Street, and in the morning it was nothing but a bunch of boards.

Calum's yard was more secluded, but Calum wasn't enchanted with the idea. When I asked if we could build a shack he grimaced first, then walked me across what everybody said was the most beautiful yard in Shean: grass, flowers and vegetables wrestled out of the unfriendly coal-mining residue of ash and coal dust. Most of Shean's houses were grim, grey and grassless in a town struggling just to stay alive, but Calum had always made his yard do what he wanted it to, and what he wanted from his yard were the flower gardens in the front with daylilies and crocuses, and in the backyard rows of carrots and turnips and onions and other stuff for his stews, along with several rows of raspberry bushes that towered above the fence and for a brief period in August, ripened with red berries that we glutted ourselves on, Duncan and I, and that Calum took into the house and boiled into jam. Between the raspberry bushes and the back fence, the furthest corner of the yard, was where Calum deeded us the land to build our shack.

Construction started in early April, scavenging what we needed from fallen sheds: old boards, posts, tar paper, asbestos siding that looked like brick. Duncan and I drove the corner posts, tied them together with framing and hammered the roof into place. We were committed but not particularly diligent, so the work went slowly, subject to any distraction that caught our interest. With school over, we were anxious to solve the problems we faced, particularly the fact that we wanted a shack with windows to watch for raiders coming over the back fence or through the raspberries, but installing windows was a construction trick that baffled us. We played with solutions from time to time, grew bored, and so through the spring and early summer our shack remained a skeleton.

"We got to finish it today," Duncan told me again as he pushed the wheelbarrow through the raspberry bushes while I held the load in place.

"Why?"

"You'll find out."

"Then we'll have to ask Calum about how to put windows in," I answered. Duncan winced but conceded that without Calum's help there would be no windows.

Calum was reading the newspaper in the sun porch when I asked him if he would help us with the shack. He put the paper aside and slowly lifted himself from the couch, standing erect. Maybe he moved slow as a funeral, but Calum walked straight as a poker. That was one of the things people noticed about him, besides his fierce resistance to fun; he walked as straight as a poker. Age never collapsed his shoulders the way it did Bartholomew and other old men. It even made him look taller, being so old and so straight, giving him a kind of humourless dignity that kept the world at bay. Most people, if they had ever known, had probably forgotten that Calum had fallen from the church roof and was unable to bend to Nature, even if he wanted to.

He followed me through the bushes to the shack where Duncan was unloading the wheelbarrow. Under the top layer of old wood from John Alex's stalls was a pile of new boards.

"Where did those come from?" Calum asked.

"I found them," Duncan answered.

"Take them back to wherever you stole them," Calum told him turning to inspect our shack. He shook a corner post and the whole structure trembled. He shook his head.

"We want to put a window in here," I told Calum, pointing to the side of the shack opposite where the door would be.

"Come with me, both of you," Calum ordered and we followed him to the wood shop.

The floor was covered with recent curls of scented pine, but the thick, scarred work bench was an immaculate filing system of hammers and saws and planes and chisels. Calum sent me up a ladder to the loft, and in the back among the boards and old stored furniture was a small, cobwebbed window, glass still intact, the paint of its white frame chipped and flaked. I lowered it down to Duncan who smiled back at me. Our idea of a window had been a glassless hole in the wall, but Calum's real window was going to give our shack a touch of class that would be the envy of every shack-builder in Shean.

"Now come here," Calum said, and the two of us approached the work bench where he stood with a pad of drafting paper and the flat carpenter's pencil he had pulled from the bib pocket of his overalls.

With a ruler and a few pencil strokes Calum drew the dimensions of our shack, then filled in where the window was going to go with lines and explanations of headers and supports that would hold the window in place. It looked possible.

"Let's get at it," Duncan said, beginning to pick up the window.

"Not so fast," Calum said, freezing us. "Do either of you know what a wedge board is?"

"Great," Duncan muttered. "He's going to give us an exam."

Calum waited for our answer which came in a pair of shoulder shrugs. He turned back to the pad, tore off the drawing for the window and drew another picture of our shack.

"When you begin boarding the walls," Calum said drawing a line, "nail the top board on first, and the bottom board on next, but don't put them on straight." It was obvious from his drawing that the top board wasn't exactly straight, which was something I wouldn't expect from Calum. Nor was the bottom one. "When you put them on, tilt them a couple of degrees toward each other. Then put the next board on under this one, and the next one on top of this bottom board. Follow that pattern until they meet in the middle and there's only room left for one last board."

"We're only building a shack, for frig sakes," Duncan grumbled, making me giggle.

"Pay attention!" Calum snapped, drawing us back to the page. "Because the top and bottom boards weren't put on level, this last board is only going to fit properly in one end of the wall. You will be able to push it in from that end about half way, then it becomes too tight. Do you understand?"

We nodded our vague comprehension, getting giddy, afraid now to look at each other.

"When you get the board in as far as it can go, you'll take the sledge and force it the rest of the way. That will pull this wall up as tight as a ship. One wedge board in each wall, understand? No carpenters today are using the wedge board; most of them never even heard of it. That's why the old houses will be still standing a hundred years from now when these new ones they're building today will be falling down in a generation or two."

"A hundred years!" Duncan said. "Who wants a shack to last a hundred frigging years? We'll be old men by then."

With a real window and Calum's instructions the shack was completed that day, including the wedge boards. It was Duncan who said we better drive them into the building or Calum would come snooping around and shake it into kindling, and it was Duncan, when we finished, who threw himself against the shack a few times trying to prove Calum wrong, but it held solid as a rock. Inside we built some bunks on the sides of the shack that had neither window nor door and made a table from the leftover wood.

"Now we can sleep in it," Duncan said as we sat inside gazing out the window at the wooden fence two feet away, thinking too late that perhaps we should have put it on the raspberry side.

Duncan, Farter and I sat in the candle-lit darkness of our first night in the shack, smoking cigarettes and laughing at Duncan's new joke.

"This guy and girl were doing it in the bushes, eh, and this tourist comes along and asks the guy, 'How far is the Red Top Inn?' and the guy tells him, 'It's none of your business'."

"I don't get it," Farter said through our laughter.

"Maybe you're never going to get it. Maybe you're never going to get your red top in," Duncan said, sending me into stitches again.

"Mother Saint Ursula was right, Farter," I said. "It's easier to tell something to the stove...," recalling for all three of us the day in school when the grade six nun got so tired of trying to teach Farter, or Farquhar as she called him, about math that she turned to the pot-bellied stove and began explaining the problem to the cracked cast-iron Warm Morning.

"Oh, I get it now," Farter added unconvincingly.

"Time to go," Duncan said, checking his wrist watch. "Smelt, you come with me, and Farter, you guard the shack until we get back."

"Where are we going?" I asked.

"Why do I have to stay here? What if Ack-Ack comes?" Farter asked.

"Because Smelt is a good lookout, and besides, you got nothing to worry about. Not even Ack-Ack could tear down this shack," Duncan said, slamming the side of his hand against the wall. "Know why? Wedge boards. That's the secret to building something solid. If Ack-Ack comes, just lock the door and wait inside until we get back," Duncan advised Farter, who had been a favourite target of Ack-Ack's bullying, so much so that Duncan felt sorry for him and let Farter hang around with us, even though he was a snot-sniffer who always wore a dirt ring around his neck.

Duncan led the way through a few backyards and across the street to Holy Family Church where the two of us served as altar boys. Moving in the shadows of the buttresses we made our way to the back of the church where Duncan dropped to one knee and reached under the vestry step. Stuffing a brown paper bag under his jacket we retreated back to the shack.

"Here's to our happy home, Smelt," Duncan said, pulling the package from his jacket, then pulling from the bag a quart of Mass wine. Farter and I stared in startled silence at the bottle of red wine, our giant shadows shivering along the wall in the candlelight. "It's not blessed," Duncan explained, seeing our faces, then unscrewed the cap and sniffed the contents like people in the movies.

"Just wine, no blood. Farter's father wouldn't have any trouble selling this if we brought it to him, would he, Fart?" Duncan said, putting the bottle to his lips. He sipped, swallowed and smacked. "Not bad. No wonder guys become priests. Try it. So help me God it's not blessed," Duncan assured us as he passed the bottle across the table. I took a timid taste and passed it to Farter.

"You're not saying Mass, you know," Duncan said when the bottle came back to him. "Here's how they do it down at John Alex's barn," he showed us, tipping the bottle back and letting the liquid roll down his throat 'til it began dribbling down his chin. He pulled the bottle away, let out a pleasurable sigh, wiped the dribble from his chin with his sleeve and passed the bottle to me. "Come on, Smelt, take a man's drink!"

Blocking my mind to all the blasphemies and sacrileges we were committing, I took the bottle and let a large swallow flow down my throat, feeling it settle, then spread like warmth through my blood. I passed it on to Farter who drank, then passed it back to Duncan, watching it circle around us until it was gone, Farter's tongue probing the neck for the last drop.

"Give it up, Farter, you're not on skid row yet," Duncan told him. "We have another one in the bag. So whadda ya think of our new shack? Best frigging shack in town. What you have to do, Roddie, is draw pictures of naked girls to hang on the wall."

Hoping to appease the Creator for my blasphemy, I told Duncan, "If I could draw a picture of something I never saw, I'd draw God."

"God's got no tits," Duncan said.

"I saw a naked girl, you know," Farter said.

"And then you woke up, right?" Duncan said.

"No, I did," Farter said, trying to out-convince our disbelief. "It ... it was my sister."

The shack fell silent as imaginations fetched a favourite topic. Everybody in the shack, every boy in Shean had at some time or another, imagined Farter's sister, eighteen-year-old Nicole MacRory, wild, beautiful Nicole MacRory, leading them into the mysteries of girls and women. Anybody who didn't would probably turn into priests. And here was Farter, still sniffing long snots up his nose, telling us he had seen her.

"Have another shot there, Farter," Duncan said, twisting the cap off the second bottle, "and tell us what she looked like."

Farter took the bottle, sipped it, studied the taste, savoring his sudden place in the spotlight.

"We got no bathtub, you know. The old man got the toilet put in last year, but he thinks bathtubs are a waste of money, you know. Aftershave's cheaper than washing if you have to pay a plumber just so's you can take a bath, he says. So we have to take our baths in the washtub in the kitchen, you know. Nicole lives in it, you know, always has a blanket hanging over the doorway, splashing and singing and getting ready to go out to a dance every night if she can, you know." Farter took a long draw from the bottle, holding onto it. "This one Friday, you know, there was a hole in the blanket she used, like when a toenail catches in it and rips it into a little square, you know, and the old lady was out to bingo, and the old man was asleep, and nobody else was in the house...."

"We don't care where everybody else in the world was at the time," Duncan said. "Get to Nicole."

"I tip-toed over so I wouldn't creak the floor or nothing, you know, and put my eye to the hole, and there she was in the tub rubbing a face cloth all over herself."

"Were they big?" Duncan asked.

"I didn't exactly see them because she had her back to me, you know, and the hole was a little high, and I had to stand on my tip-toes, and I lost my balance, you know, and had to grab the blanket so I wouldn't fall, and well, the whole blanket fell down, you know, and I fell into the kitchen, you know, and Nicole screamed and jumped up, and I got a pretty good look at her for a second before she started pounding me, you know, and kicking me and calling me a dirty little pervert, you know, but she's always calling me that, and by the time I got out from under the blanket, you know, she had a towel around her, so all I saw was her face, and it made me start running. But they were pretty big, you know."

"Give us that bottle," Duncan said, reaching across and grabbing the wine and rapping Farter on the noggin with his knuckles at the same time. "No wonder the nuns are always doing that to you. The frigging pot-belly stove has more sense. A chance to see Nicole MacRory in the bathtub and you fall down. Remember that poem we learned last year in school, 'Opportunity'?"

Farter shook his head, but I recalled, through the strange mood the wine had put me in, that I had memorized it along with everyone else in the class. "Had I a blade of keener steel...."

"That's the one," Duncan said, swigging from the bottle.

"I used to know it all," I said, trying to recall.

"You're more forgetful than Taurus," Duncan said, "but who wants to remember a poem, anyway. It's more important to remember what it's about, that's how you pass exams, and what that poem was about was opportunity. When opportunity knocks, Farter, my friend, it doesn't mean you're supposed to fall through the frigging door. That's God for ya," he slurred, taking another drink. "A nice God would have let me be the one looking through the blanket, or even Roddie here. Then the old Smelt could draw us pictures of Nicole, and we could each take one home to our rooms and commit mortal sins." He passed the bottle to me.

"So what you're saying here, Farter," Duncan continued, "is that you almost saw Nicole MacRory naked. Some story. Roddie's got a better one than that, don't cha, Smelt? About the time your aunt died. Tell us that one. This is really great," he told Farter. "I laughed my head off when I heard it."

The first time I told Duncan the story of Aunt Evelyn he thought it was so good that I began telling it to myself in my head to see if I could make it even better without really changing it, because it was true. Duncan passed me the last drink of wine.

"I have this aunt, eh, Evelyn, and she went to Boston before I was born. She started drinking a lot up there and even wound up on skid row."

"There's no women on skid row," Farter said.

"Shut up and let him tell the story," Duncan said. "Besides, where do you think Jesus found Mary Magdalene?"

"Anyway, Aunt Evelyn wound up on skid row. I know that's true because Mrs. MacFarlane told me about her, didn't she Duncan? She said my aunt was really beautiful and awfully spoiled and when she went away she fell in with the wrong crowd and ended up on skid row. Calum went to the States to get her a couple of times and took her home, but she always went back there, and the last time he went he couldn't find her. She just disappeared for years and years. I never ever saw her myself except for her picture on the wall in the parlor.

"Anyway, this night I'm lying in bed and I hear the telephone ringing. I thought it was an alarm clock first because nobody ever calls us except Duncan, and not at midnight. So I go downstairs and pick up the receiver and say hello.

"This woman says she's an operator and will I accept a collect call from Omaha. That's in Nebraska if you know your geography, and I don't know anybody in Omaha and I was pretty sure Calum didn't either, but the operator said it was an emergency, so I went upstairs and woke Calum.

"He didn't have his hearing aid in so I'm hollering 'Calum, there's somebody on the phone for you' and Calum's saying 'You broke a bone?' and I'm saying 'No, the phone, there's somebody on the phone for you,' and I'm holding my hand against my ear like I have a telephone in it, and all of a sudden Calum gets it. He jumps out of bed, and I mean jumps, and for Calum that's something, but he jumps out of bed in his pajamas and rushes down the stairs and picks up the phone, sticking his hearing aid in as he goes.

"I followed him, of course, and when he starts talking into the phone, even with his hearing aid, he keeps saying 'What?', so the operator has to talk so loud even I can hear her. 'WILL ... YOU ... ACCEPT ... THE ... CHARGES.' Loud like that and finally Calum gets it and says yes and then another woman comes on the phone.

"'Evelyn!' Calum yells, 'Is that you, Evelyn?' But it wasn't Evelyn, it was a friend of my aunt's, Christine. 'I have bad news for you, Mister Gillies,' I could hear her say. Then she tells Calum that Evelyn died, and Calum, who was standing up just sank into the chair and began talking to the woman like his hearing came back to him. Her liver killed her, Christine said. She died in the hospital there but made Christine promise she would be buried back where she was born, back where she had family. 'But it costs five hundred dollars for an undertaker to send someone in a coffin that far, and I don't have any money, Mister Gillies,' she said, crying. Calum said that wouldn't be a problem.

"The next day, Calum goes down to the train station and wires the money, and his friends come to the house, and the people who used to know Evelyn, and they begin getting ready for the wake. They brought in all kinds of baked stuff, and arranged the furniture in the parlour so the coffin would be exactly where it was when my mother and my grandmother died.

"It took four days and three nights for the coffin to come from Omaha, Nebraska, to Shean on the train, and when Bartholomew drove Calum down to the station in his panel truck to meet it, it wasn't there. That was the night train. The next morning they went again, but it still wasn't there, so John the Station sent a telegram looking for Aunt Evelyn's remains. They couldn't find her. Maybe she was put on the wrong train, they said, because there was no record of her coffin crossing the border. So they call the American train company, and they have no record of shipping a coffin from Nebraska in the last couple of weeks.

"So Calum goes to the phone and calls Omaha himself. The police first, who told him to check with the coroner who told him there was no record of anybody named Evelyn Gillies having ever died in Omaha," I said, leaving the rest to silence.

"So what happened to her?" Farter asked.

"Nothing," Duncan said. "Don't you get it? She never died. She thought up this way to get five hundred bucks out of old Calum. You have to be cagey when you're on skid row; that's what they were saying down at John Alex's barn, and that's about as cagey as anybody ever heard of anybody getting. And her a woman, too, they were saying. But didn't she pull a great one on Calum? Good for the old bastard."

I began making my way to the door, feeling the thrill of the wine turning to vomit as surely as Jesus turned water to wine. Farter followed me, and outside, standing side by side, we spewed the Mass wine over the raspberry bushes, gulped fresh air that tasted good but didn't relieve the dizziness or our roiling stomachs. Then we crawled back into the shack.

"Let's sing songs," Duncan suggested.

"Sing us to sleep," Farter said, falling onto his bunk and pulling his blanket over him. In my bunk I did the same, remembering, as I slipped away, the sound of Calum in the sun porch, after Christine had called collect to tell him that Evelyn was dead, crying like a baby. I never told Duncan that part.

5

The next day, Mrs. MacFarlane was feeding us fresh from her oven, like she did most Saturdays. Duncan tried to make her believe Calum and I only ate porridge, but she knew better. She knew Calum, she liked him, even chatted to him a little in the Gaelic when they met in Bartholomew's store. She had known my father, too, and I learned a lot about my family from Mrs. Mac-Farlane, who liked telling stories while we ate our way through her Saturday baking.

Feeding us thick slabs of chocolate cake at the kitchen table, taking a slender slice for herself, Mrs. MacFarlane listened while I told her about the earlier part of the day. Near dawn, exhausted and leaving the other two sound asleep, I went in the house, longing for my own bed.

Calum woke me, asking did I know what time it was, which I didn't because I didn't have a watch. By the time I stretched, reflected on the previous night, throwing in an Act of Contrition for drinking the stolen Mass wine, which I didn't tell Mrs. MacFarlane about, Calum was back downstairs in the kitchen.

On the kitchen table was a small package sitting on a five dollar bill: A Timex of my own, my Grading Day gift, which I set to Calum's watch. It was almost eleven a.m.

My talking about Calum's gift, showing it to her, reminded Mrs. MacFarlane again about the time I tried to hang my grandfather. It was the last birthday I had while my grandmother was alive was how she timed it. Calum and Bartholomew had driven Bartholomew's panel truck over to the Gaelic College in St. Ann's for the Gaelic Mod.

"You got the cowboy suit that summer, do you remember? You were a regular Roy Rogers with your ten-gallon hat and chaps and vest and gun and holster and lasso, and you were strutting around the yard showing off, shooting everybody who came to your birthday party, shooting everybody who walked down Culloden Street. I swear you killed more people on Culloden Street that day than were killed at the real Culloden in Scotland. Belle, your grandmother, made a nice birthday party for you, but the next day I met her in the Co-op and she told me what happened that night.

"When everybody had gone home from the party you stayed in the yard shooting caps and killing crooks and capturing Indians and God knows what until it got dark. Then Belle made you come into the house, but you were too excited to sleep. Finally she went to bed and left you to wait up for Calum so you could show him the cowboy suit.

"'The next thing I heard,' your grandmother told me, 'was Calum hacking and coughing, and at first I didn't think too much of it, but it kept up so I was afraid maybe he was having a heart attack or something, and I rushed to the top of the stairs to see.' What she saw was you on the landing where you had been hiding in ambush, and when Calum came into the house and walked down the hall past the stairway you dropped your lasso around his neck and tried to drag him up the side of the banister. Belle said it was a sight, Calum with his eyes bugging out, trying to get his fingers into the rope around his neck, and his tongue sticking out about three inches. The poor man didn't know what happened. Belle told me she just sat on the steps and laughed until her nightdress was wet with tears ... or something. She said that night she learned just how much Gaelic Calum really had, words she had never heard uttered by that upright Presbyterian came pouring out of him in a blue stream. Do you remember that?"

I was pretty sure I did, thanks to Mrs. MacFarlane's help.

"You should try that again, Smelt," Duncan suggested. "You're bigger now. Maybe you'll really hang him this time."

"Duncan, that's not funny. But what's odd," Mrs. MacFarlane said, "is that it wasn't your grandfather who took the heart attack, but Belle just a couple of months later."

The cake and the stories finished, and with five grading day bucks in our pockets, Duncan and I grew restless to be outside. "Don't go near John Alex's barn," Mrs. MacFarlane hollered after us as we charged out the door, making a beeline for John Alex's barn.

The new stalls didn't change the barn very much. It still smelled of horses and dry hay, manure and liniment, leather and saddle soap, all stewing in the summer heat to a strong odor that wasn't any one of them, but the barn's own smell. It took getting used to, and then you liked it. There was another smell too, especially on Saturdays, of alcohol.

John Alex's barn stood in his backyard on the last street of the Company Rows, giving the two horses a view of the daily sunset. One of Duncan's jobs in summer was to lead the horses down to the ocean for a swim in the saltwater which John Alex swore was good for their legs, ignoring the plague of bowed tendons and miles of bandages those particular horse problems required. John Alex's barn was Duncan's territory where I was tolerated under his immunity. No other kids were allowed in the barn, partly because John Alex, with his mean temper, discouraged it, but mostly because mothers forbade their children from hanging out with men who did little but drink, talk horses, brawl occasionally and tell stories all day long.

Duncan grew up in the barn like a colt that had been born there, discovering it only a short distance from his own house just after he learned to walk, and it was in John Alex's barn that he learned, if not how to talk, how to add to his small vocabulary a collection of words not found in any dictionary. He just blended into the hay and oats, walked fearlessly under and around John Alex's stable of horses, and by the time he was ten, John Alex was letting him help harness the horses that the horseman jogged along the roadside, sometimes with Duncan sitting on his lap in the sulky, holding the reins. He even began letting Duncan lead the horses to the beach for a saltwater soaking, sometimes for the horse's sake, and sometimes just to get rid of Duncan.

Occasionally, John Alex gave Duncan a couple of dollars for helping out, or a hot tip if he felt that one of his horses was ripe to win that night – tips Duncan learned to ignore. Duncan's real pay, though, was the beer bottles. All the beer bottles emptied in John Alex's barn belonged to Duncan for the refund. We hated to see rum or other hard liquor, although there was plenty of it. Empty rum bottles were useless for anything but target practice with Duncan's .22. Still, enough beer was drunk each week to keep Duncan in show fares, so he thought he was well paid for shovelling manure from the stalls, washing down the horses after they were jogged, remembering to feed them if John Alex got too drunk to get around to it. And on Wednesday night when the races were held, Duncan was the youngest guy in town with his own stable pass to the racetrack. He was John Alex's groom. It even said so on the score cards. Duncan dreamed of turning sixteen and getting his own licence for harness racing.

Mrs. MacFarlane didn't like Duncan hanging out at John Alex's barn, and although she warned him away most of the time, she didn't forbid him. Duncan's father, who lost his job when the coal mines closed, had gone away to work in the hardrock mines of northern Ontario, and had been working in them for the past few years along with lots of other miners from Shean. Some moved their families away from the town to live in other mining places, or moved their families and themselves far from any mines at all, to places like Boston or Detroit. Others, like Duncan's father, went away to work where the money was good but the only accommodations were bunkhouses or mining camps. Mr. MacFarlane sent money home every month and came home two or three times a year.

Duncan and I had been eating in his mother's kitchen when Mr. MacFarlane came home from working his last shift in the Shean mine. It was a day everyone still remembers. Not long before

Duncan's father walked into the kitchen, the mine whistle blew, a longer-than-ever moan that froze everyone in Shean inside its sound. Even Duncan and me. We were only nine, but we caught it from his mother who stiffened at the kitchen sink when the whistle went. We didn't chew when the whistle blew, although we didn't know why. We just listened. Then Duncan's father came home. He was carrying all his mine gear under his arm and his pit helmet was on his head, cocky-like, but it wasn't working. He still looked worried. He let the bundle of black clothes drop from under his arm, put his lunch-can on the counter and threw a brown envelope on the table. We heard the coins clink.

Mrs. MacFarlane emptied the pay package onto the table, more money than we had ever seen, and counted it. "Fifty-three dollars," she said."How long can we live on this?" She hadn't even counted the change. There was seventeen cents there. Duncan and I counted it with our eyes.

Duncan's father looked tired, his face shadowed and sunken. He scooped the change off the table and handed it to Duncan. "Go get yourselves something," he said. He and Mrs. MacFarlane never said another word until we had left. Sometime after that, Mr. MacFarlane left Duncan and his mother behind and went away to work. Before he left, he told Duncan, "Listen to your mother and be careful around those horses at John Alex's barn." So, Duncan reasoned, even though his mother didn't want him around the barn, his father had told him to be careful which meant that it was alright with his father for him to be there.

John Alex was there when we got to the barn, sitting with a couple of other men on benches made from hay bales. Angus John Rory, who had christened me Smelt at the river, was there along with Johnny Rosin. They were passing a bottle around, mildly arguing with each other, and barely took notice of us. Duncan went right to the stalls, scratching the wide foreheads of the two horses, Windspirit and Cape Mabou, checking their oat buckets and mangers, making sure John Alex hadn't forgotten. They weren't great horses even by Shean's standards, but they were two John Alex had raised from foals and hung onto while buying and selling other horses like a regular trader. Once, I would have called them smelts, but I had a new understanding of the word.

I sat on a bag of oats, wiggling it into a seat for myself, and listened to the men discuss the merits of John Alex's saltwater treatment for every injury any horse had.

"I learned it from my father," John Alex was saying, "and he was raising horses before most of the vets today was even born. Saltwater, he said, my father, I mean. That's what's best for them. Lots of saltwater! Why should I be sending good money to the United States for some vet's cure when my own horses here could put their arses up to the manure window and shit in an ocean full of saltwater? Use what the Good Lord gives you, man. That's what my father said, and that's what I do."

"Don't be giving me that, John Alak," Angus John Rory drawled. "Your father, and I'll give that to him, he knew his horses, but that didn't make him a college on the subject. You talk like he was the patron saint of hayburners, but your father thought saltwater could cure anything, and it killed him. Arthritis in an undertow! No wonder the poor man drowned, an arthritic man trying to swim in an August undertow, and when he went down for the last time he took all the good horse sense in your family with him."

John Alex leaned toward him, glaring. I could feel the tension. Duncan scooted over to watch in case there was going to be a fight.

"I'll break every bone in your body, mister, if you say one more word about my father," John Alex said slowly, like he meant every word of it.

"It's not your father I'm talking about, John Alex, just the saltwater," Angus John Rory said, reaching out to tug the bottle from John Alex's hand. It became a tug of war while Angus continued to talk. "Take those two horses of yours. Saltwater

creatures, wouldn't you say? How old. Seven? Eight? Did either
one of them ever win a race?"

"They will," John Alex whispered back. "They just need to
be classified for the right race."

"And if the whole field of horses falls down in some race,
then maybe the two of them will finish in a dead heat, pacing the
mile in 2:30." The bottle was being squeezed between their white
knuckles. "All I'm saying is that salt water doesn't seem to be
doing them much good. Maybe if you took them to Fatima...."

The tension broke suddenly as a tune rose from Johnny
Rosin's fiddle, which he had quietly retrieved from its case. Both
John Alex and Angus John Rory turned their attention to the first
notes of music, and John Alex's grip relaxed on the bottle, letting
Angus have it, a peace offering.

"That's the stuff, Johnny," Angus said, taking a drink, then
falling silent like the rest of us to listen. John Alex rolled a cigarette, a slow foot tapping to the sad air. Angus had his eyes closed.
Everybody in the barn, even Johnny Rosin, seemed to be alone
with the music. His fingers travelled the neck of the fiddle, freeing
a painful melody that rose amid the cigarette smoke and the smell
of the rum and the musk of the barn. Duncan took John Alex's
makings and rolled one for each of us, and we leaned back, copying the relaxed posture of the men. Duncan gave me a contented
wink, and I closed my eyes, letting the music swell in me.

Johnny's fiddle suddenly abandoned its lamentations and
made a turn into a strathspey, a lively tune that brought Angus
John Rory to his feet. The rest of us caught the tempo with our
feet, but stayed sitting down. Angus looked like a man hiding a
bag of oats under his plaid shirt, he had so much belly on him. It
struck me funny for a moment. Fat and half drunk, his feet shuffled under him in confusion at first, but then they began to make
sense. His belly bounced all out of tune but the rest of his body
was still, barely a tremor in his shoulders or a quiver in his arms.
He danced only with his feet, and I thought that there must have

been a time when Angus John Rory was as graceful as the tune he was dancing to. Duncan and John Alex and I clapped time for him, and Johnny Rosin reached down to draw more from his fiddle. Angus was no match for the challenge and in a couple of minutes broke stride and sat down, gasping and laughing at himself. Johnny Rosin put a flurry on the end of his tune, then hit Angus on the shoulder with his bow, a well-done tap.

"It's easy to dance when you're cranking them out, Johnny," Angus puffed. "You're one of the best."

"Bullshit!"

The voice was thicker than I ever heard it, but I recognized it at once.

"Bullshit!" Taurus MacLeod repeated, pulling himself up from a drunken sleep in the hay stall by holding onto the half-door. I didn't know he was there. He was talking to Angus.

"The man's got an iron wrist, for Christ's sake. Calling him 'one of the best!' If you don't know you're lying, Angus, you shouldn't even be listening to music because you can't hear a god damned thing!"

"Hi Taurus," I called out to him, but there was no recognition in his glance, and no distracting him from the direction he was going in.

"What I am saying," Taurus said to Johnny, "is that you're no Angus Chisholm, and Angus John Rory has no business rating you there."

"I never said I was any good. I just like to play," Johnny Rosin replied, his voice sounding hurt, not angry. I had heard him play the airs to a lot of Taurus's songs, so I guessed what Taurus had to say about Johnny's playing mattered.

"I didn't say you were no good," Taurus growled. "You're an adequate dance hall player, but you're no Angus Chisholm."

"Nobody said he was Angus Chisholm," Angus John Rory growled from his seat on an oat sack. "But you have no call to go around insulting the man, and I've a good mind to go over there and punch you for it. I don't care what kind of reputation you have," he said, standing up.

He took a couple of steps toward the feed stall when the half-door swung away from Taurus, and he started to fall forward but fought it, shifting his weight behind him so that instead of falling he sat heavily on a bale of hay. He was just a shadowy shape in the dark stall then, his arms on his knees and his head hanging on his chest. Angus dismissed him with a wave of his hand and walked back to his seat. "To hell with him," he said, opening a new bottle of rum. Johnny put his fiddle back in its case. John Alex walked over to the stalls and began rubbing Cape Mabou's ears. The fun had gone out of the barn.

"Let's go to The Turk's for french fries," I suggested to Duncan, patting the money in my pocket. The conversation that had restarted in the barn had turned itself to anything-but-music as Duncan and I started to leave.

"Com'ere, boy."

I knew it was me Taurus was calling. Duncan leaned against the barn door, waiting while I walked toward the stall where Taurus sat. He looked like a sick man sitting there staring at a spot of nothing on the floor. I stood and waited until he picked up his head and focused on me. He had to switch to one eye to do that.

"You won't tell them, will you, boy?"

I looked into his open eye so he could see that I meant it; then I shook my head. Taurus dropped his head again, smothering whatever else he was muttering to me.

6

Duncan's father came home in August driving a long, green, second-hand Chrysler with Ontario plates, the first car he had ever owned. His coming home was always the best part of summer, even better than nights in the shack, days on the beach or working with horses at the track. It meant lots of beer bottles to be turned into cash, lots of stories to listen to, and fistfuls of loose change when they wanted to be rid of us, Mr. MacFarlane and his buddies.

In the house, the men sat in the living room splashing hard liquor into large glasses and telling each other stories. Mrs. Mac-Farlane would be in the kitchen most of the time, trying to get them to eat some of her stew or drink tea, or trying to stop them from driving in their condition. She was pretty good about the drinking, not at all like the hell some of the other men would eventually stagger home to, but then again, Mr. MacFarlane's benders were pretty mild compared to some of the others.

Most of the men in the living room were the same bunch of miners who just got home from northern Ontario, and they spent the summer reminding each other of all the crazy things they did that winter. There were men with them who had come home from other parts of away, too, and men who had not gone away at all, and everybody was telling stories – stories from away and stories about what went on at home while the others were away. By the end of it they all had a pretty good picture of the whole year. The stories kept getting interrupted, though, so the fiddler could play a few tunes. They always wanted to hear a few tunes. Mrs. MacFarlane got the biggest kick out of that.

The first thing these men want to hear when they come home, she said, is the fiddle. Before he went away she couldn't get Mr.

MacFarlane to take her to a square dance if their marriage depended on it. He wanted nothing to do with the fiddle, preferring Hank Williams and Hank Snow to Angus Chisholm and Angus Allan Gillis. They're all the same when they come home, she said, but that's not such a bad thing, she added. She said they all wanted to hear the fiddle when they came home because, although they never paid attention to it when they were here, they missed the sound of the slow airs, the strathspeys, the jigs and reels the way they missed the sound of the ocean lapping, slapping, or smashing on the shore. Maybe they never noticed that the music was present all the time, if not in the fiddle itself then in the lilt of their language. When the sound was no longer there, they missed it, missed it a lot.

Mr. MacFarlane had told her about the miners he worked with, the Ukrainians, the Poles, the other displaced people, DPs he called them, who could never go back to their homes. A lot of the miners, like Mr. MacFarlane, had been through the war, had seen what happened to those countries and knew that the DPs lost everything. The further and longer the men from Shean were away, the more they sought out the fiddlers whose music they had known all their lives and were glad to find waiting and unchanged when they returned. Still, whenever the fiddler, and it was usually Johnny Rosin, started a tune, Mrs. MacFarlane couldn't help but smile and wink at us.

When the fiddle started up, and once Johnny Rosin started to play, they listened reverently to the first few strokes of the bow, then returned to their stories, everybody trying to talk above the fiddler they insisted on hearing. "Don't give a damn if they listen or not," Johnny Rosin once said in John Alex's barn, "as long as they have the booze." Usually that was how the fiddler was paid, in black rum and homemade cheese and that was why lots of mothers forbade their sons learning the fiddle, which would make them an essential figure at any house party, celebrated and indulged with liquor until it became a way of life that turned deadly for some, their music buying them swollen livers and early death.

When Johnny Rosin began to play an air to one of Taurus MacLeod's songs, though, "*Cumha nam Méinneadairean*," the room went silent. There was no conversation at all. A couple of the men, Mr. MacFarlane among them, began to hum the tune at first, leading them into the words, and they sang the Gaelic litany of names they knew, some of those dead miners these very men had carried from the bowels of the earth under Shean, and the song brought them back there again to the coal and the dust and the dark and the dampness, and when the air was finished, it brought them to the subject of Taurus himself.

"How is Taurus?" Mr. MacFarlane asked no one in particular.

"He was on a binge in July but I think he got straightened away again," someone answered.

"He's over in Calum's sun porch," I volunteered.

"Then he's certainly not having a drink," Mr. MacFarlane chuckled. "That's good, I suppose, but it would be good to have one with Taurus. Strongest son of a bitch I ever knew," Mr. Mac-Farlane said, adding that some of the Ukrainians he worked with up north were close, but for sheer power and endurance nobody could beat Taurus MacLeod. "Bet he could hold his own even today," he said.

Mr. MacFarlane's Chrysler expanded the range of his visiting that summer. With it he could drive out of Shean to other places in western Cape Breton, to the Margarees or up to Lake Ainslie, anywhere he wanted to go, and he wanted to go lots of places. Sometimes he took Mrs. MacFarlane to a square dance, and when they were leaving the house I was surprised how young and pretty Mrs. MacFarlane looked, all dressed up with lipstick on. Sometimes, against her wishes or warnings, though, he and some of the other miners would go travelling through the countryside visiting people they knew, bringing a drink and trading stories and getting drunker and drunker until they might or might not come home that night. Then Mrs. MacFarlane would walk from window to window, worrying and trying not to show it, but jumping to look out the window every time a car came down their street. The next day, Mr. MacFarlane would be as polite as could be to her. Sick, but polite.

One day, while Mr. MacFarlane was trying to calm the waters, as he called it, Danny John Campbell came for a visit. They were in the living room. Mr. MacFarlane wasn't drinking that day, just having a few beers. Danny John was having one with him and talking about people they hadn't seen for a long time, and they began talking about Tom MacPhee who had a farm up in the Shean Highlands. We should go visit Tom, Danny John Campbell said. Mr. MacFarlane said that was a great idea and came into the kitchen to talk to Mrs. MacFarlane, saying that they would like to take a drive up to visit Tom MacPhee.

Before Mrs. MacFarlane could say no, Mr. MacFarlane said he would like to take the boys along, meaning Duncan and me, that we would have fun spending an afternoon at Tom's farm instead of loafing around town all day. Mrs. MacFarlane said she didn't see the difference between us spending our time with John Alex's horses or Tom MacPhee's horses but said if he was taking the two of us with him there had better be no liquor, and she expected all of us home for supper. He promised her there would be no drinking.

Mr. MacFarlane's first stop was the vendor's. where Danny John Campbell hurried inside, coming out with two bags of liquor, and then, with the two of them in the front seat and Duncan and me in the back, we drove up the long, dirt Highlands Road, climbing into the mountains along a steep cliff that plunged to the shore below, passing all the abandoned farms along the way. Almost no one was living up there any more.

"It's a shame," Danny John Campbell lamented. "All these farms and the Americans just buying them up for back taxes. Stealing the land, that's what they're doing. My own people came from up here. Our heritage is being sold for back taxes. Piss a guy off."

"If they bought it for taxes like you say," Mr. MacFarlane replied, "then where was the family? What's the taxes on some of these places? Fifty bucks a year maybe? Most of the families up here had ten, twelve children and most of them, all of them in most cases, went off to Boston or Toronto or somewhere and did alright for themselves, and the family home wasn't worth five bucks apiece to them to hang onto it, so don't go blaming the Americans. Lay the blame where it belongs, with ourselves for not valuing our own. There's no god-damned way an American or any other foreigner would own any of this land if we cared about it."

Tom MacPhee's farm was different from most of the ones we passed where the pasture spruce was creeping through the hayfields, and the grey, weathered houses were empty, and the barns had bare spots on the roof where the shingles had been wind-stripped. His farm was hard at work growing hay and po-tatoes and onions and turnips. From the cows' milk his mother and wife and he made cream and curds and butter and cheese, and every Saturday Tom and Mary MacPhee came to town, just like Tom's parents before him, selling it all door to door, and their country cheese, according to Mrs. MacFarlane and even Calum, was the best on the island, although I couldn't get past the smell of it myself. Once, Duncan told me that his father liked to let the cheese age until it was crawling with maggots. Then he would scrape them off and eat it. I really wasn't interested in country cheese after that.

Duncan's father took the liquor out of the trunk, and he and Danny John walked up to the house, Mrs. MacPhee coming to the door, holding it open for them. Duncan and I didn't go to the house. Instead, we went to the pasture where Tom MacPhee's Clydesdales were grazing, their huge, heavy heads covered with flies, their tails making lazy swishes behind them. We knew the horses well.

At the fence, Duncan and I coaxed the Clydes to come to us, our scratching hands clearing the flies from their eyes.

Every Saturday, once the MacPhees finished selling their cream and curds they tied their team to the fence behind the Co-op, which everybody called the Farmers' Store, and went into the store to do their weekly shopping. The Clydes weren't alone. On Saturdays, the lot behind the Co-op filled up with horses, teams and singles, harnessed to hay wagons or buggies. Almost none of the farmers owned trucks, although a few had begun turning up between the horses in the parking lot.

Duncan always checked on the horses in the parking lot on Saturday night because often there were farmers who would go into the tavern after doing their shopping and stay there until closing time, not thinking about their horses at all. Duncan took to walking among the horses that had been left there, taking flakes of hay off the wagon, placing it in front of them so they could eat. He checked their blankets to make sure they were warm, and if someone didn't cover their horse with a blanket Duncan did it, even if it meant taking a good lap robe from the wagon and putting it over the horse. Sometimes, we took them for a ride around town, getting them back before their owners would even notice they had been missing.

From where we leaned on the pasture fence we could see Shean below us, a square mile of town under a canopy of white poplar, the toughest weed on the planet according to Calum, and the only tree that would grow under a daily cloud of smoke, coal dust and ash when the mines were booming. With all the sunshine and fresh air since the mines closed the white poplar was now everywhere in town, claiming every empty lot, every unkept yard. Between the town and the ocean we could see the grey and black margin of workings from the old mines, long tumours of slag that ran from the last row of company houses to the water. The sea itself with its golden band of sandy shore sloping into the August blue ocean was cool and inviting and beautiful. From up here, Shean looked like a picture out of a magazine, its unpainted, sagging reality hidden under the green leaves of the large weeds.

We picked out our own homes and eventually, because of horses flies and black flies, retreated to the house.

Everybody was laughing at a story Mr. MacFarlane had just finished telling about their army days. Duncan and I slipped in behind the table, and Mrs. MacPhee brought us each a plate and a glass of milk. On the plate were biscuits and country cheese and a couple of cookies, and their three little children watched us while we ate them, hollering to their mother when I tried to put the cheese in my pocket. I mashed it into my mouth before she had time to turn around. When she did, she noted that I really liked the cheese. With my mouth full I could only nod my appreciation while trying to swallow without having the whole thing come back up, which was when I noticed the large piece of cheese on my plate. Duncan had slipped his onto my plate. If I throw up, I thought, I know where I'm going to aim it.

"These your boys, Duncs?" Tom MacPhee asked Mr. Mac-Farlane.

"The blonde one. The other one's Roddie Gillies's boy, Roddie."

Tom MacPhee looked at me with interest.

"So how's it going with the farm?" Danny John Campbell asked, and Tom MacPhee turned to him, taking a drink from the glass in front of him.

"She's a struggle, I'll tell you that. Everything we're selling you can buy cheaper in the store. Of course, you get what you pay for, but there's not much money around since the mines went down, so people have to settle for store stuff. Fancy wrapping makes it look better to them, too. They can eat here in Shean whatever they eat in the cities."

"You're about the last farm up here, last of a dying breed," Danny John said.

"Yeah," Tom said, "but having no one on the other farms makes getting my hay cheap. The Americans let me have it just to keep their fields clear."

All the time he was talking, Tom MacPhee's eyes kept coming back to me. The conversation moved from farming to mining, from mining to who was home, from who was home to who had died, from who had died to when would Mr. MacFarlane and Danny John be travelling back to northern Ontario. All the time, though, Tom MacPhee still kept it up, the glancing at me. Eventually, the talk came around to the war again, Mr. MacFarlane telling about when he was recovering in England. He had been shot in the shoulder, although he never talked about that part, just about a funny thing that happened to him in the hospital, and that reminded Danny John of the time when his ship was subhunting in the North Sea.

"Weeks out at sea and bored silly," he said, "eating nothing but reconstituted eggs and other garbage. It wasn't the German subs we were afraid of," he said. "It was our next meal."

"Anyway, this day we pick something up on the radar, and the captain hollers for a depth charge, and they man their battle stations and fire one depth charge which exploded under the North Sea."

"We figure we're watching for signs of a German sub, oil or refuse or something," he says, "and what comes floating to the surface but thousands of codfish, all knocked out by the concussion. The captain orders us to lower a life boat, and we row out there and gather up dozens of cod. Best god-damned feed anybody ever had during the war."

That reminded Tom MacPhee of the time something happened in Italy.

"There was myself, Johnny Sandy Rankin, John Alex's boy, and Roddie Gillies. That would be your old man," he said, acknowledging me, and my father's presence in the story made me sit up. "We bought a couple of bottles of navy rum from this British sailor, and it didn't take a hell of a lot of that stuff to get you into trouble. That's when Roddie decides we're too drunk to walk, and so the first jeep we pass, Roddie jumps behind the wheel and we're away. We get to this checkpoint, and that's when we notice the American flags on the fenders, and the American soldier at the checkpoint notices them, too. He begins asking us what we're doing in a U.S. vehicle, and Roddie puts up his hands like he doesn't understand and begins explaining everything to the Yank in Gaelic, and he had the good Gaelic," he chuckled, throwing a glance my way, and I realized that even though it was Mr. MacFarlane and Danny John that Tom MacPhee was talking to, it was to me he was really telling the story.

"Of course, the American thought we were Germans in Canadian uniforms and pretty near machine-gunned us before we started speaking English, but with our accents, he still wasn't sure we weren't spies. By the time we convinced him, he was so severely pissed off that the next thing we knew, we're in the lockup for the night. I can still see his face, though, when he asked Roddie if he spoke English. 'No,' Roddie says, 'just Canadian,' and then he goes into another Gaelic spiel.

"He was a good man, your father," Tom MacPhee said, pouring a large drink for himself. The room went silent and thoughtful. "His pipes came home, didn't they? I saw to that myself. Do you play them?"

"They're under Calum's bed," I told them. "He caught me trying to play them one time and took them away and told me never to touch them again."

"Strange. You'd think...," Tom MacPhee let his thought trail away.

"Calum never taught him Gaelic, either," Mr. MacFarlane said. They all agreed this was really strange, and Mr. MacFarlane said he thought that when my father was killed Calum turned sullen and distant, but, he continued, "not that you'd notice because Calum was always that way, but what can you expect from a man who doesn't drink," he said with a laugh, passing the bottle to MacPhee.

"Well, not drinking wasn't your father's problem, kid. The Highlanders spent a couple of years in England waiting to go into action, so a lot of our training took place in English pubs.

That's not exactly true for your father, though. Every chance he got, he jumped a train to Scotland looking for people who spoke Gaelic or played the pipes. He took his pub training up there," Tom MacPhee laughed. "That's when he met your mother. We couldn't keep him in England after that, even though she didn't speak Gaelic or play the pipes. I never met her, your mother, until I got home here, and by then she was pretty sick herself, and you were barely old enough to walk.

"In forty-four we were shipped to Italy. We shared quite a few over there. Of course, being the Cape Breton Highlanders we felt it was our duty to rid the world of black rum, and we tried, we tried really hard. Italian wine, too, for that matter. If you think Cape Bretoners get soft in the heart about home when they're away working in the mines or living in Toronto, then you should see what happens to Cape Bretoners when they have to go off to war – especially when we had to bury our dead.

"It was the idea that we didn't have time to bury them right that bothered us. No wakes, I mean. We thought that was the greatest shame, not having time to hold a wake, to drink to a guy's life, to send him off with a pint and a prayer. The closest thing a lot of our men had to a priest at their funerals, I suppose, was your father's bagpipes. There were lots of pipers, of course, but when the body of one of our own went down into a hole, your father broke a few army rules. He was as good at that as he was with the pipes.

"It wasn't the 'Last Post' he'd be playing for them, but slow airs like 'Hector the Hero' or 'Lovat's Lament,' then swinging into a rousing selection of jigs and reels instead of reverie, and we all felt that we were doing right by those men. Not all the officers agreed, some were pretty regimental bastards, and more than one told Roddie to play by the rules for military burials. Roddie would just let go a Gaelic spiel, pretending he didn't understand English and the next time we had to bury somebody, what would we hear but 'Hector the Hero' again."

Tom MacPhee paused for a moment, remembering. "In March of '45, we were shipped back to France and given a week before going back into action. You father wasn't the only one to take that opportunity to cross the channel to England or even catch a train for Scotland, but as far as I know, he was the only one who got married on that leave. Then we were back into it, the pipers piping us into action and out of action, your father and the others playing the sounds of home, and we'd be trying to make them laugh, calling out nicknames or Gaelic phrases. And then this day there was a shot, a single sharp shot, and your father went down ... a sniper...."

A thick silence filled the room, the silence of men who wondered if Tom MacPhee took the story too far, the war itself so seldom entered their war stories. It was a reflective silence, one that took the men in MacPhee's kitchen back overseas. They just sipped quietly in the silence until I asked, until I had to ask, "Did anybody get him?"

Tom MacPhee looked way off again for a long time until I thought he wasn't going to answer.

"Yes," he said finally, the word coming out as an awkward cough. "Yes, somebody got him."

I knew who.

It was hours past midnight before Mr. MacFarlane and Danny John Campbell shook Duncan and me awake where we slept on opposite ends of the MacPhee's kitchen couch and led us out to the car. We walked with a groggy stumble toward the car. Danny John was stumbling too, but Mr. MacFarlane, I noticed, was walking with the false erectness of someone pretending he didn't have too much to drink. He drove the car slowly down the narrow Highlands Road, the headlights piercing the pitch darkness, the trees so close on either side of us that it was like driving through a tunnel.

Danny John began snoring right away, and Mr. MacFarlane began telling us about the ghosts along the Highlands Road to keep us and himself awake, I think. We had heard all the stories before, told them to ourselves late at night in the shack, but Duncan always swore there were no ghosts. When Mr. MacFarlane pointed out that we were coming to Annie Rosary's house, telling us maybe we better say our own rosary so she wouldn't come screaming after us, Duncan said there was no such thing as a ghost, and his father hit the brake suddenly. Danny John Campbell tumbled forward, hitting his head on the windshield. Mr. MacFarlane checked him but couldn't figure out whether he knocked himself out when he cracked his head or just didn't wake up. Then he told Duncan that if he didn't mind ghosts, then he wouldn't mind walking down the rest of the road back to town. Duncan answered that he was too tired.

"Too scared," Mr. MacFarlane teased, and Duncan opened the door and jumped out before his father could start the car again. "We're not scared, are we, Smelt?" he said, slamming the door, leaving me no choice but to open the door on my side and step into the blackness.

"The only place you really have to worry about," Mr. MacFarlane said, "is Annie Rosary's. She's been known to try to drown young boys in holy water, they say. I'll tell your mother to wait up for you," he added, pulling the Chrysler away from us, the receding headlights leaving us in a blackened world of shadows rustling in a warm breeze.

"If I could see you I'd punch you," I said into the darkness while waiting for my eyes to adjust as best they could.

"I didn't think he was going to leave us here," Duncan's voice said as the rest of him slowly began taking shape.

"Like son, like father," I answered.

"What does that mean?"

"The only other guy I know who would think this was a big joke is you."

"But I wouldn't do it to my father."

"To your best friend?"

Duncan didn't answer, but I could feel the truth smiling out of him as we began walking. The sound of the car had already faded away. Only the breeze-stirred trees and the pounding sound of the ocean a couple of hundred feet down the wooded bank was audible. Approaching Annie Rosary's, that ocean sound was all we wanted to hear.

The stories about her described a crazy holy woman who tried to turn her children into saints. Most holy mothers we knew were always trying to coax or force one of their sons or daughters into the priesthood or the convent, but Annie Rosary believed her children had a higher calling. She punished them severely in the name of God, forcing them to walk to church in the winter with only their shoes on, fasting from midnight and getting nothing to eat until they walked all the way back home after receiving Holy Communion. Some people in town felt sorry for the children and brought them food for after Mass. Annie Rosary locked them away, forcing them to pray for hours on end, year after year, until one by one they never came home from Mass, just went walking the other way, running away in some cases or being brought in by relatives. When her children were all gone and not one of them canonized, Annie Rosary took to the Highlands Road with her beads and her holy water, praying for everyone she met, trying to baptize with her holy water any Protestant children she met.

Sometimes, before her death, people passing by, like the MacPhees, could hear her screaming at night. When they went to see if she was alright, she wouldn't let them in, cursed them and chased them away. Then the screaming at night stopped, and when neighbours went to check, they found her hanging from a rope. She had hammered nails into each of her feet, and into both of her hands, although they weren't hammered into wood since she wasn't able to nail herself to a cross. Her head was covered with a crown of wild roses. She had crucified herself as best she could. Ever since then, it had been said, people passing by have heard

Annie Rosary screaming from her house, or worse, met her on the road, and those were the people she sprinkled with holy water.

I was more frightened at the thought of Calum at that hour of the morning than I was of the thought of ghosts until her house loomed on the hilltop, a scurry of clouds opening for the moon to light it up, glowing on the wind-washed shingles.

Duncan and I were walking side by side, our pace increasing with each step we took. I wanted to say something to distract us, but I was afraid that my changing voice would come out in a girl's high pitch, making me sound every bit as scared as I was becoming. Duncan wasn't saying anything either, just quickening his pace beside me. We both wanted Annie Rosary's house to be out of sight again, but before we reached the safety of less haunted sections of the Highlands Road, there was an explosion of light and sound that sent me screaming down the road, the hair on the back of my neck rigid with fear.

It took a while for Mr. MacFarlane's voice to reach through my terror and beckon Duncan and me back to the car once the horn had stopped honking. "Stand in the lights there," he said as we approached the Chrysler. "I want to see if you boys pissed your pants."

"Didn't scare me," Duncan said as we settled into the back seat.

Maybe, like he said, Duncan wasn't scared, but I noticed that for the first time in our whole lives together he had been running fifty feet ahead of me and opening up more distance as we raced down the Highlands Road.

Danny Campbell slept through the whole thing.

7

We were in the raspberry bushes, Calum carrying a dishpan in one arm into which we threw the berries we plucked. He ran his fingers through the half-full pan, cursing the birds that had stripped most of the crop. I never mentioned the milk bottles filled with raspberries that Duncan and I sold door to door for a quarter each. Calum wasn't the only person in town who liked to pour fresh cream over a bowl of ripe raspberries, but he was the only person in town who grew them. There were plenty of wild raspberries to be found in the fields and woods around Shean, but it took a lot of scratches and fly bites to pick them, so Calum's were easy to sell.

Calum, when he reached the end of the first row of raspberry bushes, took the extra few steps toward the shack. It was the first time he had come to see it since showing us about wedge boards. The structure was tall enough for Duncan, Farter and me to stand in, but the door was so low we had to crawl through it. This was Duncan's idea. With Calum's bad back, he figured the old man wouldn't be able to come inside and surprise us smoking cigarettes or even polishing off another bottle of Mass wine.

Calum stood examining the shack. We had tar-papered the roof, and the walls were covered with brick-wall siding stripped off an abandoned house. The window was covered by an old blind from the same house. He walked over to the structure, put his strong, brown-spotted hand on it and gave it a shake. Nothing happened. He nodded to himself, as if pleased that the brick-wall siding covered the well-placed wedge boards. Without a word, he started down the second row of raspberries, me walking along beside him, pulling the berries from the lower branches.

From the raspberry bushes I could see across the whole yard, the August garden bursting with colour. The flowers themselves didn't interest me much, but there were times when the colours in Calum's garden jigged my attention, the fresh orange bloom of the daylilies, the pink phlox, the yellow and red nasturtiums, and the dying purple of the last of the foxgloves beside the purple birth of asters unravelling from long, green buds. Sometimes I tried to imagine how shapes and colours such as these could be caught on paper, framed, hung on a wall where it would continue to bloom long after the season that inspired it.

Sometimes I noticed patterns that made me want to add colour to my pencil drawings. I did lots of colouring in art class when the art nun, Mother Saint Margaret of Scotland, wanted something special done to one of the Christmas or Easter murals.

Unlike other teachers who cracked my knuckles for compulsively doodling in the margins of books and scribblers, Mother Saint Margaret encouraged me, hovering over my shoulder, talking about perspective or teaching me cross-hatching and other shading techniques. She also wanted me to use colour as much as possible, sometimes supplying me with special pastels while other students worked with crayons or turned their paper soggy with torrents of water colour, and she always assigned the fine work to me while Duncan and the other guys were given the sky to colour, large expanses of blue that they could not ruin with their lack of interest. In September when school opened again we would be going into grade nine. There would be no more art instruction, no weekly afternoon of drawing and colouring, the best part of school.

There weren't many homemade pictures in Shean. Sometimes someone would cut a cute picture from a calendar – kittens, horses or kids – and put it in a frame and hang it on a wall. Holy pictures were everywhere, the Sacred Hearts of Jesus and Mary or a patron saint. In John Alex's barn, the walls were covered with half-dressed women cut from magazines and nailed to the boards, showing almost everything by showing nothing at all. Mostly, though, the walls of the houses were given over to pictures of people, those who had died and those who had gone away, like Calum's parlour wall, hung with pictures of my mother and father, Aunt Evelyn, and Calum and Belle at their wedding. I really liked the one of Belle with a drink in one hand and a cigarette in the other, laughing, and Calum beside her, his hands folded on top of the table, nothing in front of him. There was even a tintype of Calum's father and mother, both looking even more grim than he could look himself sometimes. There were pictures of other people, all dead, whose connections to our family were already becoming vague, even though I had been told when I asked who they were, but I hadn't asked for a long time.

In the classrooms, besides the crucifixes hanging above every door, there was at least one picture, people stopping work in the field to pray the Angelus or women gleaning wheat or a bearded man breaking bread. I thought they were all holy pictures until Mother Saint Margaret told us they were works of art, painted by famous people who had caught with their brush the awe of God's goodness expressed in the worship of simple people.

"What do you see in this picture?" she asked the class one time, pointing to *The Angelus*, a picture of two peasants in a field somewhere in France praying as the noon Angelus rang from a nearby church.

"Two people staring at the ground," Duncan had confidently volunteered. Mother Saint Margaret turned red as anything and wheeled around and walked out of the classroom. She came back a few minutes later stuffing a Kleenex into her large black sleeve, and told us to start drawing in our workbooks. At dinnertime, Farter, who had been thrown out into the corridor by his teacher, told us that while he was sitting there waiting for the class to be over, Mother Saint Margaret came into the corridor. He didn't want to have to explain what he was doing there himself, so he hid behind a bunch of winter coats hanging on hooks. "If I didn't know better, you know," he said, "I'd swear she was splitting a gut, you know, but she must have been crying or something because nuns can't laugh like that."

In the art room itself, the walls were full of copies of what she called "The Masters," and she laughed too, the time I asked her if all the painters in the world lived in Italy. She said they didn't, they just wanted to. She had once studied for a summer in Italy herself, she said, visiting places where great art was on exhibit. One of the pictures on the wall was of a street in Venice. It was when she was telling us about being in Italy that she also told us she painted that picture. Then I realized that her picture wasn't like all the others on the walls, pictures of pictures, but a real picture she had painted herself. What was really strange was that there was nothing of God in it, no saints, no churches, just a street filled with oddly-shaped houses and colourful roofs and white walls, and the whole neighbourhood was slightly not right, not perfectly straight, as if it was a little bit drunk the way you sometimes see somebody strolling home from the tavern humming a happy little tune. That's what I liked about looking at it – once I learned it was real and painted by somebody who wasn't even Italian. A nun, to boot.

I looked up from the garden and saw Taurus sitting in the sun porch reading the paper he had brought for Calum from Bartholomew's store. Down the street I could see Bartholomew himself making his way toward Calum's sun porch. Back in the raspberry bushes I told Calum that his friends were already here. He pulled his watch from his pocket, checking their arrival against his own schedule, and realized it was nearing noon. He passed me the dishpan to finish picking the berries and went into the house through the back door where I knew he would put the kettle on the stove, leaving the rest of the tea up to me.

Taurus burst out laughing when he saw me carrying their tea into the sun porch, drawing Calum and Bartholomew's attention to the fact that there was something not right about my appearance. With all the teacups in my hands, I couldn't check myself, like to see if my zipper was opened or something, but whatever it was, it was enough to make both Calum and Bartholomew crack a shadow of a smile.

"What do you suppose raspberry leaves in your hair means?" Taurus asked me. "We were just talking about some of the old beliefs," he explained. "You know, when a bird gets in your house there's going to be a death, bubbles in your tea cup means you're going to come into sudden money. Superstitions. So what does having raspberry twigs in your hair mean?" Taurus asked again, this time directing his question to Calum and Bartholomew while I reached up to gently pull a small nest of tangled twigs from my hair.

"Nothing," Bartholomew replied.

"An oak or elm leaf would mean something, but there are no raspberry bushes in the alphabet," Calum said.

"So does that mean anything to you, kid?" Taurus asked me with a wink, "or are we both just listening to a couple of senile old men talking nonsense?" I shook my head while twirling the raspberry twig in my fingers. Taurus took one cup from where I had set them on the sill, passed it to Bartholomew who passed it to Calum, then passed the second to Bartholomew. He took the last cup for himself and reached for the biscuits. "So what would an elm leaf mean?" Taurus asked Calum.

"A," Calum said, putting the cup to his lips.

"A what?" Taurus asked, spooning molasses.

"A!"Calum said sharply. "Just A!"

Taurus turned to me. "You sure your grandfather doesn't drink? Or does that make sense to you?" I shrugged my ignorance of Calum's remark.

"I'm sorry, Calum, but I don't understand what you mean," Taurus said more seriously.

Calum lowered his cup and looked at Taurus, who had a habit of putting his solemn friends on. It must have been clear that neither of us knew anything because Calum expanded his explanation by a few more words.

"The alphabet," he said, sounding as if those two words should remind even Taurus, who was prone to forgetting things, of what an elm leaf was. Taurus remained as unenlightened as myself. "You do know that the letters of the alphabet are named for trees!" Calum said, his words inflected with incredulity, as if Taurus and I couldn't answer the first question in our catechism.

"The Gaelic alphabet?" I asked, Calum answering with a look that asked me if there was another alphabet worth all this trouble to him.

"You mean that every letter in the Gaelic alphabet is called after a tree?" Taurus asked. He seemed almost dazed by this new knowledge. Calum nodded his assurance that the information was true.

"The elm is A," he said, "and the birch is B, and the C is the hazel. Ailm, beth, coll...," Calum began the alphabet in Gaelic.

It was obvious that what was fundamental knowledge to Calum and Bartholomew was as new to the Gaelic poet as it was to me, but as Taurus began to repeat the alphabet, the connection Calum spoke about seemed to grow clearer to him.

"There was a time in the Scottish Highlands," Bartholomew added, "when a clan chieftain who wanted to send a message to another chieftain could arrange leaves in a way that the other chieftain, when he got them, could spread them out and read them clear as writing."

Taurus didn't touch his biscuit or his tea, instead he took the makings from his pocket to roll a cigarette. After he lit it he gazed out the window at the white poplars in the yard and started talking, maybe to all of us, maybe to no one but himself.

"I didn't have much schooling, being in the mine when I was twelve, riding our old mare down from the Highlands to get to work before the sun came. It was dark when we went into the mine, dark when we came out, and dark when I put the mare to bed."

Taurus drew deeply from his making, his eyes staring at the Shean Highlands in the distance.

"I took a path through those woods up there," he said, point-ing toward the mountains with his chin, "a shortcut down the mountainside instead of the road. Probably all grown in now, but that mare could find her way in the dark while I just hung on, the trees all around me, touching me. I didn't learn a lot before leaving school, but I learned that trees make oxygen, which didn't matter much at the time but sure became important underground. There's no trees making the air down there, boy, and when we walked out, even though the mine yard was nothing but soot and cinders, it still tasted fresh. That's what I used to think about, about how the trees were what's keeping us alive in this world.

"But I never knew this," he said, nodding in Calum's direction, then went silent for a while, puffing on his cigarette.

They took him away into the Gaelic then, Calum and Bartholomew glad to be able to tell Taurus new details about the language they shared, which he devoured with eagerness and questions. I sat for a few more minutes, listening to the three of them talk to each other in a language that was twitching on their tongues the way the tail of a dead snake twitches until sundown. Then I left to find people I could talk to.

After supper, I read a page that was still in Calum's typewriter. It was the eighteen letters of the Gaelic alphabet.

A	Ailm	(Elm)
B	Beithe	(Birch)
C	Coll	(Hazel)
D	Darach	(Oak)
E	Eadha	(White Poplar)
F	Fearn	(Fern)
G	Gort	(Ivy)
H	Uath	(Hawthorn)
I	Iogh	(Yew)
L	Luis	(Rowan)
M	Muin	(Vine)
N	Nuin	(Ash)
O	Onn	(Furze)

P	Beith Bog	(Dwarf Elder)
R	Ruis	(Elder)
S	Suil	(Willow)
T	Tinne	(Holly)
U	Ur	(Heather)

I was certain that the page was for Taurus, that he had asked Calum to do this. I took a sheet of Calum's typing paper and his fountain pen and wrote down a copy for myself before Calum gave it to Taurus, but it turned out to be weeks before that happened. Duncan told me the next day that Taurus had broken out on the booze down at John Alex's barn, which is where he must have gone after he left Calum and Bartholomew in the sun porch.

8

We were back in school, and Mary Scotland was back from her summer in Boston. I was looking for her from the minute I walked into the grade nine classroom, but it was Duncan's elbow in my ribs that guided my attention to the cluster of girls surrounding someone I vaguely recognized; then I suddenly realized it was Mary Scotland. Boston had changed her. She looked taller and had breasts, and her hair looked like the cover of a music magazine, and her clothes clearly came from Filene's Basement, the most famous store in all of America. Mary Scotland had obviously been there. She was also obviously beautiful.

"All's fair in love and war, Smelt," Duncan said, waking me to the fact that the girl of my dreams was now fair game for any boy in the school, including him. I watched for the desk where Mary Scotland would drop her scribblers then placed mine on the one behind her, and Duncan slid into the seat across from her.

Her real name was Mary Cameron, but there were seven Mary Camerons in the school, three in our class alone. To identify them, an elementary teacher made nicknames to distinguish them. Mary's father loved Scottish history and had called his daughter after Mary Queen of Scotland, which the teacher shortened to Mary Scotland, along with Mary Jane and Mary French whose mother was Acadian. Mary Scotland turned to check the seats around her and saw me.

"Hello, Roddie," she said. "How was your summer?"

I was glad to hear that she hadn't acquired a Boston accent, but when I started to answer I felt the words rise high in my changing voice box and chose silence and a shrug instead, then busied myself with straightening out my desk.

"Did you like Boston?" Duncan asked her.

"It was nice but too hot. I'd rather spend my summers here at the beach than with my aunt in Watertown."

"I know what you mean," Duncan said. "What's the point of being in Boston when it isn't even hockey season. Is it as big as they say? See any Bruins?"

While they talked about Boston I pretended not to be listening, looking around the classroom. It was exactly the same as every other classroom we were ever in, or would ever be in, in Shean.

Holy Family School was a complex of three almost identical wooden buildings with four classrooms in each of them, two upstairs and two downstairs. The double doors at the front of each building brought students into a lobby strung with rows of coat hooks, brown doors leading into the two downstairs classrooms, and a stairway on either side leading to the upstairs classrooms. The first two buildings took students all the way from grade one to grade eight. In the third building, grade nine to twelve, you turned into a high school student, and the high school itself, the newest building, had a basement with toilets in it. Everybody in all of the buildings who had to go to the bathroom had to run across the street to the basement of the high school. The other two buildings, built when the mines first opened, didn't have basements. They had mud cellars where the coal for the schools was kept, and every classroom, heated by a pot-bellied stove, had students assigned to get the coal each day, two students took the empty scuttle to the coal cellar, filled it and carried it back between them. There were other buildings: the domestic science and art building and Holy Family Convent where all the nuns lived. Beside the convent was Holy Family Church and the glebe house where the priest lived. It was pretty holy ground that everybody called Catholic Hill.

Being a high school student now, I expected the building to be more special than the others, but it wasn't. The classroom was identical: a worn-out stove in the front near the teacher's desk, the tongue-and-groove hardwood walls and ceiling painted a greenish blue, pieces of the hardwood missing where the tongue-and-groove had shrunken up so much the sticks couldn't hold onto each other and dropped out of the ceiling. The corners were cobwebbed, although Ack-Ack was supposed to have cleaned all the classrooms the week before school started.

Boxes of textbooks were opened and passed out, math, science, geography, history, French and English, and when everyone had their books the teaching began, with Mother Saint Matthew-Mark telling us what she expected. She expected us to do a lot of homework, a lot. She was, as with all the lower grades we had been in, the only teacher for all the subjects.

I was leafing through our English book when Mother Saint Matthew-Mark called me to her desk. She wasn't the first teacher to beckon me on the first day of school to ask about the way I spelled my name, Gillies with an "e." There were lots of Gillis families in Shean, but we weren't related to any of them since Calum had come here from outside Sydney with no family connections on this side of the island. Besides, the Shean Gillises were Catholic.

The first time it had been pointed out to me that I was spelling my name wrong, I was in grade three. Mother Saint Benedict explained to me that there was no "e" in Gillis, so I began spelling my name without the extra vowel. That lasted until the first test I brought home to Calum. I had a perfect score in spelling but Calum wasn't impressed because he never got past the misspelling of my own name.

"Come with me," he said, leading me into his study and sitting me at his desk with a pad of paper. He wrote at the top of the first page G-I-L-L-I-E-S, and then he had me write the word what must have been a thousand times, until my wrist was sore.

"Why do we spell it different than everybody else?" I asked him.

"We don't spell it differently. We spell it correctly," Calum answered.

The very next test I had in grade three after Calum's spelling lesson, I wrote Gillies, with the "e." Mother Saint Benedict called

me back to her desk again and asked my why I was spelling my
name wrong again.

"I'm not spelling it wrong, I'm spelling it correctly," I said,
repeating Calum's words confidently. I didn't know that nuns used
to have different names before they married Jesus, and I certainly
didn't know that Mother Saint Benedict's maiden name had been
Eleanor Gillis, without an "e." We had a stubborn little war, but
I was more afraid of Calum than of her, so I stuck with the "e."

When Mother Saint Matthew-Mark pointed out I was spelling
my name wrong, I knew what I wanted to say, but for all I knew
she could have been Mother Saint Benedict's sister, so I simply
said that in our family that's the way it was always spelled, and the
way Calum wanted it spelled. She didn't make as big a deal of it as
Mother Saint Benedict, so I figured they probably weren't sisters.

Being in grade nine, we were invited to the first high school dance
of the year on the first Friday after school started. It was a dance
that was supposed to help us get to know each other, although
everybody in the class had been together since primary. At one
o'clock on Friday afternoon, grades nine to twelve lined up in
ranks with the teacher standing at the head of each class. At a
signal from the principal, Mother Saint John of the Cross, whom
the whole town called Mother Saint Cross John, we marched in
double ranks between the church and the glebe house toward the
parish hall, each boy carrying two bottles of pop, each girl carrying a plate of sandwiches or squares.

Once we were all inside the hall, Mother Saint Cross John
locked the double doors against any thoughts of escape while we
sorted ourselves out, the girls walking automatically to sit along
one wall of the hall while the boys milled in a corner of the opposite wall. A couple of the grade twelve students were on the
stage plugging in the school's portable record player, while other
students piled their favourite albums beside it. Soon the music
from the small record player was trying unsuccessfully to fill the

large cavern that was the parish hall. In Shean, only the churches were bigger.

Duncan and I, one Friday night when we were sleeping in the shack, heard the music from the parish hall and walked over there. A square dance was going on. At first, we hung around outside, eavesdropping on the men around the side of the building who were sharing a bottle and talking about where they had been working all winter, or about fights they had been in or would be in, or the Yankees and the Dodgers, or who was taking whom home from the dance. Once they stopped collecting at the door we slipped inside.

The fiddler was Johnny Rosin, seated on the stage beside his piano player, and the floor was filled with sets of square dancers, and a prompter was calling out directions which most of the dancers seemed to ignore.

The first thing I noticed was that square dancing was hard work. These people were sweating more than a farmer making hay, but they still managed to smile at each other, or whoop or whistle when the fiddler raised the stakes with another jig or reel. It didn't take long to tell who were the real dancers and who were just making it up as they went along. The real dancers step-danced all the way through the three figures of the set and, like the fiddler, never missed a beat. It was clear too that they didn't want anybody in their set who couldn't step-dance. What I found funny was that it was toward them, the good dancers, that the prompter directed his voice, although it was those good dancers who seemed to need directions the least. The good dancers also tended to be in front of the stage, in front of the fiddler, and it was for them the fiddler played. At the back of the dance floor were the larger, wilder sets made up of people who were enjoying themselves and the music but didn't know the first thing about what they were doing.

When the prompter called for couples to "fill 'er up for the last set" Farter's sister started walking across the floor. One man stopped her and asked for the dance, but she just shook her head and kept on coming, apologizing to three or four other men who wanted the same thrill and who were probably hoping that if they had the last dance with her, they could take Nicole MacRory home.

"She's shooting them down like they're MIG jets," Duncan said to me as she continued across the floor, stopping for a moment to signal to a friend. "No wonder they want to dance with her. With all the moving around that goes on on the dance floor, I bet you could get a feel out there brushing up against the women...." Duncan's observations choked to a halt when the two older girls stood in front of us, Farter's sister reaching for Duncan's hand while her friend, Stella MacIntyre, made the same gesture toward me.

I was ready to run but Duncan was already letting himself be guided onto the floor. I followed Stella, feeling the nods in our direction from women who thought it was cute, and from men who thought it was a waste of the last set, the one where all the dates were made. While we waited for the fiddler to start up, Farter's sister slowly worked her feet to a tune she hummed, showing us a basic step. All the while, she was holding Duncan's hand, which was more contact than he had ever had with her, even though, ever since Farter told us about watching his sister taking a bath, Duncan had become a fixture at their house.

The fiddle started with the piano accompanying it, and a hundred dancers began following the music. Even Duncan and I, who had never danced before, began letting ourselves go, and soon the chaos around us began to make sense, although the brief dance lesson wasn't doing either of us much good. We were walking through the figures, but Duncan was more interested in his hands than his feet anyway, trying to accidentally brush against his partner, his corner partner, every woman in the promenade. As for myself, my eyes were level with Stella's bust, and trying not to stare was taking all my concentration. Before either of us wanted it to end, it did with a flurry of a jig, and the hall began to empty.

Duncan pulled me aside and said that we should follow Nicole and Stella out of the hall and invite them over to the shack. His plan fell apart when we saw the two girls getting into a car with two guys.

The sound of the fiddle, piano and prompter had filled the parish hall that night, which was more than could be said for poor Bobby Vinton on the high school's record player. Five nuns moved through the hall, making sure none of the boys were smoking, none of the girls chewing gum, encouraging both to dance to the music. The floor remained empty. Mother Saint Cross John spoke firmly to the grade twelve students, and some of them walked self-consciously onto the floor, held each other at maximum distance and stepped forward and backward to the slow sound. Their leadership role did nothing to start a dance floor stampede, so the nuns took forceful control of the situation. Our teacher, Mother Saint Matthew-Mark, walked to where the cluster of grade nine students were all trying to hide behind each other, reached in and grabbed me by the wrist. With everyone watching she marched me across the near empty dance floor to the other wall where the grade nine girls were seated. With her other hand she reached down and drew Mary Scotland from her seat, dragging both of us to the middle of the floor.

"Teach him to dance," she told Mary Scotland, then turning to me she ordered, "I want to see daylight between the two of you at all times!" She then marched off the floor and into the rest of the grade nine boys. Other nuns began pairing off the students in their class.

The basic square dance step I had learned from Stella MacIntyre was of no use to me with Mary Scotland and Bobby Vinton. All I knew about round dancing was that you were supposed to take three steps forward and two steps back. I put that knowledge to work, aware that I was holding Mary Scotland's left hand and that my right hand was on her back and that we were dancing together. I wished the music was louder so she wouldn't hear my heart.

"Do you mind if I tell you something, Roddie?" she asked.

"No," I said, hoping it didn't require an answer.

"I just wanted to tell you that you don't have to look at your feet all the time, and you don't have to count out loud."

That left me two choices, to look at Mary, or to gawk around at the other dancers. I chose the latter, scrounging around in my head for something to say, which wasn't easy since I was trying to keep silent count of my dance steps. I felt my hand begin to sweat and hoped for "Blue Velvet" to end and prayed that it never would.

"You're good to dance, Roddie," Mary Scotland said. I figured she meant she was glad that I wasn't tramping all over her feet.

"That's because I was coming to the square dances here this summer," I explained.

"Were you? Are they fun? I'd love to go to one, but my friends think they're old-fashioned. Maybe next summer, if I don't go to Boston, I could go to a square dance with you. Would that be all right?"

"Yup," I said as the album ended, and Mother Saint Cross John ordered us to take a break and enjoy some pop and sandwiches.

After we ate, we were ordered back onto the dance floor. This time Duncan didn't wait to be assigned to a partner. He walked across the floor and asked Mary Scotland to dance, and then Mother Saint Matthew-Mark had to walk out on to the dance floor and pry Duncan away from her so that there was daylight showing between them.

At 3:30, when the school bell rang its dismissal, Mother Saint Cross John unlocked the doors of the parish hall and we fled into the street. Duncan offered to show Mary Scotland our shack, but she had to go right home. I didn't tell Duncan that I had a date with her.

9

The rink was on a flat piece of land behind the church. Every spring, the panels of fencing were taken down, and every fall they were erected again. Lights were strung from high corner posts, and the coal stove was set up in the rink shack. As soon as it was cold enough, the flooding began, creating a surface for hockey games and skating parties where the "Blue Skirt Waltz" and other songs squawked through a loudspeaker.

During the Christmas vacation, Duncan and I spent our first night flooding the rink. Except for sleeping in our shack, Calum would never allow me to stay out all night, but flooding the rink was something like sleeping in the shack. Parents, and grandfathers too, knew where you were and that you weren't likely to get into trouble because it was too cold to be just hanging around the streets all night. The best time for flooding was on still, cold nights when the water went on in smooth sheets, layer upon layer, building a thick surface that could stand people skating and playing hockey for two or three days. It took about ten people, mostly high school students, using the fire department's hoses to flood the rink, operating the hoses in shifts of two or three people while the rest stayed in the shack getting warm around the stove, smoking and telling stories.

The rink had to be flooded whenever the chance came along because winter could never be depended on to stay cold. Sometimes, the morning after flooding, a cold snap would break and warm weather would ruin all the work, or a breeze would ripple the water to a pebbly or washboard surface, or a sudden snow would mix with the water and make a slushy mess of everything. Sometimes after a snowstorm buried the ice under two or three feet of snow it had to be shoveled away; people excavated the ice surface, wearing their skates, carrying shovelfuls of snow to the fence and heaving it over. It was hard work, but eventually the rink would reappear in time for an afternoon hockey game or an evening skating party. There were a few rules that went along with flooding the rink, and the biggest of them was no cursing out loud, since we were only a few feet from the convent, and the last thing anybody wanted was Mother Saint Cross John, who carried her strap folded in her habit pocket and could draw it faster than John Wayne, coming across the church yard at two o'clock in the morning to shut the whole operation down and noting names of students she would probably call to her class on Monday morning. But as long as we were quiet, the nuns didn't mind us flooding all night because some of them liked to skate too. Strange sight.

The first time the rink was flooded that year, which was a time when almost everybody came out with their skates on, I caused a big tumble because I was skating around the rink looking over my shoulder for Mary Scotland, building the courage to ask her to skate with me, when I ran into the people in front of me and we fell in a heap. I realized as soon as I turned my head that I had knocked down a string of four nuns who were skating arm in arm.

My first thought was to pretend I was knocked out, but there wasn't time before a crowd gathered helping the nuns to their feet, and an arm was suddenly lifting me to me feet. It was Mother Saint Margaret of Scotland, and she guided me to the fence which we both leaned on. I told her I was sorry, but she said it was just an accident, that she thought it was her own fault, that her skate blade had tangled in her long skirts, slowing the nuns up, and that was why I ran into them. Without mentioning that I had been gawking around looking for Mary Scotland, I accepted her apology.

"Are you still working on your drawing, Roddie?" she asked me.

"A little," I answered, which was the literal truth because I wasn't doodling as much as I used to except in my school books, which was a habit Mother Saint Matthew-Mark was trying to break me of.

"Try to keep working at it. I'm sorry you can't come to art class any more, but you have talent, so stay with it," she said, pushing herself away from the boards and back into the flow of the rink.

The night of our first flooding, Duncan and I had taken three or four turns on the ice with the water freezing as soon as it hit the rink surface, the fine spray from the hose turning our pants legs hard as shin pads. It made for a great surface, but the fun of flooding was coming out of this adventure awfully fast in the bitter cold, and everybody just wanted to be inside the shack, sitting beside the stove, staying warm, talking and asking what time it was every few minutes. "All night" seemed to take forever.

It was well past midnight when the shack door opened and a bulky form that looked like the Hunchback of Notre Dame came in, startling us. A moment later a heavy bag came off the visitor's shoulder, and there stood Taurus MacLeod with a hundred pound sack of coal.

"I saw you fellows flooding and figured you could use some of this," he said, lifting the bag toward the bin like it was ten pounds of potatoes. He stepped up to the stove and began warming his hands. Someone offered him hot tea from a thermos which he happily took, and watching him closely I could see that he wasn't drinking.

Talk in the shack quickly veered away from hockey and sex to gather around our visitor. Taurus pulled out a polka dot handkerchief and blew his nose, exchanged it in his pocket for a package of tobacco and was soon smoking, sipping his tea, and talking with some of the older boys about ice and winters when he was a boy.

"There wasn't much time for skating," he said, "not when you went into the mine as young as we were. To tell you the truth, I never learned to skate until I was a grown man. That was during the strike of '32."

"There was a strike here?" Duncan asked, excited by the thought.

Some of the boys said they had heard a little about it. Others, like Duncan and me, had never heard anything at all.

"More than thirty years ago and it's still an open wound in this town," Taurus told us, and we began pumping him for more information.

The strike, he explained, happened when the compressor that provided all the electricity for the mine, and for the town as well, broke down. The Shean Coal Company decided they were finished with the mine. It hadn't made any money in years, and they announced that they were shutting it down. Nobody knew what was going to happen to Shean, what with no work and not even an electric bulb that would light up. The town lived in the dark while people tried to figure out what to do.

The first plan came from the parish priest at the time, Father Ranald McSween. What the priest wanted was for the town to take over the mine, buy a new compressor and begin operating again.

"There were a couple of things wrong with that plan," Taurus told us. "First, the new compressor would be paid for by deducting money from the miners' wages every week. The problem with that was that before the compressor went, I was taking home some pays that didn't amount to two dollars for the week. The town was broke, the miners were broke, and the mine hadn't made money in years, so the first problem we could see with Father McSween's plan was that the miners would be going broke trying keep their jobs. The second problem with that plan was that Father McSween was as crazy as a boxcar full of drunks in the DTs."

The blasphemy sent a shiver down a few spines, but Duncan roared out laughing.

"There was a third problem, of course," Taurus said, spitting a bit of tobacco from his making in the direction of the stove. "Even if it was a good plan, it was a Catholic plan. People don't get much into that foolishness today, and thank God for that, but a lot of the miners came from the other faith. They didn't trust the priest, not because he was crazy but because he was Catholic. If the town took over the mine, and most of the people here are Catholics, who would get all the work? So they didn't trust the priest any more than I did. The town split in two along those lines, those who were for the plan and those who were against it. It wasn't exactly Catholic against Protestant because there were quite a few like me, Catholics who sided with the Protestants.

"Our plan for the mine was that we get the government involved. We had good coal here, good mines, good miners, but there's nothing on God's good earth as shaky as coal. One day the whole world can't get enough of it, and the next day they don't need it any more. To get the mines back on track was going to take more money than this town had ever seen. Of course, right away we were labeled Bolsheviks.

"The priest began preaching against us from the altar, and ordering Catholic miners at the cost of their souls – at the cost of their souls no less – to go into that mine and man the pumps and get it ready for the town to take over. There are men who believed, still believe, that a priest had the power to damn their souls if they didn't do what he told them to do. And the women were even worse because they were holier. So we set up picket lines to keep Father Ranald's men out, and they kept trying to break through to the mines.

"Their children were cursing us and our children were throwing rocks at them, and the children were fighting with each other. The men, too, of course, especially if a bottle got involved, and lots of bottles did.

"It was ugly and it went on all winter. Darkness would fall, and the town would disappear, only to flicker awake by lantern-light in a few windows. After the first couple of weeks, not many people had enough money to buy kerosene, and those who did rationed it out.

"When they put this rink up that winter, our kids, the strikers' children, weren't allowed to skate on it. Imagine the tiny mind he had to have for Father Ranald to be standing by a rink fence on a cold winter day looking through hoods and parkas and scarves for little boys and girls whose fathers were on strike. And then ordering them off the ice, children five and six years old, some of them. So we damn well built a rink of our own down by the slag piles, near where our picket line was so we could keep our eyes on our children. Of course, on the back shift on the picket line there wasn't much to do but stand around a barrel of fire trying to stay warm, so some of the men began taking their skates to strike duty, and that was when I learned to skate. I was a sight, apparently, but I got to enjoy it after a while. Still, even though all that's behind us now, I could never make myself come up here to this rink in later winters to keep on skating."

"So how did it end?" Duncan, who had wormed his way into a seat beside Taurus, asked.

"We got what we were hoping for. I wouldn't say we won, but we got our way. An election made it the political thing to do, to take over the mine. The government needed to hang on to this seat, so a new compressor was set up, and you should have seen this town the night they lit her up. They waited, the way politicians always do, until it was dark, and then they fired the thing up and the town exploded in light. Well, the joy! For a few minutes nobody remembered anything about the past eight months. It was as if all those lights had gone on inside our heads letting us see just how foolish this whole business of trying to own one another really is, but it didn't last.

"We got another twenty years or so out of the mine until it closed ... what ... seven years ago? I still think we were right to get the government involved except they really didn't give a damn about the mine, just staying in power, so none of the right things were done to make the mines really work. I don't know if it was worth it or not to have that strike. There are men I really liked who haven't talked to me since 1932."

We sat around the stove taking in Taurus's story, wondering where our own parents or grandparents were during the strike. Maybe the fact that Calum, and Bartholomew too for that matter, weren't miners might have made it easier for them to be friends with Taurus, or maybe it was because he stood up to the Catholic Church that they liked him, but I knew at the bottom of my heart that their friendship didn't have anything to do with mining.

Duncan was doing math on his fingers. "My father would have only been eight years old in 1932. Too young to be on strike," he said, disappointed.

"Now you young fellows mind that what I'm telling you is only my version of what happened. It may be a completely different story at your kitchen table. But what you'll find most is nobody wants to talk about it. And unless you think I'm slandering the priest, you might want to know that he died two years ago in an insane asylum. Should have been in there thirty years ago," Taurus said, draining his cup and passing it back to the owner of the thermos. "Good tea, but not as good as my friend's here," he added, cuffing me on the side of the head. "I'll be by for a cup when Calum opens the sun porch again."

Duncan and I took another shift flooding the rink. Duncan was so excited about Taurus's story he couldn't stop talking about it. "Think of being on strike for eight whole months, Smelt! In the papers the miners in New Waterford and the steel workers in Sydney always seem to be going on strike, but I never thought it could happen here. Too bad we didn't still have mines. We could organize a strike of our own. The old man's in a union in Ontario, and they talk about going on strike sometimes but they never do. What the old man says is that strikes make the mine owners pay you more money for the work you do, but the best part, he says, is that it just pisses them off to think that 'rubber boot,' that's what he says the owners call them, that 'rubber boot' miners could have a mind of their own."

Once the last sheet of water had been sprayed across the ice surface we all sat in the shack waiting. It was almost five a.m., and even though going home to bed felt like a great idea, we sat around the fire and waited. Finally, someone came in and announced that the ice was frozen solid. We laced on our skates, hauled out the nets, turned on the lights, picked up our sticks and stepped onto the ice, skating through a silence broken only by the slap of a puck from the blue line tangling quietly in the mesh of the homemade net.

10

Every day all winter, except Sundays, Calum walked the few blocks to Bartholomew's store for his paper, leaving the house an hour and fifteen minutes before the train arrived with the *Herald*. Bartholomew's store was long and narrow, with still-life bowls of bananas, oranges and apples on display in the two large front windows. The displays of fruit, as fresh as we could get in Shean, were in the store windows when nothing else of importance was happening in town, because the store's windows were a living calendar.

In summer and winter the town's local and provincial trophies for baseball, softball or hockey were on display in Bartholomew's window along with a team picture of the winners who had brought sports glory to Shean. Over the Labour Day weekend, the end of summer was announced with displays of Bearcat and Hilroy scribblers, Webster's dictionaries, and math instruments; in November a black throw-cloth held a sad garden of artificial poppies, red as blood drops, with pictures among them of men from Shean who had gone off to the two wars and had never come home, a brooding memorial to our war dead; in December, the windows of Bartholomew's store grew festive and bright, lights twinkling around the edges, drawing attention to the wonders of this year's gift choices. As other occasions arose, Valentine's or Graduation Day, the store windows took on the character of the holiday, and when there was nothing to celebrate, there was always the fresh fruit.

Inside, the hardwood floors were warped and worn and the walls lined with products, the left wall holding all the patent medicines: cure-alls and cure specifics; aids for the eyes, nose, mouth, chest, stomach or limbs; tonics to grow hair; tonics to dye hair; and machines to dry hair. There were poisons and preventions, all guaranteed by doctor so-and-so. Lining the right wall were all the tobacco needs: cigars and cigarettes, chewing tobacco and snuff, pipes and lighters. Beside the tobacco display was the rich-tasting candy counter with displays of chocolate boxes rising in card-house construction, each box showing a lady holding a box of chocolates which showed a lady holding a box of chocolates which showed a lady holding a ... well, it seemed to go on forever. There were smaller glass displays of long-lasting white peppermints, known as "farmers' chocolates," and licorice and caramels and creams and maple buds. The two walls faced each other for fifty years like old foes, the health shelves versus the pleasure shelves.

At the back of the store, a marble soda fountain served strawberry, vanilla and chocolate milkshakes and ice cream cones of similar shades, and from either end of the soda fountain two long, glass showcases ran the length of the store. From behind these glass counters, their tops piled high with newspapers, recipe and pattern magazines for women, and magazines for men with half-dressed women on the cover, tiny pieces of tape holding the magazine covers closed from the prying eyes of young and curious boys, Bartholomew served his customers. The showcases themselves were filled with gift choices of china or clocks or watches.

On either side of the door where customers walked in were long, cast iron hot-water radiators that stretched a couple of feet beyond either side of the glass cases, enough for Bartholomew to rest on the waist-high radiator on his side of the counter and Calum or another customer to lean on it on his side. Like their conversations in the sun porch, the store talks were carried out while they stared through the store's picture window, studying the people and traffic on the street.

When the train's whistle sounded as it rounded the Protestant graveyard, announcing its arrival at the Shean station within fifteen minutes, it was also telling people that the *Halifax Chronicle Herald* would be on Bartholomew's counter within the half hour.

Men began filling up the store, waiting for their paper, bantering all winter about hockey and all summer about baseball and always about politics. This was the best time to be at Bartholomew's, if I could get down from school before the papers arrived and the men, including Calum, dispersed. For one thing, if I wanted money, this was the best place to ask Calum for a quarter, a trick I learned from Duncan. Parents almost never refuse when you ask them for money in front of company, he said. We never had a lot of company at our house, so Bartholomew's store at noon was as crowded as it got. I also knew it wasn't something I could get away with very often, so I never wore out my requests.

Mostly, though, Bartholomew never let kids hang around his store, shooing them off to The Turk's restaurant if they weren't buying candy or newspapers. Some kids, like Duncan, were barred from the store for life. Bartholomew caught Duncan trying to shove a *Police Gazette* with a picture of a half-naked woman on the cover under his jacket.

At noon one February day, Mother Saint Cross John sent a note to all the classes that school was cancelled that afternoon because of an unpredicted storm raging outside. It had come up quickly without warning and was welcomed by every student in the school. Outside the town was barely moving. The storm was throwing waist-deep snowdrifts across the street, lifting blinding sheets of snow on the wind, behind which the town disappeared as if it was a magician's cape. It was the kind of storm that drove adults indoors and young people out. We were free to explore the storm to the point of freezing, then find refuge in the warmth of The Turk's restaurant, slipping nickels into his pinball machines while someone worked a wire coat-hanger through a crack in the glass, hitting the 1000-point bumper until we had racked up enough games to last us the afternoon. Duncan, Farter and I were meeting there after dinner to plan our day off.

When I got home I swept the snow off myself in the back porch and went into the house, but Calum wasn't there. He had gone as usual to Bartholomew's store before the storm and was probably still there. I pulled my coat back on and headed for Bartholomew's, afraid of finding Calum in every bulge of grave-shaped snow on the street.

He was still leaning on the radiator on his side of the counter, Bartholomew on the other. Other snow-covered men huddled around it, stamping snow from their boots and slapping their snow-peaked caps across their thighs, reaching in to warm their hands on a rib of radiator, blowing drips of snot from red noses into polka-dot handkerchiefs, asking, "Paper in yet?"while assembling to stand in the store and wait for their *Herald* to arrive.

After ten or twelve people had asked, "Paper in yet?" Bartholomew walked to the phone at the back of the store, twisted the crank and asked the operator to get him the station. A few moments later he walked back to his perch at the radiator.

"John the Station says as far as he knows the train's just late. Nobody has wired to say it stopped anywhere."

"If it was caught in a drift or went off the track how would anybody know that?" Sandy Sight wondered aloud.

"Could be caught in a drift, I suppose," Archie Miller said. "Remember when the train was caught in the pass at Black Rock for three days? One slut of a winter, that one."

"Calum was on that train," Bartholomew observed, a silence following his words as the men who had come through the storm anticipated a tale. Calum seemed not to notice at first, but then nodded his acknowledgment that he had indeed been on the snow-bound train that men still recalled decades later.

"You were coming from Boston, weren't you, you and your daughter?" Bartholomew said. "How many would've been on that train?"

"Nineteen," Calum said, adding "including the crew."

"Must have been cold," Sandy Sight said, peering at Calum through his still fogged-up bottle-bottom glasses.

"Bitter enough. We spent the first night in the caboose. The cook stove in there took care of us."

"I heard something about it turning into a big party," Sandy said, trying to prime the pump for Calum's telling of the story.

"I suppose," Calum said, clamping his lips into the thin grim line of someone who was not enjoying the memory.

Bartholomew, although he was a lot like Calum when they were in the sun porch, was also a merchant who spent his days in banter with the men who came to his store to pick up their papers as ritually as they went to church on Sunday. Over the years, he had probably heard a version of the story from just about everybody on the train. He steered the attention away from his friend by taking over the story himself.

"Malkie Beaton brought his team down to the train when the storm let up and took everybody back to his place. They were there the next couple of days, Malkie's wife feeding them, but Malkie himself had a cellar full of something he didn't want to drink alone. And do you know who else was on the train? Angus Timmons and his fiddle. So I guess they had quite a time in the two days it took to dig the train out. Fifty men with pan shovels! Had to pay them mine wages to do it. Cost the train company plenty."

"Good," said Archie. "But wasn't there a hell of a fight or something?"

Bartholomew just shook his head like he couldn't remember anybody mentioning anything about that, and Calum was looking out into the storm like nobody else was in the store. I began to get it then. Calum coming back from Boston with my Aunt Evelyn, and them getting caught in the storm and all that partying and music, and her a drinker. Maybe she got away on Calum.

"Do you know a storm that was almost as bad...," Bartholomew said, taking the conversation elsewhere. John the Station phoned in the middle of that story to say the train got through, and someone was already on the way with the papers. The men fell in line along the counter as Bartholomew rationed out the *Herald* one to a customer for a nickel. One man after another buckled up and disappeared into the storm. Later, when the mail came in on the evening train and was sorted into boxes by Lick 'n Stick, the postmaster, Calum would send me for the mail, and I would see the same men gathering again, this time in the lobby of the post office, asking as each stamped snow from his feet, "Mail assorted yet?"

Calum took his paper from Bartholomew, which I took from Calum and shoved under my jacket to keep dry, and walked ahead of him, breaking a path through the drifts so he could follow me.

It may have been too stormy for school, but the storm blowing in off the ice floes covering the Gulf of St. Lawrence didn't stop many of us from fighting our way through squalls and snowdrifts to get to Tony the Turk's in the afternoon, the girls gathering in the booths and the guys around the pinball machines and along the counter, although those patterns were beginning to unravel with our growing interest in each other.

The Turk's wasn't the only restaurant in town, but it was the only hangout – when it was opened, that is. Tony, being an unpredictable boozer, occasionally fired his whole staff for some imaginary reason right in the middle of a busy day. With no one to work for him, the restaurant would have to close until Tony had apologized and pleaded with Nicole MacRory and the other waitresses to come back to work. Or, less often, in the middle of a bottle in the middle of the night Tony would decide to renovate the restaurant, ripping and tearing at counters and kitchen, while his hand-written sign in the window announced that he was Closed For Business. Most of the time, though, The Turk's was open for business, Tony dishing out burgers and fries and making change for the pinball machines and the jukebox.

I was playing pinball when Mary Scotland came into the restaurant shaking off the snow and making her way to a booth where her friends sat. After taking off her parka, Mary walked over to the jukebox, dropped her money in and began reading the music selections. I tried to stay concentrated on the route the chrome ball was following amid a noisy soundtrack of bumpers, but my knowledge of her presence was more distracting than in school.

When Mary Scotland went back to her booth, Ack-Ack tugged the upright collar of his black leather jacket and walked over to where she was sitting. With his duck-tail sweep of hair and the cigarette burning down to a butt without him ever pulling it from his lips, just inhaling and exhaling and squinting through the stream of smoke at Mary Scotland, Ack-Ack began miming the words to the song, directing them to Mary who was trying not to laugh at him. He began gesturing for her to dance with him in the middle of the restaurant floor, something nobody ever did, and she refused. He reached down and began tugging her wrist, trying to draw her from her seat into his arms. The pinball machine was racking up points and games as if it was playing itself while my peripheral vision took in what was happening, but I had no idea what to do about it. Then Duncan, who had been at the counter talking to Nicole, was standing at the booth between the two of them saying something to Mary who laughed at his joke, but Ack-Ack didn't find it one bit funny and sly-poked Duncan behind the ear, sending him crashing on top of Mary. Then he grabbed Duncan again and flung him across the floor, and Duncan went stutter-stepping backwards into the counter with Ack-Ack charging at him. Mary jumped out of the booth and tried to reason with him, grabbing his arm but Ack-Ack just flipped her off, his whole focus concentrated on Duncan and the unfinished business from the day Duncan rescued Piper from the clothesline. Whatever fear I had of Ack-Ack was sucked into the vortex of rage at seeing Mary stumbling backwards, and I pushed myself away from the pinball machine and made a run for him, tackling him from behind just as he was about to punch Duncan. With me riding on Ack-Ack's broncing back, Duncan threw a flurry of punches, and there was blood on Ack-Ack's face; and before I could let him go, I was pulled off him by Tony who, holding a cleaver, grabbed Ack-Ack by the collar and ran him to the door, throwing him into the fading blizzard.

Duncan and I began straightening ourselves out when Tony came back from the door and told us to get a move on, that we were to "Get out and never come back!" It was a common banishment but, unlike Bartholomew's, it wouldn't last past turning up at the counter with a quarter for french fries and a Pepsi.

With Tony towering over the two of us, Mary apologized to Duncan for getting him in trouble, which Duncan accepted with a nothing-to-it shrug. Then she turned to me, saying, "You're a good friend to help Duncan like that, Roddie."

11

Spring rarely comes to western Cape Breton the way poems in our school books talked about it, all flowers and sunshine. Instead, it was mostly mud and last minute snowstorms with an occasional perfect day. Calum and I left the house on one of those perfect days, a Sunday morning when the Gulf of St. Lawrence was a turquoise mirror of the sky and ghosts of the broken polar ice floes floated like gems in a liquid setting. The wharf was piled with lobster traps, the fishermen hoping they would see the last of the ice before the first of May. The town was afloat on a vapor of ground frost from the thawing earth under the unpaved streets, and the streets themselves, not yet turned to muddy puddles, were spongy and soft to the step.

We walked together up Culloden Street to where it was crossed by Church Street, and there we parted, Calum going left to St. Paul's Presbyterian Church and I turning right to Holy Family Catholic Church. At the crossroads, Calum was joined by Bartholomew while Mrs. Fraser walked with me, but I left her as quickly as I could at the front door and hurried around back with her parting words, the ones she said every Sunday, ringing in my ears: "Be sure to pray for them."

It was one of the earliest things I understood about God, that he wasn't Protestant and that my grandfather and Bartholomew and all the others gathering in St. Paul's were doomed to eternal damnation unless they learned the truth of the Catholic Church. Mrs. Fraser spent her whole life praying for Bartholomew, and for Calum too, and never failed to instruct me to do the same. She wasn't the first. It had been brought up a couple of times by nuns in school who told me I should listen for God's call to the priesthood and dedicate my life to praying for Calum's conversion. They implied that because my grandmother died too young to accomplish that miracle, the responsibility fell to me. Mrs. Fraser took it even further, suggesting my grandmother was called away because she didn't take her spiritual responsibilities seriously enough, enjoying music and laughter too much instead of praying for Calum. Mrs. Fraser's dream was to know that her husband would be buried beside her in the Catholic graveyard, saved by the grace of her prayers and God's goodness.

I used to worry about it a lot, the idea that Calum was going to Hell, and asked him once to turn Catholic. He gestured for me to follow him into his study where he sat at his desk and I sat on the other chair.

"Roddie," he said, "your grandmother and I had an understanding when we were married that we would keep our religions. There were conditions I had to agree to, and because of those you are Catholic today. I promised your grandmother, and I promised your church, and I try to be a man of my word.

"You're not the first person in this family to have my religion held over them like sword. You may pray for me if you wish, but don't expect those prayers to be answered, and don't," he said, his words rising to anger, "allow those people to convince you that God's judgement of me is in your hands. That foolishness has already destroyed one life in this family!"

After that, I didn't spend as much time worrying about Calum turning Catholic, because he didn't seem worried about it himself. Still, I never forgot to offer a prayer for his conversion, although, in spite of what the nuns said, I didn't hear God calling me to a vocation in the priesthood.

When Duncan and I talked about it, he said I better not tell any of the nuns that I didn't want to be a priest because as long as they thought there was a chance I would join up, they'd go on grading me no matter how bad my marks were. Of course, Duncan's advice was no more comforting than Calum's, because even though he was a Catholic, he was always raising some heresy in religion class, asking questions that the teachers couldn't answer. They hated that. One teacher even said he was possessed by the Devil.

When I got to the back of the church to get ready to serve Mass, the priest hadn't arrived in the vestry yet, and Duncan was rooting through the cupboards to see what he could find. I slammed the door behind me to make him jump, but it didn't scare him at all. Then I joined him. We found the collection basket from the morning's first Mass in one cupboard filled with envelopes and loose bills and lots of change, but we didn't take any. Stealing money from the church was something both of us were too scared to do. Wine wasn't the same thing, Duncan said. One cupboard was filled with the elaborate robes of High Mass, rich, colourful gold-threaded cloth for celebrating special occasions from funerals to the Resurrection. Another cupboard was filled with used candles, twisted candle holders, plaster statues of Jesus and Mary and a bunch of saints with no fingers and broken noses. Duncan said that the Church couldn't throw them away because even though they were broken they were still blessed. He said that they had to be shipped to Rome where the Pope had a big graveyard for burying blessed things from all over the world.

As we scouted the cupboards with interest, the form of a woman moved past the window: Mrs. Bruce, the grade ten teacher and the only teacher in the school who was young, pretty and not a nun, was coming to confession before Mass. Before I knew what was happening Duncan raced to the confessional, opened the priest's door, stepped inside and turned on the light above the door that signaled to parishioners the priest was waiting to hear confession.

Mrs. Bruce nodded to me as she opened one of the two confessional doors on either side of where the priest sat. A moment later, the vestry door opened behind me and Father Alex walked in, made a quick apology for being late and began preparing for Mass. I went to the altar boys' closet and began putting on my surplice and soutane.

"Where's Duncan?" Father Alex asked.

"I didn't see him," I lied, walking in front of the parish priest to keep him from looking toward the confessional and discovering what Duncan was up to. "I can do the Mass alone," I added, wanting to lead the half-dressed priest as quickly as possible through the door that led from the vestry to the altar.

He laboured over every stitch he put on, holding the vestment, making a short prayer before putting it over his head, giving the stole a humble kiss before putting it around his neck, while through all this eternity I wondered if he could hear my heart beating.

"Ready, Father?" I asked, but instead of directing me to lead him, he began to frisk himself.

"Where did I put my glasses?" he asked, looking around, his gaze stopping to study the light on over the confessional door.

"Did I leave that light on?" he asked, walking toward the confessional. Duncan and I were both as good as dead. Prayers for help were screaming through my mind, when the vestry door opened behind me and Mrs. Fraser stood there.

"Father, would you please bless this medal for me?" she asked. Father Alex turned from the confessional and went to her. Behind him, while he muttered Latin words over Mrs. Fraser's medal, I watched the confessional light go out. Mrs. Fraser was explaining that she planned to pin the medal to their mattress so that Bartholomew would be sleeping in the presence of God and might have a dream like Joseph did that would convince him to convert. When she left, Father Alex turned again to the confessional.

"I turned it off while you were blessing the medal, Father," I said, walking deliberately toward the altar door. With a shrug he followed me.

A few minutes after Mass started, Duncan came through the same door to help me serve. He was white and gave me a long, grateful exhale as if to say that that was too close for comfort. A little later, the front door opened. I took a peek over my shoulder and saw Mrs. Bruce looking surprised that Father Alex could have gotten so far along in the Mass in the short time it took her to walk from the vestry around to the front of the church.

Duncan and I served Mass by mumbling our way through the Latin responses, our voices rising confidently with *Et cum Spirito tu tuo* and a handful of other phrases we mastered. We moved through the various parts of the Mass all the way to the sermon when Father Alex mounted the circular stairs that took him into the pulpit suspended from a pillar several feet over the heads of the congregation. He began speaking to his drowsy listeners when there was a slight commotion at the back of the church. Duncan and I, seated on the altar boys' bench beside the altar, craned our necks to get a look and saw Johnny Logan's clumsy walk coming toward the centre aisle.

One of the town drunks, Johnny Logan was a more familiar figure stemming money in front of the liquor store than he was a churchgoer. Duncan looked at me and gave a knowing nod. He had changed his mind about Johnny Logan whom we used to tease, even torment, when he was too drunk to do anything about it.

Ever since Taurus told us at the rink about what Duncan always referred to as "the strike of '32," Duncan had been trying to learn more about it. He even asked the history teacher one day why we were learning about dead Romans instead of our own history, like the strike of '32. The words themselves made the nun bristle, but she never answered his question. He asked other people as well, and one afternoon in John Alex's barn, when Johnny Logan was hanging around hoping for a drink, John Alex gave him enough for a quart of wine and sent him off.

"Shame," John Alex said, and Rory John Angus agreed.

"What's a shame?" Duncan asked, and eventually wheedled the story out of them.

During the strike of '32, John Alex said, Johnny Logan had been with the Protestants, even though he was Catholic like Taurus. One afternoon when the men were meeting in the roundhouse at the train station because the priest wouldn't let them have the parish hall, Father Ranald arrived at the meeting to break it up. He ordered them all to go home, and nobody really wanted to get into it with a priest, not even the Protestants. Johnny Logan was having a few drinks of false courage, John Alex told Duncan, and he told the priest he was crazy and ordered him to get out of their meeting. He even made a few mock runs at the priest as if he was going to grab him and throw him out, and when the priest defied him, Johnny Logan let go a kick. It wasn't meant to hit the priest, and in fact it didn't, but it caught the hem of his long black coat. Father Ranald glared at him, then pointed a finger and told Johnny he would lose the use of his legs for threatening a man of the cloth. Logan laughed at him and slammed the door closed after the priest left the meeting.

Despite the strike, both sides had come to one common agreement, and that was that they would keep the mine from flooding. Each day a crew went underground, one shift from one side of the strike and the next shift from the other side. These men operated the pumps that kept the water level down. If the mine was allowed to flood, then neither side would win and Shean would be the only loser.

A few days after the confrontation between Father Ranald and Johnny Logan it was Johnny's shift at the pumps. During that shift he went into an old working to have a crap, and the roof collapsed on him while he was squatting there, burying him. He was in the hospital for months with legs so crushed they thought he would never walk again. But he did walk again, although it was on stiff legs and he was drunk so much of the time that it was hard to tell what was making him walk that way, the accident or the booze.

But he was never the same after that, John Alex said, and that incident pretty near lost the strike for the men opposing Father Ranald's plan. Everybody began saying the priest has the power, and there were wives who didn't want their husbands going up against him any more, and there were men who never said a word, just stopped turning up for strike duty. In the end, it wasn't enough to change some people's minds about Father Ranald's plan, especially the Protestants, but it came close to winning the day for the priest.

"Those mines would still be open if we listened to Father Ranald," Angus John Rory said.

"Bullshit," John Alex said, spitting on the floor, then turned to Duncan and said that Johnny Logan was only nineteen when he had his accident, but he was an old man, an old drunk man when he got out of the hospital.

"Do you know why?" Angus John Rory asked, then answered, his own question, "Because he believed it himself. Johnny Logan believed the priest crippled him. Believed it! He was still Catholic enough for that, and do you know what? So do I. That priest had the power, I'm telling you, he had the power!"

Not everyone would talk to Duncan about the strike when he tried to ask questions. It was still an unhealed wound, and lots of people told Duncan when he asked, "What do you want to go stirring all that up again for? Let it be."

After hearing the story about Johnny Logan, though, Duncan was different with him, even though the man was a mess, wearing piss-stained pants as often as not. Duncan was probably the youngest person in town who gave Johnny a few coins whenever he could.

Now Johnny Logan was making his drunken way up the aisle. Nobody in his right mind would confuse Father Alex in the pulpit with Father Ranald, Father Alex being practically a saint, but that seemed to be what Johnny Logan was doing when he began hollering as he approached the pulpit, his words mostly a slur, but you could tell he was cursing the Church and the priest. Then he was calling the Church the anti-Christ, saying that the Catholic Church had killed Christianity and nothing could do that but the anti-Christ. A hundred hands went to foreheads in a sign of the cross once people began to hear what Johnny Logan was saying. Nobody moved as he kept walking down the aisle, shifting one leg in front of the other like they were wooden ones, spittle coming out of his mouth with the blasphemies.

When Father Alex heard the word "anti-Christ" and realized that it was directed at the Church, his gentle face turned hard as stone and he glared down from the pulpit. Maybe it was that look, that look unlike anything anybody had ever seen on Father Alex's face, that triggered Johnny Logan's memory of that other priest, because he began shaking his fist at Father Alex, calling him Father Ranald, challenging him to come down off that pulpit and stop looking down on people like they were nothing but sheep, and come outside and settle this like a real man. Finally the congregation unfroze, and a small surge of men began moving angrily toward the drunk but receded again when they realized Taurus MacLeod had left his seat and was walking toward Johnny. Unlike the others, there was no anger in Taurus's approach. He simply walked up the aisle and stood beside Johnny for a moment before reaching out and touching him on the elbow. Logan turned defensively, then saw Taurus and sort of sagged. "You were there, Taurus, you were there. You know what happened. You dug me out. It was an accident, not a god-damned priest that crippled me, an accident. We were right, weren't we? We were right. Tell me we were right!"

Taurus never said the words Johnny was asking for, but there was no mistaking the certainty in the nod of his head. Johnny broke down then, his anger turning to huge sobs that seemed to embarrass all of us in the church, and Taurus walked out with him and never came back for the rest of the Mass.

In the silence that fell over the church after their departure, Father Alex did not continue his sermon. Instead, he gazed down on the congregation for a moment, the stone face gone now, and said we should all sit in silent reflection on the nature of forgiveness, think about those people whom each of us has to forgive for recent or ancient wrongs.

When the Mass resumed, Duncan and I prepared the priest for Holy Communion, bringing him the bread and wine which he blessed and offered up as the body and blood of Jesus Christ. Then he served Communion to both of us; and I took the paten while Duncan went to sit down since it only required one altar boy to help the priest. The people knelt along the rail between the altar and the pews, and Father Alex took a round white host from the gold chalice and placed it with a blessing on the tongue of each person, while I held the brass platter under each chin to catch the holy host if it was dropped by the priest or the recipient. When we came to Mrs. Bruce kneeling before the priest with her eyes closed in reverence and her tongue out to receive the sacrament, believing she was freshly confessed, I caught Duncan's eye, but he looked away and never mentioned it after Mass was over.

12

The three of them were back in the sun porch like spring birds on a budding branch, their presence obscured from most passersby by Calum's wall of plants along the windowsill. Taurus wasn't there the first couple of weeks, and Calum and Bartholomew didn't ask about him; they never did. When I saw Mrs. MacLeod shopping in the Farmers' Store I asked her to tell Taurus that the sun porch was open, and she told me he hadn't been feeling well, that he had even been a little delirious, and I couldn't help wondering if maybe she was telling me he had been in DT's. Lots of families didn't like admitting to a boozer in the house, so they invented illnesses to explain absences. But Taurus didn't like to drink alone or at home, so if he had been drinking, Duncan or I would probably have heard about it.

I was coming from Duncan's house when I saw him sitting with Calum and Bartholomew in the warmth of a late Saturday morning. I poked my head in the sun porch to say hello, and Calum pulled his watch from its pocket by the chain, a gesture that suggested I was cutting tea time too close. In the brown paper bag in my hand was a collection of squares and cookies from Mrs. MacFarlane's Saturday morning baking.

"Aren't you a good boy," Mrs. MacFarlane remarked when I told her why I had to go home. I only told her because I knew it would piss off Duncan who was always hearing from Mrs. MacFarlane that he should try to be more like me, a comparison he endured only because he knew how many times, when he did something that led his mother to praise me, I had actually been with him. But I could run faster, lie harder and hide better than he could.

Except for Mrs. MacFarlane, I never told anybody I was going home to make the tea. It was such a long-standing chore that

I never saw it as anything unusual; but once, when I had to leave The Turk's to go home to make noon tea, the teasing started about me doing women's work. It was embarrassing, especially in front of Mary Scotland, and it reminded me of how Duncan had first become convinced that Calum was weird.

When my grandmother died, there was a half-finished quilt on the loom she set up each winter in the parlour. Instead of dismantling it to make room for her coffin, Calum had some men help him move it almost intact into his study. After the funeral, he had them help him move it back to the parlour. That winter, he finished the drunken sailor pattern himself and used it to cover the couch in the sun porch. The first thing Duncan saw the first time he came to my house was Calum in the parlour stitching the quilt. "Are you Duncan's grandmother?" he asked, laughing his head off at Calum, but Calum just glared over the top of his glasses, and since then they never found anything in common that they liked except, I guess, me.

When I took the tea to them, along with some of Mrs. Mac-Farlane's baking, Calum was showing Bartholomew and Taurus something he had drawn on a sheet of draft paper.

"Stay around," he said to me, "I'll need you," then returned to his Gaelic explanation, Bartholomew and Taurus seeming to agree to something. When the tea was finished Calum told me to bring two galvanized buckets and a shovel from his workshop and meet them at Bartholomew's store, the three of them going on ahead.

"What's going on?" I asked Taurus, but he just winked and smiled, and when I got to the store Bartholomew was inside speaking to his hired clerk. When he came back out he was carrying some cardboard boxes that had been flattened, and he put them in the back of the panel truck. Then the three old men squeezed into the front seat while I sat on the floor in the back with no idea what we were up to, but with the feeling that I wouldn't be spending this Saturday afternoon hanging out at The Turk's with Farter and Duncan and wishing either of them was Mary Scotland instead.

The panel truck wound its way down the beach road past the hills of grey clay, coming to a stop near the wharf where fishermen were landing their lobster. Bartholomew backed the panel truck almost onto the beach, and we all got out. Looking along the shoreline and out at the Gulf of St. Lawrence, it was easy to forget that we were living in the dirty aftermath of an old coal town with too few jobs and no money to paint houses or do any of the things that people would like to do to their homes. The golden sand stretched in a horseshoe for more than a mile, and on the lapping waves of the Gulf, a few colourful lobster boats hauled their traps. The water was still too cold this early in June for swimming. The beach was barely visited except for couples in love who came here to walk and talk and be by themselves, but in a month's time we would practically be living here, Duncan and me and everybody else with no school.

"Fill those buckets with sand and put it in the truck," Calum ordered while the three of them walked along with their heads down, bending to pick up stones that fitted some idea they had in their mind, and carrying them back to the truck. I filled the buckets and placed them in the truck and watched as Calum approached with a stone, placed it in the truck, then arranged the flattened cardboard to cover the floor. He picked up the first bucket and dumped the sand on the cardboard, then the second, and passed both buckets back to me, telling me to keep doing that until there was enough.

"Enough for what?" I asked, but he was already wandering back along the beach, and Taurus and Bartholomew were coming, carrying more carefully chosen stones. I shoveled sand fast, hoping we would get out of there before anybody I knew came along and asked what we were doing. The sand and the rocks built up until the back of the panel truck was sagging like a hen's hole laying a goose's egg. Slowly, whining all the way, the panel truck carried its burden away from the beach and back to our house where it was left for me to unload the whole cargo onto the lawn while the three of them went their own ways, Bartholomew back to the store, Taurus to his home and Calum to rest in the sun porch for awhile.

When I had piled the sand and the rocks on the lawn and swept out the panel truck I went to tell Calum that I was finished.

I wasn't.

He sat up and told me to hook the hose to the outside tap, and when I had done that he was standing at the tower of rocks I had carefully piled up. He told me to spread them out on the grass. That done, he instructed me to hose them down, and then, with an old towel, rub them dry.

I was in the middle of drying the rocks when Duncan came by to see what I was up to. Calum, when he told me what he wanted, explained that all the salt had to be removed from the rocks and even the sand, because he was going to be cementing the stones together, and if the salt stayed on them or in the sand, it would weaken the cement. None of this proved an adequate defense against the fact that, "Old Calum's got you washing and drying rocks. It's not bad enough that you have to wash the dishes, but he's got you washing rocks, too. Next thing you know, he'll have you shampooing the lawn."

The next thing Duncan knew, though, he was washing sand in a large flat box made for hand-mixing cement, then he and I were mixing the sand with cement, adding water and with two shovels turning the concoction into a thick grey soup while Calum selected and arranged stones, then began mortaring them together in a circle that grew higher and narrower until it stood about three feet tall. At the bottom it was about 18 inches and a foot across at the top where Calum capped it with a flat stone.

"I see what he was doing now," Duncan volunteered. "He was making a pile of rocks. Senile old men do that all the time, just like babies with their alphabet blocks."

"What is it?" I asked Calum as the three of us stood around the now finished tiny stone tower.

"A cairn," he answered quietly, seemingly lost in thought, then repeated it. "It's a cairn."

"It doesn't look like any Karen I ever saw," Duncan muttered, then addressed Calum. "Want us to drive Bartholomew's truck back to the store?" Calum glared at Duncan and then walked around to the driver's door and took the keys out of the ignition.

The next morning, Taurus and Mrs. MacLeod walked down Culloden Street with me after Mass because Taurus wanted to see the cairn. Calum's church hadn't let out yet, so we walked across the lawn and stood looking at his work.

"The dictionary says a cairn is a landmark," I told Taurus. "Why would Calum need one?"

"The English dictionary told you that, I suppose," Taurus said. "To the Scots a cairn is a lot more than that, boy. It's a monument, a way of remembering something or someone important. I don't suppose Calum told you why he built this one?" I shook my head. "He probably won't, either. Your grandfather has a way of keeping things to himself. Your grandmother had a way of cracking him open when she wanted to, though. She could get to him. Whose wedding was it we went to the time Belle got so drunk?" Taurus asked his wife whose mouth fell open with shock that he would be talking that way about my grandmother in front of me. "Well, whose?" Taurus asked again.

"I don't remember, and I don't think that's what you should be talking to this young man about," Mrs. MacLeod answered.

"Not remembering is my job," Taurus replied, "but you remember every piece of juicy gossip that's gone on in this town."

"I would never gossip about Belle Gillies," Mrs. MacLeod said. "Besides, she wasn't drunk, just a little giddy."

"Anyway," Taurus continued, giving up on getting help from his wife, "it was somebody's wedding, and Belle got into the punch. She probably didn't know what kind of a punch was in that punch, but it was nothing but moonshine made sweet. It turned her into the life of the party, and it wouldn't take too much shine to lighten your grandmother up. She was a natural for a good time. I don't mean she was a boozer, she wasn't, but she always had time for a song or a story. You'd think Calum would have no toleration for that business, especially in public, at a wedding, but she danced with everybody, talked to everybody, but he never said a word, which, you know, I think disappointed some people. They thought there was a fight brewing, Calum being who he was and Belle being who she was; but to tell you the truth, I think he was getting a kick out of her himself, although whatever humour is inside Calum is as stiff as the wood he works with. Whose wedding was that?" This time the question was addressed to himself, and I thought of the picture hanging in the parlour of Calum and Belle, the two of them all dressed up and my grandmother with a drink and cigarette in her hands.

"Whatever this was built for, whoever this was built for is between Calum and God. Your grandmother would be my guess, but it's a fine piece of stone work," Taurus said, running his hand along the rounded stones. "Cairns I've come across up in the mountains, and some monuments up there are free-standing stones that will eventually topple and fall back into the earth, some already have, but this one's going to be here for awhile."

Calum came through the gate then, joining us, and invited Taurus and Mrs. MacLeod into the sun porch. I ran into the house to make tea, surprised by his invitation. Mrs. MacLeod was the first woman I ever saw in there, but when Calum invited them to stay, Taurus accepted, telling his wife that she had to see "what this boy can do with a cup of tea." In the kitchen, I put the teapot to steep beside Calum's Sunday stew simmering on the stove, then I went to the pantry and took out Mrs. MacFarlane's bag of baking. I had put out some of it with the tea the day before and hidden the rest for myself, but with a woman in the house I had no choice but to make a plate for her.

Mrs. MacLeod sipped from her cup as she watched the last of the Protestants make their way down Culloden Street from St.

Paul's Church, then she took a square from the plate and bit into it. When she took a square, so did I, having fasted since midnight for Holy Communion. She and Calum and Taurus gabbed in the Gaelic all through their tea, but when she finished hers Mrs. MacLeod asked me if there was any more. It was a compliment that made me nervous. What I didn't need was a reputation for making good tea among old women who were the grandmothers of guys I knew. It would be different if they talked about how good I was to draw or play hockey, but not as somebody that old women thought made the best tea in Shean.

Before she and Taurus left, Mrs. MacLeod brought the cups into the house, and the ooohing and aaaahing started. Not many women visited us, but when they did, they all made the same noise. Calum had built his house after he and my grandmother were married. It was nothing fancy to look at, a storey and a half under a steep-pitched roof that looked like dozens of others in and around Shean, plain brown except for the white gingerbread trim that hung under the eaves like stiff lace, Calum's own handiwork. Inside, there were lots more of Calum's touches, though. The floor of the parlour was a shiny hardwood that Calum had done himself, small oak pieces worked into a star pattern in the middle, although it was usually hidden under a mat. He had engraved all of the door frames with Celtic knots, although Belle used to tell people they were Calvin knots, they were so severely defined, like the square-topped steeples of some Protestant churches or the top of a castle tower. She would have preferred flowers. Still, people always seemed to reach out and touch and trace Calum's endless knots.

Even in the places visitors didn't see, there were pieces of Calum everywhere, including my room where, when my mother and I moved in, Calum put in bookshelves, a toy box, cupboards, including a hidden cupboard to hide my secrets, and a picture rail from which I hung my cartoons.

And when we first moved in, I got my first toy from Calum, a small, beautifully carved wooden horse. There were plenty of

888888 FRANK MACDONALD

other toys from Calum that I managed to smash over the years, kites and gangly dancing wooden men with loosely hinged arms and legs, but the carved horse still stood on the corner of the bookshelf. I used to lie on the floor and let it carry my imagination across the wild west or other exciting places, and when I had outgrown playing with it, it went up on the shelf and remained there, no longer a toy but a treasure.

When she had finished swooning over Calum's work, Mrs. MacLeod reached out and touched the carved frame around the living room door, saying to Taurus, "Wouldn't it be lovely to have something like this?" Taurus just chuckled and told her he would carve the door frame at their house that night in a coal mine pattern, picks and shovels. It wasn't until after Mrs. MacLeod and Taurus left and Calum and I were sitting down to dinner that I realized that Mrs. MacLeod didn't ask me who made the squares I served her, and she ate three of them. I hoped she didn't think I did the baking too.

13

I had my first job.

Hanging around the race track with Duncan while he looked after John Alex's horses paid off. On the first Sunday afternoon of racing, the drug-testing van, the one that travelled from track to track for the Department of Agriculture, pulled into the stables. The drug tester needed a helper.

In my job, Ken Brown explained, I would be a piss-whistler. After a winning horse was taken into the paddock and cooled down by the groom, then stabled, I had to take a bottle attached to a long handle and stand in the stall waiting for the horse to piss. When it did, I was to stick the bottle in the hot stream, fill it and screw a cap onto it, then bring it to the van to be labelled. All Brown had to do, as far as I could see, was take a cotton swab of spit from the horse's mouth then wait for me to bring the pee. He warned me not to do what his last year's helper, Archie Ack-Ack, did.

Not all horses are cooperative, so sometimes a piss-whistler has to wait a long time. One of the secrets to making horses, or even people, pee, Brown said, is to whistle. To help the horse along, besides the whistling, he showed me how to take a handful of straw and use it to tickle the horse's crotch to help the cause. Still, there were horses so shy or dehydrated that, no matter how long you whistled and tickled, they just couldn't or wouldn't pee. It gets frustrating, he told me.

"But no matter how long you have to wait I don't want you pulling out your own tool and pissing in the bottle just to get it over with the way that fellow did last year. Pretty near drove them crazy at the government lab in Truro, what with the horse's urine testing for everything from beer to baloney."

Piss-whistling paid five bucks a race day, and we raced Wednesday night and Sunday afternoon in Shean. Like Duncan, I had my own stable pass, and although no one ever asked us for identification in the loosely secure paddock area, we always flipped open our otherwise empty wallets whenever we passed through the gate. The best part of the job, though, was gathering all kinds of stories to tell Taurus in the sun porch. He got a big kick out of it when I told him about the night I was holding the bottle under the winner, hoping in the darkly shadowed stall that I was holding it in the stream, only to realize when I checked the empty bottle that the winner was a mare. The worst part of the job, though, was living in fear that Mary Scotland would ask me exactly what it was I did at the racetrack.

The beach was still a part of our summer days when there weren't races, but we weren't living on it like other summers, not with our jobs. John Alex decided that summer to stable his horses at the track instead of walking them back and forth from his barn every day, which gave us a chance to hang around the tack stalls listening to the men talk about the horses featured in *Hoofbeats* magazine, horses standing in stud with lifetime marks for racing a mile in under two minutes. Both Duncan and I devoured the magazines, educating ourselves on the bloodlines of the trotters and pacers. The marks owned by the horses in the magazine were beyond our ability to imagine. Almost all of the horses at the Shean track were there because they were too old, too sore, too slow or too cantankerous to race on any other oval in North America, according to Brown. A horse that could run a mile in 2:15 was top dog at Shean.

Horses had been racing at the Shean track for as long as there had been a town. First it was picnic racing. Taurus told me that when the mines were booming, Holy Family Parish in Shean held its annual summer picnic on Dominion Day weekend, with a special picnic train coming along the west coast of Cape Breton picking up passengers all decked out for the holiday. When it arrived at the Shean station, the town's brass band, its pipe band and half the population were there to meet it. Horses all decked out in colourful harness were led by their owners from the boxcars and walked up Station Street, followed by the baseball teams that came from towns and villages all along the coast to play in a tournament, and finally hundreds of passengers, most of them with relatives in Shean with whom they could stay for the weekend. They all joined the long parade that wound its way over Main Street, up past our house on Culloden to the top of the street where the town ended and where the picnic grounds, carved out of part of the blueberry barrens, crowded up against the evergreen forest. In the middle of the picnic grounds was the oval that hosted the visiting horses which came from the other side of Cape Breton Island, from Nova Scotia, and even from Prince Edward Island. It was a great weekend, Taurus said, one that usually ended in a massive brawl at Saturday night's dance, filling the Sunday morning church with hangovers and black eyes and a stale booze smell stronger than the incense. But the parish made lots of money.

First the war came, then the mines got in trouble and the parish picnic shrank into a one-day event that nobody but the people in town took part in. Eventually the people in Shean who owned horses leased the track from the parish, got it registered with the United States Trotting Association and started racing horses all summer long. A few horsemen from other parts of the province with stables of four or five cripples moved to Shean for the summer, but no brass bands went to the station to meet them when they arrived. The local horsemen had their stalls, as well. Since almost all the horses needed lots of care, the men spent a lot of time at the track gathering in tack stalls, sometimes to drink, sometimes not, trading truths and lies while Duncan and I sat in the corner smoking cigarettes and listening.

Unlike other tracks, the Shean paddock was located behind the grandstand instead of on the backstretch, so fans were able to look over the back of the grandstand and see who or what was going on, what stall doors were closed, which horses seemed friskier than the others. From the stands the paddock looked like fun; for me it was clear magic being in the paddock itself on race day amid the smells that were not unlike John Alex's barn, where I first encountered flesh-and-blood horses, only the track smells were larger, stronger, more wonderful. The horses sensed the excitement of race day even more than we did, their ears alert as bridles were slipped over them, as overdraws pulled their heads up proudly, as leather traces linked horse to sulky, as they felt the weight of a driver swinging himself onto a sulky, the reins grasped in one hand, colourful silks shimmering. There was a nervous excitement of horses anxious to take to the track, the pride of trotters and pacers as they were paraded before the grandstand, being introduced by owner, driver and sire. They were horses that did not know they were being paraded on a track that was at the end of the line as far as horse racing and racehorses were concerned. They quivered in their harness like colts or stood confident and cool as veterans.

The drivers, too, in their multi-coloured silks, each one registered and original as a thumb print, could have been getting their horses ready for the Hamiltonian or The Little Brown Jug, the serious way they went about their business. Even if half the drivers in a race were wearing red-and-white silks, which was often the case, Duncan and I could identify the design of each of them, the patterns of their jackets and helmets, half a track away. And the silks, when the horses charged out from behind the starting gate, clung to the bodies of the drivers like bright flags rippling in the airflow created by the horse each driver guided.

The horses too, a lot of them, stood out in their harnesses. While many of them were strapped into the sulky with cracked brown harness, others were fashion shows of bright bridles and colourful shadow-rolls, of white knee pads and ankle boots, of white traces against black, sweat-shiny flesh, and as the starting gate rolled away we hung over the paddock gate, watching our favourites and cheering. The whole grandstand stood to see what horse charged into the lead; which ones tucked comfortably behind the pace-setter; which horses were hung up on the outside unable to find a way in on the rail, being carried by the rest of the field for a long, long mile, a mile often too long for the horse to last. Which horse was at the rear of the field and was he a horse that could come from behind or was he simply taking his place in the natural order of things? As they came to the head of the stretch of the half-mile track for the second time, the wire an eighth of a mile away, every driver in the race wanted to get his picture taken. All strategies abandoned, the seven or eight horses spread across the track in a mad dash for the finish.

This was the beauty of it for me, the race to the finish line. Sometimes it was too close to call and people held their tickets while the judges studied the photo-finish pictures and the defeated horses hobbled back to the paddock, long, thirsty tongues lolling from under their bits. We hugged the winners, stood in awe in the stalls of these local greats as we would stand in the dressing rooms of our hockey heroes if we could.

I liked the track better than John Alex's barn, but the Shean track was often a crueler place to be. Because the track depended on so many broken-down horses racing two dashes a day, twice a week, not all the horses were well looked after. When the fans looked over the back of the grandstand to see what was going on in the paddock below, it was the closed stall doors that their betting eyes sought. If the stall door was closed, then there was probably someone behind it feeding spiked carrots to his horse or puncturing a horse with a needle. That was why I had a job.

Duncan and I didn't think about it much, understanding as we did that it was just part of horse racing. The drug tests tried to keep racing fair while the horsemen looked for new drugs the Department of Agriculture tests couldn't detect. Sometimes horsemen were caught, fined and suspended, sometimes they got away with it, but most horses that won weren't doped at all.

Besides, John Alex explained to Duncan and me once, if the horse is never going to win, he's going to wind up as mink food, so drugging the horses was in their best interests, although he never drugged his own horses; but neither of his horses had ever won a race in all their lives. Anyway, the horses never seemed to mind afterwards.

Except for Summer Cloud.

What captured our imagination first was the fact that a new horse at the track, 12-year-old Summer Cloud, hadn't won a race in four years. But Summer Cloud had a lifetime mark of 1:59:1, and even though that lifetime mark was made as a two-year-old, this was the first horse Duncan and I had ever met who had paced through the two-minute barrier.

"It's not fair," Duncan said when he saw how fast Summer Cloud had been as a colt. "If they hadn't cut his nuts out we'd be looking at his picture in *Hoofbeats* with a five thousand dollar stud fee. Instead, they took all the good out of him, and look where he wound up, in Eric Rundle's stall, for Christ's sake."

Summer Cloud was one of five horses Rundle brought to the Shean track that year, a sentimental favourite with the fans and with Duncan and me. The white gelding in blue-fringed harness made a striking picture on the track as Rundle jogged and turned him before the race, but his legs were shot. Other horsemen said he had an infected frog, a cracked hoof, bowed tendons, hock trouble and just about everything else that could go wrong with a horse's legs. He could barely stand in his stall, always resting on three legs while holding a fourth away from the floor, but he was so beautiful he excited us, and it was Duncan and I who brought that beauty out in Summer Cloud more than Rundle did.

Rundle was not just a horseman, he was a horse-trader, so he did what he needed to do to keep his horses making money or turning them into sales to other horsemen. But it was Duncan and I who took the brushes and the curry-comb when we had nothing else to do and went into Summer Cloud's stall and brushed and combed him to a silver shine, Duncan talking to him all the while we brushed him, asking in whispered wonder what it was like to have raced a mile in 1:59.1.

"Think about it, Roddie. We were only five years old when Summer Cloud was racing faster than two minutes. Doesn't seem fair that we didn't even know about it, does it? And here we are now taking care of him."

What else didn't seem fair was that Summer Cloud was the only drug addict Duncan and I ever knew. Because his legs were so tender that he lurched when Rundle jogged him, the horse-trader always closed the stall door on race day, and a little while later, when the horses were paraded before the grandstand, Summer Cloud pranced like a prince, walking as if there had never been a problem in his legs. And when the starting gate led the horses down the stretch the white free-legged pacer was so filled with desire to win that his mane fluttered like a banner on his neck and his chest pushed against the starting gate in his desire to take control of the race. He could still cut a thirty-second first quarter and lead the field to the half in 1:02, his ghostly form pacing fifty lengths ahead of the field. Then the fade began, with the other horses catching Summer Cloud on the back stretch, one by one eclipsing him as they hit the three-quarter mark, and coming down the stretch Summer Cloud continued to fade. All Rundle wanted from him was a finish in the top five horses, because those were the positions that shared the dash's purse money. More often than not, Summer Cloud could hang on to fifth place.

It was the day following the race that Duncan and I hated, walking to Summer Cloud's stall to find the white gelding lying down, unable to rise to his feet, his coat, stained with the mess of manure and urine in the straw, quivering with what some horsemen said was the DTs, explaining to us that drunks and drug addicts go through the same shakes when they are coming off booze or dope. Duncan would bend under the bar and enter the stall, sitting beside Summer Cloud, stroking him, his eyes filling with the only tears I ever saw Duncan shed.

"Why does he have to do this?" Duncan asked every time. "Rundle's got four horses that are hardly crippled at all. He's winning races with them. Why can't he leave Summer Cloud alone?" But we had no answer, not to that question, nor to Duncan's other longing. "I wish we could do something. Too bad he wouldn't win just so Rundle would get caught in the drug test."

Summer Cloud's mistreatment bothered us, but it didn't dim the delight we took in being at the track, not even when Calum said I was spending too much time there, but without ever saying that I couldn't go. Neither he nor Bartholomew had ever bothered with the races, and Taurus said it was probably because they still thought it was a Catholic picnic.

Taurus himself rarely came to the races, but in the summer when the town filled with people coming home from away, wanting to do all the things they missed, the track was an attraction. One Sunday, on my way to the parimutuel to place Duncan's and my bet, I saw Taurus standing with some home-from-away relatives studying the scorecard with the same furrowed brow I used trying to make sense of my Latin book. I made myself visible, and as soon as Taurus saw me he beckoned me over to a cluster of MacLeods, introducing me as Calum's grandson, because my name was apparently forever lost to him, and telling them that I was an expert.

"So where should I put my money?" he asked.

Duncan and I always pooled our pay and our knowledge of the horses, confident each race day that we were on the verge of a fortune and almost always leaving the track flat broke.

"The quinella's going to be Ann's Boy and Oradale," I told him, and he passed me two dollars to make the bet for him. By the time I got the tickets for ourselves and for Taurus, I was the last bettor before the wicket closed, and as I left the parimutuel the race was already on. I scrambled back over the grandstand to be ready to test the winner, and it wasn't until after the last race that I was able to cash the two quinella tickets, ours and Taurus's. Then I went looking for Taurus in the departing crowd, spotting him as he and his relatives walked toward a car with Massachusetts plates. I called out to him as he opened the door to the back seat, and hearing me he stopped and waited, greeting me with a wave as I approached.

"You won," I told him, "twenty dollars and eighty cents."

"Won what?" he asked.

"The race, remember? The quinella? You asked me to bet for you? I did and you won," I said, passing him the money.

"Oh, yes," he said, taking the twenty and leaving the change in my hand, but I could tell he couldn't remember why I was giving him the money.

"Excuse me," one of his relatives called out after Taurus got in the car and I started walking away. He came over to where I stood, told me he was a third cousin of Taurus's visiting from Boston, then asked if that happened often.

"Does what happen often?" I asked.

"Forgetting things. You seem to know him quite well. Does he forget a lot?"

"He never remembers my name, but he never could, not since I was little. He always calls me boy."

"But the bet, don't you think he should have remembered that? That's what we're worried about. Most of the time he's just great, but once in a while he seems to get lost."

I answered that I never noticed anything like that before, and I would know because he was always at my grandfather's.

14

Through the kitchen window I watched Taurus thoughtfully studying Calum's cairn. Calum and Bartholomew were already in the sun porch waiting for their tea, and soon Taurus turned to join them. His thoughts were far away when I brought the tray to the sun porch, and I wondered if he was drifting off like that day at the track. He leaned forward, placing his tea on the sill and taking out his tobacco, which was the way he usually began his conversations. Because I took a seat beside him he spoke English.

"Calum," he said loud enough to draw my grandfather's attention from behind his newspaper, "that little cairn of yours got me thinking about another one, a bigger one. A really big one."

"There've been some big ones built," Calum said. "But it would take more stone than Bartholomew's truck could haul."

"If you're serious, Taurus, I don't know if we'd be up to a job like that," Bartholomew added. "We're not spring chickens."

"I could draft a design for discussion," Calum replied, "but what do you have in mind, and where would it go? And why?"

"It's not stone I'm thinking about," Taurus told them, taking a puff of his cigarette. "It's trees. Remember that business you told me about the tree alphabet? Now, if I put pencil to paper it's the shape of the leaves I'm seeing on the page, the idea that our people once talked to each other through trees is really something."

Taurus was speaking slowly, like he wasn't sure he wanted to get where he was going, and I saw Calum's finger move up behind his ear to the button that turned up or off his hearing aid. He always turned it off when there was something he didn't want to hear, like Duncan and me playing cowboys and Indians in the house when we were smaller, but I didn't think he was turning it off on Taurus.

"I picked some different leaves one day not long ago, took them home and spread them across the kitchen table, trying to make words with them. Mary, of course, was watching me like a hawk. The woman already thinks I'm losing my mind. Anyway, when I spread the leaves out on the table, even though it was nothing but gibberish as far as I could tell, know what else I saw looking down at them? God's eye-view of a forest, Calum. If you can spell out messages with leaves, there's no reason we can't do the same with trees. You could ... well ... you could plant a poem. What do you think of that?" he hurried the last question and looked away from their faces.

Calum and Bartholomew didn't say right away what they thought, but I knew what I thought. I thought, if Duncan hears about this he'll blame Calum for the idea and laugh his frigging head off. "That would be like planting a whole forest," I said loud enough for all of them to hear me. "It would take forever."

"Not a forest," Calum said with his usual exactness. "Possibly several hundred trees depending on the length of the poem," he added, looking at Taurus, his raised brows making a question of the last statement. "What poem do you have in mind?"

Taurus puffed on his cigarette. "Well, none really. I was just wondering if it could be done."

"Possibly. It's like Calum said, probably a few hundred trees, but that presents a problem because a project like that would require quite a bit of land," Bartholomew added.

"I've got a couple of hundred acres going to waste up in the Highlands," Taurus said. "A lot of woods on it, but there must be seventy acres cleared, doing nothing but sinking under pasture spruce."

"Evergreen or hardwood?" Calum asked.

"Mixed. I don't know how it breaks down, but there's quite a bit of hardwood up there. Used to be our firewood in the winter, and it turns pretty as a woman when the colours change. Different colours mean different trees, so I'm thinking what you're thinking, Calum, that there's probably a lot of what a man would need right there on my own land. About the poem, though, I was thinking of writing one."

They stopped talking then, and I left the sun porch for The Turk's, hoping Taurus's idea was something he would forget about, like everything else.

Mrs. MacFarlane said she would rather be feeding the horses at the racetrack than feeding Duncan and me, especially Duncan who had shot a couple of inches and several pounds past me during the summer. Mr. MacFarlane was home from the mines again but gone all day with the car and his friends. He had better be back soon, she said, because there was a square dance at the parish hall that night, and he promised to take her.

"I'm going after the races," I said casually, Duncan looking at me like I was crazy.

"Going to a dance where my father and mother are? A square dance?" He was laughing.

"I'd like to go. I've never been to a square dance except the time we snuck in last summer. I'd just like to see one." Hiding just below the surface of my remarks was what I heard in The Turk's earlier, Mary Scotland and Mary French telling Mary Jane they were going to the square dance at the parish hall.

"I'll bet you're a good dancer, Roddie. Surely you have some of your father's music in you," Mrs. MacFarlane said.

"He does," Duncan said. "You should hear him whistle. He gets all the horses dancing."

The August night was warm and dry, and the dust raised by the starting gate covered everything and everyone. The water truck's endless tour did little to soothe the thirsty track. Still, it was better than racing in the rain.

Once the races began I became busy with my job, going to the stall of the winner and whistling to my heart's delight. I was developing into quite a whistler, trying various tunes, testing the pee-inspiring value of rock and roll versus Scottish fiddle music or the airs to some of Taurus's Gaelic songs. Some horses gave up their offering quickly, and some took their good old time, and often I had to wait between dashes to find out who the official winner was after the judges studied the photo-finish.

That night, I stood at the bulletin board where they posted the official photos of the close finishes to see which stall I had to stand in with my trusty bottle. It wasn't really necessary for me to be at the bulletin board since they always announced which horse won, but it was the close finishes that made the races exciting and I liked to see who nosed out who. A couple of photo-finishes had already been posted, so while I waited I took my scorecard and the pencil with which I recorded each dash's results, times and pays, and turning to the blank inside cover, I began sketching a wilder version of one of the photo-finishes. What I drew wasn't exactly like the photo-finish on the wall, but as I finished it, a voice behind me said, "Hey, that's me!"

It was Sammy Smith, the driver of Hobbled Up, the winning horse in the picture, who had come to look at the photo of himself and his horse, probably to see if it was a close enough finish for him to order a copy of the photo for himself, which was how the photo-finish photographer made most of his money at the track, selling pictures of winners to their owners and drivers. Standing at my shoulder, Sammy Smith recognized my drawing.

"That's me," he said again. "You can't even tell it's me in the blurred photo there, but you can tell it's me in your picture. That's better than the photo-finish. How much do you want for it?"

"A buck," I said without thinking.

"Done," he answered pulling a bill from his pocket while I tore the cover from my scorecard and passed it to him. He took it, studying it as he walked away, looking proud. Then the speaker announced the winner of the last race, and without waiting to see that picture I went to the winner's stall.

After the races Duncan and I washed the dust from our hands and faces at the tap outside John Alex's tack stall, and Duncan asked me if I was serious about going to the dance. I told him I was going, and then it took him about two more questions to understand why. "Think I'll come along," he said. He went to John Alex's tack stall and came back with a bottle of Old Spice for us to splash on ourselves to smother the smell of the horses we had been rubbing shoulders with all night.

We could hear the music long before we rounded the church and made our way to the parish hall to pay our dollar at the wicket and walk through the double blue doors that swung into the hall itself. On the floor, several groups of dancers were going through the third and final figure as the fiddler, supported by his pianist, led them toward the close of the set.

It took me no time at all to spot Mary Scotland in a set, step-dancing her way through the figure, laughing with her partner, enjoying herself. As the fiddler left the stage, though, three other musicians stepped onto it, two carrying guitar cases and an amplifier, the other carrying a tin bingo chair. They were the Moran Brothers, and they wore ducktail haircuts and tight jeans and played for the round dances between the square sets, giving people a chance to dance to the hit parade because not everybody wanted to square-dance all night long. The Moran Brothers played Ernest Tubb and Hank Williams and the Everly Brothers and Elvis and Jerry Lee Lewis.

Paul and Ray Moran plugged in their amplifier, then plugged their flattops into the amp, and Gerry Moran opened the collapsible tin chair he was carrying and set it in front of the wooden chair on which he sat. He pulled a handful of tin bingo markers from his pocket and tossed them onto the tin chair. Then with two rungs from a wooden chair he tapped the metal one, finding a snare rhythm that underscored the music his brothers were making.

They opened their set with Paul and Ray harmonizing on "Candy Kisses."

Those dancers who hadn't gone outside for a breath of fresh air or a quick sip from a hidden bottle walked back onto the floor to waltz slowly with each other as the lights dimmed. Standing beside Duncan at the back of the hall I watched Mary Scotland leave the floor after the square set and take her seat between Mary French and Mary Jane. I took a deep breath, having convinced myself that I was going to walk across the floor tonight, without a nun dragging me by the hand, and ask her to dance.

"Candy Kisses" turned into the "Tennessee Waltz" and then into "The Wayward Wind" and still I stood rooted to the floor while the other two Marys were being asked, one by one, to dance until Mary Scotland was sitting alone. She wouldn't be sitting alone very long, I knew, so as the Morans began to sing "Won't You Wear My Ring Around Your Neck," I took a deep breath just as Duncan gave me a hard push to start me on my way across the floor. Rehearsing "Would you like to dance?" in my head over and over I was making my way toward Mary Scotland when, from the other side of the hall, Archie Ack-Ack walked confidently up to her and gestured with his head the very words I was trying to form in my mouth. With a slight hesitancy, Mary Scotland stood up and followed him onto the floor, leaving me standing in front of the three empty chairs that had been occupied by the three now-dancing Marys. I was caught in no-man's land on the women's side of the dance hall with no choice but to turn and retreat across the full length of the floor with all the guys watching, smirking, wondering which girl shot me down.

"Roddie," Mrs. MacFarlane said, coming up behind me, "have you danced yet?"

"No," I said, hoping that she wasn't offering. Dancing with somebody's mother would be even worse than getting shot down. She stood with me, chatting about nothing as we slowly made our way across the floor, her company making my journey across the long hall appear to have some purpose to it. She had rescued me from ridicule. Mr. MacFarlane, she told me, had gone out to the car after the last set ... the rest left unsaid. I glanced over her shoulder to see Mary Scotland trying to keep Ack-Ack from pulling her too close as he tried to rest his head against hers.

"Is that why you came here tonight?" Mrs. MacFarlane asked with a teasing smile.

"What?" I countered with an exaggerated display of confusion.

"Mary Cameron," and we both looked toward the floor just as Ack-Ack, leading Mary Scotland, bumped into Mrs. Bruce who was dancing with her husband. They pulled away and he bumped into her again, and it seemed intentional. Mary Scotland then tried to pull herself free of Ack-Ack's hold on her, but he wouldn't let her go, and at that moment Duncan ran from the back of the hall through all the dancers moving to the music and slammed into Ack-Ack so hard he let go of Mary.

The move surprised Ack-Ack, and before he could recover Duncan was punching him with both fists so fast there was only a blur and blood. When Ack-Ack stumbled and fell to the floor Duncan dropped on top of him, still punching, and Ack-Ack was useless against the height and weight Duncan had gained over the summer. He was in full control of Shean's bully, calling him a coward and a piece of shit, but his anger was scaring everyone. Mrs. MacFarlane ran into the crowd to try to pull her son off Ack-Ack. Several people soon got over the shock of the sudden fight and tried to pull Duncan off, but the hand that finally lifted him away belonged to his father.

"Have you lost your mind!" his father was shouting, shaking Duncan.

Meanwhile, Ack-Ack was trying to squirm away from Duncan like a snake, and even dangling from his father's hand, Duncan still managed to score an occasional kick. Then, still trembling with rage but exhausted by it as well, Duncan stopped fighting, and his father, followed by his mother, pushed and shoved him outside. None of them came back to the dance.

As the crowd dispersed and a beaten Ack-Ack left the parish hall, rubbing blood from his nose and telling everybody that if Duncan hadn't sly-poked him things would have turned out differently, I found myself standing beside Mary Scotland. The other Marys rushed to her side before I could even find words to ask if she was all right. She told them she didn't know what started the fight, but she didn't want to stay at the dance. Her friends, though, their romantic fantasies still intact, didn't want to leave.

"Maybe Smelt will walk you home," Mary French said. "You can't go alone with Archie Ack-Ack out there somewhere."

"I don't think he'll bother me, so you don't have to leave on my account, Roddie," Mary said.

"I was just going anyway," I said, waiting while she got her coat. As we left, Johnny Rosin tuned his fiddle for another set.

15

The following morning Calum asked me for a hand around the yard, so I still didn't know what happened to Duncan after the dance. I was glad to be helping Calum because it gave me time to think. Living with Calum gave me lots of time to think up cartoons and pictures and day dreams, but my life had suddenly become much more interesting than my imagination. Calum knelt, stiff-backed, beside the rows of vegetables, me crouching across from him; we weeded in silence. It was the way we did everything, so I wasn't ignoring Calum just because my mind was giddy with the night before.

Mary Scotland didn't want to stay at the dance, but she said it was too nice a night to just go home so we walked the streets looking at the stars and stumbling into the potholes, as silent as me and Calum, but it wasn't nearly as comfortable. We tried to talk about the stars, but I couldn't even find the Little Dipper. We tried to talk about the Moran Brothers, but when I said how good it was to have some real music at our local dances instead of all that fiddle music, Mary said she liked the fiddle, which wasn't something people our age went around admitting. The worst part was, I liked the fiddle too. I really enjoyed listening to Johnny Rosin whenever he played in John Alex's barn, but I couldn't tell her that now that I had said what I said. We walked for a long time trying to think of things to say, and it was she who finally said what was on my mind, that maybe we could find a place to sit. I thought of the shack but I couldn't imagine taking her through the raspberry bushes to crawl on her hands and knees to get inside just so we could sit around trying to talk to each other. I thought of the beach but it seemed too romantic to mention.

I thought of the sun porch.

"We could sit in there and just talk," I said, not wanting her to think I could think of anything else we could do in there. We walked to Culloden Street and I led her up the steps and into Calum's sun porch. Knowing that he was asleep in a room above us hushed us, even though he was sleeping four feet from his hearing aid. It got easier to talk sitting on the couch almost touching, staring out the window through the plants into the darkness, and I told her about Calum and Bartholomew and Taurus always sitting here.

If you have stories to tell about Taurus you're bound to be able to entertain people, I discovered, because I had her laughing out loud at some of the things he had said, and it was because we were laughing that we touched each other, our hands finding each other under cover of that diversion. Then I kissed her and I'm almost certain that she kissed me back, and after that we fell into silence all over again, but holding each other, frozen in time, feeling warm all over.

When Mary said she had better go home, I walked her to her door and said good night and so did she, and we stood there in another silence, awkward again, and I knew I was supposed to do or say something but I had no idea what. So I said good night again, and wondered while we worked in the garden what Calum would tell me if I asked him what I should have done. It was funny to imagine what he might say, but I certainly wasn't going to risk the real thing.

Up and down the vegetable rows I had plenty of time to think, to discover how stupid I was that I couldn't find any words to say except goodbye. Not, "Can I walk you home again sometime?" Not, "I really enjoyed myself." No, just a stupid goodbye like it didn't matter if I ever saw Mary Scotland again, whom I couldn't help but see every time I closed my eyes. By ten o'clock I knew she would never want to see me again. I decided to run away. I decided to die heroically saving her from a tragic death, because only then would she come to understand my perfect love.

At eleven o'clock in the morning Mary Scotland walked by my house between Mary French and Mary Jane, pretending not to be sneaking glances into our yard, walking by as if she walked past our place every day, which she almost never did at all, and after she passed, my own look followed her for a long, long time, all the way out of sight, catching her giving one last nonchalant glance back as she walked between her two friends who didn't seem to know anything about us yet or else they would be giggling and gawking at me and teasing her. I was trying to believe this was real, but I still had no idea what to do about it.

Calum kept me at work in the yard, sentencing me to the flower garden once the vegetables were done, but I was singing all the way. Calum had such command over his garden that I was surprised weeds were allowed to grow in it at all; but they did, being even more stubborn than him. They didn't live long, though. Reaching for any growth I was unsure of, I would catch Calum's eye, point to it and whether it lived or died depended on whether Calum nodded his head or gave it a shake.

Sometimes it seemed Calum and I had our own language, like a secret Gaelic. Calum was always inside himself, thinking, and not talkative enough to share much of what went on within him. He was always absorbing something, newspapers, the books in his study, but none of it ever came back out in any way I could see. Probably it did with Bartholomew, maybe even with Taurus, but I couldn't be sure. We sure weren't alike that way. As soon as I found out anything interesting, I couldn't wait to tell somebody just how much I knew. Not Calum. He could hold his tongue longer than a cloistered nun. Duncan said that when there was as much silence in his house as in ours, it was because his mother and father were mad at each other. That's not what it means at our house, I told him, but Duncan wasn't so sure. He decided that Calum wasn't talking to me because I never learned to speak the Gaelic.

"He never taught me," I reminded Duncan. "How could I learn to speak it if he never taught me?"

"Maybe he tried when you were so young you don't remember. We've been taking French in school since grade seven. How much of that do you speak? None. And Latin? I bet it was the same with Gaelic. You're either born with it or you're not," Duncan reasoned.

I found myself wondering more and more often why Calum never did raise me in the Gaelic. I had already thought about the very thing Duncan said, that I was too stupid to learn, so he never bothered. I wasn't convinced, though, and while I wondered about it, I was not about to ask Calum to teach me. If I did, and he said okay, it would be worse than going to school because there was no way Calum would let me learn a little bit of the Gaelic, not Calum. I'd probably have to be writing exams and everything.

When I had questions, Calum usually had answers. Sometimes he would just tell me what I wanted to know, and sometimes a single question would lead to me having to read a whole book, so I was cautious with my questions, asking only what I seriously wanted to understand. Through Calum, though, I learned about Scottish history and our own family's history inside that larger one, the two being inseparable in Calum's eyes, as they were inseparable in the eyes of everyone in Shean whose people came from the Highlands and Islands of Scotland. All of us were descendants of people driven out of their homes in great numbers to fend for themselves on shores owned by the same British tyrants who took the land from the Highlanders, because it was more profitable to raise sheep on the land than people. Then they shipped those people to foreign shores to settle new lands for the Crown.

That fact wasn't lost on Calum, even if others didn't make a big deal of it. Often, at community events he was a lone figure in a crowd refusing to rise for God Save the Queen unless he happened to be standing up anyway. If he was sitting down he stayed down and people who noticed this said that Calum's back must be hurting him, but if they knew Calum at all, they knew why he remained in his seat. In his private revolt he would not rise to the sound of royal music, although he never tried to remind other descendants of Highlanders that they were standing to sing the anthem of the nation that had destroyed their own.

He and Bartholomew fought their own war, speaking in the once damned language of their ancestors, but Bartholomew did not refuse to rise for the royal song that served as our own colonial anthem. He was different from Calum in that way because he was a businessman and never intentionally offended anyone who might be coming into his store. Even in the store he was different than in the sun porch, chatting with those who came to buy his tobacco and medicines. In the sun porch with Calum you would swear they were exactly alike, but if you watched them closely you knew they weren't.

Through Calum I would not forget the story of our people's banishment or the story of Calum's family, the Gillieses, who settled in their home near Sydney generations before I was born, clearing land and farming it. Belle's family who came to western Cape Breton about the same time, carved out a similar existence in the Shean Highlands and all along the coast. My grandmother's people settled in the Shean Highlands, and she was born up there before her father bought a house during the boom in Shean and brought his family down where her mother opened their home up as a boarding house.

Belle had been born on a farm not far from where Taurus was born, and somewhere in the crisscross of marriages within the large Catholic families Taurus and I were distantly related. Among the Cape Breton descendants of Scottish Highlanders, a hundred, two hundred years after their migration, people still saw themselves as Scottish Highlanders and held the clans intact by claiming whatever cousins they could unravel from the genealogical memories of those who knew the bloodlines of families and clans, and I liked the idea that Taurus was my fifth or sixth or seventh cousin, if my counting was right. The fact that my mother came from Scotland two hundred years later and didn't tell Calum or Belle a lot about herself meant I didn't know what family, if any, I had still living in Scotland.

The difference between what I knew and what Calum knew, Taurus once told me, was that Calum knew what he knew in the Gaelic. I only knew it in English. "I can't explain the difference," he said, "but it's a big difference, a big difference," his remark reminding me of all the times that Taurus told Calum and Bartholomew stories in the Gaelic, some that would make even those two laugh out loud, and Taurus would turn to me and apologize. "I'd tell it to you, too, but it doesn't mean anything in English." So, since we spoke different languages, I guess Calum and I spoke best in silence.

It wasn't as if Calum never talked except in the grunts Duncan liked to mimic. He just never talked for the sake of talking, so we worked together in the garden or the workshop, then went into the house and made lunch, ate and returned to our chores with hardly a word being spoken. Sometimes, though, Calum would be reminded of something, and that would make him talk, telling me the difference between when he was growing up and when I was; what it was like to live in a world without radios; how his family took a horse and buggy over the miles to St. Columba's Church in Marion Bridge for several hours of Sunday services, then came home and sat in the parlour for the rest of the day of rest, reading and memorizing the Bible; the story about how his family or my grandmother's family survived those first frightening winters in Cape Breton's deep snow, growing a living from what was often barely fertile land.

Sometimes, Calum spoke very slowly when he told me these things, more slowly than he normally spoke to me, which I thought was just his way of telling a story, since he wasn't much of a storyteller anyway. One day in school I had to stand up and translate into English for the class a passage from Caesar's Latin writings. To translate it, I had to take it piece by piece in words and familiar phrases so that my English telling of the Latin text reminded me a little of the way Calum told me about things from his past, and I wondered if that was because those memories were so old and only known to him in the Gaelic that in repeating them to me he had to actually translate them slowly into words I could understand.

Once, I asked Mrs. MacFarlane, who also spoke the Gaelic, why she never taught Duncan, and she said there was no point to it really.

"Who would he use it with? His grandmother, maybe, and myself. His father doesn't speak it. It won't get him a job. It's a shame that the language is disappearing, but its time is past. I feel sorry for the old people like Calum and Bartholomew, but the world is English now," she said.

When she said that, I found myself thinking not of Calum and Bartholomew but of Taurus, remembering the way he reacted when Calum told him about the tree alphabet, and the picture he made in my mind when he told us about going out to the woods and gathering up leaves and taking them home and trying to write something in the Gaelic with them on his kitchen table, his wife thinking he had lost his mind. Besides, they were his songs that nobody would be singing any more.

But I couldn't help wondering, too, what Calum would say to Mrs. MacFarlane's reason for not teaching the Gaelic to Duncan, or was there any difference in their reasons? Whatever it was he would have to say, it would be said in the Gaelic so I would never know. I also wondered how different things would be between Calum and Duncan, that first time they met, with Calum sitting at Belle's quilting frame, if Duncan had been able to ask him in the Gaelic, "Are you Roddie's grandmother?"

By late afternoon Calum and I had finished the gardens and replaced the back fence boards, and this time it was I who examined the shack that Duncan and I had only slept in once all summer, and I guessed that it was the last shack we would ever build together. I shook it the way Calum had a summer earlier, and it was still sturdy. When I looked up Calum was watching me, and I nodded the same approval to him that he had given me a year earlier, and we continued until we finished the fence. Then I went to see what happened to Duncan.

"Is Duncan home?" I asked Mrs. MacFarlane when she answered my knock.

"No, he isn't," she replied sternly. "We gave him away!"

Looking at my confusion she couldn't hold her face that way for very long. It cracked into a smile. Duncan and his father had gone to Duncan's grandmother's farm in Margaree to help put a new roof on the barn. They wouldn't be back until Sunday.

"Come in anyway, Roddie." she said. "I want to talk to you."

It wasn't hard to guess what she wanted to talk about.

"Do you know what happened last night? We couldn't get a word out of him. He can be so frustrating sometimes. I know Duncan has trouble living within the rules, but he's never been violent. I doubt if he's fought with other boys more than two or three times in his life." Then, as an afterthought she added, "Has he?"

I assured her that Duncan never picked fights, but I did tell her about the one at The Turk's which I thought she didn't know about.

"And Mary Cameron was there both times," she said, also voicing something I didn't want to talk about even to myself.

"I hope that won't mean trouble for you two."

16

In September, the Shean track cut out Wednesday nights, racing only on Sunday afternoons, which meant that even though school was back in I was able to keep my job as a piss-whistler, and I was making just as much money from my drawings. Once Sammy Smith nailed my sketch to the wall of his tack stall other drivers and owners started asking me to draw pictures of their horses' winning races. A couple even asked me to draw a picture of them holding their horses by the halter, and one horseman asked me to draw a picture of his little girl sitting on the back of his racehorse. Often, when there wasn't time to draw the pictures at the track, I worked at home, using as my model the carved wooden horse that Calum had given me. Even though drawing pictures was making me money, I wasn't about to give up a sure five bucks a week to try to live on orders for horse pictures, not when I wanted money in my pocket in case I ever asked Mary Scotland out on a date.

We kept meeting each other everywhere, and I was walking her home almost every night from a dance, a party at Mary French's house, The Turk's, but I couldn't find the courage to ask her to go to a movie or a dance with me, leave alone go steady, not even on nights when we necked and even got into petting in the sun porch. People said we were going together but we never talked about it. Duncan kept telling me I had to ask her to go steady before she got tired of waiting and decided to go out with somebody else. I wasn't sure if he was telling me or warning me.

After he came back from his grandmother's Duncan never talked much about his fight with Archie Ack-Ack. The town's bully still tried to throw his weight around and govern The Turk's like he always did, telling people that Duncan sucker-punched him and that he would get him back someday, but whenever Duncan walked into the restaurant Ack-Ack never started anything. Duncan hardly ever said a word to him, but sometimes I would see him staring at Ack-Ack, and if looks could kill Ack-Ack would be nothing but maggot meat.

We had gone into grade ten after Labour Day, and it was really different having Mrs. Bruce instead of a nun standing in front of the class teaching us. Not all of our teachers had been nuns, but those who weren't were either grandmothers or spinsters, with terrifying reputations as ear-twisters and strappers. Mrs. Bruce wasn't cross, but she didn't give an inch either. She taught us every subject except religion. Duncan and I guessed that because she was young and pretty and married, with her and her husband probably doing it every night, she wasn't allowed to teach religion. So every morning, for the first half hour of school, the art nun, Mother Saint Margaret of Scotland, taught our religion class. Then Mrs. Bruce took over.

Most afternoons after school Duncan and I went to the track where he changed the bandages on the legs of Cape Mabou and Windspirit. Then we checked out the rest of the stables.

The horse we checked out most, though, was Summer Cloud. Over the summer we had become aware of just how much he was hurting, and Duncan and I talked about stealing him, knowing that in the whole spectrum of the movies we had seen, stealing horses was the worst crime of all, even worse than murder, because sometimes killing people wasn't really murder, Duncan said. In the war his father killed all kinds of people, but it wasn't murder. Stealing a horse, though, was always a hanging crime.

A lot of the other drivers and trainers, even though some of them sometimes gave their own horses a little illegal help to win, knew that what was happening to Summer Cloud was terrible. They talked about it, said it was a shame, but did nothing, claiming it was none of their business. Once, in John Alex's tack stall, Duncan said somebody should report what Eric Rundle was doing to Summer Cloud, but John Alex said it was no different than if Rundle was beating up his wife. "It's nobody's business but his own," John Alex said, "but I'd never sell him one of my horses, I'll tell you that."

Nor did anyone but Duncan have the heart to open Summer Cloud's stall door on the mornings after he raced to look at the suffering animal. Duncan, who went to the paddock every morning to feed and water John Alex's horses on his way to school, always went into Summer Cloud's stall to kneel beside him and pet him.

One Sunday afternoon late in September, I was whistling the hit parade to that day's winning horses, including Starstruck, one of Eric Rundle's stable. It had been a photo-finish, and when the picture was posted and the winner announced I carried my bottle over there and waited while Rundle stripped his horse down, washed him and put him in the stall. He then took the little mare, Gina Jean, from her stall and began harnessing her for the next dash.

I was serenading Starstruck, waiting for him to fill my bottle for me. In the next stall, I could hear Summer Cloud shivering with the false energy of the drugs in his system. He had already run his two dashes, finishing fifth and then last. The drugs were probably already wearing off, and by morning I knew he would be writhing in pain on the stall floor. I whistled louder to drown out the sound of him next door and the image of him tomorrow.

Starstruck wasn't very cooperative, not even when I resorted to tickling him with a handful of straw. I did become aware, though, that my methods were working on Summer Cloud whom I could hear producing a strong stream in the stall beside us, making me wish that he had won one of his races. Then Rundle would be caught and punished for doing what he was doing to that horse. My thoughts, though, were half a step behind my instincts because before I had even had time to think about it, I was squatting under Starstruck's stable bar and stepping into Summer Cloud's stall, rushing my bottle under him, getting a full sample before his stream stopped. Petting the roan gelding's quivering neck, I capped the bottle and took it to the van where it was marked as Starstruck's urine sample.

After the races Duncan and I went to The Turk's for french fries, and it was while we were sitting in a booth with Duncan banging the bottom of a stubborn bottle of ketchup that I told him what I had done. When he heard, he hit the bottom of the bottle so hard that it squirted across the booth covering me like a hem-orrhage. Duncan's laughter brought everyone's attention to my splattered face and shirt, giving the whole restaurant a reason to enjoy the joke, but nobody laughed as hard as Duncan; but then, nobody knew why Duncan laughed so hard.

It was late that same Sunday afternoon that I got home to find Calum, Bartholomew and Taurus in the sun porch, Taurus read-ing from a sheet of paper in a slow cadence that told me it was a poem. It was the first time I ever heard Taurus speaking one of his poems instead of singing it, but as he read, his foot kept time to the rhythm of his voice and I knew it was the one he planned to plant on the family land his grandfather had settled when his MacLeods migrated to Cape Breton. I told Taurus that even though the poem read very slow, it didn't sound as sad as some of his songs.

"It's a poem about my grandfather and the other people who came to the Shean Highlands when they were driven from Scot-land. It's not a sad poem because, in spite of what they suffered, they made a good place for us all. I suppose it's a celebration of some kind," Taurus said, passing the poem to Calum who took it and folded it carefully and put it in the top pocket of his bib overalls.

The following Saturday, Calum woke me early and, sleepy-eyed, I followed him down the stairs where Bartholomew and Taurus were waiting in the kitchen eating biscuits and drinking tea. I took a glass of milk and a biscuit, and then Calum led me to the workshop where he pointed out the shovel and the axe, which

I picked up. Calum hung a galvanized bucket on the end of my shovel while he took shears and clippers and his long tape measure and put them in his pockets, and we walked to Bartholomew's panel truck parked in front of the house. Bartholomew was already behind the wheel and Taurus beside him. Calum squeezed into the front seat, and I got in the back, sitting on the inverted bucket.

The panel truck made its way up the highlands road past Tom MacPhee's, up past the block of forest that Taurus pointed out as once being the farm where my grandmother was born, up further than I had ever gone before, past farms abandoned or turned into vacation homes by their new owners. Near the top the road became narrower, the boughs on either side of the road brushing against the truck until Taurus directed Bartholomew to take a left along a narrow wagon track that suddenly opened up, and Taurus said, "Here we are!"

Bartholomew drove the panel truck up to the house which still stood straight but with most of its windows broken, some of them covered up. Inside there were signs of life more recent than Taurus's family's last days here. He pointed out through the kitchen window to the apple orchard, explaining that the window was an ideal spot for hunters to sit and wait for deer. They could light a fire in the rusty but still intact stove, drink tea, which the tin cups beside the sink suggested they had been doing, and wait for the deer to arrive. It would be easy to pick them off from here, he said. Then leaving us looking out the window, he wandered toward one of the doorways and stood there gazing into what must once have been a living room, remembering things we couldn't imagine.

Taurus then stood in other doorways, one leading into a second downstairs room that could have been a bedroom off the kitchen, and the other obviously leading into the pantry. He stood and looked but never went into any of the rooms, and then he walked down the hall and up the stairs while we waited in the kitchen. Calum examined the workmanship of the people who had built the house, and when he walked into the living room he called to me.

I went in, and he was standing at the front wall between the two windows. Several of the wallboards had been pulled off, probably to burn in the kitchen stove, and through the gap we could see the boards of the outside wall.

"What's that?" he asked me, pointing to one of the boards. At first, I didn't know what he was getting at, but when I looked closer I could see that the board was slightly wider at one end than the other and that it had been driven into place with a hammer or a mall.

"A wedge board," I said, remembering what he had told Duncan and me. The wedge board tightened up old houses so that they stayed standing for a hundred years. Taurus's old home seemed proof of Calum's claim, the windows gone, the inside trashed and the walls being torn apart, and still the house felt as straight and true as a parable from the Bible. Calum walked away, looking at other features. A little later he pulled out his pocket watch, checked it, and said, "Go upstairs and see what's keeping that fellow."

I followed Taurus's path down the hall and up the stairs to the second story where a small hall faced three doors made of boards that were as old as the rest of the house. "Taurus," I called, but there was no response. I pushed one of the doors, and it opened into an empty room. There was a bed with a rusty spring on it and a tangled mildewed blanket, several broken beer bottles scattered around the floor, but no Taurus. I pushed the second door and found a room not unlike the first one, except its window didn't overlook the orchard, so it hadn't been used as much by hunters. I went to the third door which still had a latch on it and knocked, but there was no response. I lifted the latch and, feeling uncomfortable, swung the door open. Taurus was sitting on a rocking chair that was missing one of its runners. He didn't hear my knock or respond to the door opening, and was sitting so still that for a moment I thought he might have died in the chair, but then a rise and fall of his shoulders told me he was breathing.

I touched his shoulders, startling him, and he looked up at me from somewhere far away, and I knew we were in the same room together but not at the same time.

"Calum and Bartholomew are downstairs. They sent me to get you," I told him, and I could see him trying to take in this information and give it meaning while still trying to come back from wherever his memory had been visiting. Then it came to him, and he pushed himself up from the chair. "This used to be my room," he said, closing the door behind him.

Outside the house, the four of us surveyed a pasture growing over with ragweed and spreading spruce, broken by a small brook rambling through it. Taurus's farm was near the top of the highlands, and it looked everywhere. To the west it looked out on the Gulf of St. Lawrence, and from this high up I thought at night you would be able to see the flickering lights of Prince Edward Island. To the north, we looked down on the town of Shean. It was even more remote and picture-like than it had been from Tom MacPhee's. You could also see all the way up the valley where the highway led south through the villages of the county, and at the foot of the mountains directly across the valley we could see the Protestant graveyard beside the little St. John's Presbyterian Church. It was older than Shean itself. The trees were showing the first tinge of colours and, in a few weeks, would surround the small white church with a beautiful leaf-weave of red and gold.

The Catholic graveyard was right in the middle of Shean, not far from the church, but dead Protestants had to be taken out of town to the cemetery we were looking at, a graveyard filled with headstones a lot older than any you would find in Shean itself, the graves of those who had died long before coal or the town. While we looked, the Saturday train skirted the graveyard on its way into town.

"That's the field I was thinking of," Taurus said, leading us into what had once been a large hayfield. "What do you think, Calum?"

"There's a good bed of soil here for this high up," Calum said, poking at the ground with the sharp shovel as he paced off the field, walking through thigh-high hay and thistles and rag-weed and young spruce. After getting his feel of the field Calum stopped, looking toward the hardwoods that crept toward the top of the mountain.

"Is there a path you remember?" he asked Taurus who nodded and led the small parade of us in that direction, all but Bartholomew who eased himself down on the front step, saying he would wait for us there. Taurus seemed to be guessing for a minute, having stopped to look, then suddenly started off and in a moment disappeared into the woods. When Calum and I got there he was already well along a well-defined path, humming as he walked. Calum wasn't trying to keep up with him, and I was following Calum who was walking among the birch and maple and mountain ash, stopping to examine trees that interested him, testing saplings, making notes in a small hard-covered journal while shafts of cool sunlight streamed through the leaves, highlighting him like a Catholic statue. I wondered what Calum would say if I told him that. Probably just grunt.

Taurus came back, and asked, "So what do you think?"

Calum looked at him over his glasses, finished writing, then put the notebook away.

"A lot of what we'll need is right here. But there's quite a bit of planning to do, and it looks like we might need to get some of the saplings we'll need elsewhere, but by next spring we should know just what we need and how best to begin."

Taurus looked around and smiled.

"I feel just like a kid with all those little play blocks with letters and numbers on them. This pasture is our playbox, and these," he added with a sweep of his hand, "are our letters." He punched me lightly on the arm. "We're going to do this, boy."

I wasn't as keen on the idea as they were, knowing that the three of them would be the talk of the town if word got out about

Taurus's poem, and it wouldn't be great talk, just giggles and gossip. Before I had time to give much thought to it, though, or to Duncan's inevitable remarks, Calum led me to a small ash sapling, defining a circle around it with his heel in the leaves.

"Dig around there," he told me, and as my foot drove the spade into the earth, he watched and instructed until the two of us were able to lift the sapling from its home. Then with Calum carrying the shovel I transported it back to Taurus's house. Calum led us all, including Bartholomew, back across the field, this first venture defining a new path of knocked down hay. He led us near the fallen fence at the northeast corner, and when I put the sapling down he passed me his garden shears and told me to clear a circle substantially larger than the one he had me dig. The three of them stood watching as I clipped yellow weeds and yellowing hay, gathering them in my arms and throwing them as far as they would carry from the clearing.

When the circle was cleared to Calum's satisfaction he nodded, then passed me the spade. Having Taurus watching me use the shovel and knowing the weight of the pan shovel he wielded underground in the mine was making me ashamed of the sweat I could feel seeping out of my forehead.

"Go to Bartholomew's truck and get that bucket you were sitting on and take it to the brook over there, fill it, and bring it here," Calum ordered when I was finished.

It was becoming quite clear why I was along on this trip. I ran to the truck, retrieved the bucket and jogged to the brook. With the bucket full I started across the field, walking lopsided with the weight of it.

The three of them were standing around the sapling Calum had already set in the hole. Taurus was filling in around the roots by returning the rich-looking earth I had earlier unearthed, scraping it with the shovel. Bartholomew broke loose lumps of ground with his foot and kicked the results into the hole as well. Calum directed me to pour the contents of the bucket around the sapling's roots, where it disappeared, the ground gulping thirstily at my offering. He sent me for a second bucket.

This time I didn't hurry back, lingering instead, thinking that I was doing all the work while they just stood around remembering, but there wasn't much sympathy for me, not even from Taurus who had been working in a coal mine for three or four years by the time he was my age. Watching from the brook, they could have been three men standing at the grave of a fourth friend, or old pirates burying treasure. Although he was taller than the other two, Calum didn't tower over them, standing there in his salt and pepper cap. Bartholomew and Taurus were about the same height, but Bartholomew was a wisp beside Taurus's thickness. Even the kind of braces that held up their pants was different, Bartholomew's dressy ones coming from the men's clothing store, Taurus's from the Farmer's Store where they hung among the rubber boots and thick flannel pants, the same kind of pants he was wearing. Calum seemed to be doing all the talking, his hands building images in the air of whatever he was saying. A sweeping hand took in the whole field, and Bartholomew's and Taurus's eyes followed it; and it was easy to guess they were seeing the oak and the ash, the birch and the elder, pushing into the October sky, carrying words that turned almost vocal with colour before falling silent through the winter, only to begin humming again in the spring and bursting fully into summer.

By the time I got there, Taurus was quoting the poem he had written from a page Calum had typed. While he read, I watched Calum's hand reach down and caress the small leaves of the ash, ash standing for N. The first letter in Taurus's poem had been planted.

17

The racing season was almost over before the judges at the Shean track received the results of Starstruck's urine test, a test that showed that the horse was drugged the afternoon he won his race. Only two Sundays of racing remained of the track's season, so Eric Rundle was suspended for the rest of that season and half of the following one. Rundle was livid, threatening to punch the judges and accusing other horsemen of sabotaging the best horse in his stable. In the end, though, there was nothing he could do but sit out his suspension, which applied to all USTA tracks. For him, it meant that for almost a year he wouldn't be able to drive. For Duncan and me, it meant that Summer Cloud wouldn't need to be drugged any more, at least not until Rundle was able to race again.

It was Duncan who brought me the bad news, dragging me up to my bedroom for privacy even in front of Calum, who always turned off his hearing aid whenever Duncan was around. Summer Cloud would never have to worry about being drugged again, ever, he said, because Rundle was not allowed to race for the rest of the season and most of next summer and didn't plan to winter any of his horses if they couldn't pay their way. He was selling all of them, and Summer Cloud he was selling to the mink farm.

We had hoped once Summer Cloud was no longer of any use to Rundle, he would sell the horse to someone who could look after the roan gelding, maybe even heal him, or at least never hurt him again. He still had two years of good racing left in him if somebody took the time to get him sound. It never occurred to us that Rundle would just turn a horse with a mark of 1:59:1 into mink meat.

"He's going today," Duncan said. "Rundle's selling him to the mink man for twenty dollars. Twenty friggin' dollars and nobody at the track was willing to buy him. Even John Alex told Rundle he wouldn't take Summer Cloud for free! How much have you got, Smelt?"

"Forty-five dollars," I answered, confessing the figure I often counted, had just counted again that Saturday morning. Saying the figure, though, I knew it was gone.

"Together that gives us fifty bucks," Duncan calculated. "Let's buy him. I can take him to John Alex's barn for now; then I'll ask my grandmother if we can take him to her farm. My uncle just fixed up the barn this summer, and there's lots of room and lots of hay, and my uncle will look after him like a pet. What do you say?"

I looked at Piper asleep on the pillow and thought of what Calum would say about me buying a horse.

"If you don't want to do it, then loan me the money. I'll pay you back. Don't I always?" I didn't bother saying no; Duncan never paid back money he borrowed because we never kept those kinds of accounts. Still, forty-five dollars was a lot different than one dollar or even five, but this whole thing was my fault. An image came into my mind of Summer Cloud being put in a large cage where hundreds of hungry, weasel-like minks devoured him alive, a nightmare worse than any he might have had withdrawing from the drugs Eric Rundle gave him twice a week. It wouldn't happen that way, I knew, but that was how I saw Summer Cloud being trucked away to the slaughterhouse. I took the money from my drawer and passed it to Duncan who charged down the stairs and up the track faster than poor Summer Cloud had run in years. I didn't try to catch up to him, but I was glad Duncan was in this mess with me. If I had learned alone about Summer Cloud going to the mink farm I wouldn't have known what to do, except perhaps pray for a miracle, but Duncan was that miracle. He heard about Summer Cloud going to the minks and figured out exactly how to save the doomed gelding.

Following Duncan's route at a walk, it occurred to me that I didn't need to tell Calum anything about buying a horse since Duncan had already worked out how we could stable him. It wasn't like Calum was going to walk out to his workshop some morning and find a horse standing in it. If Summer Cloud rested all winter, and if Duncan and I could go see him often enough and work on his legs with every kind of liniment from Tuttles, to blistering him; by next summer we might have Summer Cloud sound enough to bring him back to the track, maybe as fast as he ever was. It suddenly seemed natural for Duncan and me to become the owners of the horse we loved, as if everything that happened was God's way of helping us help Summer Cloud. The story could go anywhere from here, I thought, maybe even the track record. Growing excited, I found myself hurrying, breaking into a run, wanting to see Eric Rundle's face when Duncan offered him fifty dollars for a horse he was going to sell for twenty. There was no way a horse trader like Eric Rundle wouldn't take fifty dollars instead of twenty, but before I got to the track I met Duncan coming back, walking slower than Calum. When we faced each other, he passed me my forty-five dollars, and I could tell from his face if he tried to say anything he would cry. Summer Cloud was already gone. In trying to save him, I had killed him.

I didn't go piss-whistling the next day, telling Calum I was sick. I kept to my room, plagued by Summer Cloud's death. I tried to sleep the day away, although I could hear the loud-speaker voice of the race announcer tracking the position of each horse in each race, calling their names out from wire to wire. Piper curled up like an act of forgiveness inside my own fetal curl but I wasn't in the mood to be forgiven. I carried my imaginary sickness and real sadness through the sleepless night and into the morning when I told Calum I was feeling too sick to go to school.

Calum, his sun porch now locked against the coming winter, made his morning journey to Bartholomew's store an hour and fifteen minutes before the noon paper arrived, and when he returned he noticed that my stomach ache had healed enough to account for the missing half of an apple pie that Mrs. MacFarlane had sent over to us. It was enough evidence to convince him that I had healed from whatever affliction had kept me in my room for two days. As the afternoon bell called students back to school, I was among them.

When the bell rang dismissing classes for the day, Duncan asked me to walk over to the domestic science and art building because he had to see Mother Saint Margaret for minute. She met us at the door, and before I knew what was happening Duncan was talking a blue streak.

"Mother," Duncan began, "my grandmother in Margaree is really, really sick and our whole family is going down to be with her, and we're leaving right after school, so Roddie offered to scrub the building for me. Is that okay?"

Before his words had time to sink in, Mother Saint Margaret was gushing all over me about what a good friend I was and how thoughtful and responsible Duncan was, considering the circumstances, to think of his duty in the middle of family problems and, promising to pray for his grandmother, opened the door herself to let Duncan out, then closed it again trapping me inside with the bucket and mop. The last thing I saw through the closing door was Duncan's smile which would soon, I knew, be a loud laugh filling The Turk's.

"You and Duncan have been good, good friends for a long, long time, haven't you?" Mother Saint Margaret said as I filled the scrub bucket with hot water under the sink tap, watching the soap form a heavy head of white bubbles. We used to be, I told myself, but not wanting to lower the esteem that Duncan's lie had brought to both of us, I agreed.

"When he asked me to help him, though, he didn't tell me what he did. I wasn't in school this morning, remember?"

"Duncan likes challenging his teachers, Roddie, which isn't always a bad thing, but he's a boy who won't accept anybody's rules until he's tested them for himself, even his faith, which he's forever questioning," Mother Saint Margaret said. "I don't mean his silly little ideas like 'If God can do anything, can He give a bald-headed man a hair cut?' or 'Can He make a rock so heavy He can't lift it?' I hear those questions at least once a year, but there are other, more serious matters that can't be tolerated.

"This morning, it was animals. He wanted to know if animals have souls, and if not, why not, because any God who would make something alive only to wind up as dog food is just cruel. He was quite passionate about it, but grade ten is no place to be questioning God's intentions and when I told him so, he made a blasphemous remark I won't repeat. For punishment I ordered him to come here after school and scrub the building. I didn't know his grandmother was sick or I would have asked him to write an essay on faith. Maybe it was worrying about his grandmother that made him so angry. We don't always know what other people are feeling, do we? Anyway, Duncan is lucky to have a friend like you."

Mother Saint Margaret showed me the well-tracked hallway and domestic science and art rooms that needed to be mopped and how to wring the mop, which I already knew how to do since I did all the mopping at home, but I wasn't about to admit that. I swished the wet mop across the floor, wrung it, wiped the linoleum again to soak up the excess water and stroke by stroke the floor began to surface from under the traffic of hundred of pairs of feet coming and going from art class and domestic science all day. It wasn't difficult, and it didn't take long, and I hoped that down-on-my-knees waxing wasn't part of Duncan's punishment. Knowing Duncan got into trouble with Mother Saint Margaret because he was angry over what happened to Summer Cloud made my scrubbing of the floor a proper penance for us both.

"I'm finished, Mother," I said, knocking on the door of the room she had entered when I started scrubbing.

"Come in," and I opened the door. Mother Saint Margaret was standing at an easel painting. She placed her brush in a bottle of liquid while I looked at what she was doing. Pinned to the side of her easel was a landscape picture from a magazine that she was copying.

"I still have a lot of work to do on it," she said, wiping her hands on a paint-stained towel she carried over her shoulder. "Have you finished already? Then have a glass of juice with me."

Mother Saint Margaret left the room and returned from the domestic science room with two glasses of orange juice.

"Are you still drawing, Roddie?"

I told her about the racetrack and the pictures I was drawing and selling there, but aside from that there wasn't much else I was doing with what she called my talent.

"Would you like to learn more?" she asked. I shrugged, not sure what she was asking.

"If you are serious about your talent, and I believe you should take it very seriously, perhaps I can help. It wouldn't be during school, so you'd have to make a commitment to come here after school one or two days a week. Would you care for that?"

I realized what she was saying, that at least once a week I would have to come here after school instead of making for The Turk's to sit with Mary Scotland. Right this minute, I thought, Duncan is sitting with her while I'm scrubbing his floor.

"Would I learn to paint?" I asked, indicating her own work on the easel.

"Certainly. Do think about it, Roddie. Please. You won't be sorry."

I walked into The Turk's, and everybody in the place started laughing, including Mary Scotland who was sitting in a booth with Mary Jane, Mary French and Duncan. I raced across the floor and jumped on him, shoving him down in the booth and punching hell out of his arm but he couldn't stop laughing. Neither could I. We sat up then, making a giddy peace while I promised him that his time was coming. "I'll get you back, Duncan, so help me God, I'll get you back."

"You're going to have to keep this secret," Mary Scotland scolded. "If my mother finds out you scrub floors she'll try to make me marry you."

"You mean Smelt is just the daughter-in-law she's looking for?" Duncan joked, not mentioning what only he knew, that I mopped the floors at home. "It could get even worse, you know. If all our mothers find out about it, they could go on strike, marching over streets with their mops on their shoulders, and Smelt here would have to walk through the picket line to scrub everybody's house because the men would tell him it's his fault, and their floors better be clean and their suppers on the table when they get home from work. Wouldn't that be something to see, women on strike?"

Duncan had never lost his interest in the strike of '32, and wanting to shift the conversation away from its current subject I asked Duncan if he knew the army had been sent to Shean in 1909 to stop a strike. Duncan obviously didn't know.

"Calum told me about it when I asked him about 1932. He said the army was in all the coal mining towns in Cape Breton in 1909. They had tents set up at the shore in Shean and kept their eyes and their guns on the miners. Nobody got shot, though."

"The army! You know what, we were born at the wrong time. There used to be strikes right here in Shean, organized labour telling the big bosses to go straight to hell. There's no strikes now. There isn't even any work now because the big bosses took all the money and told us to go screw ourselves, if you'll pardon my Gaelic, ladies."

"But there was no money in '32," I reminded him. "The town was striking against itself as far as I can figure."

"But we won, didn't we?"

"Who won?"

"Our side. The side I would have been on, Taurus's side. The same side you would have been on. You're not going to tell me you'd go against Taurus, are you? Nope, it would have been me and you and Taurus against the whole frigging army if they sent it in here.

"Know what I'm going to do next summer," Duncan said to us generally, "organize the stable boys at the track. If the horsemen didn't have us to shovel their shit for them they wouldn't be able to race, and all I get for it is what John Alex happens to give me whenever he thinks of it. If we had a union of stable boys and piss-whistlers, then we could get treated better. What do you think?" he asked me.

"Stable boys and what?" Mary French asked, shaking her head as if she hadn't heard right, and my heart sank, wondering if Duncan was sinking it on purpose.

"Oh, they're guys that just stand around the stables doing nothing but whistling and trying to look useful. They might get a few bucks for helping the drug tester or something like that," he said, drawing his explanation out slowly, keeping his eye on me like a threat. "Anyway, I'm going to unionize them next summer so we can have a strike."

Walking Mary Scotland home, she said, "Duncan told me what happened."

"Yeah, he set me up pretty good, and I fell for it; but I'll get him back."

"I don't mean what happened today. I mean about the horse. He told me what you did to try to stop it from being drugged, that you're one of those whistlers, and he said he would never think of doing what you did in a million years, find a way to get rid of that awful horseman."

"I got an awfully nice horse killed doing it," I pointed out.

"I know, but it wasn't your fault. Maybe he's better off dead than being a drug addict."

"Would Johnny Logan be better off dead than being the town drunk? Duncan had a plan to rescue Summer Cloud. He was just too late," I said, surprised to find a distance already growing between me and Summer Cloud's death. "He was a beautiful horse. He had a mark of 1:59.1. That's only a couple of seconds slower than the world record. If Duncan had gotten to the track a few minutes earlier.... Last night I drew a picture of Duncan standing beside Summer Cloud, holding him. I'm going to give it to him for Christmas, and Mother Saint Margaret is going to make me her art student," I added, my decision to take the art nun's offer coming in the act of telling Mary Scotland about it.

18

It took awhile for me to tell Mother Saint Margaret I would become her after-school student, because even though I already told Mary Scotland and even though I wanted to learn how to paint, I wasn't so sure that's how I wanted to spend my after-schools. Finally, on a Friday morning in late November after religion class, I followed her out into the hall and told her I wanted to be her student. Because it was so close to exams and the Christmas holidays, she said we would begin in January.

When I told Calum I was going to take art lessons he didn't bat an eye, so I wasn't even sure his hearing aid was plugged in until I got home from serving Midnight Mass on Christmas Eve. Calum was already in bed, but wrapped under the tree was a spectrum of oil paints, a variety of brushes and an easel he had made himself, with legs that folded up like the two-foot wooden ruler he carried in the leg pocket of his bib overalls. The easel stood on three legs when it was unfolded, but it closed up like a suitcase, including a handle for carrying it, the paints and brushes fitting inside.

Calum wasn't easy to shop for, already owning about fifteen bottles of Old Spice, my offerings on previous Christmases and birthdays, and he didn't smoke so I couldn't buy him a flat fifty of Player's. He wasn't a person for ornaments and knick-knacks, either, or even winter socks, since he knitted his own and mine. Stumped, I had to settle for a pound box of chocolates from Bartholomew's store, one of the boxes with the endless woman holding the endless box of candy. Calum wasn't fond of candy, but I knew they wouldn't go to waste.

A turkey for just the two of us and we would have been eating it for Easter, Calum said, buying instead a chicken which we stuffed with my grandmother's recipe of bread crumbs and spices, and just before Calum left for Christmas morning services at his church, we put it in the oven to roast. I set the oak table in the dining room where we seldom ate, spreading the white tablecloth across it and taking the good dishes from the china cabinet, making a place for Calum at one end and me at the other, putting out the fancy salt and pepper shakers and the gravy boat, placing little glasses for our tomato juice which we only drank at Christmas. From the top of the china cabinet I took down the carved oak case that held the Murray silverware, taking forks and knives and spoons from the velvet-lined grooves that held them in place, putting the largest spoon in the gravy boat, and in a large bowl I put the fresh rolls that Mrs. MacFarlane sent over.

As she did every year, Mrs. MacFarlane invited us to have Christmas dinner with her and Duncan and Mr. MacFarlane who was home for the holidays, and, as he did every year, Calum thanked her and refused, telling her we would get along just fine. When he got home from services, the chicken was ready to come out of the oven.

Calum sat at one end of the table, and I sat at the other, and he carved the chicken, putting both legs on my plate. There were houses, I knew, where there was never enough legs to go around, one of Shean's favourite Christmas stories being the one about Farter's father carving the Christmas turkey with his seven kids hollering, "Give me a leg! Give me a leg!" and him shouting back, "Whadda ya think I got here, a spider?" So getting both legs was one of the great things about living with Calum. When our plates were full of potatoes and turnips and carrots and chicken and stuffing, and covered by a thick brown cascade from the gravy boat, Calum stopped and put his head down to thank his God, and I lowered my head to mutter my Catholic grace, and then we started.

Calum didn't eat much compared to me, but he ate a lot more than he usually did, and when we were finished, including Mrs. MacFarlane's apple pie of which Calum even had a sliver, we gathered the plates and carried them to the kitchen and did them right away, placing them clean and dry back in the china cabinet for another year. We did the same with the Murray silver, too, and then Calum went into his study to lie down, and I pulled on my jacket and headed for Duncan's house, carrying my gifts for them.

Mr. MacFarlane thanked me for the bottle of Old Spice, and Mrs. MacFarlane thanked me for another china cup, this one with a picture of the Queen on it, and Duncan, when he opened the first gift I gave him, looked at it quizzically. "Protestant socks! Not a chance I'm going to wear those," he mocked; but his mother said, "Duncan stop that silliness and be sure to thank Calum for them the next time you go over to his house." But the first chance I got I told Duncan not to thank Calum at all since the socks had been knitted for me. I just wanted to see his face when he opened a package of Calum's knitting.

I also wanted to see Duncan's face when he opened the drawing I made of him and Summer Cloud. He recognized the horse and himself right away but asked when he had posed for it. I told him that he didn't, that I just drew a picture of the horse, using for a model the carved horse that Calum had given me, and then I drew a picture of Duncan standing beside it.

"You're allowed to do that, just make it up?" All the time he was asking me how I did it he held it in his two hands as far away from him as he could, just looking at it. He liked it, and so did Mr. and Mrs. MacFarlane who, when Duncan said he was going to hang it in his room, suggested it should be hung in the living room where everybody could see it.

With Mr. MacFarlane home, Duncan's house was where we wanted to be, because there were lots of visitors in and out, lots of drinks being passed around, lots of stories being told, and one day Mr. MacFarlane landed home with Taurus who was having a few over the holidays. It was just Mr. MacFarlane and Taurus and Duncan and I in their living room, and Mrs. MacFarlane in and out of the kitchen depending on what story was being told. Mostly they talked about the Shean mine and the things that had happened to them underground. Duncan pumped them to talk about 1932, but they were more interested in the last days of the mines, and whether or not there would ever be any more life in them. There's still lots of coal down there, Mr. MacFarlane said. Taurus said it didn't matter, the mines were gone for good. The last mine was almost two miles under the sea when they pulled the pillars.

"Once you pull the pillars, that's it," Taurus said, reminding me of the movie where Samson was chained to the pillars of a palace by the Romans, and he pulled at them with all his strength until the pillars crumbled and the whole palace collapsed.

"When you're mining coal," Taurus said in reply to Duncan's question about pulling the pillars, "you leave huge blocks of coal, called pillars, standing there to help hold the roof up. When the mine reaches the end of the coal vein, they begin back-mining, which means taking out the pillars, starting with the one at the very bottom of the mine and working backwards. Once you remove the pillars, the mine begins to collapse, closing it off forever. Sometimes, mine owners order the pillars to be pulled, not because they reached the end of the coal, but because it is costing them too much to mine it. Pulling the pillars is much cheaper. That's what happened here. There was still lots of coal, but it was costly, so they had us pull the pillars and we did, even though every miner down there knew that by pulling the pillars we were working ourselves out of a job. Now nobody will ever get the coal that's left down there."

"Maybe that's not a bad thing," Mr. MacFarlane said.

"Maybe not," Taurus answered, "but it was a damn waste of a lot of good coal, a damned waste."

Seven years earlier, in the summer of 1954, several weeks after the last mine whistle blew and Mr. MacFarlane came home with his last pay envelope, Calum and I walked down the mine road along with almost everybody else in Shean. The mine yard, once full of machine shops and boiler rooms and change houses and a towering bankhead, full of train tracks and trains and men and smokey noise, was just an empty geography of red ashes and grey clay. People stood among the desolation, whispering their conversations like people at a wake. There used to be eight hundred men working in the mines here, someone said. Up in the bankhead had been the largest hoist in North America, so big they had to build a special flatcar to bring it in to Shean. Not even Pennsylvania ever saw anything like it, someone else said. Six decades earlier, there were newspaper advertisements all over Europe, in Ireland and England and Belgium and Germany, looking for miners to come to Shean, and they came in their hundreds to work in the mines. Now they were gone, most of them anyway, following whatever mine needed them next.

A few times when the mine was still running, Duncan and I had ventured down to the mine yard, begging ball-bearings from Duncan's uncle who worked in the machine shop where there were barrels of them, ball-bearings of every imaginable size, a marble player's paradise. Walking back home, our pants would be almost falling off from the weight of our wealth of steelies. Once or twice we were there when the rake, the train of small cars that carried the miners to the surface, came up from underground with its cargo of men as black as the coal they dug, carrying lunch cans under their arms, unhitching their pit belts from which hung the batteries for the lamps on their pit helmets, and when they took their helmets off there was a ring of sickly white skin at the scalp just where it disappeared into the hair, and the eyes of the men seemed to shine out of the blackness that covered their faces. I couldn't tell one miner from the other and was amazed that Duncan spotted his father in the middle of them and ran up to him. Mr. MacFarlane picked him up and gave him a big whisker burn which left the side of Duncan's face as black as the miners', and Mr. MacFarlane's teeth, when he laughed at the look of Duncan, were the whitest I ever saw.

That day, as Calum and I stood with the rest of the town, about a dozen of the miners were dressed in their mining gear, walking in and out of the pithead. Taurus and Mr. MacFarlane seemed to be the ones giving the orders. It had been the laid-off miners who were hired to dismantle the buildings, to disassemble the hoist, to load it on the train that carried it away, and now they were preparing for the last step.

So many people stood watching in the mine yard that several of the helmeted miners formed a loose circle to coax people a safe distance from the pithead itself while Taurus and Mr. MacFarlane walked down the pit carrying explosives. They spent a long time down there, but nobody left, and when they emerged they were rolling wire from a heavy spool which they connected to a plunger. Taurus called out "Fire in the hole!" and then one of the miners keeping people well back from the pithead called the same thing, "Fire in the hole!" which was repeated by the miner closest to him, the words travelling the perimeter of the mine yard until they came back to Taurus, telling him everybody was accounted for. Then he signaled Mr. MacFarlane who pushed down on the plunger.

The explosion was remote, like distant thunder, and the earth trembled under our feet, followed by several seconds of silence before the blast tore out of the mine's mouth, roaring and spewing a dark cloud of dust while the slope below collapsed. The cloud rose almost in slow motion high over the town before it began to fall like a black mist on us all as we stood there, nobody trying to get away from it. We stayed that way, motionless and silent, for a long, long time before people began to shift and move away, Calum pushing me in front of him. I saw Duncan and Mrs. Mac-Farlane waiting for Mr. MacFarlane, and when I looked back to where they were looking, Mr. MacFarlane and Taurus were both slump-shouldered, standing beside each other.

It wasn't long after that that Taurus sang his "*Cumha nam Méinneadairean*" for the first time for Calum and Bartholomew and me in the sun porch, and nobody in Shean could count how many times the song had been sung since then by just about everybody. And it wasn't long after that that Mr. MacFarlane left for northern Ontario.

Once we were back in school my art instruction began. It was hard, harder than I thought because there was a lot more to it than just putting paint on canvas. I never knew art had a history, just like war, and Mother Saint Margaret talked about it as if it was just as important. She gave me thick books to read that fortunately had more pictures than writing in them. At least, I reminded myself, I wasn't going to have to pass an exam. Still, even with my own easel and oils, Mother Saint Margaret stayed with drawing for the first few weeks, giving me exercises in plants and animals and people, telling me it was important to master drawing skills because the more confident an artist was in his fundamentals, the more creative he could be when he let go of them. I wasn't sure what she meant, but she said not to worry about it, just keep practicing. I was fortunate, too, she said, because my natural ability to draw included an instinctive sense of perspective – how much talent that meant I had could only be discovered by me.

Mother Saint Margaret also taught me to mix the oils, take care of my brushes, stretch canvas, but every day began with her questioning me about my impressions of the art in the books she lent me, followed by our regular – but growing shorter by the week – drawing lesson.

Finally, on small canvases we began painting still-lifes from pictures in the books, with her pointing out the language of light and shadow as spoken by the Masters, and we painted little still-lifes she composed herself, raiding the domestic science room for fruit that she called our models, arranging them for our session, the two of us eating them afterwards.

She showed me how to let light fall onto the subject and how to make the light radiate from the subject. My efforts were clumsy but improving every week, and I took my canvas home with me to work on it in my bedroom. Mother Saint Margaret commented on how well I was coming along one afternoon when we were eating the oranges from a still-life. Turning from my easel, which she had actually been admiring more than the picture I had on it, she said that I obviously got my talent from Calum.

"Calum doesn't draw," I said.

"Maybe not, but your grandfather is an artist. It's a pleasure just to walk by his yard when his garden is in bloom. The rhythm of colour that goes on in that yard all summer doesn't just happen, Roddie. That garden is as well thought out as any painting. He obviously works with wood in the same way," she said, running her hand over Calum's handiwork the way Mrs. MacLeod did with his carved door frames. "For some people, there has to be a practical point to everything they do. Your grandfather seems to be like that. Maybe it's what they call the Protestant work ethic, but no matter how practical he tries to be, your grandfather is an artist."

It didn't take long before I was looking forward to my art class more than anything else, except maybe walking with Mary Scotland, and even then it was mostly art I was talking to her about, telling her the things I was learning from the books, from the things Mother Saint Margaret was telling me.

"I think she enjoys it as much as I do," I once said.

"Why shouldn't she? Every day she spends her time with children who don't really care very much about what she's teaching them, and now she has you to teach. She's been trying to teach you for years. I remember when we used to have art classes. She was always giving you the hard things to do, always spending ten times as much time at your desk as anybody else's. I bet she's really happy to have you all to herself now."

Mary was the only one I told when Mother Saint Margaret made me draw a copy of a nude woman from one of the art books, me trying to draw the breasts while pretending not to be looking at them. "If I took that drawing to class and got caught with it, Mother Saint Cross John would pound me to pulp with her strap," I said, "but Mother Saint Margaret acted like she didn't even notice the woman had no clothes on."

"Were you as red drawing the picture as you are now?" Mary Scotland asked, her smile teasing me, and when I hunched my shoulders to say I didn't know, she said that Mother Saint Margaret was probably standing behind me the whole time I was drawing. Yes, I answered, realizing it was true, Mother Saint Margaret was behind me most of the time.

"I bet she was looking at those red ears of yours and laughing her head off," Mary said.

19

The persistent ringing of the phone, two longs, one short, woke me from my sleep. It took a long time to recognize the sound because the phone so rarely rang in our house, and never in the middle of the night. Groggy, I threw back the blankets only to grab them instantly around me again. The coal furnace in the basement sent its heat into the downstairs rooms through a four-foot square register in the dining room floor and into the upstairs through much smaller registers, too small to prevent the frost from drawing thick, leafy designs on the bedroom windows or to keep February at bay beyond the blankets. I wanted to hide inside my quilted cocoon, but the ringing wouldn't go away. I reached out with one arm, groping around the floor beside the bed until I found one sock, pulled it on under the blanket, then felt around until I found the other. With my socks on, I threw back the blankets, reached for my shirt which was carefully laid out on the chair beside me for exactly this reason, so I could jump up when Calum called, and hurry into my clothes with minimum exposure to the cold, but it was a lot colder in the bedroom at two in the morning than eight. I chased the ringing down to the living room and lifted the receiver.

"I thought you were all dead over there," Sally Fortune, the backshift operator, said. "I was about to call the police. Calum has a long distance call from Omaha. That's in Nebraska, and that's in the United States, so if somebody is calling from the United States I thought I better put them through."

Simply hanging up wouldn't make the phone call go away because Sally would just start ringing the house all over again. Besides, she was just dying to listen in and find out who would be calling Calum at this hour, if she didn't already know, and chances were she already knew. "How many people from Omaha, Nebraska, in the United States, call people in Shean?" she wanted to know. "I don't know," I answered, then told her I would get Calum.

I went upstairs and knocked on Calum's door, which was a useless gesture. I opened it and walked into his frosted room, feeling for him under the blankets and when I got my hand on his shoulder I shook him. "The phone!" I said when he opened his eyes, holding my hand to my ear in pantomime. "It's from Omaha!" That news did not spur him to the sudden action it had inspired a few years earlier. He took his time, sitting up in his long underwear, knocking his finger through the thin shell of ice in the glass beside his bed, retrieving upper teeth. I left him there and went back down to the phone.

"He'll be here in a minute," I told Sally, wondering if Aunt Evelyn could hear me on the other side of the phone and listening too to the slow steps coming down the stairs, turning to see Calum pulling the straps of his bib overalls over his shoulders. He had no shirt, just the grey top of his long underwear. Calum took the phone from me, adjusting his hearing aid with one hand as he raised it to his ear.

"Hello," he shouted loud enough for someone in Omaha, as deaf as himself, to hear. He listened, and in the middle of listening he signaled to me to go into his study and get a pen and paper. When I came back with his fountain pen and a writing pad, he was nodding.

"When?" Calum asked. He wrote the answer on the pad I placed in front of him. "Where?" he wrote down that answer, as well. I could tell it wasn't Aunt Evelyn on the phone, but that Calum was having a conversation so similar to the last time there was a call from Omaha it could have been a recurring dream. Looking down at his shaky scribbles, I could see that he wrote Time of death, followed by an 8:55, and the name of the hospital, followed by the figure $500. Calum then asked for a number where he could get in touch with the person who was calling, and then hung up.

I had moved over to stand on the register's warm wafting of air, barely more than a baby's breath exhaled by a furnace banked with coal to last through the long night. Calum turned away from the phone and looked at me. He hated stating the obvious, saying to me one time that most conversations were made up of it, but eventually he said what I already knew.

"She says Evelyn's dead."

"Again?" If he heard my sarcasm he didn't acknowledge it. Instead, he went into the kitchen and poked at the coals in the kitchen stove, flaring it to life, added coal, took off one of the lids and replaced it with the kettle. Then he came into the dining room.

"I want you to ring me Omaha, Nebraska, and ask the operator for St. Joseph's Hospital," Calum said, and I rang Sally Fortune who answered almost before I finished turning the crank on the side of the phone. At two o'clock in the morning in Shean there probably weren't all that many people phoning each other, which accounted for her quick response. Either that or she was waiting for Calum's call. In the meantime, she had probably called anybody who was awake at that hour to tell them that Aunt Evelyn was dead. Like me, I imagined that everyone she told answered, "Again!" I told Sally I wanted to phone St. Joseph's Hospital in Omaha, and she told me if I wanted to hang up, she would ring the house when she got through.

"It might take a while," she said, then asked, "How is Calum?"

"Fine," I told her, watching him back at the kitchen stove, angrily forcing the fire out of its listlessness the way the phone had forced me awake a little earlier. I said it, but I wasn't at all sure Calum was fine. I sat at the kitchen table in silence while he waited for his water to boil. I had nothing to say that he wanted to hear, nothing that wasn't already shouting inside him.

When the phone rang again, I answered and Sally told me she had St. Joseph's Hospital on the line. I passed the phone to Calum who explained as precisely as a telegram who he was and what he wanted to know, and he was given the information he asked for, confirmation of the death of a patient, Evelyn Gillies. She had left a request that her remains be sent home to Shean, Cape Breton. The undertaker would make those arrangements if there was someone to pay the cost. Evelyn Gillies had died destitute. Then Calum phoned the number he had written down and that's when I realized that it was an undertaker who had first phoned.

The following morning Bartholomew came to the house even before he opened his store, so fast was Sally Fortune at spreading the news, and he drove Calum to the station where my grandfather wired $500 to Omaha, Nebraska, for the second time in his life. Between Sally and John the Station, everybody in Shean soon knew Evelyn Gillies was coming home for real this time.

Mrs. MacFarlane practically moved in, getting things ready, filling the pantry with food from women all over town. It's not often, she said, that you have three days to prepare for a wake, so she was making the best of it.

Calum seemed to go on as usual, grooved as he was into his routine. Bartholomew came to the house every day, which he almost never did when the sun porch was closed, but what they talked about I had no idea because they spoke a language I didn't understand. Still, I was glad Bartholomew was there. I'll bet Calum was, too. Taurus didn't come.

My Aunt Evelyn's death started a small debate in town: Should Thursday night's bingo be cancelled the way bingos or dances were automatically cancelled whenever someone in Shean died, or could they get away with holding it? It wasn't like she was living in Shean at the time, some people said, pointing out that the jackpot was over one thousand dollars. There hadn't been a jackpot that big in a couple of years, and it had been the talk of the town until my aunt provided a new topic. Other people on the bingo committee, though, went to school with my aunt and said they remembered her as she was, not as she had become. In the end, they voted to treat her death with respect and cancelled the game, although it was probably more for Calum than anything, who wouldn't have noticed anyway.

On Thursday, the third day after we got the phone call, there she was at the station, and I stood beside Calum watching while four men unloaded her from the baggage car and placed her carefully in the back of Bartholomew's panel truck. Then we drove to the house. There was a small, silent crowd waiting, men in their suits, women in their hats, and Aunt Evelyn was carried into the well-prepared parlour.

When the coffin was set down Calum walked up to it and unclasped the locks that held it closed. I pretty near fainted. I thought, after all that time, that he would just take down the pretty picture of her hanging on the wall and place it on the coffin for people to see, the way they do when somebody gets smashed up in a car accident and they have a closed coffin at the wake. I don't think anybody wanted to know what the train ride had been like for Aunt Evelyn, but Calum lifted the top and set the metal arm that held the lid open. The smell of death came then, no different than it smelled around the coffins of others whose wakes I had gone to, and my aunt's face was still all there, thank God, and we were only waking her overnight with the funeral in the morning. Calum stood and stared for a long time at his daughter, and after a while I found the nerve to go over and stand beside him, staring at the remains of an aunt I never met.

The house filled up and stayed that way pretty well all day, with Calum and me sitting side by side beside the coffin, and people came in and shook our hands and said things to Calum, and he nodded his acknowledgment, but I'm sure he had his hearing aid turned off. Then they walked to the coffin, and I started getting giddy because so many people would look over their shoulders when they went to bless themselves, like they wanted to be sure they weren't going to offend the Presbyterian household in which she lay, or maybe they were just afraid Calum would throw them out, rosary and all. Death makes people so polite.

Calum never moved until he saw the nuns come in, three of them, Mother Saint Margaret, Mother Saint Ursula and Mother Saint Cross John. When they did, and while they were still in the hall before they got to the parlour, Calum stood up and walked out of the room and up the stairs. The nuns said a decade of the rosary aloud which, of course, made everybody in the house have to get down on their knees except for the Protestants who slipped into the kitchen and sipped tea. When their prayers were done, the three nuns gave me their condolences, asking me to be sure to share them with Calum. Mother Saint Margaret squeezed my hand, and then they left. Calum, who must have been watching from his bedroom window, came back down to the parlour.

Pretty soon, I got restless sitting there trying to look sorry and wondering if maybe I really was, because this was the first time I had ever seen my aunt. She didn't look at all like I imagined her, not like someone evil enough to steal $500 from her father by faking her own death. She was desperate; that's what Mrs. MacFarlane said when we talked about it once, and that must have been it because I couldn't find any of the hate I had felt or imagined for so long. But I didn't feel a lot of anything else either so I went to the kitchen. It was almost dark already and snowing outside. Mrs. MacFarlane gave me a plate of food at the kitchen table and, taking the chair across from me, asked if I was all right. I told her about Calum going upstairs when the nuns came in, but she already knew.

"Calum told me one time that the nuns ruined one life in this house because he's Protestant. He was talking about Aunt Evelyn, wasn't he?" I asked her. There were other women in and out of the kitchen, but they left Mrs. MacFarlane and me to ourselves.

When Aunt Evelyn was a child, she told me, more than once nuns had taken her to the convent after school and sat her down at the table and told her she had an obligation to join the convent and devote her life to praying for Calum's conversion. That sounded familiar. It happened more often, she said, as Aunt Evelyn was

becoming a teenager and a very beautiful young woman, and the
nuns who were in Shean at the time stepped up the pressure. She
was praying all the time, Mrs. MacFarlane said, going to Mass
every morning, and the friends she had then said that the reason
she was praying hard was for Calum to convert before she finished
school so she wouldn't need to join the convent. Then Calum
found out. He went up to the convent and told the superior and
all the nuns to leave Evelyn alone and leave him to God. Nobody
knew exactly what Calum said to the nuns, Mrs. MacFarlane said,
but knowing Calum it would be short and sharp as the knife he
carried in his pocket.

Evelyn had only entered high school then, but after Calum's
visit to the convent the nuns began treating her like a leper, and
she stopped going to church, stopped praying and stopped studying. When she turned sixteen she quit school and went to Boston
to work. People from Shean who were also working in Boston
used to see her all the time at down-east dances and parties, and
they could see she was drinking a lot and not behaving like a
lady, and then she found new friends and they saw less and less
of her. Occasionally when someone saw her they became alarmed
and contacted Belle who would tell Calum, and Calum would go
after her. Sometimes he would find her and bring her home and
sometimes he wouldn't. Eventually she just disappeared out of the
city and was lost for years until that first phone call from Omaha.

"The nuns today aren't like that, but it was different then,"
Mrs. MacFarlane said.

Duncan was his mother's errand boy during the wake, so I didn't
see much of him during the day. Neither did Mrs. MacFarlane
since sending Duncan for milk or bread wasn't the same thing as
sending the Pony Express. Even if Mrs. MacFarlane just sent him
across the street to borrow an egg, Duncan had to check out the
whole town on his way. It wasn't just the wake, it was the way he
was, willing to do anything for anybody, but not in a hurry. Even

though there wasn't much of him around the wake during the day, the two of us had volunteered to stay up all night with the remains. There were always a few people in Shean who took the backshift during a wake, sitting up all night with the corpse, and Duncan and I were going to get in on this one.

It was into the evening when Taurus MacLeod came through the back door into the kitchen. I thought he must be drinking, but Mrs. MacFarlane didn't think so. He was wearing his suit but he had no shirt or tie on, just his long underwear under the jacket with the braces holding up the pants and rubber boots on his feet. When he saw me he came to the table and said he had tried the sun porch door, but it was locked, so he went to the workshop to see if Calum was there. He wasn't so he came to the kitchen.

"Is Calum here?" he asked me, and when I told him he was in the parlour with the coffin he looked at me strange, as if he didn't know about the wake. But just then Mrs. MacLeod came into the kitchen through the living room door and saw her husband and looked suddenly relieved, but still worried.

"That fellow!" she said in exasperation to Mrs. MacFarlane. "We were getting ready to come to the wake and I was ironing his shirt, and when I turned around he was gone. What in the name of God possessed you to come out looking like that?" she asked her husband, pulling a folded shirt from her large purse. "Now you put this on before we go see Calum, and ... oh, look at your feet," she added suddenly, noticing the knee-high mine boots. "I don't know what I'm going to do with this man. I swear he's losing his mind," she chuckled to Mrs. MacFarlane, but her voice wasn't as light as her words.

Taurus put his shirt on in the pantry and fixed his tie in the mirror over the kitchen sink. Then I walked back to my chair ahead of both of them to sit beside Calum who hadn't yet moved except to avoid the nuns – not to eat, not to go to the bathroom. Taurus and he exchanged a few Gaelic phrases, and Mrs. MacLeod did the same with Calum. Then taking her husband by the arm they walked to the coffin. As they stood there I saw Calum's eyes do a double-take as they took in Taurus's footwear. It was snowing out, people were coming in with little white caps of it on their own caps and kerchiefs and bare heads, but it wasn't snowing so much that anyone else was wearing rubber boots. Whatever Calum thought about the look of his friend was just swallowed up inside him like everything else, and Mrs. MacLeod guided Taurus out of the house and home as soon as they had finished their prayers.

About nine o'clock that night, as the evening wave of visitors was waning, the three Marys came into the wake, telling Calum and me they were sorry, and Mary Scotland took my hand and held it for a minute while she gave us her condolences. The three of them said their prayers beside the coffin, and then Mary French and Mary Jane left, but I saw Mary Scotland circle back from the hall to the kitchen, which made me think it was time to see if Mrs. MacFarlane needed any help. Mary was already washing dishes with Mrs. MacFarlane drying them. I started saving the dishes, saying, when they told me not to bother, that I knew where everything went so it would be easier. Mrs. MacFarlane twigged right away and said, passing me the dish towel, in that case, I may as well dry them, too, and she left us alone at the sink while she made more tea and put out more sandwiches and squares.

Duncan came at ten o'clock, just ahead of John William Connors and Michael John MacLean, a couple of old bachelors who didn't live together but were good friends and always sat up all night at all the wakes. John William was a dainty bachelor, but Michael John wasn't nearly as neat. Mrs. MacFarlane said wakes were the only time either of them got to eat something besides their own fried baloney, curds and potatoes, which was evident by the way they loaded up on biscuits and ham in the kitchen. They weren't afraid of the sweets, either. At eleven o'clock, Calum came into the kitchen to say goodnight and thank Mrs. MacFarlane; he thanked John William and Michael John for coming, and gave Mary and me, sitting at the table, a long, absorbing look. I followed him upstairs, worried because he looked so tired and hadn't eaten a bite or drunk a sip all day to my knowledge, but he said he was fine and told me to be sure to get some rest. I replied that I would, adding under my breath, "but not while Mary Scotland is in our house."

Back downstairs, Johnny Logan had come in, drawn to the wake and the inevitable bottle. I guess he was late coming because he figured Calum wouldn't have a bottle handy for visitors, and he didn't. It was Mrs. MacFarlane who stocked the pantry with a forty-ouncer of rum for hot toddies, so somebody must have told Johnny, or he was just desperate to get in from the cold. He was covered in snow, and we could hear the wind howling. The evening's snowfall had grown to a storm.

Once John William Connors and Michael John MacLean had been settled, and Duncan and I were accounted for, Mrs. MacFarlane hurried to get herself home before it got too cold. All of the other visitors were already gone. When I was holding the storm door open for Mrs. MacFarlane to leave, another shape came through the blowing snow toward the house, Nicole MacRory coming to pay her respects after closing Tony the Turk's restaurant.

When I told Mary how bad the storm was getting she said that she had better start for home but didn't move, and I didn't offer to get her coat. Instead, she went to the stove, checked the tea, and offered more food to John William and Michael John, John William saying, "That would be dandy, just dandy," and Michael John said, "Just a little bite," but meaning a lot more than that, and Johnny Logan asked if there were any other choices besides food. I told him I could find a drink, and asked the others. "A little one would be just dandy," John William Connors said, holding his fingers a good inch and a half apart, "and put it in a cup in case anyone comes in. Or downstairs," he added as afterthought. With food and drinks we moved from the kitchen to the parlour and settled into the couch and the chairs beside Aunt Evelyn's coffin.

John William sat in the armchair, Michael John on one of the straight chairs. Duncan sat on the couch beside Nicole who had decided to stay until the storm eased, and Mary and I crowded onto the couch beside them, pushing us into a tight fit against each other just as the lights flickered.

"They're going to go," Michael John predicted as the lights blacked out a second time, then died on their third and final attempt to stay lit. We were engulfed in total darkness in the same room as a dead woman. "Candles?" Michael John asked quietly.

I pushed myself up from being squeezed into the pleasant presence of Mary Scotland and groped my way toward the kitchen and the oil lamp we kept there. "Be sure she doesn't follow you out there," John William joked, sending a chill down my spine as his remark changed the content of my thought from Mary Scotland to Aunt Evelyn. A moment later I jumped as a cold hand took hold of my own, Mary giggling at the pathetic whimper that rose from my near failing chest. "I don't want to stay in there without you," she said, her hand growing warmer in my own.

Holding closer than we needed to, we made our way to the stove where I removed the lid, the glowing embers emitting enough light to define the corners of the kitchen, and the play of shadow and light on Mary Scotland's face was irresistible. I kissed her, and she moved against me in sudden passion against death and darkness and night, allowing my hands to travel the length of her body without the sudden chaperoning of her hands. John William Connors's voice broke through at last, calling out whether or not we had found a light. Reluctantly, I released Mary and found matches and then the lantern and several candles, which we lit and left stuck in their own wax on saucers in the kitchen and the living room.

The lantern, when we brought it into the parlour, turned everything into gigantic shadows that swept the room like a ship rocking on a stormy sea. We settled in again, and I realized the smell of liquor in the room wasn't just coming from Johnny Logan and the two bachelors. Duncan, when he leaned across Nicole to remind me of the time we had been at Annie Rosary's house in the middle of the night, had the smell of rum on his breath. Realizing that I knew, he winked and touched a mickey in his belt, offering me some with his eyes, but I refused. My thoughts were still in a roil over my moment in the dark kitchen with Mary Scotland, the two of us clinging in a way we had never before held each other. I wished everyone in the room was gone, including my aunt, but Mary was the one who said she had to leave.

She assured me she would be all right walking home in the storm, but I wouldn't let her leave alone. I put on my parka, and the two of us walked through the blizzard breathless, turning our backs to the wind to gasp enough air to go on, losing our way in the white-outs, stumbling over snowdrifts, watching behind us for the flashing amber lights of the snowplough that might come along and not see us, as sometimes happened to someone, and to cars stuck and buried in the snow.

When we got to Mary Scotland's door we necked in the corner so long we almost froze, before she had sense enough to send me home and go inside. But before she went in, I steeled myself and asked her, or more accurately, blurted out, if we could go steady. She said she had been doing that since last summer, and didn't I know that?

Going home through the same storm seemed no problem at all as I sang into the wind and shouted wind-snatched words of love, knowing no one could hear, and by the time I got to the house I was even thanking dear old Aunt Evelyn for having died and making this night possible. John William and Michael John and Johnny Logan were still in the parlour, accompanied by the rest of the forty-ouncer they found in the pantry, but Duncan and Nicole were gone and I wondered if Duncan, whom John William said had walked Nicole home through the storm, would ever dare to try anything with an older woman, her being nineteen.

The men in the parlour talked about death while shadows trembled on the wind-shaken walls, and they told ghost stories to each other, all intended to make me tremble, but my mind was still singing songs of the living – and their tales, which would have enchanted Duncan and me at any other time, were suddenly stories to be endured until I could endure no more. At four in the morning, I said good night, stood beside Aunt Evelyn's coffin, said a silent thank-you and went to bed. Scratching away enough frost from the pane to peek outside, I saw that the blizzard had worsened: Wind-driven clouds of snow almost obliterated the street light that normally backlit the frost's ferny pattern on the window. I suspected Duncan would never come back through the storm to sit the rest of the night with the others.

20

Calum nearly had a stroke the next morning, and it had nothing to do with Aunt Evelyn's death or funeral. Duncan and Nicole might have been almost frozen when Calum found them in the sun porch the following morning, but their circulation started pumping in a hurry when he hollered at them, and they threw back the quilt they were huddled under and began buttoning buttons and buckling buckles, and then, Duncan said, his empty mickey bottle slid out from between them onto the floor. That's when Calum took a swipe at Duncan with the snow shovel.

After Mary Scotland and I left, Nicole MacRory said she had better leave, too, and Duncan offered to walk her home. Going out the front door, though, he took the skeleton key to the sun porch off the nail in the hall and invited her in for a sip to keep them warm before they started out in the storm. It felt warm in the sun porch, Duncan said, and so they sat for a while sipping black rum. Then it began to get chilly, so he pulled Calum's quilt off the back of the couch and around their shoulders, and they started getting warm again, and then ... and then Calum got up at six in the morning with the blizzard still raging, and he took the shovel from the back porch and went to the front verandah to clear the steps for anyone who might come to the wake before the funeral that morning. That's when he made his discovery and drove them both off into the storm, telling Duncan he didn't want to see his face around our house again.

The funeral was scheduled for ten in the morning, but the blizzard wasn't letting up. Mrs. MacFarlane came back to our house about nine o'clock, waking Duncan up to come with her, and when Calum saw him in the kitchen a big vein in the old man's forehead started throbbing, but he didn't say anything in front of Duncan's mother because she had been so good to us all through the waiting and the wake. When the phone rang, it was Mrs. MacFarlane who answered it, and we heard her telling Father Alex she was worried about my aunt's remains. The priest, I could tell from their conversation, wanted to cancel the funeral for a day, but she said that Calum had kept the furnace blasting heat during the wake, and my aunt wasn't embalmed, and it was five days now since she passed away. Mrs. MacFarlane didn't feel the poor woman had another day left in her.

A short time later Father Alex arrived, having walked through the storm carrying what he needed to hold a funeral service right in the house instead of taking Aunt Evelyn to Holy Family Church. Then Bartholomew phoned to say his panel truck was buried in his driveway and the roads were closed, and he couldn't even make it to the funeral. We had no way to get my aunt to the graveyard where the grave had already been dug, Calum having paid a couple of men to pick and shovel their way through two feet of frost and four feet of mud beside my grandmother's grave in preparation for Evelyn's burial.

Everybody at the house, Calum, Mrs. MacFarlane, Father Alex, John William, Michael John, Johnny Logan, Duncan and I, stood or sat in the kitchen drinking tea and eating more of the funeral food, trying to think what to do.

"Well, we have two altar boys to help me hold the service," Father Alex said to Calum. "Maybe we could close the casket afterwards and place it in the sun porch. It would be protected from the weather, and your daughter would be kept cold. Tomorrow, when the weather breaks, we could take her to the cemetery."

Calum bristled when the priest suggested the sun porch, and I thought it was because Calum didn't want to have to remember his dead daughter's coffin every time he went in once he opened it again in the spring. Duncan had yet to tell me about what happened there earlier that morning.

Then Duncan had an idea that even had Calum nodding in approval. Together, he and I set off for John Alex's house, explaining to John Alex what we needed and John Alex pulled on his own overcoat and came out to the barn with us, helping hitch Cape Mabou to his flatbed sleigh, and then he turned the reins over to Duncan, telling him to be careful and watch for the snowplough. Cape Mabou pulled us through the streets of Shean, her wide chest bulling through snowbanks, both of us hollering through the wind that she was better at this than racing. When we got to the house I tied her to one of the few pickets I could still see on our front fence while Duncan pulled a big rug and a flake of hay off the sleigh and put the former over her and the latter in front of her, and we hurried inside.

With neither surplice nor soutane, Duncan and I helped Father Alex with the funeral Mass and graveside service right there in our parlour, and then the priest left, leaving Duncan, John William, Michael John, Johnny Logan, who was shaking pretty bad by now, and me to carry the coffin out to the sleigh and then up to the graveyard. With Calum and Mrs. MacFarlane watching from the front steps through a veil of blowing snow, the five of us, along with two shovels, got on the sleigh, wrapping ourselves in old blankets and overcoats that Calum had gathered and given us to stay warm.

"Thank Jesus she wasn't a Protestant," Johnny Logan said, leaving the rest of us to imagine what the three-mile trip out to the Protestant graveyard in the Glen would be like in this weather.

Nothing was moving in Shean except Cape Mabou and her cargo of living and dead as we made our way through the snow-clogged streets toward the cemetery. Duncan, with a scarf covering everything but his eyes, pointed the mare through the storm, guiding her up the hill past the church and the school buildings to the graveyard itself, which, as we approached it, was visible and invisible in turns, the storm howling across it, only dark shapes of the larger monuments to tell us it was there at all. Instead of stopping at the gate and carrying the coffin as we expected to do, as was always done, Duncan coaxed Cape Mabou to use the piled-up snow as a bridge over the fence, all of us tense with worry that she would tangle a leg in the wires and wood below. Suddenly, though, we were inside the graveyard itself, the horse pulling us in the direction I pointed out to Duncan, the direction in which my grandmother and my mother were buried, and beside whom we would be burying my aunt.

Cape Mabou kept pulling like she was enjoying the adventure, as if she had really been born to the wagon, not the sulky, but Johnny Logan finally had enough. "Stop this god-damn vehicle right now or I'm going to crawl in there with that poor woman and die," he begged.

Duncan pulled on the reins, stopping Cape Mabou, and a desperately dry Johnny stumbled out and fell to his hands and knees, and, driven by the dryness of his hangover, began eating the cold, clean snow like a horse in a hay field. Duncan suggested we let the horse rest anyway and walk from where we were. Cape Mabou seemed to sense it was the end of the road, because while Duncan was wrapping her reins around the arm of a headstone shaped like a cross, the mare lifted her tail and dropped a barrage of steaming green balls. We all laughed until Michael John looked closer, rubbing snow from the headstone, and said, "Aw, Jesus, she shit on my old man!"

Our laughter, already started by Johnny Logan's desperate hangover, turned to belly laughter so contagious that even Johnny forgot his great thirst long enough to join us. We laughed until the tears froze on our cheeks, and when we finally regained control, Michael John, who preferred to be the purveyor rather than the subject of gossip, gasped, "For the love of God, don't tell anybody about this," as we lifted my aunt from her old-fashioned hearse and began carrying her to her final resting place.

Carrying the shovels and leading the four of them while they carried Aunt Evelyn, two on each side, I walked ahead to find our family plot, but when I got there it was gone, so I changed directions and checked a more likely looking section of the cemetery, but neither my grandmother's nor my mother's nor my aunt's waiting grave was there, so I took new bearings and was marching in a new direction when I heard my name fly past my head in a snatch of wind. When I turned, the four of them had Aunt Evelyn resting on top of a large headstone protruding from the snow. They were all collapsed and gasping across her coffin. Walking back to see what they wanted, Duncan screamed, "Will you find that damn grave or we're going to leave her right here!" and behind them I could see the snow already filling in the long, random path along which I had led them and my aunt. I assured them with hand signals that I knew exactly where she was to be buried and started off again, but when I looked behind they were still sprawled on the coffin no longer believing in me.

When I found the plot, scraping the snow away to read Belle (Cameron) Gillies on one stone and Theresa (MacDonnell) Gillies on another, I turned to signal the weary pallbearers but tripped over a mudpile camouflaged as a snowbank, realizing only as I sank through the snow that this was definitely the location of Aunt Evelyn's grave. I hoped, as I treaded snow up to my neck, one foot resting on the edge of the already in-place rough box, that they saw me disappear and became curious. Wallowing in snow, I hollered hopelessly against the wind until they finally arrived, dropping the coffin in the snow so they could pull and lug and tug at me, growing giddy again, but without me joining in to enjoy the joke this time.

Once I was out of the grave, my boots full of snow and my feet turning cold, Duncan and I had to shovel the snow out of the grave, half of every shovelful blowing back against us, fine powder filtering down our coat collars. Eventually, with no ropes to lower her, we managed to drop, bump and slide my aunt into her grave, our prayers more a plea that the coffin would stay closed than petitions to Heaven for my aunt's soul.

There was still enough snow at the bottom of the rough box to cushion her arrival, and with Aunt Evelyn now safely and finally interred, Duncan and I took the first shift on the shovels and nearly broke our wrists when we drove them into the frozen solid mudpile. It took more than an hour to pick-and-shovel enough rock-hard lumps of earth to feel confident that Aunt Evelyn wouldn't surface in the spring, and then I said goodbye to her while the others hurried away. I caught up to them where Cape Mabou was hitched to Michael John's father's headstone; the horse's shit was already frozen hard enough for Michael John to kick it away.

"Should have left it, Michael. Maybe there would have been nothing but flowers all over your father's grave in the spring," John William said, and Johnny Logan said, "For the love of God, get me to a bootlegger," which wasn't hard since Farter's house was on our way.

We let Johnny off at the MacRory house, then let John William and Michael John off at their doors and drove the mare to John Alex's barn where we made her comfortable, and it was while we were unharnessing her that Duncan told me about Nicole, the sun porch, the rum bottle and Calum.

"You should have seen his face, Smelt. I thought he was going to take a stroke right there in the sun porch and die. I don't know if he was talking Gaelic to us or choking at what he saw because it all sounds like the same thing to me, but we were out of there in a hurry, boy, and the old bastard even took a swing at me with the shovel when I ran by him at the door."

The storm let up in the late afternoon, and I went out to shovel it away from the front step while Calum made supper. The pantry was still half full of funeral food, but I came in from outside to the smell of salt cod boiling on the stove. It was Friday, and Calum wasn't going to let me forget my Catholic menu. We sat to our supper and afterwards, while I washed the dishes, Calum retreated to his study.

The knock on the door wasn't Duncan's, as I expected, but Mary Scotland's. I had almost forgotten that we had been going steady since the night before, and I hadn't given any thought at all to how Calum would like the idea of a girl becoming a regular visitor, but there was nothing to do now but let it happen. Mary followed me into the kitchen and sat in my grandmother's rocking chair, Piper leaping into her lap and settling there, while I, putting away the last traces of supper, told her about the funeral. I knew from the way she was laughing that Duncan and I were going to be telling this one for a long time. When I was finished Mary suddenly stood up, carrying Piper in her arms, and walked into Calum's study before I could warn her about the cat.

"Hello, Mr. Gillies. How are you now?" she said, causing Calum to look up from his seat at the roll-top desk, his eyes, over the top of his glasses, taking her in as she sat in the chair beside him, looking down at the graph paper Calum was working at, pencil and ruler carefully set upon it. I stood in the doorway feeling helpless as Calum's eyes, flaring slightly, fell on Piper whose tail flared slightly.

"Is that a garden you're planning?" she quizzed my grandfather, trying to read the graph paper upside down, and Calum must have decided that she was more interested than nosey because he answered her, not sharply as he might have, saying instead that he was translating a poem.

"Oh, we have to do that in Latin this year," she said, "but it looks more like math than poetry. What are you translating it from?"

"The Gaelic."

"Into what?" Mary asked, trying to make sense of the sheet of paper in front of my grandfather.

"Trees," Calum replied.

"What?"

"Trees."

Mary's glance shot over my grandfather's shoulder to where I stood, and I nodded a quick signal that he was serious. Her first hint of laugher at Calum's joke faded, and she asked how he could do that and why. Calum picked up his typewritten version of Taurus's poem and began explaining to her about the Gaelic tree alphabet. He seemed to be measuring her interest with each phase and phrase of his explanation, and obviously finding it sincere since, even when Piper struggled loose from her arms and stepped onto Calum's desk, he continued to explain the correlation between trees and the letters of the Gaelic alphabet much as he had explained it to Taurus and me in the sun porch. Mary's hand reached out and began scratching behind the cat's ears while she listened, and Piper settled comfortably down on the desktop, basking in the attention of whatever gods allowed her to be here under Calum's increasingly tolerant gaze.

"This exercise," he said finally, nodding at the work in front of him, "is to translate the poem into the trees the letters represent."

"The way you're working it out on the graph paper, you could almost plant the poem in the ground, couldn't you?" Mary commented and Calum turned slowly to me but I shrugged that I hadn't told her anything. He turned his attention back to Mary Scotland. "I suppose you could do that," he said, and I knew he liked her.

21

They're all leaving, the young ones. Pretty soon there'll be nobody left here but us old bastards, and when we're gone then there'll be nothing but sheep grazing on our graves," Angus John Rory was saying as we walked into John Alex's barn. The barn smells, smothered by frost all winter, were letting go with the spring thaw, the manure pile out back steaming to life again, its awakening being sniffed out by John Alex's neighbours in the Company Rows who would have to get used to it all over again.

"Wouldn't that be the cruellest trick of all," Johnny Rosin said, "sheep grazing on our graves. After all, what is it but the sheep that drove us here, the British valuing a sheep more than a man."

"More than a Scotsman you mean," John Alex added, taking a drink and passing the bottle to Johnny Rosin. "It was my ancestors' land they stole, drove my great-grandfather and grandmother and six children onto a ship, and here we are today."

"So do you think we'd be better off today if it was us they chose to keep instead of sheep?" Angus John Rory asked, going on to answer, "I was there during the war, up there in Scotland, all the way up to them there Clearances. I saw the highlands and the islands and the fog and the rain. I even saw Culloden, for God's sake, and you know what I got to say," Angus said, lifting his own bottle in the air. "God bless the god-damned sheep!"

"Now that's not the point," Johnny Rosin said to Angus. "You yourself was the one who just said that all the young people are leaving and are going to leave us in a ghost town, but it's more than the town they're leaving behind. It's everything we stand for."

"And just what noble cause does your life stand for?" John Alex asked Johnny Rosin, winking across at Duncan and me who had settled ourselves onto comfortable bags of pliant oats, moulding them under us like chairs. Barn furniture, John Alex called bags of oats and bales of hay.

"Music," Johnny Rosin said. "I play the music that my father played and his father before him all the way back to over there where you were just talking about. My son, if I had one, would be doing the same, don't you think, learning the old tunes from his old man? The truth, though, if I had to admit it, is that my son probably wouldn't even pick up the fiddle, if I had one, a son that is. No, he'd probably be wanting to bang on some jeezly guitar. Look what's happening to the dances." Johnny Rosin drank deeply from the bottle, leaving the rest of us hanging there on the edges of our oat bags wondering what was happening to the dances. After a moment, Angus John Rory prompted him on, asking what he meant.

"Where were you boys last night?" Johnny Rosin asked Duncan and me in response.

"At the dance," I answered.

"Not at my dance, you weren't."

"We went to the Broken-hearted Lovers' dance out in Glen Ian," Duncan said.

"You heard that, Angus? John Alex? You heard where they were, and how many were with you?" Johnny Rosin asked, returning to his cross examination of us.

"It was packed," Duncan volunteered.

"And I had barely two sets on the floor of the parish hall. Why? I'll tell you why. Because these young ones would rather go out to the Glen Ian dance hall and listen to a bunch of juvenile delinquents banging on three chords of an out-of-tune guitar than come hear a real musician playing in Shean's parish hall. Broken-hearted Lovers, my foot! You'd think their own name would be good enough for them. It was good enough for them when I was paying them for playing the round dances between my square sets. I gave them their first break, and look how they turned on me."

The Moran Brothers had bought themselves three white sports coats and a set of drums, changed their name to the Broken-hearted Lovers and were playing all the songs on the hit parade. The Glen Ian dance hall wasn't just full, it was packed so tight people could hardly dance.

"What else can you expect from them, though. They're Irish." Johnny Rosin said. "They're the ones, don't you see, who are ruining the music, and worse, ruining the young ones, so I'm saying it's not just that the young ones are going away, but they're taking their hearts away with them. They don't want the old ways, the old music; they just want to follow that wiggle-worm of a thing they call Elvis Presley. What's a name like Presley anyway? Irish, I suppose. What is it about that music," Johnny Rosin asked, directing his question to Duncan and me, "that makes you betray your own people's music for rock and roll?"

"The girls," Duncan answered.

"Well, there you have it, Johnny," John Alex said. "It's the girls who are ruining your dances because they want to see some young fellow in a white sports coat singing like a hound dog. To tell you the truth, if I thought there was anything in it for me, I'd be at the Glen Ian dance hall myself. There's some pretty stuff goes out there. Now why don't you just shut up and have a drink and play some of that music you think is so precious."

Johnny Rosin reached for his fiddle, and I walked into Cape Mabou's stall and started stroking her mane, my eyes exploring the spring day through the manure window behind the mare. The ice was almost all gone from the Gulf, only a few white fragments drifting in the turquoise blue. What I seemed to be seeing for the first time, though, was the slag piles, acres of grey clay still holding white snow in the hollows of their folding hills, Nature's own study in black and white. Losing interest in the barn banter, I took a hard-covered sketch pad from my back pocket, one Mother Saint Margaret had given me to carry at all times. It was small, and its black cover was cracked and broken from being sat on, but it was filling up with rough ideas, a diary of drawings.

I was lucky. Not everybody in Shean could get away with taking out a sketch pad whenever he wanted without being teased or tormented. All my horse drawings the past summer saved me. The fact that grown men paid me money for my drawings of their horses was what made guys my own age let me doodle without bothering me very much. I thought they respected the talent Mother Saint Margaret was encouraging me to develop, but Duncan said nobody bothered me because they thought I was weird, just another Shean character in the making. "At least nobody's calling you an artist or anything like that," he consoled.

Still, the way Mother Saint Margaret was making me look at things, then look again and again, had me forever reaching for my pad, which was practically full of scenes and people I wanted to turn into paintings sometime. There was even a bunch of pages of sketches of the men gathered in John Alex's barn, but it wasn't them who interested my pencil that day. Nor was it Cape Mabou, my favourite horse for practicing on to perfect next summer's drawings at the track. What caught my attention was the last traces of white winter cradled in the gullies of the grey hills, and although I could see them from Cape Mabou's window, I wanted a better perspective from which to sketch them.

Telling Duncan I would see him at The Turk's later on, I left the barn and walked down to the slag piles, the thawed clay clinging to my shoes, making my feet larger than Tom MacPhee's Clydesdale's. Not much was left of the industry that had once given birth to Shean, just acres of slag embedded with broken pit props and other abandoned mining equipment. Although the town council forbade it, the clay hills had also become the town dump, household garbage and store trash being trucked there and thrown into piles anywhere that was convenient.

Sitting on the fender of an abandoned car body, I was sketching pages of possibilities when I noticed someone walking across the slag. I included the figure in my efforts, pondering whether or not a human presence was something I wanted in my final drawing, the one I would bring to Mother Saint Margaret for her "critique" as she called it. What I didn't want was for the spell of the moment to be broken, so I sat and sketched, trying not to attract the interest or company of someone else who was out experiencing and exploring the spring slag piles.

It was a good day for just drawing and daydreaming, my pencil running under its own steam, my mind wandering around the world, coming back from time to time to check on the progress of the current page. I had never been anywhere beyond the world I could see, beyond those distant hills and horizon where I would eventually travel. I knew that. What John Alex said in the barn about the young people going away might as well have been in the Bible it was so true. It was the most exciting thing we knew, Duncan and I and everyone our age, that we would eventually be going away. And it wasn't just the young people. Mr. MacFarlane must have been in his thirties or forties, and he was still leaving. Duncan and I would go off somewhere after we finished school – Toronto, Sudbury, Boston, who knew where. Our destination was a whim that changed with every new set of plans.

As the figure walking among the slag heaps drew closer, it took the unmistakable shape of Taurus MacLeod and his presence became an important feature of the sketches I was making. My pencil busied itself trying to capture him until he got so close I could no longer ignore him. I lowered my pad and looked up to meet him, welcoming him with the universal Gaelic greeting. He didn't reply, just looked at me the way I must have been looking at the lunch can under his arm.

"What are you up to, Taurus?" I asked.

"Work," he answered, his gaze swiveling around like somebody in a panic. When his eyes fell on me I could tell he didn't know who I was. He didn't just forget my name this time. "I'm on the afternoon shift," he continued without much confidence in his voice, and I realized Duncan and I had been wrong. We hadn't seen him since my Aunt Evelyn's wake, and people were saying Taurus MacLeod was going senile, but we argued with everybody who said it, reminding them who they were talking about, reminding them that the man was a legend.

"There's no mine, Taurus," I said, feeling uneasy and alone at the moment. "They closed it, remember? You blew it up."

He heard what I said because it brought realization to his eyes. He took the lunch can in his two hands, studying it like he was trying to make sense of a math problem. He knew now that the mine was gone, but it didn't seem to help him much, because even knowing it and knowing where he was, he still didn't know how to get home from there.

"My house is, uh...," he said, waving an embarrassed hand in the direction of the town, hoping for a hint from me.

"I'm going up there now," I said, pocketing my pad, wanting to get the two of us off the slag pile, get Taurus home where it wouldn't be my fault if something happened to him. "I'll walk with you," I offered, solving for him the problem of which way to go and where. We started walking together, but Taurus seemed to be keeping half a step behind, like he was following me but wasn't sure he should. He didn't know me, and I didn't know what to do about it except to go on as if nothing was wrong, talking a blue streak to keep myself from even thinking about the two of us out here on the clay hills.

"Calum's been busy with your poem, Taurus," I said. "He's been working on it quite a lot, every night almost, turning it from words into trees so that next summer we can go up to your place in the Highlands and plant it. There are four hundred and seventy-nine letters in your poem. One hundred and fourteen words. Calum and I counted them. There are six stanzas with four lines each in them, but I guess you know that, since you wrote it. But I bet you didn't know how many words or letters, did you? The way Calum is working it, he's making the spaces so they are equal to the room the largest trees need in order to grow. They may be as much as twenty or thirty feet apart. That's to give the oaks room to grow, the oaks and the elms, and then he's going to plant each of the trees an equal distance apart just like letters in a book, except for the 'h's, of course, because they'll be beside the 'B's and 'M's, like 'Bh' or 'Mh.' Calum calls the h" an aspirate. And he's going to skip a space whenever a new word starts. That's so people will know when one word ends and another begins.

"But you should hear the two of them, Calum and Bartholomew, going at it about the alphabet. Remember when you and I didn't know there was even one tree alphabet? Well, there's more than one. More than one source, anyway, Calum says, and they're not all the same. In one version he looked up, it says the 'A' is the elm tree, and in another, it says it's the pine tree. And one of Bartholomew's sources says the 'U' is the yew tree. In another source he looked up, 'U' isn't the yew tree, it's heather. I said I thought it should be yew because they sound right, U and yew, but I don't think they're going to listen to me at all. Besides that, in the alphabet that says the U is the yew, what do you suppose the 'I' is? The yew tree, too. And one alphabet says that 'T' isn't even a tree. It says it's fire, unless there's a fire tree but I never heard of it. Not Calum either, and another alphabet says that the 'T' is the Holly. Anyway, they're studying it.

"When fall comes and all those trees, all those letters, I mean, start changing colours, I bet we'll be able to see just how beautiful the Gaelic is. That's what everybody says, that it's a beautiful language. Remember I told you that Calum told me that Gaelic was the language that Adam and Eve spoke in the Garden of Eden, and you said that must mean the apple tree stands for all the letters in d-a-m-n-e-d, the way they were damned by God to go east of Eden? Anyway, I think the oak trees are going to be great because your farm is going to be full of them. I think I counted fourteen of them in your poem. They're going to take a long time to grow, though, but when they do, they'll live for hundreds of years. I've practically memorized the alphabet now...."

I glanced over my shoulder and saw that Taurus had fallen behind. Maybe I was scaring him in my effort not to be scared myself, but I couldn't let him just wander away from me. I walked back to him where he stood staring at the old mine workings, but there was no way for me to know what he was seeing or not seeing.

"It's not far to your house, Taurus," I told him and he timidly began following me again until we got to his street, and his pace quickened with recognition. When we got to his gate Mrs. MacLeod came out of the house.

"There you are! I didn't know where you went...," her voice faltering as he passed her his lunch can.

"It was very good," he said, and she looked at me, both of us knowing that Taurus MacLeod had just come home from a shift in the mine, had eaten the lunch in his can, and was tired after all that work.

"Thank you, young Roddie," she said, as Taurus kept on into the house, and she started after him. "He doesn't seem to be getting any better. I hoped once the winter was gone and he could get out and see his old friends again...."

22

Duncan and I made our way along the beach, with Farter sniffing along behind us when he wasn't doubled over in coughing fits like somebody with a winter flu in late June, but it wasn't the flu. His father had taught Farter to smoke cigarettes about the time he started school, a way of entertaining his bootleg customers. People started predicting that sickly little Farquhar MacRory would be dead before he was twelve, but he had made it to fifteen, so current predictions claimed he wouldn't last to twenty before TB or cancer or something else would eat his frail form. And they told him that, the men drinking in his father's house, scaring him with their sad assurance that he was going to die young, and offering the boy cigarettes. Keeping him from craving tobacco was the least they could do, they told him.

It was Duncan who told him that nobody but God knows when somebody is going to die, unless he's a horse thief about to be hanged. He predicted that Farter would live longer than Doc Holiday, the gambling gunslinger in the westerns who used to hang around with Wyatt Earp, coughing all the way through the movies. It gave Farter a new hero, and he tried to talk people into changing his nickname from Farter to Doc, but his request never stood a chance. Shean had two Docs already, Doc MacRae, a mechanic, and Doc Aucoin, who had been a medic in the war, not to mention the two real doctors who lived in Shean; but the town had only one Farter, so there was no escape.

Duncan stopped and waited for Farter to catch up while I scanned the beach for clusters of girls. Every June, as the hot days collided with final exams, students took their studies to the fine warm sand of the Shean beach. Girl students were more serious about studying despite the sunshine, asking each other questions out of the texts and talking about which questions could be on the exams and which wouldn't. As for the boys, well, it was like the time Duncan told Johnny Rosin why he went to rock and roll dances: because that's where the girls went. We weren't interested in spending a nice afternoon in the books when we had all night to cram for an exam, so it wasn't for the sake of geography that Duncan and I were standing on the shore waiting for Farter to stop coughing and catch up.

I watched Farter slowly walking toward us and couldn't help but wonder what Duncan was up to. He had always made room for Farter, but for the past couple of months he had been encouraging Farter to come along with us, calling for him at his house, standing inside waiting for him, watching the poker games at the kitchen table, the liquor being sold by the drink and by the bottle, and watching beautiful Nicole MacRory float above it all. I guess I wasn't wondering at all, but Duncan had never said exactly what, if anything, had gone on between them since the night of Aunt Evelyn's wake.

"You okay?" Duncan asked.

"Yip," Farter said, suddenly drawing a six-shooter from the imaginary holster and firing at a flock of seagulls drifting like kites overhead. "Let's find some girls," he instructed, blowing smoke from the phantom gun, twirling it around his finger before reinserting it in its holster, more notches for Doc Holiday.

It wasn't "some girls" I was looking for, but I wasn't about to say that. So I led the walk over the beach. All along the shore there were several "clumps," as Farter called them, of girls sitting on driftwood or lying on towels in eroded coves along the bank, above which was piled the black slag and red ash of the mines, which only occasionally washed down onto the beach in rivulets of rusty water trickling across the sand when it rained. It seemed as if the slag itself, which covered once-green fields, didn't have the heart to ruin Shean's beach, its last beautiful belonging.

We stopped and chatted with different groups of girls, moving along from one group to the next until someone mentioned where the three Marys were, and we found them crouched on a large outcrop of sandstone that had been bared by the movement of tides. They seemed to be more interested in the sandstone than their books.

"What are you looking at?" I asked.

"Fossils of old trees," Mary Scotland answered.

"Big trees," Farter said, looking up into the sky as if he was trying to see the tops of them, making us laugh. Fossils were common sandstone discoveries along the Shean shoreline, stone imbedded with the ancient shape of a leaf or a bug, but Mary Scotland, Mary Jane and Mary French were convinced that what they found were fossils of trees, pointing out to us dozens of small, knobby protrusions on the sandstone.

"What do they look like to you?" she asked.

"Lumps of sandstone?" Duncan ventured.

"They don't look like any tree I ever saw," Farter teased.

"Whole trees don't turn to stone, do they?" I asked.

"Yes they do," Mary Scotland said. "Where do you think all the coal in Shean came from? From whole forests that turned to carbon millions of years ago," she answered, then drew our attention to the patterns and features of the sandstone lumps, and it grew obvious to all of us that she was probably right. It was as if something had sheared off the trees in what must have once been a small grove, leaving only the short stumpage Mary had recognized.

"You mean in a few million years we'll be able to open the mines here again?" Duncan asked. "That's good luck for you, Farter. That'll be just about the time you graduate. There'll be a job waiting for you and everything," Duncan said to Farter who had started school with us but was now lagging behind.

My own thoughts were trying to picture this lost forest that had been transformed into a small stone monument of itself. Like everyone, I grew up knowing the coal under Shean was composed of old jungles and forests and marshy ferns that got covered and smothered with ice ages until they were compressed into seams of coal, but I never once thought of those jungles as something that had been real, not the way these sandstone fossils suddenly turned into a real forest before me. These fossilized stumps were the ancestors of the same forests that still grew all around Shean and up into the Highlands, like the worn sandstone headstones of our own ancestors fading away in half-forgotten graveyards as old as the first Highlanders to come ashore at Shean.

The stone forest was older than that, older than the Mi'kmaq who had lived here for centuries before us. With an urge I couldn't explain, I put my hand on one of the stone stumps, resting it casually, trying not to attract anyone's attention, just trying to touch the place, imagining towering forests tens of thousands of years before Shean came to be, before anyone of us sitting there came to be.

"Roddie!" Mary Scotland's slightly exasperated voice said, and I knew that I had been asked a question.

"What?"

"Do you think she's all right?"

"Who?"

"Mrs. Bruce. Do you think she's all right?"

This was the most talked about thing in our class all year, whether or not our teacher, Mrs. Bruce, was all right. She could teach better than any teacher we ever had, but some days she wouldn't teach us at all, just tell us to open our books and study by ourselves while she sat at her desk staring into thin air or else trying to hide the fact that she was crying. The girls in the class said that when you are going to have a baby you get moody at first, but after months she was still moody, but her belly wasn't any bigger. So then they said she was having her change of life, but other girls said that couldn't be true because she wasn't even thirty yet. Lots of days she never came to school at all, and we had to have a substitute. And almost every day she arrived at school at the last minute, rushing and flustered. Our class was the best behaved we had ever been because everybody liked Mrs. Bruce, and she seemed so fragile that even Duncan, who had a way of driving teachers batty, never gave her a hard time. The substitutes didn't get off so easy.

"My mother said Mr. and Mrs. Bruce are fighting all the time," Mary French said. "Maybe that's why she's upset so much."

"She's frigid," Farter said.

"I bet she was supposed to be a nun but now that she's married she can't be," Mary Jane said.

"She's frigid," Farter said.

"How do you figure she's supposed to be a nun?" Duncan asked Mary Jane.

"Well, almost all the teachers we know are nuns, so what if she was supposed to be a nun but fell in love before she could go into the convent? Then she would be in the wrong vocation, wouldn't she, and she wouldn't be happy because she didn't answer God's call."

"She's frigid," Farter said, finally drawing some attention to the fact that he was among us.

"You mean she's cold?" Mary Jane said.

"No, I mean she can't do it with her husband," Farter said.

"A woman as beautiful as her, of course she can," I volunteered.

"Do what with her husband?" Mary Jane said, and Mary French whispered in her ear and Mary Jane got red.

"Where did you get a stupid idea like that?" Duncan asked Farter.

"I heard her husband tell it to my father one night when he came to our house for a bottle, you know. He came and drank his bottle there because he told my father, you know, he couldn't take the bottle home or Mrs. Bruce would break it, so he was sitting at the table, you know, drinking, and then he began looking at Nicole, you know, like that."

"Like what?" Duncan asked him.

"Like that, you know, the way everybody looks at Nicole, you know. Anyway, my father said he'd have none of that, you know, and besides, what was Mr. Bruce doing looking at his daughter, you know, when he had a beautiful wife of his own, and Mr. Bruce shrugged and said Mrs. Bruce was frigid, and that's what my father said," Farter told us, looking at Mary Jane. "'You mean she's cold?' the old man said, and Mr. Bruce, you know, sort of laughed and took a drink and said, 'In a way I suppose that's what I mean,' and then he told my father that his wife couldn't do it any more. The old man said, 'Oh, you mean she gives you the cold shoulder. Well, they all do that, but that doesn't mean you can go around leering at Nicole the way you are, you know'."

"He said all this while you were sitting there?" Duncan scoffed.

"No, I was upstairs lying over the register, you know. It's a great place to listen to people, and just about everybody who comes to my house talks about things. The old man said once, you know, 'You'd think I was a priest, not a bootlegger.'"

"Maybe she's having a nervous breakdown,' Mary Scotland said.

"This is all just gossip," Duncan said. "She's okay. Maybe she just needs a rest."

"You're just saying that because she likes you so much," Mary Jane said. "She must. She's the only teacher who never kicked you out of class at least once since grade primary."

"Maybe Duncan has a crush on her," Mary Jane teased.

"We know who Duncan has a crush on," Mary French said, hinting at Duncan and Nicole MacRory, the worst kept secret in Shean. Nicole told everybody they were just friends, but nobody believed her or blamed Duncan for waiting at The Turk's until closing time to walk her home whenever he could. He didn't even talk to me about it, but he didn't pretend it was a secret, either.

Duncan stood up, saying he was going to The Turk's, asking Farter and me what we were going to do, his announcement causing a few knowing smiles among the girls who knew Nicole was working that afternoon. Farter stood up. I moved much slower, not sure what I wanted to do, go with Duncan or stay with Mary Scotland, which meant with her friends, too. Actually, I wished they would all leave, leaving the fossils to me, but I decided for Duncan, instead, leaving the three Marys with their books and their studies.

When we walked into The Turk's, Nicole was behind the counter arguing with Archie Ack-Ack who said that he put a quarter in the pinball machine which should have given him five games, but it just rolled right down the slot, and he wanted his quarter back. Nicole was saying that she wasn't allowed to refund money and he would have to ask Tony who was cooking in the kitchen.

Duncan walked right over to where the two of them stood on either side of the counter and drove his fist into Ack-Ack's face, staggering him backwards while Duncan just kept coming at him with rights and lefts. It was happening so fast that Farter and I were frozen, and when I looked at the look on Nicole's face, she was just as surprised as I was. Trying to retreat from the flurry of punches, Ack-Ack backed up against the pinball machine, and Duncan had him cornered there. Ack-Ack dropped to the floor, but it wasn't like he had been knocked out, more like he wanted Duncan to think he was, curling up there with his arms over his head as Duncan let a kick go that caught him in the back and when Ack-Ack reached a hand around to cover his kidneys, Duncan jumped on top of him, putting both hands around his throat and began squeezing.

Nicole was the first to move, running from behind the counter screaming at Duncan to stop. Tony the Turk came from the kitchen and, seeing what was happening, jumped over the counter and grabbed Duncan by the shoulders, trying to pull him away, but Duncan's grip, no matter how hard Tony tried to pull him away, was like a white-knuckled death grip, like the hands of people we had heard about who died when their cars plunged over cliffs, their grip on the steering wheel so tight that their fingers had to be cut off to free their bodies from the wrecks. That thought and the sight of Ack-Ack's tongue protruding and thickening from his blue face, shocked me into action.

With Nicole screaming and Tony hollering and everyone else making some kind of noise I hauled off and kicked Duncan as hard as I could in the hands, but my first kick missed and I pretty near tore Ack-Ack's ear off; the second one connected with Duncan's fingers, but did no good. Ack-Ack's eyes were rolling back in his head by the time I landed a third kick on Duncan's knuckles, and this time his hands let go and The Turk was able to haul him away while Ack-Ack just lay there trying to breathe but couldn't. The Turk took one look at him and let Duncan go and, getting a protesting Farter to help him, hurried Ack-Ack out to his car and off to the hospital. Duncan, when Tony let go of him to tend to Ack-Ack, just sort of collapsed into a booth screaming for everybody to get away, to stop crowding him, making Nicole and me back off while he gasped himself back under control.

We just stood there, Nicole and I, looking at each other, our eyes asking silent questions, both of us a little scared of something we had never seen in Duncan before. But before he could calm down enough for us to approach him again, the restaurant door opened and the Mounties walked in, two of them. They told Duncan he was under arrest, and when Nicole asked what the charges were, the oldest one, Constable Kennedy, told her, "Attempted murder!"

It was all over town in an hour that Duncan MacFarlane had tried to kill Archie Ack-Ack, and the police had him in jail. I went straight to Duncan's house to tell Mrs. MacFarlane before she heard it from someone who couldn't wait to tell her, and there was no shortage of those in Shean. She was pale by the time I finished my tale.

"Why, Roddie, why would Duncan do something like that?"

Duncan's mother asked me as she put on her coat to go to the police station, asking me to please come with her. "Do you think the fight was over that girl?" I shrugged, noticing that Duncan's secret wasn't even a secret from his mother, but I was wondering the same thing, wondering if Duncan was so jealous that nobody was allowed to talk to Nicole any more.

The Shean jail was in the basement of the building shared by the town hall and the volunteer fire department, three damp cells usually occupied on Saturday nights by Johnny Logan and friends, but rarely, if ever, by attempted murderers. Through the metal grill that was the door of the second cell we could see Duncan sitting on a rusty bunk under a dim and naked light. Mrs. MacFarlane began crying, and Duncan looked up at us coming down the narrow cement stairs. The Mounties had told Mrs. MacFarlane, when we went to see them, that they couldn't release Duncan until bail had been set; and besides, they said, Duncan refused to make a statement about why he had assaulted Archie Ack-Ack. They had received a complaint by telephone from the hospital where Ack-Ack was a patient being kept overnight for observation. He had rasped out his charges, and Tony the Turk confirmed that Duncan tried to kill one of his customers. The RCMP picked him up, but Duncan refused to talk about the crime he was being charged with.

Duncan wasn't any more talkative with his mother than he was with the police, but he stood up when he saw us arrive and gripped the cell door. He didn't look one bit scared as he said hello to his mother and gave me his "I'm in deep shit now" wink, the one that usually came as a teacher was throwing him out of class or his mother was grounding him for some shattered rule. I noticed a definite difference in the depth of the shit he was now in, even if he didn't.

"Why, Duncan? Why did you beat that boy?" Mrs. MacFarlane asked.

"Because he tortures cats," Duncan answered and beyond that had nothing more to say about the subject, so Mrs. MacFarlane asked him what he wanted or needed, finally deciding she was going to the Justice of the Peace, Daniel MacKinnon, to see if she could get him out. She also supposed she would need to call a lawyer from Sydney – the last lawyer to live in Shean had been starved into moving to Ottawa to practice law. She said she would have to call Mr. MacFarlane, too, and with all these tasks to keep her busy I accompanied her up the steps while Duncan called to me to bring him some cigarettes when I came back. I suppose he was telling his mother that if he was old enough to be in jail he was old enough to smoke in front of his parents.

When we got outside Mrs. MacFarlane gave me two dollars to buy a couple of packs of smokes for Duncan, telling me she could take care of things herself now. She would be happier if I stayed with Duncan as long as I could. By the time I got back with his cigarettes, Dan Doyle, the jailer, and Duncan were playing crib through the cell door, while I sat watching and helping smoke Duncan's cigarettes until Dan pegged out and then went out for a walk, leaving the two of us alone.

"What are they saying?" Duncan asked.

"Your mother thinks it's over Nicole," I answered.

"And you think it's over Mary Scotland," he added, his insight embarrassing me, recalling that on two previous fights, Mary had been bothered by Ack-Ack, once at The Turk's and once in the middle of the parish hall dance floor.

"Just what the hell is it over, Duncan?"

"If I tell you, you'll be just as responsible as me."

"I didn't do anything," I said defensively.

"No, but you would be bound to secrecy just like a priest who has to go to jail or be martyred rather than tell the things he heard in confession," Duncan said, and a light went on in my head as I remembered a light going out over the confessional one Sunday when we were serving Mass. Both of us had been steeped in the wonder of the sacraments and had heard religion teacher after religion teacher tell stories of saints and priests who had died protecting the absolved sins of others. Reveal what he heard in confession, even under torture, and a priest was damned forever.

If a person is at an accident and someone is hurt and wants to make a confession, a nun once told us, then any Catholic can hear that person's confession but is bound by the same sacrament as an ordained priest. It's just as good as the real thing in the eyes of God. Later, especially if the person in the accident dies, you can repeat that person's confession to a priest, but you will always be bound to secrecy over what you heard, or be damned forever if you betray it to anyone else. Duncan was forever driving nuns and teachers crazy with religion questions that bothered him, but that didn't mean he didn't believe. Now he was offering to ordain me.

I wasn't sure I wanted the vocation, but without it I would never learn what was behind Duncan's fights, and I already knew enough to know that it had something to do with Mrs. Bruce. Duncan was ready to go to jail, even prison to protect her. I had to know why. I had to hear her confession.

"It was just a lark," Duncan said of his going into the confessional that Sunday morning, but his light beginning of the story soon turned into a flood of words.

"Holy Jesus, Smelt, I had no idea what was going to happen. She started to say her confession, and then, even before she finished her Bless Me Father she started crying, and then this story blurts out of her like she was bursting a boil: she was assaulted by a man. That's how she said it, 'assaulted by a man.' It happened weeks before she came to confession, though, because she was too ashamed of what happened to her, but on her way to Mass she found herself walking around the back of the church and into the confessional as if she had nothing to do with the decision.

"I'm sweating, Roddie, I'm really sweating, and then I hear Father Alex come in and you two talking and she's still whispering through the cloth between us about what happened. She can't hear your voices, but I can see you and Father Alex through the mesh in my door, and I see him look up at the light and my heart stops. Then Bartholomew's wife comes in and distracts him and I turned out the light, praying he won't open the door, and just then Mrs. Bruce starts telling me that when she came to school one morning Archie Ack-Ack was lighting the fire in the stove, and she said hello to him and they talked for a few minutes. Then she sat at her desk to prepare for class, and he came up behind her and started rubbing her shoulders and slipping his hand down her front. She told him to leave her alone and tried to push his hands away, but he wouldn't let go, just kept grabbing her tighter and rougher. Finally he ripped her blouse, and then he went crazy and grabbed her and made her lay on the desk and exposed her boobs and tore her underwear off and hit her when she tried to push him off her. Then he raped her, and afterwards he told her to stop crying because he could tell she enjoyed it just as much as he did, and she had been asking for it for a long time, looking like she did. Was she? That's what she asked me, Smelt, was she asking for it? She pulled her coat over her torn blouse and went home, telling Mother Saint Cross John she was sick, and when she got home she burned all her clothes and sat in a bathtub so hot it burned her skin, and she cried all day and all night, too. She changed the way she wore her clothes, not wearing anything that wasn't as modest as possible, and no makeup, but she didn't know what to do, who to talk to, how to forget what had happened to her. She was ashamed to go to the RCMP, and she couldn't tell her husband, and she wouldn't let him touch her anymore because she was ashamed of betraying him, but it was more than that, though, she said. She couldn't stand the thought of being touched that way, and so she and Mr. Bruce began having lots of fights, and her mind has been getting sick with thoughts of revenge on Ack-Ack, she said, and then she went quiet.

"By this time, Roddie, I was terrified she was going to learn that it wasn't a priest she was talking to but me, so I had to go on pretending but I didn't know what to say, so I pretended that I had laryngitis and talked real low like this and told her that her sins were forgiven and for her to say three Hail Marys and everything would be alright, and she just knelt there on the other side of cloth like she was waiting for me to say something more and crying and I told her to go in peace, and after a long while she got up and left.

"Every time I see that bastard I want to kill him, Smelt. That night when Ack-Ack was dancing with Mary Scotland and I fought him, it was because I saw him jostling Mrs. Bruce and the look on her face, her dancing with her husband and him tormenting her like that. What am I going to do, Rod?" I had no answer, so Duncan went on. "She won't go to the police, and she can't tell her husband, and she thinks she went to the priest but she didn't get any help there, did she? So what am I going to do? I'm afraid she's going to go crazy, Roddie. I think about telling Father Alex, but do you think he could help her? He's a priest, for Christ's sake. They're virgins. What do they know about sex, rape even? But that's not the only reason, Smelt. What do you think he'll do to me if I tell him? Excommunicate me for impersonating a priest? And that bastard's still lighting the fires in her classroom!"

23

By July, we had gone twice to Taurus's farm.

Spring was already a deep green the first time Calum, Bartholomew and I drove up there with the rutted road bumping the bottom of the panel truck and bouncing me off my upside-down bucket in the back. When we reached the abandoned farm, Calum and Bartholomew got out and started walking across the field, leaving me to follow carrying an awkward armful of bucket, shovels, shears and axe. I didn't try to catch up to them as they made their way, carefully choosing their footing in the middle of all these once cleared but overgrowing-again acres. It was a warm Saturday afternoon, and Calum wasn't wearing a jacket, just his wine coat-sweater over the bib overalls, Bartholomew, beside him, looking almost dressed up in the same kind of clothes he wore working in the store, dress pants, white shirt and tie with a brown pullover pulled over it. I had hardly ever seen them together when they weren't sitting in the sun porch or bent over the radiator at the store, so watching them cross the hayfield I was surprised by the vigor of the two old friends, not fast but determined, stopping every few steps, Bartholomew's hand sweeping the landscape in aid of his side of the discussion, Calum's finger pointing in more specific directions. They seemed to be recreating the history or geography of Shean lying below them, but whatever it was they were talking about, I bet to myself it wasn't Taurus.

Taurus hadn't been in the sun porch since Calum unlocked the door on May fifteenth, and I missed him. Most of what I knew about Calum and much of what I knew about Shean I learned from Taurus's stories, but Calum and Bartholomew never mentioned his name or absence. They discussed his poem, though, continuing with their plans to plant it, although I was left out of most of it now, the two of them gabbing away in the Gaelic when they were together, only using English when they wanted me to do something, like carry shovels, dig up saplings or lug water. When I reached them they were nodding sagely at the little ash we had planted the autumn before.

"I was afraid it was too late last year, but it took," Calum said, fingering the young buds that both men seemed to consider a good omen. Calum put me to work chopping down the scattering of spruce trees creeping across Taurus's land: Nature's reclaiming of the world once we are done with it. First, the hayfields, cleared a hundred, maybe two hundred years before and worked for generations, go to ragweed and thistles, then the encroaching spruce forest begins re-staking its claim with a wide scattering of young, cocky trees that, if not fought back, soon become dense and dark green, filling up with the comings and goings of deer and partridge and other wildlife until the signs of settlement are buried as deep as the settlers themselves. I hacked at the slender trunks and hauled the fallen spruce off to the side of the field while Calum and Bartholomew walked back and forth, measuring tape stretched between them and four hundred and eighteen trees still to plant.

Back at the truck, where I went for a drink from a large bottle of pop Bartholomew brought from the store, I stood watching them in the field and took the sketch pad from my pocket and quickly penciled their images in the field with trees towering around them. I had my own reason now for being enraptured by trees we planned to plant. Mother Saint Margaret all through the year had lent me books by the Renaissance painters, the Dutch Masters, the French Impressionists; and then, at the end of May when our class was coming to an end because she wanted me to use June for studying for exams, she leant me a book about the Group of Seven to keep over the summer. I had heard of them, of course. What Canadian hadn't heard of Tom Thompson and the Group of Seven? But a bunch of Canadian painters didn't really mean much to me until I was squinting through the eyes Mother

Saint Margaret was trying so hard to get me to open. I saw the same trees that grew around me, trees I was learning to recognize and name, and the same coves and bays, the same shape and colour of winter ice that Duncan and I had walked on on the frozen Gulf, all turned into art by the brushes and imaginations of these Canadian artists. It was even more exciting than discovering that the painting of Venice hanging in the art room had been painted by Mother Saint Margaret, but it was an excitement that frightened my own dreams away.

"I'll never be able to paint like this," I told Mother Saint Margaret, who asked me why I would want to.

"I want you to learn from works like these, even to be influenced by them, but your job is to concentrate on being able to paint like Roddie Gillies, no one else," she said, then asked if I was interested in keeping on with our classes when school started again in September, and I said yes.

"Good," she said, "because I want you to think about a painting you would like to begin in the fall. Come up with an idea and work at some preliminary sketches this summer, and we'll see how it turns out when we get together again."

I carried the quart of ginger ale down to Calum and Bartholomew. Each of them took the bottle, rubbed a palm across the top, took a swig and passed it along until it came back to me. I rubbed my hand over the top and took another drink, watching Calum, who was in better shape than Bartholomew, using his foot to force the shovel into the soft earth and lift out small scoops of earth, making a place for another ash sapling a carefully measured distance from the first one. Following Calum's instructions, I took the second shovel and went into the hardwoods to find a little tree. Altogether, we planted seven letters that day, one ash, two mountain ash, and four birch. It was slow work, having to re-measure each time to find out exactly where each tree belonged in the lyrical scheme of Taurus's poem. On our way down the mountain road Calum said we needed a better way of marking out the poem.

The next time we went back to Taurus's farm was the day of our final exam. Mary Scotland and I thought we were on our way to the beach. Stopping at our house to get my bathing suit I saw Bartholomew's panel truck parked in front, the two of them sitting in the sun porch, and I knew what they were up to and who they were waiting for, and for the first time I told someone else what they were doing.

Calum told me to load up the panel truck, which this time required several trips to the workshop. When we came back from our previous venture Calum set to work making sharp stakes, more than four hundred of them, each one numbered in red paint with a letter painted on it in blue. The stakes were bundled in bunches of fifty, and by the time I finished carrying them and the tools out to the truck, Mary was sitting on the turned-over bucket talking to Calum and Bartholomew, all of them waiting for me. I sat on a bundle of stakes as Bartholomew, squinting over the wheel, drove up a much smoother highlands road, the Department of Highways having graded it for the summer residents who had already begun to arrive.

Mary Scotland, when I told her about planting the poem, didn't roar out laughing the way Duncan would have, and while I was loading the panel truck she visited with them in the sun porch, asking Calum if the plans she had seen him draw in his study that first evening she visited us were the plans for the poem. He told her they were, and she asked if she could help with the planting. On the way up to Taurus's place she told them about her plans for the summer. Her aunt had a job waiting for her in Boston, looking after two doctor's children. She was leaving right after Dominion Day, a fact that didn't make me very happy, but it was news that didn't settle well with Calum, either. When Mary began telling him, my grandfather had his ear cocked to her voice while he stared ahead at the road. When she told him where she was going, though, he made himself turn in his seat enough to look at her, even though it was hurting his back. "Be very careful there," he told Mary, his voice softer and fuller with those four words than I had ever heard it sound before.

At Taurus's, I took Mary on a tour of the old house. Signs of life were all through it, mostly the garbage of hunters. In Taurus's boyhood bedroom looking out across the field I told her that when he was twelve years old Taurus used to ride horseback down the side of the mountain every morning to the mine. He worked in those mines almost from the day they opened until the day he blew up the last entrance.

"What do you suppose he was like as a little boy?" Mary asked. "I bet he was bad in the way that makes you laugh, you know, mischievous. But I guess it wasn't much of a boyhood if he had to work in the mines when he was twelve. That's so sad. We're not even out of high school yet and he was in the mines four or five years by the time he was our age. And now look at him," she added with a sad shake of her head.

People barely saw Taurus any more, and if they did it was because he had wandered away and was lost in the same streets he grew up on. Every Sunday, though, Mrs. MacLeod dressed him in his suit and took him arm in arm and walked with him to church like a young couple in love, but all through Mass people were more aware of Taurus than the priest. He mumbled his prayers, or began singing Gaelic songs. Young children in the church, and some not so young, giggled and snorted at Taurus's distractions, and I was afraid that some Sunday Father Alex was going to order him out of the church, or gently ask Mrs. MacLeod to take him home, or maybe tell her to keep him home.

"If he ever does that to Taurus," Duncan promised, "we'll organize a strike against the church."

Father Alex, who never even asked mothers to take their crying babies from the church, never banished Taurus for his mindless outbursts, either. It wasn't something I liked to think or talk about so instead I imagined Taurus running through the field below us, a boy barely learning to walk and already running headfirst into his life, thinking for a second I could hear his laughter until I realized it was Bartholomew pressing on the horn of the panel truck, hurrying us along. Grabbing a few seconds to neck in the privacy of the house, Mary and I then ran to join them.

There wasn't a lot of planting done that afternoon. Instead, with Calum and Bartholomew carrying a tape measure, Mary dropped one numbered stake an exact distance from the one before it, while I followed along, driving them into the ground with the back of the hatchet, all of us a bit bloodied from blackfly bites.

"Why do some of these stakes have two letters on them?" Mary asked, pointing out the ones that had 'bh' or 'mh' painted on them. The question brought both men to a halt while they explained that the 'h' was what they described as 'an aspirate.' It wasn't really a letter at all but a signal that the sound was changing. Although there was an 'h' in the eighteen-letter Gaelic alphabet, no words began with 'h.'

"'B' followed by an 'H'," Calum said, means the sound will become a 'V.' The same is true for 'M' followed by an 'H.' The 'H' is represented by the hawthorn. The birch and the hawthorn have to be planted closer together where there's an aspirate. The same is true of other letters that change their sound."

Through Mary's questions I was learning a bit more about the Gaelic than I knew before. She had more questions than me, and even if it was me asking them I don't think Calum and Bartholomew would have stopped and taken the time to stand on either side of me explaining Gaelic grammar. What I was really learning a lot about, though, was trees. How to tell them apart when I walked through the woods, the different shapes of their leaves, the texture of the various barks, and how to carefully uproot a sapling and carry it from its random place in the forest to its proper place in Taurus's poem.

We drove more than half of the stakes that day before Calum and Bartholomew grew weary. While I brought three birches down from the highlands forest, Mary carried buckets of water from the brook to soak the roots into their new home. The four of us then stood in Taurus's field, which now seemed to be growing a scraggly mixed hardwood forest, and looked down over the scarred old coal town below.

Nothing came of the attempted murder charge against Duncan, much to the disappointment of almost everybody in town who was looking forward to a big trial. His mother had him out of jail on bail the night it happened, and Ack-Ack never came near the police station to follow up his complaint from the hospital, so the Mounties let it drop. Mrs. MacFarlane got her bail money and her son back, but she was still worried about Duncan and Nicole MacRory, thinking it was Nicole who brought out the killer instinct in him. There was nothing I could tell her because now I was just as bound as Duncan by Mrs. Bruce's confession. Still, Duncan would rather have gone to prison than do what he finally had to do: tell Father Alex.

He decided to tell Father Alex about his impersonation of a priest the same way he got into the mess, in the confessional, because then the priest would be just as bound as he was to Mrs. Bruce's confession.

"That way," Duncan reasoned, "once I get out of the confession box, Father Alex won't be able to raise the subject again. He's not allowed to. He won't be able to do anything about it except maybe make me say a million rosaries or something."

He waited until the first Friday of July when half the Catholics who go to church would be crowded into the vestry to make their monthly confession. Duncan stood in line with them and went into the confessional with all those people sitting out front waiting their turn, and he spilled out the whole story like a big black sin, which it was to Father Alex.

"He was snorting like an old horse, Smelt, probably because he knew that in the end he'd have to forgive me since I was confessing, and with all those people sitting outside the confessional he couldn't very well holler or come around and open the door and drag me out and punch me or anything like that. I'm just glad it wasn't Father Ranald, that crazy priest from the strike of '32. He'd probably have killed me. He asked me if I understood the seriousness of what I did, and I felt like telling him to ask Ack-Ack about that, but I figured it wasn't the place to get cocky."

Father Alex was no dummy, though. For his penance he ordered Duncan to come to the glebe house that evening and tell him all over again exactly what had taken place, that and a hundred rosaries.

Duncan asked me to come to the glebe house with him. Father Alex couldn't pound the shit out of him in front of a witness, he said, but I was suspicious. I knew Duncan so I knew this could backfire on me, like the day I had to mop out the domestic science and art building. I wasn't anxious to be in the line of Father Alex's fire, but it was too good a story to pass up, so I went, saying that I was doing my share of Duncan's penance since I was the third piece of this puzzle, the other person who shared Mrs. Bruce's confession. Duncan said it was probably a good idea not to mention that to Father Alex, but he also wanted to know, since I was sharing his penance, how many of his rosaries I was planning to say.

Father Alex looked at me strangely when he answered the door and saw the two of us standing there, but he didn't ask any questions. He hadn't forgotten who had distracted him in the vestry that Sunday morning. He nodded for both of us to come in and led us into the living room. Who should be sitting there but Mrs. Bruce. It was too late to run as Father Alex motioned us to two chairs.

"Young Mister MacFarlane, has something to tell you," Father Alex told our grade ten teacher, and then nodded for Duncan to start.

This was one story Duncan didn't try to improve with his telling of it, but he told her all of it right up to the fight with Ack-Ack, and Mrs. Bruce turned as white as a communion host as she learned from Duncan what had happened to her. I thought she was going to tip over for a minute there when he got to the part where she was confessing to him that she and her husband weren't doing it any more.

"If Smelt here hadn't stopped me I might have killed him," Duncan said, finishing up, and Mrs. Bruce buried her purple, teary face in her hands to hide her crying.

"That day, I thought...," she said at last to Father Alex, "I thought you thought it was my fault. I thought that was why ... why ... oh, I don't know, why I didn't know where to turn, who to turn to. After confessing to you and being left there in the awful silence of that confessional, I wouldn't dare talk to anybody else. I thought you didn't care." Then she looked at Duncan. "The fact that I only had to say three Hail Marys for a penance made me think that what happened to me didn't matter, that you didn't care that it happened ... that it was...." She shook her head. "Does everyone in town know?"

"No!" Duncan said quickly. "Nobody knows. I only told Smelt here a few days ago when I was in jail. Nobody else knows. We can't betray a confession. We'd have to let ourselves be martyred or go to Hell. Nobody else knows, honest."

"That holy martyrdom you mention should happen right here!" Father Alex said, slapping his fist on the arm of his chair. "What you have done is a sacrilege! It is almost unforgivable.

"As for the three Hail Marys that Mr. MacFarlane gave you," he said, turning to Mrs. Bruce. "There should never have been a penance considering you haven't committed any sin." Then turning his attention back to us: "Do you see what you've done?"

I nodded along with Duncan because the question was directed at both of us, and so was his decision to kick us off the altar: Duncan for violating a sacred sacrament, me for being his accomplice by not telling Father Alex what was taking place in the vestry that morning. He made each of us apologize to Mrs. Bruce, then told us to leave, which we did as quickly as we could because even though Father Alex spoke through it all with a calm voice the veins in his neck were distended with angry blood. Holy martyrdom isn't far away if we stay around, I thought.

"Well, that's the end of our wine supply," Duncan said as we walked down the driveway.

24

Duncan's father and his crew came home from the mines early that summer because of the trouble Duncan had gotten into, but it was pretty well over before they arrived, the attempted murder part, at least, and Duncan wasn't about to tell Mr. MacFarlane about hearing Mrs. Bruce's confession which he considered a matter between him and his priest.

While he was home, Mr. MacFarlane took Duncan, who sent for his beginner's the February day he turned sixteen, out driving every afternoon until Duncan took his driver's test and passed both the written and the driving part without a single mistake. "I'm a perfect driver," he told me when he came to our house to pick me up fifteen minutes after getting his licence.

When Mr. MacFarlane went back to the mines in Ontario he drove back with Danny John Campbell, leaving the Oldsmobile home so Duncan could drive his mother to the store and places like that. It wasn't for tearing around town in, Mr. MacFarlane said.

"Time me," Duncan said as we tore out 'the Stretch,' a mile of straight road outside Shean where people went to match the speed of their father's car against the speed of someone else's father's car. I looked at my Timex and gave Duncan the signal the moment the second hand hit 12 on the watch face. While a blur of trees whizzed past us I listened to Duncan's voice, trying to recognize words, but I may as well have been listening to Calum and Bartholomew speaking the Gaelic in the sun porch. Nine and a half minutes later I heard a clear "Amen!" as Duncan crossed himself, kissed the crucifix and hung the rosary back over the rearview mirror.

Since Duncan had to say his one hundred rosaries, he began testing how fast he could say them. The first time, he told me, saying all the Hail Marys and Our Fathers so that you could make out every word, took him twenty-one minutes. Since then, he had been trying to get down to a five-minute rosary.

"Mark that one down, will you?" he asked, pointing to the cubby-hole where he kept a scrap of paper with strokes on it. I entered his most recent rosary, making it a total of forty-three.

We sped through the summer of 1961 doing 80 miles an hour, Duncan at the wheel, me tagging along for the ride, the windows down and the wind whipping around our hair and cigarette ashes and the radio's hit parade. Life had accelerated. Our days were spent between the track, where Duncan was still working for John Alex's stable, and the beach where our winter-white skin turned red, then welted with water blisters, then peeled, then browned. Our nights were spent driving back and forth over town from the gas tanks at the Fina station to the gas tanks at the Esso, waving, nodding or tooting a hundred times to the same people. Our money was spent on gas because Mrs. MacFarlane, who couldn't keep Duncan out of the car, decided he would have to pay his own way if he was going to drive it. He didn't mind, and besides, he was good at offering people a drive to a dance in Glen Ian if they would put fifty cents worth of gas in the Oldsmobile. Then he would drop off his cargo at the dance hall, me included, and race back to town just before The Turk's closed to pick up Nicole. They weren't hiding it any more.

I didn't have a job. After what happened to Summer Cloud I couldn't go back to piss-whistling, so I hung around John Alex's stable with Duncan and picked up a few dollars drawing horses. When I wasn't driving around with Duncan I was usually drawing or playing with my paints, trying to come up with an idea or two for Mother Saint Margaret in the fall – or I was walking over to the post office after supper.

The mail arrived on the six o'clock train, and it wasn't sorted before seven-thirty, but sometimes I would take the key off the wall and walk over to the post office in the middle of the afternoon, open the box and stare into the empty spaces. It wasn't as if there was a special mail train from Boston that came earlier than the regular one, but I was beginning to wonder if there was ever any mail from Boston.

I never expected to miss Mary Scotland as much as I did, but from the day she left for her job in the States I was counting the days until she came home, and counting, too, all the things that could go wrong between now and then: every one of them a grinning, blond all-American, growing taller and more handsome with each letterless day.

As for myself, I wrote Mary long love letters, pouring out my heart on illustrated pages that I stuffed into envelopes only to stuff into the kitchen stove, promising myself to stamp the next one.

Mrs. MacFarlane was stuffing us with her baking and her stories, which were just as good as her date squares. Ever since Duncan got the car and I got a girlfriend, she said, we spent less and less time in her Saturday kitchen eating her out of house and home. But we weren't going anywhere that Saturday, not with the car in the garage and the rain hammering the windows. Duncan had a little accident trying to take the Devil's Elbow on two wheels. Except for Nicole banging her eyebrow on the windshield and Duncan cracking his chest into the steering wheel, nobody else got hurt. I was the nobody else, bouncing around in the back seat when he lost control on the hairpin turn and the car turned circles, just missing the guardrail, and eventually sliding backwards down the side of the cliff without rolling over. A torn-off muffler and a twisted front wheel were about all the damage the car sustained. I was the only one to get off scot-free.

Since I wasn't hurt, unless you count throwing up a supper of curds and potatoes all over the side of the road, I told Duncan not to tell anybody I was in the car. I didn't want Calum to hear about it and put an end to my riding shotgun for Duncan through the rest of the summer, so I took the first ride that came along, sent a tow-truck out from the Esso, and went home. Calum told me about the accident the next morning after it had had all night to grow, Bartholomew offering the juicier version to his morning customers.

"That fellow pretty near killed himself and a girl last night," Calum announced when I woke up the next morning. I asked who he meant, as if I didn't know that "that fellow" was Duncan and always would be to my grandfather.

"That fellow! That fellow you hang around with! Last night he drove his car through the guardrail at the Devil's Elbow and rolled it over and over. They had to cut him out of the car with an acetylene torch, and the poor girl, whoever she was, split her head open and pretty near bled to death."

That was the version I brought to Mrs. MacFarlane's kitchen. She was haywire enough as it was with Duncan, but she was a little giddy, too, because she was so happy he hadn't been killed, which we all could have been. Knowing his reckless nature the way she did, she probably knew that this wasn't the end of her car worries, so she was feeding us well while she had us alive.

The rain pelting the window made this the most different Saturday I had all summer, having grown used to going with Calum and Bartholomew into the highlands to transplant trees. Neither man would work at it on a Sunday, so Bartholomew began taking Saturday afternoons off and driving the three of us up to Taurus's farm. I was learning a lot from Calum about growing trees, although I think he was only a few pages ahead of me in the book he ordered. The saplings would probably have been doing better if we were able to go up and water them a couple of times a week. Some had to be torn out, thrown away and replaced with new ones. Still, we were getting somewhere with it. Oak by birch by elm, Taurus's poem was slowly getting ready to be read. By whom, I couldn't help wondering – the man in the moon? We had hammered in all the stakes, and we must have dug up and planted a hundred trees. We wouldn't finish this summer.

The letter in the mailbox stood out among the regular envelopes Calum received, and I could see the American stamp on it before I even got it out of the box. I also recognized the handwriting, Mary Scotland's, but reading the address once caused me to read it again. And again.

Mr. Calum Gillies
Culloden Street
Shean, Cape Breton
Canada

Mary Scotland must have meant to address the letter to me care of Calum and forgot, I told myself, anxious to rip it open right there and read it, but I couldn't. I couldn't open mail that had Calum's name on it any more than I could tell people about Mrs. Bruce's confession, not in our house. The best I could hope for was that Calum would open the letter and see that it said Dear Roddie and pass it to me before he started reading all the gushy stuff that would only embarrass both of us.

"This letter's addressed to you," I told him, passing him his regular mail first and making a special delivery of Mary's letter. He put aside the other envelopes and examined the letter from Boston. With all the slowness he could muster, Calum got up off the sun porch couch and walked into the house, with me following his slow-as-a-snail progress down the hall to his study where he sat at his desk, picked up the imitation claymore sword that was his letter opener and slit the envelope. He extracted the letter, examining the quality of the paper before he even got around to unfolding it. I couldn't just stand there watching him read my letter, so I got busy at the kitchen sink where, in the mirror above it, I could see backwards into Calum's study. As soon as he realized he was reading my mail he would look up for me, and I would only be a few steps away.

Calum began reading the letter while I watched in the mirror. When he finished the one and a half pages, he looked thoughtful and then read the letter again, this time even slower than the first. Then he folded the letter, put it back in its envelope and stood up, tucking the letter into a pocket of his bib-overalls as he came into the kitchen.

"The girl said to say hello," he said.

The next afternoon when I brought their tea into the sun porch, Bartholomew was just folding Mary Scotland's letter and passing it back to Calum. Bartholomew shook his head doubtfully, and said something to Calum in the Gaelic. Calum's reply seemed to contradict Bartholomew's doubt, and the two men got into a discussion that left me standing there feeling left out by all three of them, Calum, Bartholomew and Mary Scotland.

It wasn't until the following Saturday that I learned what was in the letter, and that was when Calum sent me into Taurus's woods to bring back a small red maple. The maple tree isn't in the Gaelic alphabet, I enlightened him, a remark which caused him to peer at me over his glasses.

"The T's the problem," Calum said finally. "There's confusion over whether it's gorse or holly or fire. I assume you've explained this to her, because the girl's letter suggests we settle it with the red maple. It turns red as fire in fall and would bring something of over here to an alphabet from over there."

They must really like her, I thought as I dug around one of the plentiful maple saplings in the woods. If Calum and Bartholomew would listen to somebody who doesn't even speak the Gaelic telling them how to plant Taurus's poem they must really like her. That night I sat down and wrote Mary a letter telling her that Calum and Bartholomew were using her idea about the maple trees, telling how the poem was coming along, and rambling a lot about the poem itself and how I felt that by helping Calum and Bartholomew plant it, I was helping Taurus's last words get said, even though he was still alive. I told her about Duncan's accident and the other news from around town. She answered it almost right away.

25

It took nearly the whole summer to come up with an idea for Mother Saint Margaret. My walls were filled with drawings I made while I was trying to find a picture to paint, but they were just images of landscapes and faces until one night, as I was falling asleep, the various fragments swam together for a moment, and I realized in which direction they were pushing me. I got up and started drawing and couldn't stop until the sun was up. Even then, every time I tried to sleep I would get another idea, another detail, so I was up and down, driving Piper crazy with my restlessness. It wasn't anything I thought I would ever be painting, and I hoped it would be all right with Mother Saint Margaret when school started again.

Mary Scotland came home from Boston, and you should have seen Calum's face when she gave him a big hug hello! He turned red as one of his garden beets, not knowing what to do with her arms around him, his own arms wavering like they didn't know if they should hug her back or just hang there pretending they didn't care. I was describing the look to Duncan while the three of us sat in a booth at The Turk's waiting for Nicole MacRory to get off shift. Because it was Friday the place was full of people going to the dance at the parish hall where the Trembling Hearts, the newest incarnation of the Moran brothers, was playing.

"I thought he was going to take a stroke," I was telling Duncan, and then seeing Ack-Ack sitting at his usual place at the corner of the counter, I added, "I hear he's going to Toronto."

"Who? Calum?" Duncan asked, lost in the shift of my conversational direction.

"No. Ack-Ack. I hear he's going to Toronto to look for work,"

I said nodding in his direction. It was from that seat at the counter that he used to flirt and even try to cop a feel from Nicole and the other waitresses, order people around, decide who to pick on. Since Duncan's last pounding, though, Ack-Ack seemed to shrink whenever Duncan turned up, not just in the restaurant, but at dances, anywhere. Duncan never said another word to him after the fight at The Turk's, just ignored him altogether; but all the same, things had changed. Guys that used to ask "how high" when Ack-Ack said jump, just ignored him. Nicole and the other waitresses were apt to slap him now if he grabbed them going by, and of course with Nicole spending her time with Duncan she wasn't in any danger at all from Ack-Ack.

"Good place for him," Duncan replied. "There's some people around here who can maybe get on with their lives if they don't have to look at the smirk on his face every day."

"Like who?" Mary asked Duncan.

"Oh...," Duncan fumbled, "anybody he bothers, I guess. Me, for example. I'm lucky I'm not in Dorchester Penitentiary because of that bastard."

After three hours of dancing to the Throbbing Hearts and their latest versions of the hit parade, we drove to the beach, Duncan and Nicole in the front seat, Mary and me in the back. It wasn't an original idea. Just about every car parked at the dance hall was now parked at the beach, and we could barely find a place to put the Oldsmobile. With neighbouring Fords and Chevs so close to either side of us, we got out of the car and went walking along the blackened beach, looking for privacy. Duncan and Nicole lagged behind us then veered away in the dark without us even noticing. Mary and I continued walking until I guided her toward a sandy alcove where we could catch up on our summer of missed romance.

Once there, I drew her down to sit beside me on a dark hump of driftwood, triggering the loudest screaming and screeching session in the beach's history. The driftwood, when we sat upon it, was warm and naked and had two voices that went "Ugh!" in the darkness. The two people under us rose in a mad, screaming scramble for their clothes while Mary and I leapt up, our own voices joining the chorus of terror until we discovered they weren't ghosts but only people who had beaten us to the privacy of that coveted spot. Trying to undo our intrusion, we ran from the small cove, holding hands to avoid losing each other in the darkness.

With hearts still pounding from the fright, our laughter turned hysterical. We walked back to the car along the edge of the tide, the most unlikely place to encounter more naked passion at the Shean beach. Neither of us could identify whom we sat on.

"Did you recognize the voices? I don't think I've ever heard that 'Ugh!' before," Mary said as we reached the Oldsmobile. I opened the door, setting off another scramble for clothes in the front seat where partially clad Duncan and even less clad Nicole had come for their privacy.

"Are we the only people in Shean wearing clothes tonight?" Mary whispered as we stood outside of the car, allowing some semblance of decency to be retrieved within the vehicle. A moment later, Duncan rolled down the window. "Get in." Any resentment over disrupting them was quickly washed away in the flood of laughter our story induced.

"I thought they were ghosts," Mary said finally, describing our panic.

Nicole wanted to stay parked right there and watch to see who came up from the beach to get in the cars, giving a clue to who the naked strangers were, but Duncan had other ideas. He started the car and pulled away from the beach. Twenty minutes later we were slowly climbing up the highlands road. The narrow dirt road, lined on either side by a regiment of evergreens which sheltered it from even the faintest glimmer of starlight, moved under the car. Duncan was barely crawling in first gear, making the most of the car lights and shadows and occasional glint of eyes within the forest.

"Where are we going?" Mary asked at last.

"You said you wanted to see a ghost," Duncan said. "I'm taking you to one."

"I nev ... I never said I wanted to see a ghost," Mary said. "I said I thought they were ghosts we sat on at the beach, but I never said I wanted to see one. Where are we going?"

"Just up here a little piece," Duncan said, and with those words he turned the car into a closing-over wagon road. The car lights caught the tumbling grey shape of Annie Rosary's house, slowly being swallowed by a growth of wild roses and rhubarb and alders.

Duncan turned out the lights, and for a moment it was darker than the cove at the beach until the amber light of the quietly playing radio redefined us in shapes without detail.

"Remember, Smelt?" and the two of us told Mary and Nicole the story of the night Mr. MacFarlane left us on the road with Annie Rosary.

"You were pretty scared that night," Duncan said. "Are you still scared of her?"

"Duncan, you're not serious," Nicole said, but the way Duncan said it didn't give me much choice.

"The way I remember it, I was trying to catch up to you that night. Besides, there's no such thing as a ghost," I said.

"Well, come on then," he said opening the door. I opened mine, and Duncan stayed suspended between getting in and out while he looked at Mary and Nicole. "Coming?" he asked. They looked at him like he was crazy.

"Okay," Duncan said, "but would you do us a favour? People often see her walking along this road saying her rosary or scream-ing for her children that ran away. If she comes along, would you just toot the horn to warn us?"

I caught Duncan's wink, but neither Mary nor Nicole did be-cause they were out of the car before I was, clinging to each other.

"This is stupid," Mary said.

"Really stupid," Nicole added, as hand in hand, we formed a human chain led by the flashlight Duncan had taken from the car's cubbyhole. We walked through the thigh-high hay in the middle of the wagon road leading to the weathered, windowless house. Duncan worked open a door that hung on one hinge, its bottom dragging noisily across the wood floor, and we followed him into the musky interior. Plaster dust hung in the air from shattered walls, but the house still had solid floors as well as ruined furniture that hadn't been worth stealing before the weather itself took up residence. It was a house of nooks and crannies, made more shadowy and spooky by the flashlight, with small doors that opened to storage spaces under the stairs and in the walls. Without anyone mentioning it, we all remembered the stories we had heard of Annie Rosary locking children under the stairs and in closets, cold and hungry and forced to pray for the love of God.

"I heard she tried to strangle a man with her rosary," Nicole whispered.

"Before or after she died?" Duncan asked.

"As a ghost," Nicole replied. "Apparently this man, he was from away, wanted to buy this property. He came up in the daytime and looked at it and liked it. Then that night he came up because he wanted to get a feel for what it would be like at night up here, and that's when she attacked him with her rosary, tried to get it around his neck, but he escaped. The next morning he left town and nobody's seen him since."

"Is that true?" Mary asked.

"As true as you want it to be," Duncan answered. "Must have been a Protestant. Could you imagine if a Protestant family moved in – what's that?" Our eyes followed Duncan's question down the shaft of light to where it circled the small, skeletal remains of a dead bird, tufts of feathers still clinging here and there. In the light, its oversized shadow stretched out and quivered in the tremor of the beam, sending a shudder rippling through us all.

"What killed it?" I asked, pointing out that there were no windows so the bird couldn't have flown into one and broken its neck. No one answered, but unspoken speculations loomed all around us in the shadowy walls, under the stairs, in the imagined mumble of Annie's Rosary's prayers. The logic we needed to explain away the bird's death deserted us.

"What do dead birds in a house mean?" Mary asked.

"Sunday dinner," Duncan said, taking us away from the growing terror in a sudden burst of silly laughter that grew silent as quickly as it had risen from our throats. The flashlight had fallen on a stack of pages stitched together and swollen with weather. Even before examining it closer we could all tell it was a section from the Bible.

"That's enough for me," Mary said, squeezing my hand, trying to lead me away from the room and the house, but I resisted, held us in place and stepped toward the pages, squatting down to read what I could see.

"What does it say?" Nicole's voice trembled.

"And Pathruism, and Casluhim, (of whom came the Philistines,) and Caphthorim. And Canaan begat Zidon his firstborn, and Heth.... It's just a list of names," I reported, relieved. "It's from Chronicles."

"No end of the world shit, eh?" Duncan asked.

Moving more gingerly than ever, we followed the beam of light into the kitchen where it reflected off a shiny set of black rosary beads hanging on the wall behind a rusty stove with no oven door.

"That's enough for me!" Nicole gasped, grabbing Duncan's wrist and swinging the flashlight around to find the nearest door through which we dragged each other out of there, making a beeline for the car, right through a field dense with thistle.

The sound of the engine starting up, the darkness being pushed back by a burst of headlights, the eerie silence shattered by music from a New York radio station formed a new, safer world for us to hide in and catch our panting breaths. Duncan reversed and drove us out of there, but instead of turning toward Shean, kept going up the highland road, past Tom MacPhee's farm which was dark at this hour of the night. Morning, really.

Mary, shivering, had snuggled in under my arm, so I didn't care where Duncan was going, although I sat up straight when he turned into the field road leading to Taurus's farm. The Oldsmobile's headlights caught the house as Duncan rolled to a stop beside it. In the fast fade of headlights I caught a nighttime glimpse of the field and a scattered bunch of saplings, dark spindly shapes that looked like they were drawn by a primary student. I leaned over the front seat. "What are we doing here?"

"Do you know this place?" Duncan said.

"Yeah, it's Taurus's farm. He grew up here."

"Is that right?" Duncan asked. "I used to come up here a long time ago hunting with the old man. Last week, I was exploring up here and found it again. The house has a few bedrooms in it. Beds, too, come to think of it. Anyway, I thought we could at least take a look around."

Duncan, having discovered Taurus's place for himself, didn't know anything about what was going on here, and I squeezed Mary tight, hoping she would feel my plea not to say anything.

"Come on and look around," Duncan invited, turning the flashlight back on. "No ghosts, I guarantee it."

"We'll just stay out here and talk," I answered, after we all got out of the car. "Okay?" I asked Mary. Her head nodded agreement.

The altitude and the hour took us into temperatures that had cooled off quickly and I pulled the Navajo blanket that once used to cover Mrs. MacFarlane's couch and now covered the Oldsmobile's back seat and wrapped it around us as we leaned against the car.

"You didn't tell Duncan about the trees, did you," said Mary Scotland.

"No, I guess not."

"Why?"

"It's just that Duncan and Calum don't get along very good. Duncan thinks everything Calum does is stupid or crazy, so when they started planting this forest I never said anything. I know he'd get a big kick out of it, but ... I don't like him laughing at Calum. Besides, when I started digging up the trees and replanting them and ... I don't know, Mary, the idea that we were writing a poem. I can say the poem from hearing Calum read it, and he told me what it was about, but that isn't the poem, just the translation. Anyway, I can't explain it, but I want to help these guys do this, and I don't want Duncan making fun of them, so I never told him."

"Come on," Mary said pulling me along by the blanket that wrapped us together. "I haven't been here since I got home. Let's walk through the poem." We walked down into the field, and I was glad to realize that even in the dark I had a good idea where to walk, when to take a giant step across the brook, when to go west around a patch of spongy swamp. A couple of times we bumped into stakes with letters on them, and when one fell over we stooped to pick it up and stuck it back in the ground. We didn't trample any trees walking through our literary forest.

At the broken pole fence at the end of the pasture we leaned and looked down on the streetlights of Shean flickering within a setting of inky mountains. Somewhere in our silent watching we moved closer, and then our lips found each other, and slowly we lowered ourselves to the grass and with a surprising lack of fear undressed each other for the first time.

A lost length of time later, the blare of the Oldsmobile's horn as Duncan leaned on it, coupled with the sweep of his flashlight searching the field startled us into realizing it was time to leave. Like prison escapees ducking the spotlight in the guard tower, we tried to find our clothes and dressed enough to return to the car. Jarred from the romance of the moment, we had no time to reflect on what had happened between us. Walking through the field toward the flashlight that now guided us to the car, its light bouncing off small maples and birches and ash, I didn't say anything to Mary Scotland, but I wasn't at all sure whose underwear I was wearing.

26

Duncan parked the Oldsmobile behind the Co-op while we waited for Mrs. MacFarlane to do her shopping. The parking lot was pretty-well filled with cars and half-ton trucks, but there were two or three teams of horses tied there, including Tom MacPhee's Clydesdales. We got out and went over to them.

The ring of mountains around Shean had gone to autumn colours. Calum had turned the key in the lock, closing the sun porch for the winter, and instead of Bartholomew bringing the paper to him, Calum walked to Bartholomew's store at noon. Most of the men around the Co-op and the tavern, including Duncan, were wearing red hunting jackets and caps. One car had a twelve-point buck lashed across the fender.

Mrs. MacFarlane came back from the Co-op, so we left the horses and walked to the car, noticing, as we got closer, her worried look.

"I heard in the store that Taurus MacLeod is missing," she said. "Some of the men are organizing a search. I hope he's okay. When you think of all the hunters in the woods...."

Shean's fire alarm, a Second World War air raid siren, had replaced the mine whistle which once marked everything from the changing of the shifts underground to alerting the town of a fire. The air raid siren started with a low moan that increased second by second until there was nobody within the town limits who didn't know from its high-pitched scream that there was an emergency. People told stories about it going off in the middle of the night to alert volunteer firemen, many of whom were veterans who had spent time in London during the Battle of Britain and who found themselves jumping under the bed instead of into their fire-fighting boots. Most often, the siren blew for a fire, but it also called the town to the beach when there was a drowning or when someone went missing.

A large crowd had gathered at the fire hall even before the siren stopped. Since the fire truck wasn't outside with its rotating red light leading the way to a fire, those who didn't already know Taurus was missing figured it was a drowning or a lost hunter. Sam MacPherson, the fire chief, explained that men were needed to go searching for Taurus. "Time is important here. It gets dark early, and we've already had some frost at night, and Taurus isn't all that healthy anymore. If we don't find him soon, he could be in a lot of trouble. Any ideas?"

Almost everyone thought he had seen Taurus that day. The problem was, everyone saw him somewhere else, walking to the beach, wandering near the woods, strolling over street. So many people claimed to have seen him, or thought they did, that their information was useless. We pooled what we did know, me telling them about the day I found Taurus on the slag piles with his lunch can, going to work. Duncan told them about Taurus's old farm. Other people had their ideas. Sam MacPherson broke us up into groups. Duncan and I wanted to go up to the farm, but the fire chief said he didn't need a couple of sixteen-year-olds wandering through the woods during hunting season. Another group was sent to patrol the beach in case Taurus wandered down there, and Paul Angus Cameron, a fisherman who hadn't yet taken his boat out of the water for the winter, took some men aboard, and they puttered up the coast in case Taurus had fallen off one of the cliffs where the highlands meet the sea. Another group agreed to follow the river from the mouth back toward the power plant, and Duncan and I were put with the men who would be searching the old mine site.

As we prepared to go our several ways, the church bell at Holy Family began to ring, a long, slow, steady rhythm calling the women and the men too old to join in the search to a special Mass that Father Alex was offering up for Taurus's safe return.

Driving past Bartholomew's store on our way to the mine site, I saw Calum and Bartholomew leaning on the radiator, looking out the window. It was the middle of the afternoon, a time when Calum was almost never there, so news about Taurus must have reached him. Bartholomew would have gathered up all the bits and pieces, all the rumours and facts about Taurus's disappearance from people coming into the store, each adding something to the existing version. They were too old to go looking for Taurus and too Protestant to go to Mass to pray for him, so all they could do, I figured, was keep each other company and hope for the best.

Duncan and I and four other men spread ourselves across the mine site, starting at the very beginning where the slag stopped. From there we fanned across the gullies and grey hills, calling Taurus's name, looking anywhere a person, or a body, might be hiding. I never realized before how easy it would be for someone, especially a senile old man, to be hurt or even killed in this land-scape of clay hills with rusty streams of water trickling between them. It had been the place where the mine dumped the garbage it brought up from below, the slag, broken pit props, twisted narrow gauge rails, busted machinery, shattered underground coal cars. Since the mines closed it had become the unofficial town dump, its ravines filling with car bodies, bedsprings, plaster and slats from gutted houses, and over it all a carpet of broken glass. Although I searched the car bodies and looked in the ravines and under the few groves of green growth that managed to stay alive amid the slag piles, I didn't want to be the one to find Taurus.

I kept looking toward the others, hoping they would signal their success. From the clay hills I could see the group searching the shore and even hear the faint putter of Paul Angus Cameron's boat. I could also see Duncan staring into the old mine reservoir, the bottomless hole in the ground that was the grave of count-less drowned and still-sinking kittens and puppies. Could Taurus have slipped in there, I wondered, wandering across here with his lunch can under his arm looking for the bankhead and the rake that would take him underground, looking for the pithead he had blown up with Mr. MacFarlane that day so long ago? I imagined him sinking down through the water in the last hole at the mine site. Would he think it was the rake taking him under? Duncan walked around the small, deep pond, poking at the edges with a long stick, trying to see something like footprints around the clay rim that would tell him if Taurus was there.

It was almost dark by the time we had gone across the slag piles and reversed our positions so that everybody was searching a different part of the site than we had searched on our first pass. By the time we had walked across the clay again, the beach crew joined us, having searched the shore from the harbour to the river. We didn't know whether to be happy or sad that the search resulted in nothing. All twelve of us, cold and hungry, piled on top of one another in Duncan's car, and he drove us back to the fire hall with the backend of the Oldsmobile making strange scraping sounds on the road. The searchers from the river and the men who had been in Cameron's boat were also there. Nobody found anything to hint at Taurus's whereabouts.

"That just leaves us with the woods," the fire chief stated. "There's been no word back from those who went up Taurus's old place, so we can assume they haven't found him, but it's the only lead we have left. We'll just have to keep looking through the night. How many of you can take part?"

Just about every man there volunteered to keep looking for Taurus. Nobody wanted to say what we were all beginning to fear. Instead, people began telling stories about Taurus, remembering the time he fought the seven pulp cutters from Newfoundland who were staying in a camp in the Highlands and came to Shean to drink their pay (the first time I heard the story, it had been three pulp cutters), or the day underground when he lifted a derailed coal car, full of coal, back onto the track.

"Don't worry, we'll find him," MacPherson said, and began loading gear into his car, humming the tune to *"Cumha nam Méinneadairean."* I don't think he realized what he was singing.

The fire chief told everybody to go home, get warm clothes, some food, thermoses of tea and meet back at the fire hall within half an hour. Duncan grabbed my wrist and examined the Timex. With the racing season over, John Alex's horses were back in the barn. Duncan drove to his house, told his mother we needed sandwiches for two, then we stopped at Bartholomew's store and I told Calum where we were going and what little I knew, which was no news at all.

On our way to the barn I started wondering how Taurus could make his way to the farm. It seemed so far for an old man to walk, and if anyone picked him up they would have known him and known that he should be taken home ... to his Shean home, not the one in the highlands where he grew up and where in his lost mind he might believe he still lives.

Following Duncan into the barn and holding the flashlight, unable to share my thought with him, it occurred to me that Taurus may have gone to the farm for another reason, one only Calum and Bartholomew, Mary Scotland and I understood. Maybe he had gone there to plant his poem, having forgotten....

"Jesus Christ!" Duncan screamed, jumping back from the door of the hay stall. I jumped back with him but swung the flashlight toward the darkness that had frightened him, the beam falling on a crumpled form.

"Taurus," I said, no louder than a whisper, but it was Duncan who made the first move toward him, poking the old man with his foot at first, the way he might check on a dead snake, ready to jump back if it was playing possum. Nothing happened. I tried to hold the light steady while Duncan lowered himself slowly beside the body, his hand reaching out unwillingly.

"Is he alive?" I asked as Duncan's hand touched Taurus's.

"He's still warm," Duncan informed me, leaning closer, checking for a breath. "He's ... he's pissed to the ears," Duncan said as he got a whiff of Taurus's breath.

We brought Taurus around a bit until he was garbling sounds we couldn't make out. He didn't have a clue who we were as we carried him, one on each side, over to the Oldsmobile and put him in the back seat, then drove to the fire hall where the searchers were regrouping. They all took turns gazing through the back window at the man they had been looking for all day.

"Found him in John Alex's barn, huh?" Sam MacPherson asked. "Should've been the first place we looked."

"Who would give him the booze?" one of the searchers asked.

"This is Taurus MacLeod we're talking about," Sam said. "The mind may be gone, but the instincts are still sound. If Taurus got it in his mind he wanted a drink, he'd know where to find one. He must have been drinking in the barn all day. Where the hell was John Alex?" he asked Duncan.

"Took his wife to her cousin's funeral in Sydney. I was feeding the horses for him. Taurus wasn't there this morning."

"I don't know about the rest of you, but Taurus has a great idea there," Paul Angus Cameron said, faking a shiver to remind people it had been a long, cold afternoon. "Anybody interested in getting hammered at the tavern?" Most of the men voted to follow his lead while Duncan and I were dispatched to Taurus's farm to tell the men searching up there that Taurus had been found. On our way, we brought Taurus home to Mrs. MacLeod who was just getting home from praying in church. She was happy but not surprised, saying it was a miracle, in a voice that seemed to be expecting one.

Although it was still only October, school had been cancelled for the grade eleven class. Normally, it wasn't until the big snowstorms started that school was cancelled, and that was never before late November, but that October day there was no heat in the classroom. With Ack-Ack gone to Toronto, a new janitor was in charge of lighting the morning fires in the twelve potbelly stoves, one in each classroom. In our classroom, the new janitor broke the broken grates in the stove. The ancient grates had been broken and pieced together countless times, and all that kept them in place now were the two bricks they sat on, but the new janitor found a way to break them beyond his ability to improvise solutions. Instead, they had to be sent to Billy the Blacksmith who would try to rescue the old ones or forge new ones. Outside, while it wasn't snowing, a cold, autumn wind drove freezing rain against the windows, and the windows, several of their panes cracked, rattled against the sill. The only way to quiet them was to fold up a scribbler cover and stuff it between the window and the sill. It stopped the rattling but enlarged the space the wind whistled through.

A well-stoked fire was an absolute must if the people in the class were going to stay warm – at least the people at the front of the class who managed to sit within the radius of the stove's circle of heat. The students at the back of the class made do with their sweaters and, when the teacher was feeling tolerant, a stocking cap and even jackets. The suspicion of students sitting from the middle of the class to the back was that as long as the students in front, believed to be the best or favourite, were comfortable, the rest of us didn't matter. With no fire to keep them warm, our class was let out by nine-thirty.

Duncan was angry.

"That's frigging crazy. Every place we go they got new schools made of bricks with furnaces and gymnasiums and everything, and we have to sit in this rattletrap: no heat, potbelly stoves, boards falling out of the ceiling, shingles blowing off the sides of the buildings."

"You want to be in school?" I asked him as we huddled out of the wind and rain behind the school, sharing our last cigarette. I couldn't remember when we had ever gone anywhere where there were schools like he described, since neither of us had been more than twenty miles from Shean in our lives.

"Not really, but Smelt, don't you think something's wrong when we have to go to a school like this. They're building new schools all over the province, and we're still sitting around stoves that came over on the Ship Hector. I don't give a damn about being cold. Hell, I slept in old Calum's sun porch in the middle of the winter, didn't I? But I hate thinking that maybe there's no reason we can't have a new school in Shean."

"No money, that's what everybody says," I replied, scratching around in my memory for reasons I had heard others give. "Shean's a poor town. Nobody's working, and almost nobody's paying taxes, Bartholomew says. That's why we have old schools and open sewers and no pavement."

"That's like saying somebody has to be dirty just because he's poor, but a bar of soap's only twelve cents, for frig's sake! There's no excuse for being dirty, and there's no excuse for us to have to go to schools that are falling down." He passed me the end of the smoke and suggested we spend our unexpected holiday at The Turk's pinball machines.

"I'm going over to the art room and ask Mother Saint Margaret if I can work on my painting," I answered. "If she won't let me, I'll meet you down at The Turk's."

"This art stuff's really getting to you. What are you drawing over there anyway?"

But I had already acquired the artist's superstition that no one should see what you are painting until it is finished. So nobody did, except for Mother Saint Margaret, and talking about it was the same as showing it, so all I gave Duncan for an answer was a shrug.

Even though she had classes from the elementary grades, which had heat, coming in all day, Mother Saint Margaret let me come in and work. Our easels were set up in her studio room off the art room, so there was no one to bother me, and not even Mother Saint Margaret to look over my shoulder every minute.

Mother Saint Margaret wouldn't let me take my painting home, knowing, as she did, that it would get more attention than my homework. When school started I brought her my drawings and my idea for a painting. She said it was awfully ambitious for a first effort, but she didn't discourage me. Instead, she spent the first month instructing me, making me draw and paint horses and boats and even paint a sketch I made of Calum lying on the couch in the sun porch. Several times she took the sketch of my idea for a painting and went over it with me, and then she told me to ask Calum to make a frame four feet long and two feet high. She and I stretched canvas over it. When it sat on the easel, blank and white as a field of snow, she told me I could start my painting.

I couldn't.

It was like I froze all of a sudden, standing there looking at the blankness, feeling that it wasn't fun any more, not like sketching horses at the track or doodling ideas onto paper to impress Mother Saint Margaret. I didn't know where to begin or what to do. I may as well never have had a moment's instruction in my life. I lost track of the time I stood there, but when I became conscious of myself again it was because of the sudden awareness that there were tears on my cheeks. I was scared, not knowing what to do, where to begin. Before Mother Saint Margaret or anyone else could see me, I just gave the easel an angry shove and ran from the room.

All that week, I never put pencil to paper except to write the barest ingredients of my homework. I took all the drawings off my wall and shoved them in a drawer, avoided Mother Saint Margaret, and skipped every afternoon I was supposed to be there. I'd never been so scared in my life. It occurred to me one day that I might never do it again, try to draw, that is, but that was emptier and more frightening than the thought of my painting. I knew I had to go back and fill that canvas.

I went back and nothing happened. I just stood and stared, and Mother Saint Margaret knew enough to leave me alone. It wasn't until my third visit to the easel that I reached out and drew a line. Every free minute after that was spent in Mother Saint Margaret's studio. Our studio.

I thought, as I pulled on the smock Mother Saint Margaret had given me, that I had never before had a whole day to do nothing but just paint. The painting was on the canvas by then, a blurred outline I had yet to define. I already felt the painting was going to do what I needed it to do as it emerged from its rough state toward a freeze-frame of the smelt fishermen.

The day I fell into the Big River, something in my mind clicked like a camera, but it was only during the past summer that the image had begun to make itself felt in bits and pieces, inexplicable portraits of faces, a detailed sketch of a fish, small glimpses until that summer night, falling asleep, I saw them all "gather at the river," as the song says. There were eight smelt fishermen that I could see just as the water closed over me, each with a different expression, some casting back into the water, one reaching to pull a smelt off the jig, others lifting jigged smelts from the water. What they shared in the watery vision I had of them were the same glazed, almost hypnotized eyes. Mother Saint Margaret said my perspective was that of the smelts, not of myself falling. I just wanted to paint the image in my mind, whosoever it was.

That afternoon, Mother Saint Margaret came into the studio with some egg sandwiches from the domestic science room and a glass of milk. When I looked at my watch it was well into the afternoon. I hadn't heard the church bell ring the "Angelus," hadn't been aware of time, and I had missed being home to make Calum's lunch.

"You made some serious progress today," she said, studying my work while I bit into a sandwich. "I can even recognize some of these men already, and this is Duncan. It's not going to be very flattering to any of them, though, is it?" she added, taking a seat across from me and picking up half a sandwich.

It was almost three o'clock when Mother Saint Margaret told me to cover my painting with the drop-cloth and go home. I wanted to stay until it was finished, but she warned me that rushing to finish something was a common mistake that crippled many good efforts. The painting would tell me when it's done, not the other way around.

27

November 11th drizzled over the former soldiers assembling for their annual Armistice Day parade. There were the old men in their long blue Burberrys, the ones who fought in the First World War and who didn't look like soldiers at all. Many of them had been gassed in the trenches or had come home to lose their lungs to the mines, Mrs. MacFarlane said from the back seat of the Oldsmobile. Duncan parked across from where the parade would begin, pointing the car over street so he could shoot ahead of the soldiers, and then we could be waiting nice and dry and warm when they got to the cenotaph.

"They look too old to have fought a war to me," Duncan said, and Mrs. MacFarlane said she was born after the war, but when she was a little girl she remembered the veterans gathering to commemorate Armistice Day or to bury one of the veterans who had died, usually from bad lungs.

"When I was a child, those veterans looked at lot like the ones from the last war do now, young, strong, glad to be alive," she said. None of the old men I knew, not Calum, not Bartholomew, not even Taurus who loved a good fight, had been in World War I.

Behind the old vets were the men from the Second World War, most in blazers and tams, some in original uniforms from the army, navy and air force. Mrs. MacFarlane said it was always interesting to see who could still wear their original uniforms. The war had been over for more than fifteen years, she said, and every Armistice Day there were fewer and fewer men in their uniforms.

In uniforms or blazers they were milling around, passing pints among themselves like they were cigarettes. There was a lot of laughing going on. Duncan was sorry Mr. MacFarlane wasn't home to march in the parade, but Mrs. MacFarlane said he probably wouldn't have marched anyway. Some men just don't like ritual remembering, she said, while others felt it had to be done. If my father hadn't been killed, I said, he would be there among the pipers.

I saw Tom MacPhee in the ranks of men who had gone overseas, and watching him I remembered the night we had been at his house and I learned how my father was killed, and I got a pretty good idea that night that Tom MacPhee took care of the sniper who killed him. I really liked him for that, and for how well he treated his horses.

At the front of the parade the Shean Pipe Band, veterans all, tuned up, drones humming in the wet air, snare drums rolling, the bass drummer giving his instrument a few practice blows. Pipe Major Willie John MacDonald barked his instructions, and all the random noise fell into sudden harmony, the band leading the smaller contingent of First World War vets, then the much larger group of Second World War veterans, followed by firemen in their dress uniforms, the nurses in their uniforms, caps and capes with some wearing army uniforms, the newly formed Shean Army Cadets, then the Boy Scouts.

As the solemn parade marched over Main Street, an army of kids followed, and along the sidewalk hundreds of adults stood watching. When they got in front of Bartholomew's, the old storekeeper stood there on the sidewalk rhythmically clapping his hands to the soldiers' steps, and soon people standing around him began doing the same. It caught on all up and down the street until everyone in town who wasn't marching in the parade was applauding the men who had gone off to war.

And don't forget the women, Mrs. MacFarlane said from the back seat, the nurses who had saved more lives that anyone could count, themselves stationed just behind the front lines, tending to the wounded.

Calum wasn't standing beside Bartholomew while the parade was going on. I knew he wouldn't be. He never went to a single

Armistice Day parade that I could remember, but when I told him I wanted to lay a wreath during the ceremony for my father, he took out his wallet and slowly counted out enough money to buy a large one.

At the cenotaph, the drizzle turned to rain, but the veterans stood at attention while the Legion president read out the names of those who never came home, the names engraved in the granite monument, and when he was getting close to the "Gs," I got out of the Oldsmobile holding the wreath and waited.

"Roderick Calum Gillies." I followed where the others had gone, along a narrow, white stone path with veterans standing on either side like an honour guard, to place my wreath of pine bough and poppies among the dozens of others piling up there. As I walked between the veterans I heard footsteps falling in behind, and when I laid the wreath among the others and stepped back for the moment of silence I was standing beside Tom MacPhee in his original uniform, saluting my father. I lifted my own hand uncertainly toward my brow and saluted, too. Then we both turned and went back as the next name was called, MacPhee stepping back into his place among the vets, me running back to the car out of the rain.

After the service at the cenotaph, we followed the veterans to the Holy Family Church for the Armistice Day service there, and all the soldiers went in, even the Protestants, and Duncan said maybe we better not go in because the roof might come crashing down on all those Protestants, but that possibility interested us enough to go inside.

At the end of the Catholic service, the pipe band led the veterans to Saint Paul's, the Protestant Church, where they all went inside again, even the Catholics, but Mrs. MacFarlane said she had to go home and bake something for the lunch at the Legion after the services were all over. We drove Mrs. MacFarlane home and went in with her while she was baking, knowing that even if we didn't get fresh-from-the-oven squares, we would score the trimmed-off edges.

The parade put Mrs. MacFarlane in a remembering mood about the war, and you should have seen Duncan's face – mine too, I suppose – when she talked about working in a shipyard in Pictou. We had heard lots about the war from Mr. MacFarlane, but whoever thinks to ask a woman what she did during the war, and who expects his mother, or his best friend's mother, to be a welder.

"Oh, yes," she said, "I was a riveter for a while, and I was a welder for a while. Most of the people building those ships were women like myself. The men were all overseas, remember, so we had to do the work they used to do, and we did it very well, let me tell you."

I couldn't imagine Mrs. MacFarlane, who was still pretty when she got all gussied up, working construction. Duncan couldn't imagine it either, or the fact that she had to quit working when she was going to have him.

"Did you ever go on strike there?" Duncan asked.

"No, Duncan, we weren't in a union, we were in a war. Think how the soldiers would have felt if they were overseas and heard that there were no more ships coming across the Atlantic because the women in the shipyards were on strike. Besides, we were paid very well. I was making more in the shipyard than your father was making after the war back here in the mine."

By the time we drove Mrs. MacFarlane and her baking to the Legion, it was full of veterans and other people. We carried her sandwiches inside for her, and once we got in there we just stayed. Five long bingo tables were placed end to end like a runway and covered with food. Duncan and I made for the sweets, and there were lots of them. One thing you could count on at a wake or a parade like this was that when the women in Shean had to provide the food, each bringing a dish or a plate of something. It was a food war, everybody trying to bake their best and outshine even their best friends. So Duncan and I made our camp at the sweets end of the table. Then Duncan went over to the bar and came back with glasses of pop which we used to wash down the food while we watched the men mingle in their blazers and medals and tams and glengarrys, and they were becoming old buddies again, men we never saw talking to each other for two minutes in Shean while we were growing up were now trading stories about when they were overseas together and laughing with arms around each other's shoulders, all smiles and drinks and cigarettes.

The women were clustering in the Legion kitchen making huge vats of tea that nobody seemed interested in, even themselves, because as soon as Father Alex and Reverend Smith left the hall it was like a great sigh of relief, and everyone relaxed. The men who already had a head start on the drinking didn't take long getting just plain drunk, loosening their neckties, hugging women not their wives, and making trips to the bar.

When Mrs. MacFarlane, carrying her now empty plate under her arm, wanted to go home, Duncan drove her. I waited for him to come back, taking a plate of squares and sitting close to Tom MacPhee who was sitting with some men around a table. When he noticed me, he told me to pull my chair in beside him and he introduced me to the others, who already knew me anyway, as "Roddie Gillies's boy." I was sitting there when Duncan came back, bringing me a glass of pop from the open bar. The first sip pretty near took my breath away, and he gave me that wink of his from the other side of the table and lifted his own glass of black rum to his mouth.

The Legion was loud with the laughter of men telling their stories, good or funny memories of the places they had been and the things they had seen and done. Not all of their memories were good ones, of course, but the worst ones had been dealt with during the 11 o'clock silence that punctuated the Armistice Day ceremonies, during the lowering of the flags, and during the promises they made when they said together, "We shall remember them...," but they remembered lots of other stuff too, and that was what was flowing around the Legion hall all afternoon along with the free liquor, men reminding each other of things that happened before Duncan and I were even born, and we sat there gathering up the stories.

Tom MacPhee told about the time they found a barn full of cheese in Italy and how homesick it made him thinking about his own father and mother making cheese at their farm up in the highlands. He sampled a lot of that Italian cheese, he said, and even though the other men in the Cape Breton Highlands were biting into it and spitting it out and saying it was nothing like the homemade cheese back home, Tom had to admit, at least to himself, that the Italians were almost as good at making cheese as his mother was. "I thought until then that I didn't want to be a farmer, but standing there that day there was nothing I wanted to do more, and there never has been since. I would have liked to have met whoever made that cheese, though," he said. "I would like to be able to make that kind of cheese."

"You don't need no Italians telling you how to make cheese, Tom," Steve Hunter said, emptying his cup. "Your cheese is as good as it gets, and that's what you fought for, wasn't it, the freedom to make your own cheese, not some Italian's? Right? Freedom, mister, freedom, that's what it was all about, right, the right to vote for your favourite cheese, and I'm voting for yours, Mister Tom MacPhee! I'm voting for yours.

"You boys," Steve said to Duncan and me, "you're what it was all about, about freedom for our children, isn't that right, Tom?"

"Hell, no! I was just looking for a job. Remember the depression? The army was a way to get three squares a day," Tom said, winking at me.

"Bullshit, Tom, don't be telling these kids that; they'll get the wrong impression. The war and the reason we fought it was because freedom was at stake," Steve argued.

"I guess you guys in the navy were just floating around out there with lots of time to think about what the politicians were saying, but speaking for the guys in the trenches, this guy in the trenches anyway," Tom said, "I have to tell you, Steve, at Casino

I never thought too much about anything but getting out of there alive. Not all of us did get out alive, you know."

"Look Tom," Steve said, "we've got to tell these boys what it was about."

"Wasn't that what today's parade was about?" Tom asked. "Let's leave it out there and enjoy the rest of the afternoon."

"Yeah," Steve said, "but a lot of good men died, this boy's father included, for freedom and the right to vote and the right to make cheese and the right to...."

"Strike?" Duncan asked.

Steve looked at him kind of funny. "What did you say?"

"The right to strike," Duncan repeated. "Wasn't that one of the things the war was about?"

"Damn unions, you mean? Communism?" Steve said. "That's not why I went to war, not for the right to strike."

"Why not?" Tom asked Steve.

"Unions are just Communists, that's why," Steve replied.

"Well, our miners weren't Communists in 1932 when they went on strike, and the boy's right. The right to strike is one of the things the war was about," Tom answered.

"Damn unions! You're a farmer, for Christ's sake, what do you care about unions for?" Steve asked him.

"Unions are just a bunch of workers trying to protect themselves from the greed of the owners," Tom said. "Nothing wrong with setting up a picket line and trying to get a better deal for yourself. I remember my father bringing cakes of cheese and eggs and milk to strikers' homes in '32 because their children had nothing to eat, and neither did the men on the picket line."

"Well you better not set that picket line up around me, because I'm walking through it."

"Not through my picket line, you're not," said Tom MacPhee, emptying his glass.

"The army!" Steve sneered through his nose, shaking his head like the word was a big mystery.

"What do you mean by that?" MacPhee asked, menace in his voice. Duncan dragged his chair up close while I slipped mine back a little.

"Just what I said," Steve answered. "The army! Nothing but people too stupid to get in the navy. You'll never hear union talk from sailors because we appreciate the people who give us work. What would the world be like if there was no owners to operate the mines...."

"Or close them," Tom said.

"...or the factories or the other things that give us work?"

"So, tell me, Steve, when was the last time you drew a pay-cheque, or are you still faking a war injury?"

"My work's none of your damn business, MacPhee, so shut your god-damned mouth before I shut it for you."

Tom MacPhee laughed and dismissed the navy man, telling him, "Drink up, Steve. You couldn't handle me before the war and nothing's changed."

"I was in the navy," Steve said, "so I know a thing or two now that I didn't know then, and so screw you and your strikes. That goes for you boys, too," he said to Duncan and me. "I didn't go over there and fight a war so a bunch of young bastards like you could ruin the country with your unions and your strikes."

"No need of talking to these boys like that. These boys can decide for themselves what their fathers fought for," Tom MacPhee said.

"Well, the same goes for you, MacPhee. You'd fight to save a country and then ruin it with unions and strikes."

"Careful, Steve," Tom said, quiet-like, "or I'll make you eat those words."

"You and what army?" asked Steve, and before anybody knew what was happening he pushed the table over on Tom's lap, the beer and rum spilling all over him, and Steve jumped up and hollered out that the navy was under attack and took a swing at Tom, but Tom was falling backwards to get out of the way of the spilled booze, so the punch missed and landed right on Duncan's chin, and all I saw were Duncan's feet going up as his chair tipped over. Even before Duncan hit the floor Tom MacPhee was swinging at Steve, and when somebody jumped in to stop it and grabbed Tom from behind, Tom thought he was being attacked so he flipped him round and punched him, and so the fight spread through the Legion hall, one table after another.

I took a few rum-woozy steps backward to the nearest wall, and a moment later Duncan crawled through the fray to stand beside me, one hand rubbing his jaw. "I started this," he declared proudly, watching the place let loose, blood and booze everywhere.

The women who were still there tried to get between their men, but I noticed they weren't all peacemakers, not after watching a couple of them slip in a few slypokes. One dinged her own husband when he wasn't looking, and another one grabbed a fistful of hair from the guy who was pounding her husband. After hearing that Mrs. MacFarlane used to be a welder, I figured anything could happen, including bare-knuckle wives. Most of the women, though, were trying to stop it, hollering like nuns in a classroom for those drunk soldiers to settle down. It wasn't much use. Finally, Pipe Major Willie John MacDonald had to pick up his pipes, tune them while ducking bottles and fists, and played "The Last Post," the sad, lonely music settling over the Legion hall, laden with all the unspoken memories of the morning. Fight by fight the place fell silent as the vets remembered where they were, and why.

That's when the Legion president told the men, who were sheepishly picking up tables and chairs or nursing sore spots or stopping blood, that the best thing would be for everybody to go home and get a little sleep, because, he reminded them, there was a big dinner and dance that night, and he expected to see everybody there, sober and friendly.

"What's that?" Calum asked, coming into the kitchen through the living room, his head indicating the snoring bundle on the kitchen couch. I was sitting at the table pretending to read something while squinting through the worst headache of my life. The glass of rum had made me dizzy, but the punishment for that crime was way out of proportion to its pleasure. It hurt to talk, but I told him it was Tom MacPhee, hoping I would get away with that. I didn't want to have to think up something to tell him, and I didn't want Calum getting within ten feet of my breath, which I could taste. But Calum wanted to know a little more about the bundle on the couch.

"Taking a nap," I told him.

Calum's stare turned into a glare. "I suppose he grew on the couch like a fungus."

"Not exactly," I answered.

"It's not that fellow, is it?" he said, walking toward the couch where he stood for a second then leaned over and lifted the blanket off Tom MacPhee's face just as Tom opened his eyes. They both gave a start.

"I'm sorry about this, Calum," Tom MacPhee told him, sitting up, and even I, standing behind Calum, could smell the liquor that had been spilled all over Tom. "I got a little tight after the parade, and the boy here took me home to sleep it off. I hope you don't mind," he added.

"Tea?" Calum asked.

"Please," MacPhee answered, and Calum passed the request on to me with a wave of his arm toward the kettle.

Tom MacPhee took his time standing up, clearing his head and running his fingers through his hair, trying to groom the gloom away. I had an idea how he felt, but I made their tea, had it ready about the time Tom, who had gone to the bathroom to try to freshen up, joined Calum at the kitchen table.

"I always meant to come here," Tom said, taking a sip from his cup. "To talk to you ... you know ... tell you...." He shrugged, leaving a door ajar for Calum to come through if he wanted to.

It was almost as if Calum never heard, he was so slow getting around to it. "I know all I need to know," he said finally, firmly, but Calum's words to Tom weren't as blunt as they could have been. To my disappointment they said no more about it. When they did come around to talking again, it was about Tom's farm, and that was when the two of us learned it was Calum who built the barn for Tom's father. Tom told us about the cheese and eggs and milk, the beef he would be slaughtering in the fall, the hay he would be able to sell for a few bucks late in the winter. "You eat well, but not everybody thinks that's the same as living well, I guess, so that's why most of the farms are empty now. Can't blame anybody, really. My customers can buy most of what I sell them cheaper at the Co-op. I'll keep doing it as long as I can, and then we'll see. You should come up sometime, take a look at the barn. It's still as sound as the day it was built. Wish to God you had built my house. The barn's warmer." The tea was fixing him up.

Tom MacPhee had been pretty drunk by the time we got out of the Legion. He got roughed up a bit in the brawl to boot, and he didn't want to drive his Clydes in that condition, "puking over the side of the wagon, I mean," he added, making Duncan and me laugh. "I'd just like a place to lay down for a couple of hours."

I owed him that much, I figured, no matter what Calum thought, so Duncan, who wasn't doing so well himself judging from his green-faced silence, drove the two of us to my place. He just dropped us off without a word and pulled away from the house like an old woman, not wanting to make any more noise than he had to. When we got in the house, Calum was still in the workshop, and before I got to throw a blanket over Tom MacPhee, he was snoring, and continued snoring until Calum woke him.

"Did you ever find any hazel trees on your property?" Calum asked him.

"I can't say I'd know one if I saw it, Calum. I cut maple and birch for firewood, some spruce for the mill, but I really don't know trees. They're just fence posts and firewood to me, but there's seventy acres of woodland on my property, so you're certainly welcome to come whenever you want and look around."

28

The Smelt Fishermen was finished by the end of November, but if it wasn't for the fact that exams would be happening in a couple of weeks I don't know if Mother Saint Margaret would ever have let me say it was done. She didn't want my painting interfering with my schooling. It had been a rough few weeks, with her becoming more and more picky the better and better I thought the painting was getting. Somewhere during that time it stopped being fun and became work, a series of troublesome details. The ones I tried to ignore myself, Mother Saint Margaret was quick to point out.

"If Angus John Rory's left leg is that far out in front of his right one, would they both be the same length?" she'd ask. "Do Duncan's eyes look off in different directions like that?" "If the sun is coming from the west why would that fish be shining on the east side of its body?" All she had to do was just ask the question, and the problem would drive me crazy; and not all of them were easy to fix. The oil paint made it slow to begin with. There were times when I didn't have a clue what to do, and she would leave me there for the whole period until it was time to go home, and then she would tell me what I could do, but by then it would be so late I would have to wait until the next day to make the change. I figured out her technique, though, what she was doing. When I left the art building, my mind would be on the problem she had just told me how to correct, and how to fix it would be about the only thing on my mind until the next time I got back to the art building. By then, it was usually a simple matter, I had rehearsed it so often in my head.

For her part, Mother Saint Margaret said that through my painting she was getting to know things about Shean she never knew before. As it took shape she learned from me the names of all the smelt fishermen in the painting. I told her stories about them as I was painting them, because it was impossible to be painting a picture of Angus John Rory and not remember that it was he who christened me Smelt, or recall and tell Mother Saint Margaret about the time in John Alex's barn when Johnny Rosin took out his fiddle and big fat Angus got up and stumbled for a minute to the music and then turned into this graceful dancer. It was the same for them all, all the grown men towering around Duncan, but in the painting, according to Mother Saint Margaret anyway, it was Duncan who was larger than life, and once I got his eyes straightened out, she said, there was more to him in the painting than she had ever seen in the classroom.

One afternoon in the art building, I stood in front of the painting trying to figure out what to do next. Mother Saint Margaret stood beside me.

"What should I do next?" I asked her.

"What do you think you should do?"

"I'm not sure," I answered, searching my work for a place to begin.

"Roddie, is this the best you can do?" she asked me.

"I ... I don't ... I don't think so. I mean I hope not."

"Roddie, right now, is this the best you can do? What do you want to change about *The Smelt Fishermen*?"

"I ... I'd like to make it.... I ... I guess so," I stuttered.

"You guess what?"

"I guess I'm finished with it."

"Are you pleased with it?"

"Ah...," I said fumbling for the right answer.

"This is not a test, Roddie. I'm not going to mark you. I just want you to answer the question honestly. Is this the best you can do with this painting right now?"

"Yes," I said, sagging.

"Then we'll have to declare it finished, won't we? It's very good. It's not the best painting you'll ever do, but at this point, I don't think you can ask much more of yourself. Congratulations, Roddie," Mother Saint Margaret said, squeezing my arm.

The sag reversed itself in a hurry. The painting was finished, and it was good, according to my teacher. I had stopped trying to finish it weeks before, believing it never would end, that Mother Saint Margaret would keep finding things wrong with it, keep me going over it and over it until I quit or graduated or died. And now it was finished. There was nothing more I wanted to do to it.

"What will you do with it now?" she asked me.

"I don't know," I said. I hadn't thought that far ahead, that once the painting was finished I would have to do something with it. "Take it home, I guess."

"Before you do that would you let me find a place to exhibit it for a little while? People might enjoy seeing it."

I thought she meant one of the classrooms, not above the main door of the Co-op, but that's where it wound up.

"It was either that or the post office, Roddie," Mother Saint Margaret told me, but apparently Joe MacIsaac, the Co-op manager, wanted to hang it as soon as she showed it to him. He knew everybody in the painting, she said, and hundreds of people go in and out of the Co-op every week.

Joe MacIsaac was so anxious to have it hanging in the store that *The Smelt Fishermen* got hung up even before Mother Saint Margaret had time to tell me. I learned about it first from Mrs. MacFarlane who said, when she came out of the Co-op and into the parking lot where Duncan and I were waiting for her, that I should have told her I had a painting hanging in the store. I thought she must be wrong until she began describing it, Duncan and all. Duncan, sitting behind the wheel, sat up and said, "I'm in it?" Mrs. MacFarlane said to drive her home first, so they left me there in the parking lot trembling and terrified of having to go inside and see for myself.

I pretended to be as disinterested as possible as I walked through the door, two people standing in my way looking up. I stepped around them without glancing over my shoulder and walked past the checkout and down the first aisle, my heart hammering, and I turned the corner and walked up the next aisle knowing that when I came to the far end of it I would be facing the door. I grabbed a can of tomato soup off the shelf on my way and made straight for the checkout, sneaking a nonchalant glimpse at the space above the door. It was my painting, all right. No frame but I didn't care.

I got my best look when Florence MacDonough at the checkout said, "That's a nice picture you made," as she rang in the price of the soup.

"Oh, right, that's hanging in here, isn't it?" I said, suddenly remembering, turning then to critically assess my work. Hoping I looked appropriately unimpressed, I stared at the painting.

"Everybody who comes in here says you got Angus John Rory down to a tee," Florence said. "Just about everybody has something nice to say about it."

"I'm glad," I replied, and asked her if it would be okay to use the store's washroom which was only for staff. She said sure and pointed me in that direction. On the way, Mr. MacIsaac called out from his office door that he really liked my picture, and when I got inside the washroom and locked the door, I looked at myself in the mirror, stuck out my happy hand to congratulate the image of myself, and let out a joyful but not too loud yelp, jumping up and down and hugging myself as if Mary Scotland was there with me. People liked my painting.

When I got back to the checkout, Duncan was standing under *The Smelt Fishermen* telling Florence, "It's a picture of Smelt falling in the river just before he got jigged in the leg," which, in a way, it was.

The painting was the talk of the town for a few days, people stopping to tell me they liked it, or to tell me about the kind of things that happened to them smelt fishing. Angus John Rory didn't think too much of it, though, the first time I met him in John Alex's barn, telling me that he wasn't nearly as fat as I made him out to be in the painting. Looking at his stomach while he was talking, I knew I had been too flattering, but there was no point in mentioning it. Duncan, on the other hand, had no trouble bringing it to his attention.

"Oh, come on, Angus, you took up so much room in the picture there was hardly any space left for the rest of us," Duncan said from the stall where he was brushing Cape Mabou.

"That's enough from you, MacFarlane," Angus said.

"Are you going to play cards or fight with the young fellows?" John Alex asked Angus. The three of them, John Alex, Johnny Rosin and Angus John Rory, were seated on hay bales around two other bales stacked on top of each other. Lying on top of the two bales was a broken-hinged half-door from one of the stalls, serving as a tabletop. They were playing 45s with a deck so swollen with age and moisture it stood about four inches tall, and shuffling the cards was the hardest part of the game. In front of each stood a quart of beer, occasionally used to chase down a sip of shine from a jam jar that John Alex was rationing among them.

"What's trump?" John Alex asked, bringing his attention back to the game.

"Spades, Ace of Hearts to beat," John Alex said, and Angus dropped the Jack of Spades, the second strongest trump in the hand, on top of the John Alex's Ace, but the smile was quickly wiped from Angus's face by Johnny Rosin's Five of Spades, the boss of the whole hand. It was Johnny Rosin's game, and he was growing weary of winning, which he had been doing all afternoon. He withdrew from the game, and Duncan suggested a four-hander of Auction 125, he and I against John Alex and Angus John Rory.

"Can you boys play?" Angus asked skeptically.

"We don't need to know how to play since we're only playing you," Duncan said, sitting down on the bale of hay Johnny Rosin abandoned. I sat across from him.

Mrs. MacFarlane had taught us to play Auction 45 and Auction 125 so that during snowstorms or even when Duncan was grounded, she would have people to play cards with. Every kitchen in Shean had its Auction players, or its crib board, and cards were as serious as church with a lot of people. I learned enough to play like a real amateur, and I didn't like to play with a picky partner who would criticize my mistakes, because I could make a lot of those. Duncan caught on much faster, keeping track of the cards played, making confusing leads – leads that confused everybody but himself.

What Duncan learned about cards, though, didn't all come from Mrs. MacFarlane. While I was learning about painting from Mother Saint Margaret, Duncan was studying cards at Nicole's. Once they started seeing each other, going out in public, Duncan was spending lots of time at her house where her father was selling booze, and there was usually a poker game going on. Duncan went pretty fast from watching to playing, and he had a perfect face for it, according to Nicole's father. He had something more than a poker face, though, the bootlegger said. Duncan was a winner.

There were people to whom winning just came naturally, Mac-Rory said, and Duncan was one of them. Soon, Nicole's father was wise enough to realize that even though Duncan couldn't afford the bigger games, when the pot would sometimes be more than a hundred dollars or so, he could play with the men, so instead of playing himself, he began staking Duncan that winter, splitting the winnings. Duncan was winning lots – too much, some of the players thought.

I never went to Nicole's with him unless it was just to pick her up or see Farter. I wouldn't have been allowed anyway. Nicole's father didn't like too many people hanging around, because he was always watching for a raid from the RCMP and didn't trust a lot of people. Most of what I heard about the poker games came from Duncan who, one Monday morning on our way to school, showed me over three hundred dollars that he had in his pocket.

"You won all that?" I asked.

"That's my half. Nicole's father got the other half."

"Six hundred bucks! You won six hundred bucks in one night?"

"No, the game started Friday night. I slept a little bit late Saturday afternoon, and played all night Saturday, too. Yesterday, the game broke up in the afternoon. I figure I earned it," Duncan said, stuffing the roll of bills back. "But I'd like to get in a game just for myself."

The next time I asked him about poker, he told me he lost one hundred and forty dollars.

"The cards just weren't coming my way, and besides, Farter had the flu and stayed in bed all weekend."

"What does Farter have to do with it?" I asked. "I thought it was his old man who was staking you."

"He does, because he thinks I can win most of the time, and I do, but it's more interesting to have an angle, so I worked out a deal with Farter who's always around the table dumping ashtrays or bringing a new bottle or glass when somebody asks for it, and nobody pays any attention to him. What we did was work out a bunch of signals because he gets to see just about every hand at the table. It works, that's how I won the six hundred. I really hated splitting it with Nicole's father since I won it myself."

"You could get the shit kicked out of you if you get caught. What's Farter get out of it?"

"I give him twenty bucks if I win."

So Angus John Rory shuffled the thickened deck of cards and dealt them out, calling for bids. We played a few hands, almost evenly winning, our side and theirs, when Duncan said we should play a little penny ante. We were all for it, all except Johnny Rosin who tapped his fiddle case and said, "This is the only thing I play for money."

"Do you rehearse for free?" John Alex asked him.

"Of course, I do."

"Then why don't you rehearse. I'd like to hear a little music but I'm not going to pay you to hear it," which made Duncan and me laugh. I spilled a little change onto the makeshift table, knowing I was going to risk very few pennies with Duncan playing. Johnny Rosin started up.

"Just like Las Vegas," Angus John Rory said. "Poker and entertainment. Well, boys, you may as well hand over your allowance right now because I'm going to take it all and go to the bootlegger's and get a good bottle of rum with it."

Duncan won the cut and called the first game. In an hour he had forty-three dollars, all the money at the table except for the five bucks I refused to bring out of my pocket.

"Beginner's luck," John Alex said, disgusted. He hated losing money.

"So how's the shine there, John Alex?" Angus asked, two nervous hands keeping time on the table to Johnny Rosin's music.

"It's gone," John Alex answered, while I watched him slip the half-full jam jar behind his bale of hay. He had a night to get through himself now with no money. The time for sharing had passed.

"You wouldn't think about lending a fellow ten bucks, would you?" Angus asked Duncan. "It wasn't really fair, you know, grown men like us taking advantage of boys like you."

"I won," Duncan pointed out.

"Yes, yes, but that's because you had us at a disadvantage. We didn't want to take money from young fellows like yourselves, so we wound up losing our own. It shouldn't even count, you know. It should have been just for fun, everybody getting their money back."

"When would I get the ten bucks back?" Duncan asked.

"What's that?"

"The ten you asked for. If I loan it to you when would I get it back?"

"Soon as the cheque comes in," Angus tells him. "End of the month."

"I'll go get the bottle for you, if you like, and bring it back here. I have a car."

"That's kind of you, and mark my words, the end of the month you'll have the ten."

I followed Duncan out to the car, and he started it up and drove over street a couple of times and then back to John Alex's barn where he reached under the seat and took out a bottle of Black Diamond.

"Here you go," he told Angus, "but it cost me twelve bucks, not ten. End of the month?" he said, asking for Angus's reassurance once again before he released the bottle.

A couple of evenings after *The Smelt Fishermen* went up above the door in the Co-op, I had a call from Mrs. Fraser, Bartholomew's wife, asking me if I would come to their house after school the next day. Mary Scotland came with me, curious to see inside Bartholomew's house, one of the biggest in Shean. I had only been in it a couple of times myself and barely got past the front door, even though Calum had built it.

Mrs. Fraser invited us in and led us, with white-haired dignity, to her kitchen while we caught glimpses of the dining room and living room on our way. It was a big house with high ceilings and dark wood floors and Acadian hooked rugs from Cheticamp spread around them. The table in the dining room looked like it weighed a ton, surrounded by six strong chairs. The living room was furnished in heavy, dark blue couches and chairs, with an upright organ in the corner with sheet music on it, and photographs on the walls of men with moustaches and women with grimaces.

In the kitchen, Mrs. Fraser brought out two glasses and a quart of milk and placed it on the table along with a plate of peanut-butter cookies and told us to help ourselves. When she was finished serving she sat with us.

"Roderick," she said, "I saw your painting in the Co-op yesterday afternoon. I was quite impressed with your talent."

"Thank you," I mumbled through a mouthful of cookie.

"The reason I wanted to see you here when Bartholomew isn't at home is I have a favour to ask. Do you think you could paint Bartholomew's store?"

"In December?" I asked, astounded. Mary Scotland burst out laughing, and even Mrs. Fraser made a smile.

"I mean paint a picture of it," she clarified. "When you've been married as many years as we have, finding a Christmas gift that matters gets more and more difficult. When I saw your painting, the way you painted that MacFarlane boy, making him mischievous and likable at the same time, I wondered if you would consider painting a picture of Bartholomew's store for me.

"He loves that store. He's been married to it a lot longer than he's been married to me, and he spends more time there than here except for sleeping. I thought it would be a nice present. Can you do that?"

I had to do a rapid calculation. Mother Saint Margaret made me finish *The Smelt Fishermen* so it wouldn't interfere with my exams, which were just a couple of weeks away, but it was only a store. If I took my easel home, and worked at it in the evenings after I finished studying, it would be finished in lots of time. I told her I could do it.

"Do you need me to pay you now?" she asked. "Do you need to buy anything?"

"You don't have to pay me," I said, embarrassed.

"Yes she does," Mary Scotland broke in. "If she doesn't pay you then it's your gift to her, and she won't be able to give it to

Bartholomew, will she? And besides, you need to buy canvas and paints and things." Mrs. Fraser was nodding her head, and I surrendered. She gave me twenty-five dollars and said I would get another twenty-five if she liked the painting. There were still some cookies on the plate.

"Tell me about the store," I said. "I know what it looks like and everything, but ... I don't know.... It's.... How old is it?"

"Bartholomew's store is the oldest business in town, the only one still operating that was here when the mines were booming and the town was incorporated," Mrs. Fraser told us. "He came here as a young man with a head for business and sold patent medicines and newspapers and magazines and tobacco and anything else there was a demand for. It's been the gathering place for I don't know how many years, especially for the men. They would come every day, and they still do, to pick up their newspapers at noon and meet and talk and argue and tell each other lies.

"Do you know that Bartholomew has never taken a vacation? Not one day out of that store in more than fifty years except for holidays and snowstorms so bad nothing could move. If anything in Shean was moving, then you could count on that being Bartholomew making his way to the store. I don't suppose there's a soul who ever lived in Shean who hasn't been in that store for some reason or another, and whom Bartholomew doesn't know by name and family and job and clan going all the way back to Scotland.

"I think a painting of it would surprise him nicely at Christmas."

29

I asked Duncan to park across the street from Bartholomew's store while I sketched the building, colouring it with crayons, recording details I never noticed before, the scrollwork under the eaves, the jagged rhythm of the shingles.

"You could do pretty good at this, Smelt. Fifty bucks for painting a picture. Lucky to get that for painting a house, know what I mean, real painting," Duncan said.

"Mother Saint Margaret says there's an art college in Halifax."

"College? To learn to draw? You paint pictures and you sell them. What do you need a college to teach you that for?"

"There's a lot more to it than just drawing pictures. There's a lot about art I don't know but I'd like to know."

"What's to know? As soon as somebody can't make a poem rhyme or a picture make sense they call it art. Believe me, what you're doing is not art, so you don't have to go to college to make excuses for it. College's an awful lot of money just to learn what you already know. What would Calum say to that?"

That was a question I had been thinking about ever since Mother Saint Margaret told me about the Nova Scotia Art College: What would Calum say to that? He never said much about my drawing and painting, and when he did look at something I did it was with a face harder to read than one of Taurus's Gaelic poems. I never showed Calum *The Smelt Fishermen* because Mother Saint Margaret took the painting straight from the school to the Co-op. I told him about it, but I wasn't sure he even heard me until I went for groceries and Mr. MacIsaac, the manager, told me he hadn't seen Calum in the Co-op more than half a dozen times since I was old enough to get the groceries. "But he's been in three or four times this week. Why do you suppose that is?" he asked, giving me a wink.

So what would Calum say?

"I'm probably not going to go to the art college anyway," I answered, "so it doesn't much matter what Calum would say."

"You should go if it will piss him off," Duncan said.

Mary Scotland and I walked through the first snowfall of the year, the first real snowfall, not the November snow that falls small and hard then swirls along the frozen ground like white dust, but the December snow descending in fat lazy flakes that we caught on our tongues as we walked the streets of Shean, looking at the lit-up houses. Lights and wreath-ringed candles hung in windows beyond which was the living room glitter of fir or spruce trees. Yards were occupied by carrot-nosed snowmen or plywood Santa Clauses; eaves and doorways were trimmed in colourful blinking rainbows; and even an occasional poplar tree in someone's yard sported a garland of Christmas lights. At the Holy Family Church a life-sized manger scene, lit by a flood light, showed Mary and Joseph, the shepherds and wise men, angels and sheep all gathered around an empty crib. The Baby Jesus wouldn't be placed in it until Midnight Mass on Christmas Eve.

Between the snow covering the unpaved streets and the lights on the houses hiding the fact that so many of them were unpainted, there was a lot to enjoy. Mary Scotland said that Christmas was her favourite time of year because the town seemed enchanted.

"Every year, people say it's such a fuss and that next year they're not going to bother, but they always do," she said.

All Calum and I ever did was hang a wreath on the front door and decorate a small tree in the living room, but this year Mary was directing things at our house, asking Calum if it would be alright to put up some outside lights. Using some of Mrs. Fraser's money we went to Bartholomew's to buy enough strings of lights to trim the front door and across the top of the sun porch. Coming back, we saw Calum walking across the yard carrying the ladder from the workshop. He rested it against the house and told me to follow him back to the shop where he sent me into the loft, rooting through dusty boxes that hadn't been moved since the day I was up there getting the window for our shack. I found the box marked "Xmas" that he had described and brought it down, carrying it behind him as he led me back to the house. We opened it on the kitchen table.

The box, stuffed with decorations I hadn't seen for ten years, contained long garlands of red and green paper, strings of tangled lights, boxes of small, fragile, colourful globes, each carefully wrapped in red tissue and put away until next Christmas, boxes of silver tinsel that had hung on who knows how many trees, picked off strand by precious strand and replaced in their original boxes, several childish, hand-drawn, crayon-coloured pictures, each with a strip of yellowed tape embedded with fir needles, proof that these too had hung from Christmas trees past, and an angel, a veteran of many, many Christmases, its white dress yellowing and the silver paint peeling from its bent and broken wings. Rising from the dusty box, as well, were images of a large tree in the living room and music and sweet-smelling food and my grandmother humming and reaching as high up the tree as she could, my mother lying on the couch pointing out gaps in the symmetry of our decorating, Calum lifting me to reach to the top of the tree with the angel; all those early Christmases gelled into that single memory. I became a running narrative of what Christmas was like when I was young, telling Mary about my mother, my grandmother, the gifts Santa Claus had left under that big, magic tree.

"You're going to need a big tree for all these decorations," she said.

A few minutes later, tacking the lights along the sun porch eaves I grew aware of movement below me. Calum had done something I had never known him to do before except for that time during Evelyn's wake when he chased Duncan and Nicole out of there. He had broken his own schedule and opened the sun porch door. While Mary untangled some of the strings of lights from the box, Calum, a row of thumb tacks trapped between his compressed lips, was carefully trimming the inside of the sun porch windows with lights. When we were done, we plugged our work into a wall socket, and the front of the house exploded in light. The three of us walked out in the middle of the street and stood there looking at it. Then Mary and I began our walk around town.

It was still two weeks until Christmas and one week until exams, but the night wasn't for studying or even for shopping, even though it was Farmer's Night in town with all the stores open, nor was it a night for painting Bartholomew's store. It was a night for roaming around the streets of our changed world, discovering it for each other, pointing out festive features and letting the weather push us closer together while we walked.

Through the still air we could hear the shivering jingle of bells from the Co-op parking lot, and a moment later we were standing in front of Tom MacPhee's Clydes, their winter harnesses making random music each time one of them flicked snow from its face with a shake of the head. They were the only horses in a parking lot filled with cars and trucks.

The snow in Mary's long hair was highlighted by the street light behind her. The Clydes, their white-blazed faces trimmed in leather and musical brass, enveloped her in the wintry mist of their breath. Mary Scotland's beauty took on a mystical presence that seemed to come from one of Calum's Gaelic histories or one of Taurus's songs. If I turned the street light into the moon....

"I'm starting to get cold," Mary said, interrupting my imaginary painting. We made our way down to Main Street, walking past the decorated store windows until we came to The Turk's, where Brenda Lee was "Rockin' Around the Christmas Tree," and the restaurant was filled with Friday night people like ourselves playing the jukebox and the pinballs, eating french fries and talking above the volume of the music. We slipped into a booth with Duncan who was dragging his fork through a hemorrhage of ketchup like a boat dragging for a drowned man. He found the last elusive fry and popped its bloody body in his mouth.

"Check the end of the booth," Duncan said, looking toward Ack-Ack's old seat. Wearing a hairnet and his greasy white apron, sat Tony the Turk. When Tony was out front sitting with his young customers it meant only one thing.

"He broke out, eh?" I asked Duncan.

"Getting a head start on his Christmas bender," Duncan said. "I ordered a twenty-cent plate of fries before, and he told me if I made them myself I could have them for a dime, so I went into the kitchen. I had half the potatoes on Prince Edward Island piled on this plate," he added, sweeping his fork through the crimson remains, searching for another lost fry.

When Tony went on the booze he always abandoned his kitchen, leaving it to his waitresses to fill in for him. We could see a harried Nicole through the serving window between the counter and the kitchen. She was cooking in the kitchen then running out front to take more orders. Unlike Tony, she wasn't sending customers into the kitchen to cook for themselves.

"Is Nicole working alone?" Mary asked Duncan.

"Yup," Duncan said.

"Why don't you help her?" Mary said.

"Waiting tables?" Duncan asked, incredulous.

"Or washing dishes or cooking. You didn't have any trouble making something for yourself, did you?" she said, nodding toward his plate.

"Yeah, Duncan, why aren't you helping her?" I joked.

"Are you crippled?" she said to me. "Come on, the two of you. I'm not kidding. She needs help."

Both of us followed Mary into the kitchen where she asked Nicole how we could help. The kitchen was a disaster zone, dishes and food everywhere. Nicole said she needed clean dishes in a hurry. Since Nicole was the only one who could confidently tell the difference between pork and beef, lettuce and cabbage, she stayed with the cooking. Mary took Nicole's pad and went out front, and Duncan and I found ourselves standing side by side at a sink piled high with a greasy mess of plates and glasses and cups and pots and pans.

"I really appreciate this," Nicole said, leaving a burger sizzling on the grill as she came over and gave a Duncan a thank-you kiss. "And thanks for talking Mary and Roddie into helping."

"No problem. They had nothing better to do," Duncan said, turning on the hot water.

We couldn't empty the sink. No matter how fast we wiped the dishes, Mary kept piling in more.

"Keep an eye on her, Roddie. I think she's bringing dishes in from the houses across the street," Duncan said at last.

Through the serving hole a mixture of music and voices filtered into the kitchen, Tony's voice growing louder and less friendly by the minute. He had already passed through his earlier, amiable Christmas spirit and was now reaching the dark depths of his drinking. By Christmas, most of the houses in Shean would have somebody in residence who had fallen off the wagon. Few of them would reach New Year's and sobriety without leaving a trail of damage and broken homes or friendships. Some would wind up in a 28-day detox program somewhere, but nobody in Shean raced through those moody stages faster than Tony the Turk, changing in a few hours from a half-drunk and suddenly generous businessman into the noisy and nasty voice we could hear above the jukebox, arguing with his customers, ordering whomever he was arguing with to get out while other voices baited him.

Tony's voice took a sudden leap in pitch, and a moment later Mary Scotland came through the swinging doors into the kitchen, eyes wide and terrified, and behind her stormed in Tony, hollering, "What you do in my kitchen?" Then he saw the rest of us and repeated the question, a sweep of his hand taking in all of us. "What you do? Go! Go! Go! All of you go! You fired!"

"That's a new one," Duncan said, "fired before we're hired."

"Listen, Mister Mac," Tony said to him, grabbing a sharp knife from the table. "You maybe kill little Ack-Ack, but you no kill Tony. Now you drop that and go!"

The "that" that Duncan was holding was a stack of plates. "Who am I to argue with a man with a knife," Duncan said, letting the stack leave his hands. "Oh, look, Tony, you got a jigsaw puzzle for Christmas," he said.

"I'm not a-scared of you, Mister Man, boy," Tony said, holding the knife toward the ceiling for all of us to see. "You're fired! Now go, all of you, go!" His gesture took in Nicole who undid her apron and threw it on the floor. "Wonderful! Another Christmas without a pay."

Tony turned and walked back into the restaurant waving the knife. "We're closed! Go! Go!" shooing everyone, even those who were only half through their burgers and fries, out into the snow.

"How much does he owe you?" Duncan asked, looking toward the till.

"Don't even think about it, Duncan. It's alright. I'll just look at it like a Christmas vacation. In a few days he'll sober up and ask me to come back, and he'll have to pay me then."

"But he owes you the money now, and he's only going to drink it," Duncan said. "We'll just take what he owes you."

"If you touch that till he'll call the cops and you don't need that. I don't need that. Besides, when he locks up, he's just going to take the money and go over to our house and spend it buying liquor from the old man."

"Does he play cards when he's drinking?" Duncan asked.

"Sometimes."

"Good."

I walked Mary home from The Turk's, our giddy attention grabbed this time by what had happened in the restaurant instead of the decorated houses. Then I kept on to Culloden Street. Even from the bottom of the street I could see that Calum left the Christmas lights on, although the house itself was dark. I slowed my steps to enjoy it a bit longer.

There was no reason not to tell Calum about my commission to paint Bartholomew's store. I thought he might enjoy knowing what Bartholomew was getting for Christmas, and I was right. As soon as I brought the easel home from school and got set up to start, Calum measured the canvas and began working on a frame.

When the painting began, what kept popping into my mind was one of Taurus's songs, "*An Stòr aig Pàrlan*," about Bartholomew's store, a song, Calum said, where the singer tells people that if they are ever feeling lonely and want company they will always find a friend leaning on the radiator at Bartholomew's store. The air and the sounds of it had more to do with what went on the canvas than I did.

It was nip and tuck, my race against the calendar. I was cramming for exams and seeing Mary whenever I could. Still, I made myself work at the painting a little every day, and there was the occasional day when that was all I wanted to do, so I was able to finish Bartholomew's store in time to get it down to Mrs. Fraser before the store closed early on Christmas Eve and Bartholomew came home. The last thing I did was put Calum and Bartholomew, impressions of them, behind the window pane, leaning over the radiator, looking back at you. They were vague enough that you could miss them if you didn't know they were there or didn't look closely. Calum had scrolled a frame for it that resembled the staggered pattern of the store's shingles. Mrs. Fraser loved it, so I had no trouble getting the other twenty-five bucks.

Bartholomew liked it, too, and hung it up in the store right after the holidays. Duncan said that Michelangelo might have a monopoly on the churches, but I had the stores in Shean sewn up.

30

Bartholomew took his stroke in February.

He was talking to Johnny Neil Kennedy who came for his paper every day and who gave regular progress reports on his single-handed and heroic efforts to make coal king once again in Shean. In fact, a rich seam, known only to him, ran under his own property. When he was drinking, it wasn't uncommon to see him in his hayfield at the edge of town swinging a pick, but the bulk of his prospecting was carried out in Bartholomew's store. His unfarmed field also held secret pockets of gold, silver and oil, and when the uranium boom in Blind River and Elliot Lake was all everybody was talking about, Johnny Neil discovered some of that, as well. Bartholomew used to kid him about what he called "Johnny Neil's stockmarket report." That was what he was listening to when his eyes closed and he slowly slid to the floor, according to Johnny Neil, who took time to finish telling the prone proprietor the latest news from his mineral field before he went to the store's phone, cranked it and told Sally Fortune to find Doctor Proud and send him to Bartholomew's store.

Dr. Proud asked for help lifting Bartholomew into the back seat of his car, and then raced to the hospital, leaving behind quite a commotion at the store. Even though it was only a stroke, no blood or anything, people got busy finding excuses to go to the store to ask Sarah Campbell, who worked for Bartholomew, what happened. It could have been one of the best days the store ever had for making money, but Sarah locked up, right after she called Mrs. Fraser, and went to the hospital herself; so the men milled around the front of the closed store, pondering for the first time in their lives the possibility of living in a town that had no Bartholomew Fraser in it, and wondering, too, where they were going to get their papers tomorrow.

It was me who brought the news home to Calum, having heard about it on my way from school at noon. Calum was sitting in his study reading the paper he had picked up at Bartholomew's not long before, so he must have left just before the stroke, but it was almost like he had been waiting for that news, the way he lowered his paper and sat back, staring, not saying a word. I just left it like that and went into the kitchen to make his tea. There was a nameless knot in my stomach. By the time the tea was steeped, Calum was standing in the doorway with his coat on, telling me he was going to the hospital.

For the next three days I didn't see much of Calum. He was gone early in the morning, and then he would come home, eat a little bit, browse the shelves of his library, take down a book or two, and bring them to the hospital. Once, I saw him going through his folder of Taurus's songs, choosing certain ones, although I couldn't imagine him singing them to Bartholomew in the hospital, or anywhere for that matter. The only time I went to the hospital to visit, I got as far as the door of his room but didn't go in. Bartholomew was lying in the bed, looking smaller than ever, all covered in white, bags of fluids hanging above him, tubes running up his nose and in his arms. Even from the hallway I could tell by his gasping breath that he wasn't awake. Calum was sitting in a chair beside the bed, reading aloud in the Gaelic from the book he was holding. There was no place for me in there.

On the way out I passed Mrs. Fraser, but she didn't even notice me, and I couldn't help wondering if Calum was visiting his friend at the hospital or guarding him, protecting Bartholomew from getting baptized by Mrs. Fraser while he was in a coma.

I heard Calum stamping the snow off his overshoes on the front step, then taking off his overcoat in the hall, hanging it on a hook, the gloves carefully placed in the right hand pocket, the cap hung on top of the overcoat on the same hook. He sat on the boot bench to unsnap the buckles of his overshoes, and when they were removed he removed his shoes, put on his slippers, and shuffled down the hall to the living room where I was toying with my homework.

"He's gone," Calum said.

"Oh. That's too bad," was all I could think to say.

After a long silence, Calum said, "Yes, that's too bad," and walked into his study where he lowered himself tiredly onto the couch and stretched out on it, hands crossed over his chest, and stared at the ceiling, same as in the sun porch.

Bartholomew's wake was more formal than others Duncan and I had gone to. It was quiet in the house, even though it was filled with people. Everybody knew Bartholomew, but the fact that most people had never been in Bartholomew's big house made it a big wake, but a quiet one.

Mrs. Fraser stood by the coffin all dressed in black and holding her rosary. The whole room was walled with holy pictures. I had seen the room before, and the pictures on the wall used to be family photographs. About the only thing that wasn't covered in holy pictures, crucifixes or palm leaves was Bartholomew in his coffin. No rosary twined through his fingers, no holy medal on his lapel. Still, surrounded by all those *Last Suppers* and *Sacred Hearts of Jesus* and all those angels and saints, it looked like Mrs. Fraser was mounting a last ditch assault to save her husband's soul.

Mrs. Fraser's friends from the Catholic Women's League, who catered weddings all summer, looked after bringing the food and serving it at Bartholomew's wake, and they moved through the visiting mourners with a temperate eye, weeding out potential troublemakers. There were lots of Protestants from Bartholomew's church coming in to pay their respects, especially the men from the International Order of Odd Fellows, and the women from the CWL were determined that their own husbands would make a good impression for Mrs. Fraser's sake, so there was no drinking and no loud laughter.

Under the spying eyes of so many CWLers, the people with whom Bartholomew traded gossip, jokes and news every day were forced to file through quietly, give their condolences to the grieving Mrs. Fraser, have a cup of tea and a sandwich and were then guided toward the back door. The midnight vigil had been arranged with an eye toward a well-mannered evening, so John William Connors and Michael John MacLean were thanked for their offer to sit the night with Bartholomew, but Mrs. Fraser told them that other arrangements had been made. There were more chaperones than mourners in the house after midnight. Duncan and I came down to Bartholomew's house late the first night but we were shooed home, and while we were walking home Duncan said wouldn't it be great if Taurus got loose and got hold of a bottle and got his mind back for a night. It would take more than the CWL to keep him from mourning his old buddy in his own way.

Calum spent a lot of time at Bartholomew's wake. He sat quietly in a big armchair in the corner of the room across from the coffin, taking an occasional cup of tea when it was offered, almost nobody talking to him, which wasn't unusual, I guess. I found it kind of sad because the only thing Mrs. Fraser asked Calum to do was arrange for the digging of Bartholomew's grave, and that was when Calum came and got us, Duncan and me. I got the shovels and a pick from the workshop and loaded them in the trunk of the Oldsmobile, and we drove out to the Protestant graveyard.

"They're suppose to pay us for this, you know, but I bet old Calum doesn't come across with a cent," Duncan was saying as he leaned on a shovel waiting for me to pick enough sod and earth to employ him.

"Why should Calum pay us when it's Mrs. Fraser who has all the money?" I asked. I lifted the pick above my head and put all my force into opening Bartholomew's grave but the pick hit steel-hard ground, bounced back and pretty near took my eye out while pain shot through my hands and up my arms. I dropped the pick and began dancing around, babying my aching fingers while Duncan pointed out that we were also supposed to get a bottle of rum for digging the grave but what were the chances of Calum buying us that, he wondered, while I picked up the pick again and more timidly poked at the frozen earth.

"Know what we should do, Smelt?" he said almost two hours later as we stood up to our knees in the slowly deepening grave. We had just broken through the frost line and were predicting that the next four feet would be a lot easier. "What we should do is go on strike. How would they like that, the minister and widow and the pallbearers, if they got here and the two of us were walking circles around a half-dug grave with picket signs nailed to our shovels that said 'Unfair to Gravediggers?' I bet they'd pay us then. There should be a gravediggers' union, you know that," but we managed to get the grave dug without going on strike. Still, Duncan had a point. Nobody paid us a cent.

The day of the funeral, Calum and I dressed in our suits and walked together up to St. Paul's Church for the service. We were standing in a pew close to the front when they rolled Bartholomew's coffin down the aisle and began the funeral service. I had never been to a Protestant funeral before. Duncan wouldn't come, saying that he was in enough trouble with the Catholic Church without going inside St. Paul's. Besides, he said, Bartholomew never let him back inside his store, ever since the day he caught Duncan trying to steal a *Police Gazette*. So Duncan missed Taurus's performance.

I heard him, everybody heard him, when the hacking started from the back pew, the strangling cough caused by his smoky and coal-dusted lungs. The Catholics were at least familiar with Taurus and the fact that in Holy Family Church, where Mrs. MacLeod brought him every Sunday, Taurus could often be heard above the priest, his coughing or his Gaelic prayers rising and falling with his uneven breathing, or his sudden snatches of song disrupting a sermon. It was a quirk that made children giggle, and Taurus was quickly shifting into a character very unlike the man we had known, and the new stories about him began to eclipse the earlier ones, his brawls, his drinking, his songs.

When the service began I kept looking over my shoulder at Taurus and wondering if I would recognize him on the street; he got so small over the winter and looked even smaller in his suit that was bought for a man with a thick chest. His hair was still there, wetted with water and parted on the side the way a mother combs a little boy's hair before he can do it himself. His nose looked larger, too, because his face was thin and sucked-in, and the lower rims of his watery eyes were red and runny. I would recognize his hands, though, which hadn't shrunk at all, still tattooed with coal dust and stained with nicotine as he steadied himself by gripping the back of the pew in front of him. Mrs. MacLeod was standing beside him, a handkerchief in her hand that she used to reach over and wipe the water when it ran like tears from his eyes, as if he was crying for Bartholomew – but I knew he wasn't.

We sat down as the minister read from the Bible, Calum stiff beside me, his hearing aid turned on, taking in every word, but my restless attention continued to roam around the strange, stark church that had no statues and no altars and no incense and no Latin, until it came to rest on Taurus again, fidgeting in his seat. With everyone listening to the minister, even Mrs. MacLeod, nobody noticed Taurus pull his Player's tobacco from his pocket, slip the cigarette papers out of the cellophane that encased the tobacco package, run a portion of fine cut onto a paper and begin rolling it. I could never count the times I had watched Taurus rolling cigarettes in the sun porch, and for all that happened to him since he went senile, his hacking and spitting, his mindless mumbling, his wandering away and getting lost, this action was as confident as ever. Sticking the cigarette between his lips, his hands began searching his suit coat pockets for a match. I suppose I was expected to warn Mrs. MacLeod about what was going on, but I was on Taurus's side. I willed him to find a match, my thoughts following his hands from pocket to pocket until he drew a sulphur-tipped wooden stick from a pocket in his pants and began then fumbling for his fly, exposing the zipper and striking the match, raising it to his mouth with cupped hands.

In the unscented air of the church, the smell of the match and, a moment later, the smell of cigarette smoke, seemed to find their way everywhere at once. Mrs. MacLeod was the first to know, almost without looking toward her husband to confirm her fears, her embarrassment. Taurus was puffing on the cigarette, leaving it dangling from his mouth, inhaling and exhaling without removing it. I expected him at any moment to break into a story.

Mrs. MacLeod, ashamed of having not noticed what her husband was up to, reached over and pulled the cigarette from Taurus's mouth, the paper tearing some skin from the lip, leaving a raw and bloody spot. She crushed it out in her hand, crumbling the tobacco into powder that she let fall quietly to the floor, but she also began rubbing her hand on her red coat, the black ash smudging it. There were tears in her eyes, and they weren't from the cigarette burn she was trying to rub away.

Taurus just reached back into his pocket as if he had forgotten already what had happened and Mrs. MacLeod snatched the tobacco away. Taurus just kept on searching himself, wondering where he put his tobacco.

By now, the attention of everyone in the church had been drawn by the cigarette smoke to the pew where Taurus and Mrs. MacLeod were sitting, and everybody was trying not to look, or pretending not to look, and the minister went on trying to send Bartholomew to Heaven, but only Calum, and maybe Mrs. Fraser, seemed to be hearing his words.

Johnny Neil Kennedy got up from his seat in the pew across from Taurus and Mrs. MacLeod and came over to them, pulling a plug of Old Chum from his suit coat pocket. He took out his pocket knife and cut a hefty chew of tobacco and passed it to Taurus, who stopped searching for his Player's and began chomping on the plug of tobacco instead. The mourners turned their attention back to Bartholomew's departure from our midst, rising to sing another hymn, but Taurus still had my interest.

Mrs. MacLeod was so pleased with Johnny Neil's gesture of a piece of chewing tobacco that neither of them nor anyone else, me included, thought about the fact that you should always have a spittoon or a cup or an open window handy whenever anyone is chewing tobacco. It came to me slowly as I watched him chew, his cheeks swelling with juice. Taurus never chewed tobacco, when he could smoke a cigarette instead, but every coal miner who smoked chewed tobacco underground where no matches or smoking was permitted. Taurus seemed to remember that, or maybe he thought that, because of the chewing tobacco he was underground again and as his cheeks began to grow ever larger his rheumy eyes sought out a place to squirt his tobacco juice, settling on the large purse on the pew in front of him belonging to a woman who stood singing with the others the next hymn in the service. Taurus gripped the back of the pew in front of him and calmly streamed a dark quantity of juice into the open purse.

Reverend Smith then turned to words of praise for Bartholomew, who, he said, had been leaning on the radiator of his store from the day Shean was born. Shean has a history, the minister said, and a large part of it lay in that coffin. Bartholomew had taken with him the generations of people he had known, the stories he had heard and passed along, his way of conducting business (if you made your whole transaction in Gaelic he gave ten per cent off). There are still a few memories around that reach back as far as Bartholomew, he told the mourners, that go back to the Beginning of Time in Shean, but they are becoming fewer and fewer, these founders and fathers of the place we call home. Then he prayed for Bartholomew's salvation, and the choir, in the singing of its hymns, also sang "An Stòr aig Pàrlan," Taurus's song about the friendship found in Bartholomew's store. I knew then that while Mrs. Fraser hadn't consulted Calum about any of the funeral plans, Calum had spoken to the minister about Bartholomew's wishes, this one at least. Taurus coughed and hacked all through his words.

Outside, we stood on the steps and watched the pallbearers place Bartholomew in the back of his own panel truck for the drive to the Protestant graveyard three miles outside of town, beside a small church that had been built before the coal mines were opened or the town was founded. Duncan was parked across the street, and when the parade of mourners began to move, Calum and I walked over to the Oldsmobile and got in, Calum in the front beside Duncan, me in the back telling Duncan about Taurus, and the two of us laughing at the thought of that woman looking for something in her purse later on.

At the graveyard the pallbearers carried Bartholomew over a crust of ankle-deep snow to the grave, where the minister said more words about Bartholomew, prayed for his soul, and sprinkled frozen mud over the lowered coffin. People began leaving, and when the cemetery was empty except for the three of us, Duncan and I got the shovels out of the trunk of the Oldsmobile. Walking back we saw Calum standing beside the open grave letting a hand-ful of loose earth that he had warmed and crumbled in his hand fall like rain onto Bartholomew's coffin. When we got there Calum turned and walked away from us and the grave, moving among other snow-capped headstones, reading names, while we shoveled a mound of mud over Bartholomew, patting it smooth with the backs of our shovels. Finished, ourselves as frozen as the ground, we walked back to the car, Duncan letting it idle to warm us up while we watched Calum make his way back to Bartholomew's grave and stand there.

Duncan played with the radio, looking for music to keep us company in the car, and I watched Calum at the graveside, real-izing for the first time since the wake just how dead Bartholomew was. It seemed almost wrong to be watching Calum say goodbye to all those years of friendship that Taurus had told me about, their lives forged together by their language and their religion and the similarity of their marriages. But I also knew it wouldn't have been possible for me to intrude on this moment, not even if I was standing beside Calum and he was speaking aloud the thoughts that must have been going through his head. Calum's final farewell must surely be in the Gaelic.

Nor had I considered before that Bartholomew was lost to me now, as well. All through the stroke and wake I thought of Bartholomew's death as Calum's loss, but he had been there all my remembered life, never chatty the way Taurus was, but always singling me out for an acknowledging nod when I walked past his store with my friends or brought him his tea in the sun porch. That memory brought to me an image of Calum's sadness when he would open the sun porch the following spring with no friend to speak with in the language he loved, no friend to bring him the daily paper from May until October, sit beside him, reading and trading sections, sometimes never saying a word to each other, waiting for me to bring their tea from the kitchen.

I had a sense, watching Calum standing beside the grave, that this was a grave he would probably never visit again, because he would need to ask someone to drive him out here and to wait for him while he stood alone, as he stood now, and Calum would never do that. So he lingered in the cold, eyes and nose running, knowing that this was goodbye in a way that was immeasurably hard to accept.

I realized, too, I was going to miss Bartholomew.

31

Duncan was dead wrong about how much money I was going to make selling my paintings. After Mrs. Fraser paid me for hers at Christmas, I started making all kinds of paintings, fruits and flowers, sunsets and landscapes. Duncan talked to Nicole who got her job back after New Year's, just as she predicted, and Nicole talked to Tony the Turk about letting me hang my paintings in his restaurant. She told him it was a way to decorate the restaurant for free, but it wasn't until Duncan suggested Tony get ten percent of every sale that he became an eager sponsor of the arts. I worked all through the Christmas vacation and January to get ten paintings for Tony's restaurant where, just like new calendars, they attracted a lot of early attention. Then everybody stopped noticing them except for the occasional person travelling through Shean.

One customer, when he was placing his order at The Turk's, told Nicole that the frames on my paintings were worth more than the paintings. It was a compliment for Calum, I guess, but I was happy to hear Nicole let the traveller's dinner sit on the serving window until the gravy on his french fries turned to a cold scum.

"You know what the difference is between you and your ... whachamacallit ... your Masters, Smelt?" Duncan asked. We were sitting in a booth where I was trying to rub a greasy film off the frame of one of my paintings with a napkin, wondering what the air in The Turk's was doing to the paintings themselves which had been hanging there since January. It was now May, and not a single sale. "Bare naked women, that's what. You look at those old pictures, nothing but tits, even in the Bible. No wonder they sold so many of them. They may have called them goddesses or saints or the Mother of God, but who do you suppose was doing the posing? Not the Blessed Virgin Mary! Bare naked women, that's who, and that's what those dirty old priests and rich people were buying. Bare naked women. That's where the money was. See, they had no cameras."

It wasn't painting I wanted to talk to Duncan about, though. It was a lot worse than that.

After Bartholomew's funeral, Calum moved into the study where he lay asleep with one of his books open across his chest or staring at the ceiling. He didn't start any of the projects that occupied him most winters, making furniture or fixing things around the house. He didn't seem to care that Piper strolled in and out of the study, walked across his desk, slept at the foot of the couch even while Calum was lying on it. He came out to eat and to make his share of the meals, but mostly he just lay there reading or sleeping and going for a walk to the post office every evening. Without either of us saying anything, we had traded jobs.

When Bartholomew's store opened two days after the funeral with Sarah Campbell, who had worked for Bartholomew for about a thousand years, now managing it for Mrs. Fraser, Calum said to me at lunchtime, "Go get the paper," which I did. That evening after supper he took the post office key off the hook in the hall and went for the mail, and that's how our new routine remained.

Calum read his paper and his mail and his Gaelic books in the study, and he never went back to Bartholomew's store. About the only visitor he had was Mary Scotland who went into the study to say hello whenever she came to the house, which was just about every day. The rest of the time, the silence in the house was tinged with Calum's brooding, and I began playing the radio a lot more, and louder.

In early May, though, when the weather broke, Calum went out to the workshop, picked up his pitch fork and began turning earth for his garden. One noon in mid-May, I picked up Calum's newspaper on my way home from school and found him waiting for it in the sun porch. He had taken the Christmas lights down and lined the ledge with plants and lay there thinking or daydreaming and twiddling his thumbs. I guess I hadn't expected him to open it again with no Bartholomew or Taurus to keep him company, but finding him there hissing at Piper who was sleeping in a patch of sunlight on the sill seemed to bring life back to normal in our house. I brought him his tea and my own along with it, sitting there with him, leafing through the sports pages.

By late May, just after the long weekend when Calum and I were having supper, chicken soup and bannock that Mrs. MacFarlane made for us so she could be sure Calum and I were getting something healthy to eat, Calum asked me if "that fellow" could have the car whenever he wanted. I said yes.

"Would he take us up to the farm?" Calum asked.

My spoon froze halfway between my bowl and my mouth. With Bartholomew gone along with his panel truck, which Mrs. Fraser sold, I thought Calum would forget about Taurus's farm. I had managed to hide that secret from Duncan for two years, and now Calum wanted me to make him part of it. My mind scrambled around for an alternative, only to realize that besides Duncan there was no one we knew who had a car who would take us there. There were people in Shean we could ask once maybe, but not every week or whenever Calum wanted to go.

"Probably," I answered, carrying the spoon to my mouth.

"Would you speak to him?"

So that's what I was doing in the booth at The Turk's that day, rubbing a film of grease from the frame on one of my paintings while I tried to figure out how to tell Duncan about Taurus's poem.

"Duncan, if I tell you something, will you promise not to laugh?"

"If it's not funny I won't," Duncan said, cocking his head with interest while I stumbled around for words.

"Mary Scotland's not knocked up, is she?" he asked, growing tired of waiting for me to get to the point, and that idea proved more frightening than telling him about Calum's trees, so to nip his suspicion in the bud before it became a rumour growing like the white poplars all over Shean I plunged right into the story.

"You know where Taurus's farm is, the place you and Nicole and Mary and I went that night up in the highlands, well, there's something I have to tell you about what's been going on up there."

Duncan's interest grew.

"Calum is planting trees in the pasture there, well, they're not trees exactly, they're letters. You see, in the Gaelic every letter in the alphabet is called after a tree, like A is an elm and B is a birch and C is a hazel tree, but there are only eighteen letters in the Gaelic alphabet, and Taurus wrote this poem and then Calum and Bartholomew started planting it. Well, Taurus did too that first summer, but then he went senile and Bartholomew and Calum kept on, taking me along to do the digging, and sometimes we would stop on our way to the farm to find saplings that we could plant, and we put these stakes all over the field that Calum made and marked, and when all the trees are planted then Taurus's poem will be...."

"Wait! Wait!" Duncan said, "Talk to me like I'm stupid."

"Oh, that'll be easy," I answered, backing up and beginning from the beginning, starting with the afternoon in the sun porch when Calum told Taurus about the Gaelic alphabet, then about Taurus bringing Calum the idea about planting a poem, then the poem itself which I could now quote without understanding, like making the Latin sounds when I was on the altar, and then telling him about the day all of us went in Bartholomew's panel truck to the farm and put in the first tree, and everything that happened since that time.

"No wonder you never told anybody. That's the craziest thing I ever heard." Duncan was laughing. "Nicole's father has this rule where nobody is allowed to speak Gaelic during a card game to keep people from cheating. Maybe there should be a rule where nobody is allowed to speak Gaelic to keep people from going senile. Look at yourself! Here you are out running around the woods with a shovel planting Gaelic poems and you don't even speak

Gaelic. You only know people who do. Christ, Smelt, how do you get into these things anyway? Never mind, I know. Calum. I bet you're going to be the same way when you're old, so you better die young, buddy. So this famous poem is up in Taurus's field, is it?"

"Yes," I replied. "Part of it. Calum still wants to finish it."

"And you have to help him," Duncan added.

"Well, yes, but he wants to know if you'll help him, too."

"Me!" Duncan said. "Me planting trees with old Calum? Why would I do that and why would he want me? He doesn't even like me."

"The Oldsmobile," I answered and the tumblers all clicked into place for Duncan. "We don't have a car," I said, explaining the obvious. "Calum would buy the gas," I added, trying to fill in Duncan's lingering silence, and I realized I had gone about asking him in the wrong way. I should have asked him in front of Mrs. MacFarlane when we were in her kitchen. She would have made him go.

"When?" Duncan asked.

"We used to go with Bartholomew every Saturday," I replied, explaining our routine.

"And you never said a word about it," Duncan noted.

"Well, I thought it was kind of dumb at first, and then I kind of began to like it and...," I shrugged the rest of my explanation away.

"And you thought I would shit all over it," Duncan said, completing my sentence. "Well, shit's good for making things grow, you know, even trees. Would you be coming with us all the time?" I told him I would be. "What exactly do we have to do?" I explained to Duncan that my part of the job was to find saplings that we could move to Taurus's farm. There were lots of hardwoods on the farm, and we found a lot of our Gaelic letters there, but not all of them. Sometimes we drove to crown lands in the highlands and walked through the hardwoods there, Calum and Bartholomew pointing out what we needed, me digging it up and carrying it back to the panel truck, then we would take it back to the farm and plant it where there was a marker for that kind of tree.

"I can't tell an apple tree from a spruce tree," Duncan said.

"You don't have to. I couldn't either, at first, but now I'm pretty good at reading the different kinds of leaves. You don't even have to dig if you don't want, if you'll just take us up there. Will you?"

"I can't go on race days or when I have to work out the horses," Duncan said. "And I can't believe I'm going to be doing this!"

With *The Smelt Fishermen* finished, Mother Saint Margaret had me start another composition after Christmas. She was becoming pretty picky about the way the sketches I showed her were structured. It had been like that with *The Smelt Fishermen*, getting me to shift and change people around on the page. When she asked me to try putting Angus John Rory further back than the others and get him to stand at the end of the line of fishermen instead of in the middle, I told her that wasn't where he was standing when I fell in the river. She asked me to try it anyway, and while the picture wasn't real any more, it looked a lot better with him standing at the end of the line, solid as the anchor in a tug o' war, framing the edge of the painting. With my new painting, she coaxed me to find a balanced composition, but she didn't tell me what to do as much as she did with *The Smelt Fishermen* unless I was really screwing it up.

Even though she had me working on a big canvas, Mother Saint Margaret didn't let up on my exercises, still making me draw and paint for a part of every day I went to the art building, and she still had me reading about artists and talking about what I had read. If she knew about my paintings hanging in The Turk's she didn't let on.

I knew what my new painting was going to be. At Christmas, Catherine Cameron, Mary Scotland's oldest sister, received her diamond from John Ian MacDonald who drove a pulp truck hauling softwood to the new paper mill at the Strait of Canso. There were four diamonds given out in Shean that Christmas, with one of the weddings held in February, which told everybody what they wanted to know; and one in May, which was pretty suspicious; and two for the summer, which meant there was no hurry. Catherine Cameron and John Ian MacDonald were getting married in late July, the weekend before Shean Days when everybody from the town who was working or living away would be home on their summer vacations, making it about the biggest wedding of the year.

On top of the fact that it was going to be a July wedding with an open invitation for the whole town to attend the reception, Catherine Cameron was also one of the best known step-dancers in all of western Cape Breton. She had been dancing at summer concerts ever since she was a little girl, the same ones where Taurus used to sing his Gaelic songs. At the square dances, Catherine was always in a set because good dancers sought each other out. While lots of people liked to square dance, not everybody had a clue what their feet should be doing, and Cape Breton fiddlers would rather play for a good dancer any day. With a popular dancer like Catherine Cameron getting married, there was a pretty good chance some of the best fiddlers on the island would turn up for the reception because, Mary said, Catherine was inviting them all.

Almost as soon as Catherine got the diamond and started planning for the wedding (she asked me to be an usher), Mary Scotland started thinking about what she was going to give them for a gift. I was going to have to come up with one, too, a cheap one that didn't look too cheap.

"Where will they live?" Calum asked Mary Scotland on Christmas night when she told him about her sister's diamond and her own worries about what to give them for a gift.

"There's an empty house in the Company Rows that John Ian's aunt and uncle used to live in before they moved away, and they're going to live there."

"Furnished?" Calum asked.

"No. They took everything with them when they moved to Boston, so they just left their junk behind."

"Then get this fellow to paint them a picture," Calum said, Mary answering, "Of course," as if it was the most natural thing in the world. "What can we paint for them?" she asked me, settling on what the gift would be, but not what the painting would be.

It took a while to come up with something Catherine might like. What John Ian might like was just a token afterthought. So while I had been painting pictures for The Turk's restaurant, I kept thinking about the wedding gift, and so did Mary. And it was Mary who came up with the solution. Catherine Cameron didn't like the idea of moving into the Company Rows with their streets of repeating architecture and where her view from the kitchen window was the ash-pile in the backyard of the house behind them and the view through the living room window was the front yard of the house across the street, a yard identical to the one in front of their own company house. They planned to be there only a little while, she told Mary, until they could build a house of their own.

What she was going to miss most was the view of the Shean Highlands that she had woken up to in her own bedroom every morning all her life. It seemed simple enough until Mother Saint Margaret looked at my sketches, listened to my reasoning, then grilled me on how I planned to execute the painting.

I had tried out a dozen different ideas before I came up with the idea of a painting of Catherine Cameron's bedroom window, the gentle mountains quartered by the cross sticks of the window through which she had looked upon the world every morning, and each of the four panes of glass would catch a different hardwood season. The painting would show the reddish, budding fuss of spring, the lush green of summer, the blazing beauty of autumn, and the stripped and stark white mountains of winter, while amid these changing seasons the enduring forest of evergreens would assert its permanent presence. The canvas measured the same size as Catherine's window, and we were going to ask Calum to frame it by recreating the window frame and sash inside her bedroom.

Mother Saint Margaret thought it was sentimental, but she also thought it was enough of a challenge to be worth taking. By the end of May, it was just about finished, which was when she wanted me out of the art building and at home studying for exams.

The first Saturday after I talked to Duncan, Calum began getting ready for our trip to Taurus's farm. He made a neat pile of the shovel and the pitch fork, a water bucket, shears, bags of fertilizer and other tree food, and we waited for Duncan who was supposed to pick us up at ten in the morning.

Calum sat in the sun porch, craning his neck toward every approaching car as his watch crawled toward eleven o'clock, and then toward noon. I kept busy everywhere but near him, because I knew Duncan was capable of not showing up at all without ever making excuses for himself, and I wasn't looking forward to Calum coming to that realization.

About the time I had decided he wasn't coming, the Oldsmobile pulled up in front of the front gate and Duncan got out. Calum came out of the sun porch and I came around the corner of the house, angry with Duncan but glad he had come at all. Calum had his own way of dealing with Duncan's tardiness, standing on the top step and slowly pulling his watch from his pocket, popping the cover and studying the face of it.

"I slept in," Duncan offered, but it looked more like he hadn't slept at all, which he hadn't, having been up all night with Nicole or playing cards with her father's friends. Duncan opened the trunk, and I began loading Calum's supplies into it. Calum opened the front passenger door and sat down waiting for us to finish.

"He can shove that watch up his arse," Duncan said, walking around to the driver's side while I opened the back door, wishing that Mary Scotland was with us, but her absence was both good news and bad news. Sally Campbell had hired her part-time at Bartholomew's store, which meant that she would be staying home for the summer instead of going to Boston, but it also meant she worked Saturdays which was why she wasn't with us. She was a smoother peacemaker than me, I thought, as Duncan pulled away from the house and the three of us set out for Taurus's farm.

"To really see the poem, I guess you have to be in an airplane or something," I explained as we drove up the highlands road. "It probably won't look like much from the ground since oak trees can grow to be a hundred feet and elders are really just bushes, not trees at all, and ivy is just a vine. But from up above, if you're looking down on it the way Taurus imagined it, then it's going to look great."

32

Everybody was working – Calum in his shop, Duncan at the racetrack, Mary Scotland at Bartholomew's store and Nicole at The Turk's – so I had a whole Saturday to study for provincial examinations, but the sun was hot and books made me drowsy. I should have been more scared than I was, considering that every grade eleven and twelve student in Nova Scotia was given a number and wrote exams anonymously. The exams were then sent to Halifax and marked by unknown teachers who didn't have any reason at all to give a guy that extra point or two he might need to get through chemistry.

On the other hand, the way Duncan saw it, provincial exams meant a teacher who didn't like you couldn't shave a point off your mark here and there to make sure you failed the exam. Of course, Duncan had more to worry about from teachers than most students, especially in chemistry.

In grade eleven, for the first time since we started school we had four teachers instead of just one: a teacher for English and French, one for history and social studies, one for algebra and geometry, and one for chemistry and physics. It was because of Mr. Steele, the chemistry and physics teacher, that Duncan was counting on provincial exams to get him through. He hadn't passed either subject all year, falling a few points short each time he was tested. There was a good reason for that, considering Duncan hardly ever opened a book at home. On the other hand, he listened hard and asked more questions than anyone else in the class, some of his questions being hard enough to make Mr. Steele turn red and tell Duncan he would have to look up the answer and get back to him. Duncan wasn't his favourite student.

What really put them against one another, though, was our chemistry laboratory. There was none. Instead, at the back of the classroom stood a tall cabinet with glass doors, and inside the cabinet were jars of chemicals and samples of rocks, test tubes, pestles and crucibles, and a Bunsen burner that wasn't hooked up to anything. Inside the chemistry book, though, were numerous laboratory tests students were supposed to use as experiments, writing down their procedures and observations. As far as we knew, every school in Nova Scotia except ours had a lab. All we had was Mr. Steele's word for what would happen if we were to mix some of the chemicals that were in his cabinet. If sulphur was to be used in the experiment, Mr. Steele would pass around an uncapped jar of sulphur for us to smell while he explained what would take place if the sulphur was added to another substance. If you smelled rotten eggs, he told us, then that's what sulphur under certain conditions would smell like. While he explained what we would observe during an experiment if we had a lab to observe it in, we had to write down what he told us about the procedures and observations, and draw our own conclusions. On the strength of these pretend "experiments" in chemistry and physics we would be tested and marked anonymously in a province-wide exam that assumed every student had actually performed the laboratory experiments.

While the rest of the class grumbled under its breath about the unfairness of not having a lab, Duncan raised the problem in the class in front of Mr. Steele every chance he got.

"You've made your point, Mr. MacFarlane!" Mr. Steele said the third or fourth time Duncan asked him what was the point of studying experiments if we didn't have a lab to experiment in. When a teacher starts using a student's last name he has been pushed to the edge of his temper.

"What's the point of me making my point if nobody's going to do anything about it?" Duncan asked.

"And just what do you think I should do about it, build a laboratory?"

"You and the other teachers could go on strike for a decent school to teach in, one with a lab," Duncan said.

Mr. Steele's face went from red to purple, and things never got any better between them for the rest of the year, with Duncan not passing a single quiz. So his only chance, he figured, was provincial exams.

Unable to make myself cram for chemistry's phantom experiments, I took the textbook along as a disguise when I went to the beach. Despite the heat of the day, the water in late June still hadn't fully recovered from the effects of being covered all winter by a thick carpet of polar ice. I plunged in, shivered like a wet dog, then sat in a sandy cove, opened the chemistry book, closed it after five hopeless minutes and walked the beach. Wavelets barely broke at the edge of the tide, and a few boats, each followed by its own flock of screaming and scavenging gulls, putted offshore, pulling traps, removing lobsters, re-baiting and re-setting the traps as the season wound down toward its end-of-June closure. All along the hot sand students sat in clusters, laughing and gossiping, while a few sat in the lonely discipline of actually studying.

At the fossil forest where we had met the three Marys a year earlier, I stopped. I had come back twice before, once within days of its discovery to draw the stone stumps. The second time was during the winter when the polar ice had drifted in, laden with seals whelping their young. I walked out among them, thinking I would get some good drawings, but all I got was fingers frozen around a pencil and angry, threatening mothers barking their annoyance. When I came off the ice, I was at the site of the fossils where the action of tides and ice had scraped away the sand, exposing a much larger section than had been revealed the summer before. I stopped to study it briefly with frozen hands cupped over frozen ears. In June, though, the large expanse of fossils was once again almost completely concealed by the tidal pileup of summer sand,

and it was there I took a seat among the small patch of exposed fossils as if I were taking a seat in a grove of shady trees.

Calum had suspended our trips to Taurus's farm before our exams began, but in the first couple of weeks of June we had been there a half dozen times. With Bartholomew, it had been every Saturday if it wasn't raining, but Calum was more anxious now, I guess, and Duncan and his car were available far more often than Bartholomew and his panel truck had been. Still, it was slow going because no matter how fast Duncan drove over those tortured, not yet graded roads trying to get a rise out of Calum, and no matter how quickly we searched the woods for saplings, in the end our quickness was governed by Calum's meticulous pace, his examination of the saplings we brought him, his critical foremanship as we dug holes to plant them in, his careful placing of the trees, his caution with the roots, his careful refilling of the hole, his measured efforts to enrich the soil around the little trees with fertilizers, the long soaking welcome he gave them as we brought him buckets of water to pour like a baptism around the freshly dug earth.

We also had to accommodate Calum's slow stroll through the pasture at the beginning of every arrival, his examination of the trees we had already planted, some having taken root and flourishing, others struggling hopefully, still others standing lifeless. These last ones he would pull, re-marking the spot with a stake, adding a new birch or mountain ash or whatever to our scavenger hunt in the wooded hills surrounding Taurus's farm.

Although Calum still snapped at Duncan the way he had for years, and although Duncan still mumbled under his breath his own opinions of Calum, Duncan did more than just drive us there. He knew the woods around Shean better than either Calum or myself, having hunted them with his father and his uncle and alone, and having driven up every side road he could find with the Oldsmobile, looking for safe places where he and Nicole could be alone. Taurus's farm wasn't the only abandoned place he had explored, so he was able to take us places to search for trees that were not abundant or available in the highlands themselves.

Since Duncan couldn't stand not knowing the answer to the questions that occurred to him, he began quizzing Calum the way he questioned our teachers. The biggest difference was that Calum gave him answers, sometimes long answers, about the Gaelic alphabet and the meaning of the trees. It wasn't long before Duncan knew more than me, and he was even offering to take Calum up there whenever he was free, not just waiting for Calum to ask. Sometimes Nicole came with us and sometimes Mary Scotland when they weren't working; but none of us, even though we never said anything about keeping Taurus's poem a secret, none of us ever said a word about it to anyone else. We just went there with Calum, helped plant his trees, and after that first couple of weeks getting in the car to come home, we would just stand for a moment, looking out at the pasture, seeing it slowly fill with words none but Calum understood.

Sitting among the fossils, the blank pages of my chemistry scribbler became a sketch pad as I tried to imagine with my pencil the full forest they must have been a million years ago or whenever. The fossils would have been part of a forest that grew along this shore before it was a shore, a forest that grew out into the Gulf before it was a gulf, a forest that grew over the slag heaps and the houses, grew higher than the church steeples, and it made me think of our own forest, Calum's and Bartholomew's and Taurus's, and mine, too, and Duncan's now, and Mary Scotland's and Nicole's, and I saw it in my mind standing for a million years, turning to stone along the way, the trees forming themselves into natural cairns marking the fact of our having been here, their message as impenetrable to the future as the fossils I sat among, wondering if they, too, had once been someone's song.

Duncan told me that Peter Shawl, a horseman from up the mainland, was looking for somebody to look after four horses he brought to the Shean track for the summer, mostly to look after the morning feedings, shovel manure and bandage legs. Two of the horses, Epsom Salts and Jerry Dale, were workbenches whose legs needed lots of attention, and two were sound. Duncan said they were sound because they were so slow they couldn't injure themselves. That was true of Jollity Roger, I guess, but Diamond Skies was sound and fast enough to earn his own oats. It was a typical Shean stable, three of the horses couldn't or wouldn't be able to race anywhere else because they were too slow or too temperamental. I went to see Peter Shawl who was setting up to live in his tack stall for the summer. He offered me ten bucks a week to do pretty much what Duncan described, along with working through the Sunday afternoon and Wednesday night races. He would throw in a few hot tips, too, he said, but I knew I wouldn't be risking much of my wages on his horses.

The best thing about the job with Shawl was that it brought me back to drawing horses again, even selling a few, and for the first time I began painting them, pictures of five or six horses at the finish line, one of a dead heat. I brought them to the track to show them around, and the track manager asked if he could hang them in the parimutuel for the summer. I thought it would be a good place, telling him if anybody was interested in buying them he should send them to me. Actually, I thought the track should buy them if they wanted to hang them, but without Mary Scotland or Duncan nearby to negotiate for me, I was tongue-tied. They hung there all summer.

Except for the track and Taurus's farm, I wasn't seeing much of Duncan that summer because he was spending a lot of his nights playing cards at Nicole's father's house and drinking a lot of those nights, not to mention selling a few bottles out of the trunk of his car at the dances. He could go two or three days without sleep sometimes, playing cards until feeding time at the track, go home to eat, go to the beach, back to the track on race nights, then take Nicole to a dance or go back to playing cards.

A couple of times when I dropped by his house to see if he was home, I could tell Mrs. MacFarlane was worried about him. She never said a lot, never digging for betrayals from me or stuff like that. She knew Duncan, though, and unlike so many of our teachers, she knew there wasn't a lot she could do to change him, but that didn't stop the worrying. I think she was sorry Mr. Mac-Farlane had ever left the Oldsmobile home with Duncan. When a peaceful night's silence in Shean was broken by the sound of someone peeling rubber up on Main Street, everyone had a pretty good idea whose car it was.

The biggest reason I wasn't travelling much with Duncan, though, was Calum, who seemed to be finding the summer days long, and I found myself wanting to be around as much as possible, as if my being there would keep anything from happening to him. His mornings were spent in his gardens, and he began claiming more of the lawn for flower beds just to keep himself busy. I learned quickly that Peter Shawl hired me because he was a boozer who couldn't always be sure of crawling out of the sack early enough to feed his horses. I was his guarantee they would be looked after through his worst hangovers, so I was always home at noon, bringing the newspaper with me, and then just hanging around, bringing my own tea into the sun porch along with Calum's, sitting there sketching or reading while he read his paper and napped for an hour before going into the workshop to keep himself busy with projects like planing and varnishing frames for my paintings.

Mary Scotland was busy with her job and her sister's wedding plans, so it was mostly in the evenings we saw each other, and even though Calum didn't know it, he was sharing the sun porch with us – Calum using it through the day, Mary and I through the night, curling up cozy or growing hot with summer love.

One day while we were in the sun porch, Calum lying on the couch working out the crossword puzzle with his carpenter's pencil, me watching the flowers knocked around by a pelting rain, Duncan's Oldsmobile pulled up in front of the house.

"What happened to you?" Calum asked when Duncan ran into the sun porch, his face freckled with mud except for a clean oval around his eyes where the goggles had been. He told Calum that he had been splattered jogging John Alex's horses on a muddy track.

"I guess we're not going up to the farm today, huh," Duncan said, opening his track jacket and wiping the mud from his face with the bottom of the white T-shirt he untucked from his belt.

"Those trees need this rain more than they need to see us," Calum said, but that didn't stop him from drawing his watch from his pocket by its chain and checking the time. Duncan was supposed to have come for us three hours earlier, but it had been raining then, too. Calum just had to make his point which Duncan, sitting on the car seat beside me, ignored.

"Do you think we're going to finish it this summer?" Duncan asked Calum who lowered his paper and looked thoughtfully through the window, weighing his answer.

"It's possible," he said, "but it's not something to think about finishing as much as doing well." Calum brought himself upright, lowering his feet to the floor. "It takes nothing to plant a few hundred trees and hope they take root, but not all of them will. For our purposes, it's important every tree thrive. If they don't, then the poem will look like a typewriter with a missing key. If this summer gets away from us, we'll still have next summer. One well-planted tree at a time."

"Like wedge boards?" Duncan said, his comparison surprising Calum who could probably remember Duncan's derision the day we were building the shack.

"Like wedge boards," he replied. "Like anything meant to last."

33

C alum!"

There was no answer and no one in the sun porch. I called his name through the house and out the back door to the workshop which had a padlock through the hasp.

"Maybe we better look upstairs," Mary Scotland said when I returned to the kitchen. "It might be he's just lying down."

"Maybe," I answered, having never known Calum to go upstairs to lie down during the day, not with a couch in his study and one in the sun porch. Walking down the hall and starting up the stairs Mary stayed one step behind me, following my slow-as-Calum ascent to his bedroom. When Bartholomew took his stroke, he had just crumpled to the floor of his store, and my grandmother had dropped dead suddenly in her kitchen but after being sick with a bad heart for a long time, and I tried not to think of what might have happened to Calum while Mary and I were at the beach.

He had been fine when we left, sitting in the sun porch with his noon tea and newspaper, reading about the rest of the world. He wasn't there or anywhere in the yard when we got back in the late afternoon, and reaching the upstairs hall I saw Calum's door ajar, but it revealed little. I pushed it, and the door swung away with a slow, heart-stopping groan of hinges, a noise Calum wouldn't be aware of because he always removed his hearing aid on his way upstairs to bed, followed by his upper and lower teeth.

The bed was empty and made; there was no sign that he had laid on it after he got up that morning. I let my eyes fall to the floor, looking for the wine coat sweater, the overalls, the shoes that would define my grandfather's form. There was nothing.

"The bathroom," I whispered as if we were in church.

Mary waited while I drew a deep breath and left Calum's doorway and moved toward the bathroom, recalling his confident straight razor strokes every morning, made suddenly lethal by an uncontrollable tremble of an old man's liver-spotted hand, imagining a stroke in the bathtub, a drowning, or being pitched off the toilet bowl by the crushing pain of a heart attack. Mary grabbed my arm in a tight two-fisted grip. Holding my breath, I looked through the open door. There was no bloodied Calum on the bathroom floor, no drowned Calum in the bathtub, and no Calum with his pants indignantly down, pitched headfirst off the toilet bowl. Relief welled through us.

"I think I need to go in here," Mary said, closing the door on me. I walked toward my own room, relieved but still troubled by Calum's absence. Downstairs, I went back out in the yard, checked among the high raspberry bushes, and even knelt to poke my head inside the spider-webbed shack we hadn't visited all summer.

"Is he in there?" Mary asked, startling me so that I banged my head on the top of the low door and withdrew, rubbing the bruise.

"It doesn't make sense. Calum doesn't go anywhere except to the post office, and the mail isn't even in yet. He doesn't go to Bartholomew's store anymore or get the groceries," I said. "He's not like Taurus, wandering away all the time so that you can begin to look for him anywhere. Calum doesn't go anywhere, so I don't know where to begin looking."

I phoned Mrs. MacFarlane and Mrs. Fraser, but neither of them had seen Calum.

"Maybe he went to the graveyard," Mrs. MacFarlane said, and Mrs. Fraser said the same thing. It gave us a place to look.

Before we reached the cemetery gate we could see Calum wasn't there, unless he was crouching behind a headstone waiting to jump out and scare us, which I doubted, but we went in anyway, visiting our family plot, with Belle in the middle and my mother and Aunt Evelyn resting on either side of her. The family plot wouldn't get any bigger, not with Calum going out to the Protestant graveyard someday. His only presence in this one would be on my grandmother's stone, Loving wife of Calum Gillies. I was glad to see that Aunt Evelyn was resting peacefully, retelling the story of her funeral to Mary Scotland while I examined her grave, which hadn't caved in, and she hadn't floated to the surface despite the trouble we had getting her in the ground on the stormy day of her funeral. She was safe.

"The Gillies women seemed doomed to rest in peace alone," Mary noted, reading the memorial stone that lay at the foot of my mother's grave, a grey military stone with my father's serial number on it and the date that he had been killed in Europe where he was buried. "I'm not sure I want to be one."

"Be one what?"

"A Gillies. I'm not sure I'd want to marry somebody who's going to get himself buried somewhere else," she said, filling her words with enough tease to say she was kidding.

"You found out our secret. The Gillies men hand it down generation to generation, how to get yourself killed away or converted to a religion that makes sure you don't have to lie beside the same woman forever," I replied. "So does this mean you were thinking of marrying me before you found out that we wouldn't be resting in peace together?"

"We'll talk about it in ten years' time if we're still going together," she said.

Whew! I thought. "Okay," I said.

Wandering among all my other relatives, I had almost forgotten about Calum, but when old people go missing you don't completely forget about them, so I said a silent prayer, or made a quiet plea to my relatives assembled there that I would find Calum safe and sound.

"Maybe he came home while we were gone," Mary said, reading my thoughts. "Why don't we go back."

Going home worried me because I didn't know what I'd do if he wasn't there, but he was. They were sitting in the sun porch,

Calum with a cup of tea, Duncan, who hated tea, with a glass of milk and a plate of his mother's cookies he found in the pantry. Duncan had a smile on his face that was just begging me to ask him what the hell's going on. I held out for about thirty seconds.

"What the hell's going on?"

Calum got up, carrying his cup, and walked past Mary and me with a nod that obviously hadn't given a moment's thought to being "lost" and worried about. "Makes me feel like a parent," I said as he went inside, then asked again, "So what the hell's going on?"

Duncan made a big thing of chewing on the cookie in his mouth, using the time to find the most dramatic way to say, "Calum and I went planting trees. I was down at my grandmother's this morning, and I dug up three oak saplings about this high. I was telling my grandmother about the Gaelic alphabet. Not the poem, though, just the alphabet. She didn't know that, about the trees, I mean, and she speaks Gaelic as good as Calum does, but what she did know was that the oak used to be considered a sort of holy tree. I thought that was really important, and I thought Taurus's poem should have some trees from my grandmother's farm, so I asked her if I could go out in the woods back of her place and dig some up for Calum, and she let me. You weren't here so I showed them to Calum, and he was ready to go plant them right away. So I got the gear out of the shop and away we went.

"You know, the old frigger knows a lot. You have to give him that. When I told him about what my grandmother said about the "D," the oak tree, and how it used to be a holy tree, he told me that long ago before Christianity, the Druids, these pagan priests or something in Scotland and Ireland, used to worship oak trees. They even made bread out of acorns and ate it like squirrels. Anyway, we drove up to Taurus's and here didn't some son of a bitch go and tear up all the stakes and throw them all over hell's creation. That really pissed me off. Anyway, I gathered them up, and Calum set them back where they belong, and then we planted the oak trees.

"Then old Calum says, 'Let's take a walk in there,' meaning the woods, and stupid me, I let him get ahead of me when we got to the path, so I wound up having to follow him. I'm telling you, Smelt, a telephone pole moves faster. If he was a horse, he'd be somebody's mink coat right now, but following him slowed me down so I began to look around, and, boy, I couldn't get over all the trees I know by name now. When you're hunting, eh, you're looking between the trees, not at them, looking for something to shoot.

"Anyway, while we're walking through there Calum stops and steps off the path to this little ash and examines it, and then he takes out his polka-dot handkerchief and ties it around the sapling, saying that it was too late to dig it up now but told me to look for that tree the next time we're there and bring his handkerchief back to him. I hope he wasn't using it. Think if Farter asked us to pick up his snot rag! That little ash made me think, though, and I told Calum when the trees we planted start growing they're going to start having little trees of their own, and in no time Taurus's field is going to be just as dense as the woods we were in. Between saplings and suckers and acorns – and, hell, we even planted some white poplar, the 'E,' remember? The place is going to be a jungle. Calum just nods like he knows this already.

"Anyway, it's an awful lot of work to waste, so I said next summer you and I could go up to the farm and clear around the trees until they get a good grip on growing up. That gave me another idea. In a couple of years when the trees are a little higher, maybe Mrs. MacLeod could make some money out of them. Christ knows they need it, with Taurus gone senile and all. Maybe she could put up some posters in town and hire somebody to keep the field clear and collect money from tourists who want to walk right through the middle of a Gaelic poem. Maybe she could even sell sandwiches and tea out of the house."

"Maybe she could rent out the bedrooms upstairs," I said, but Duncan didn't bat an eye, just included it in his plan.

"Yeah, she could. They're good bedrooms. The roof doesn't leak or anything. She could fix the house up. Maybe even put in a campground. Anyway, I said to Calum we could call it the Taurus MacLeod Memorial Park, and do you know what the old bastard says to me? 'It would be polite to wait until Taurus dies before you call it that.' That made me laugh. Once I got it, that is. Memorials are for dead people, you see, but it was just the way he said 'It would be polite....' You'd never figure Calum to have a sense of humour like that. I'll have to listen harder. Sometimes dry jokes can go right past you if you're not listening. But I think he thought it was a good idea. So what were you up to today?"

"We went looking for Calum's body," I answered as Duncan, standing to leave for the track, drained his glass.

Calum made enough supper for the three of us, and it was while we were eating that Mary Scotland asked him about Duncan's idea for a park. "He's an ambitious boy," Calum said, but when Mary asked him again if it could be done, "That's for some other generation to decide," was all Calum said, so she asked him again. I was getting uncomfortable with the way Mary kept asking Calum the same thing, afraid he was going to snap at her, make the Gaelic sound of his, but Calum just put down his fork and said that yes, it could be done, but it would require a commitment from somebody since it wouldn't be him and he didn't expect it to be us. He didn't spend a lot of time worrying about it, he told Mary.

Mary asked him what it would take to turn our work into a park, and Calum said it would take Taurus's family, but they never had any children who lived, so that meant Mrs. MacLeod would have to make a promise not to sell the land, or maybe turn it over to a society that would become responsible for looking after it forever.

"What's a society?" Mary asked him.

"It's a group of people who have the same ideas and form a legal organization. That way, they can raise money and give receipts and...."

"Could we organize one here?"

"Possibly," Calum said, but he was hesitant. "Shean's not a great place to form a society right now because the town is dying for want of work and for want of any real interest in it. There are Highland societies in Nova Scotia that might be interested."

I just about fell off my chair. Calum and Bartholomew, and even Taurus, who never seemed to dislike anything, despised Highland societies, making fun of their Queen Victoria tartans and two words of Gaelic and their Saint Andrew's Day balls, and here was Calum saying that maybe a Highland society could turn Taurus's poem into a park. Calum seemed to notice my shock, so I rubbed my chin, thinking maybe my supper was dribbling out of my open mouth.

"Highland societies have been here for a long time," he said, this time to me, remembering, I suppose, how often I had been in the sun porch when they were making their remarks, Taurus translating. "No matter what someone might think of them, they have the organization and the means to take on something like this. It would appeal to their sense of Highland romance."

"Why don't we do it then," I asked. "Why don't we ask the Highland societies, or one of them anyway, to look after the poem?"

"There are two reasons why we shouldn't do that at the moment," Calum said. "First, there's the planting to complete, and second, there's Mrs. MacLeod to consider. When we finish the former, I'll speak with her. If she agrees, I'll write some letters."

34

Friend of the bride? Friend of the groom?" I asked as I met the wedding guests at the door of the church, ushering them to pews on the left or right according to family or friendship affiliations.

"Friend of the priest," Duncan replied, giving my suit a double-take. He wasn't the first person to do so, but he was the first to remark on it. "When did you wear that last, your baptism?" I hadn't worn the suit since Aunt Esther's wake, and hadn't tried it on until the morning of the wedding to discover that there wasn't quite enough of it to cover my ankles and wrists. Taking Nicole's arm I guided both of them to a pew near the back of the quickly filling church.

When I returned to my post by the pillar near the main door the bridal party was arriving. The groom and best man were already at the front of the church, fidgeting and pawing the floor like a couple of horses in their stalls on race day. They just wanted this to be over with, which, I guess, is the big difference between brides and grooms. While her husband-to-be waited anxiously, Catherine Cameron and her bridesmaids were preparing their entrance. It wasn't what I expected, although Mary Scotland had told me that her sister designed her own wedding gown and it was going to be different, "because she wants to be able to dance at her own wedding, not sit there like Queen Elizabeth listening to the music."

Instead of a billowing gown, long train, and a veil to hide her face, Catherine Cameron's white wedding dress was shaped around her, long and white and tight. It reached down to her feet and had slits in the sides up to her knees. In her piled-up hair she wore a narrow tiara with a half veil attached. It wasn't very traditional, but it was elegant. Still, I would have liked to be able to read what was on some people's minds when she walked down the aisle in it, flanked by her three bridesmaids, they too wearing no crinolines, just sleek blue dresses not quite as long or wedding-y as the bride's. Wedding-y enough, though – that once I saw Mary Scotland I would have married her right there if I had a suit that fit. Instead, trying to tug my sleeves down to my wrists, I was on the groom's side. Just get this over with. The more dressed-up people looked the more I felt like Ichabod Crane in my too-small suit, and I wasn't even tall or gangly.

By the time it was over, Catherine Cameron was Mrs. John Ian MacDonald, and with the priest's last blessing we left the church to go to the wedding dinner at the parish hall. Since I was part of the wedding party and Mary's escort, I had to leave my suit on through all the clinking of glasses with spoons calling for bride-and-groom kisses, all the toasts and compliments, and all the opening of the gifts including my painting of the bride's bedroom window, which she found "interesting," while John Ian scratched his head and didn't say anything. When it was over, I practically ran home to change clothes for the reception that evening at the parish hall.

"We'll need to get you fitted for a new one of those," Calum said when I came in carrying my jacket over my arm, my necktie stuffed in a pocket, but there was nothing I could do to hide my white-stockinged ankles.

People arriving for the reception had to pause outside the parish hall just to bring each other's attention to the sun going down over the Gulf of St. Lawrence, blazing red in scattered billows of white cloud. Then they came into the hall, men in black slacks and white shirts open at the neck, their sleeves at a three-quarter turn, cigarette packs in the pockets, hair creamed back. Their wives and girlfriends wore fresh hairdos and their best summer clothes. Couples separated as soon as they came in, into two groups like it was a high school dance, the men talking in one corner and the women gathering near the coat rack. They couldn't very well gather in the kitchen with the CWL in there catering the reception, putting out plates of sandwiches and sweets for people to eat, along with bowls of punch safe enough for the children who pitched camp around the food table – the boys, like their fathers, in their white shirts and black slacks and cowlicked hair slicked back with water, the girls in their best summer dresses, bows on the back.

A couple of men would be talking and decide to go outside for a smoke, signalling a friend or two on their way. They would go out among the cars, gravitating toward the open-trunk ones where groups of men stood around swigging from bottles of hard liquor or gulping from cold bottles of beer while complaining about the heat, everybody keeping an eye out for the RCMP cruiser that would eventually prowl through the parking lot, causing trunks to slam shut like beaver tails slapping out danger signals. From inside the hall they could hear the tuning of a fiddle and watched as one car pulled up to the front door, and the Moran brothers, now known as The Rocking Horses, began carrying their guitars and amps and drums into the hall to set up for the round dances which they would play between square sets so there would be some music for everybody, the older people who loved the fiddle and the younger people who wanted something modern.

People were at the wedding from all over: Johnny Mac -Lellan home from Sudbury, Jerry MacKay and his wife and kids home from Scarborough, Jimmy the Flyer home from Detroit, and dozens more catching up with each other in the parking lot, while inside the hall women with large purses took turns going into the ladies' washroom in twos and threes, coming out giggling and laughing and glassy-eyed.

Duncan and Nicole came into the hall. Duncan, carrying a Coke bottle, gave me a wink and a smirk from across the floor that told me he was half-lit already, and Mrs. MacFarlane, sitting with Mr. MacFarlane, caught the look then caught Duncan's eye, beckoning him and Nicole to join them at their table. I guess she figured if he was sitting with her, he'd be less likely to drink a lot. Duncan and Nicole ambled over, and then Mary Scotland and her family came in, and I joined them. It took about another hour before Catherine and John Ian arrived at the reception, making everybody think that they probably started their honeymoon already. By the time they got there, bows were already flying across fiddles and a square set was underway but everything stopped, and everyone turned and started clapping for the bride and groom. Catherine was still in her wedding dress, looking like she just came from the church. John Ian still in his suit, didn't look so fresh.

Since the fiddler had stopped in the middle of the set to honour the bride and groom, the dancers broke up, and The Rocking Horses took the stage, starting off with "Rock Around The Clock" which got a bunch of people, including Mary and me, onto the floor, but the music had the older people shaking their heads. Pretty soon, Catherine had to go up to the stage and ask them to play "The Tennessee Waltz" and a few others like that because of the people who wanted to waltz, which caused most of the young people to walk off the floor, except for those glad for a chance to hold someone, the chance to make some romantic moves. For The Rocking Horses, the night was pretty confusing, trying to play to two audiences. Finally, Bobby Moran, the oldest brother and lead vocalist, told the people at the reception that the band would play slow, old music between the first couple of square sets and rock music when the old people got tired and went home to bed. Mrs. MacFarlane, who loved to waltz, didn't much care for being called an old person, and neither did a bunch of other people, so it put some in a foul mood. The next fiddler changed that, though.

True to predictions, there were quite a few fiddlers who showed up at the wedding of their favourite dancer, including Johnny Sandy Something from over near Iona, who could hardly ever name the tunes he played, and whenever anybody asked him what the name of that tune was, he'd answer, "It was something slow" or "It was something fast," but he played those somethings as sweet as anybody, and it was Johnny Sandy Something who played for the next set which Mary Scotland dragged me into. Nicole led Duncan onto the floor. Through the first figure, everything went smoothly, even though Catherine was my corner partner, which scared the daylights out of me, but I managed to avoid stepping all over her. As we waited for the second figure to begin, Duncan told Catherine that Calum taught me everything I knew about dancing. "So that's his secret," she replied with a smile, knowing Calum probably didn't even dance at his own wedding.

Anything else Duncan had to say about my dancing he let drop, catching my eye instead, drawing it toward the doorway which framed Archie Ack-Ack in a brand new black leather jacket, standing there looking around for somebody to talk to or a place to sit. Both of us then looked toward the table where Mr. and Mrs. Bruce were sitting, him sober, her swollen big as a house and both of them looking happy. We never learned what happened after the meeting at the glebe house, but over the next few months in school we could see a change in our last year's teacher that made Duncan and me feel good. It also made us feel less guilty because she was never anything but polite to the two of us, despite what had happened. Then late in the school year she began showing and the rumour went around town that she was going to have a baby. "They must be doing it again," Duncan concluded.

We went through the next two figures of the set just wanting the music to end, and when it did I followed Duncan down to the end of the hall where Ack-Ack was leaning against the wall, trying to look cool in that home-from-Toronto way some people have. He shifted to a tough stance when he noticed Duncan coming toward him, but he kept looking the other way, pretending not to notice. I saw his Adam's apple bob, though.

"How are things in Toronto?" Duncan asked, leaning against the wall beside him. I stood in front, making it look like a friendly get-together.

"Oh, hi, Duncan, Smelt. Good, everything's good in T-O," Ack-Ack answered.

"Working?" Duncan asked.

"Yup. A factory where we make cardboard boxes. I bet we make just about every box that comes into the stores around here. Boxes for cans of peas, cans of tomatoes, cans of everything. Potato chips, too. If you ever come to Toronto looking for work, I know the foreman pretty good; we have a beer together sometimes after work, and he says the way I work I'll be a lead hand in no time. I can put a word in for you. Two bucks an hour. I got a car, by the way, a good one. Want to see it?" Ack-Ack was talking fast like someone who knew that something was up but didn't quite know what, and hoped that if he talked fast enough and long enough Duncan would forget why he was standing there.

Looking from one to the other, I began to see what Ack-Ack saw, not my life-long buddy whom I knew like a brother, but someone who had grown tall and filled out in a way that had nothing to do with the fact that he was only seventeen. Duncan looked and acted a lot older than me, leaning there with a match stick in his mouth, spitting onto a bare part of the floor, a confidence about him that he seemed to have with everybody, not just with Ack-Ack. I understood then why Ack-Ack, who was older than Duncan and still a little bigger, was scared to death. Ack-Ack dealt with the world by intimidating it and didn't have a clue what to do with those people he couldn't intimidate. Duncan wasn't intimidated by Ack-Ack, not when he saved Piper from the clothesline, not when he fought him at The Turk's. It didn't matter that there was a time when Ack-Ack could have punched the shit out of Duncan. He could have beaten Duncan every day for a year and not intimidated him. The same was true for some of the teachers. They just didn't scare Duncan. It was what Nicole saw, too, I suppose, when she started going out with somebody four years younger than her, and it was probably what Mrs. MacFarlane understood for a long, long time, that Duncan had his own way of dealing with the world, and he wouldn't be bullied by it.

"Listen," Duncan said, squirting a stream of spit through the small gap in his front teeth onto the dance floor. "This is somebody's wedding, so we're not going to screw it up, but if I see you on the same side of the hall as Mrs. Bruce I'll finish what I started at The Turk's, okay?"

Ack-Ack seemed glad that Duncan had choices to offer instead of picking up where it had been left more than a year ago.

"I'm just home from Toronto for a couple of weeks," he said. "Vacation," he added with an innocent shrug. "I'm not looking for any trouble. Why would I bother her anyway?"

Duncan pushed himself away from the wall to look Ack-Ack in the eye. "There's no reason in the world why you'd bother her anyway, but I'll kill you myself if you do. That's all I have to say on the matter, nothing more. So what are you driving?" he asked Ack-Ack, moving into more neutral territory. When Ack-Ack told him a '55 Chev, Duncan asked him if it could take the Oldsmobile on the Stretch.

"We'll try it sometime," Ack-Ack said, relieved, but we all knew that the two cars would never meet on the Stretch.

The Rocking Horses had finished their music, and a new square set was getting organized. I wanted to be out of it, but the bride and groom and the three bridesmaids and their escorts were forming a wedding party set, and several other sets were forming all over the floor. Johnny Rosin hit the strings with his bow, and the music started.

The first two figures moved along just the way you would expect them to, and I was growing more comfortable with the movements, even trying to imitate a step or two the dancers around me were using. Then Johnny Rosin left the jigs behind and started into the reels of the third figure, and we began to move through the four quarters of that figure, moving in and out, going through half a grand chain, swinging our partners until it was time to promenade, then Catherine and John Ian turned back into the promenade, splitting the couples until we met our partners again at the end of the line. Then the men and women cast off from each other to form lines of the same sexes facing one another, moving in and out until the music told us it was time to dance again with a waltz or two-step with our partners. The figure repeated itself left and right through the second and third quarters, and into the fourth when the full grand chain brought the dancers past their partners and all the way around again, then the promenade that brought us all back to join hands and step it off.

This was where I thought the music should have ended, but I didn't understand a lot about dancing. I was just drafting along behind the guys dancing next to me, mimicking whatever they were doing, because they seemed to know what they were doing. The dancers in the hall moved in and out to the music, repeating the first quarter again, flowing through the movements, and I was beginning to appreciate that you had to be in good shape to do this, the sweat pouring into my eyes and someone on each side holding a hand so that I couldn't wipe the sweat away, but the sweat didn't blind me to the fact that I wasn't alone in my growing weariness.

I hadn't square-danced often enough to become familiar with how long the third figure should be, but it seemed to be going on a long time. I looked at Johnny Rosin, and he was sitting there, eyes closed, the bow moving in short, sharp strokes, his face peaceful as a sleeping child's. Finally, one of the sets quit, all eight dancers walking off the floor, hair, shirts and skirts pasted to them with sweat. Still Johnny Rosin played on, actually taking the music up another notch when he noticed the set leave the floor, and about a minute later it happened again; another set left the floor.

I never thought about my heart before, but I was thinking about it then because it was beating louder than the music. Still, nobody seemed to be giving up in our set, not even after every other set had left for the sidelines, leaving us alone on the floor. Looking around at the people in our set, it was clear that the bride and her three bridesmaids were in for the long haul, with nothing to keep us guys going but shame. Johnny Rosin wasn't stopping, and I grew vaguely aware that everyone at the wedding reception had been drawn out of their conversations and their drinking to watch what was taking place. The fiddler was challenging the dancers, and I was caught in the middle of it, the weak link trying to soldier on with legs of jelly. Please God, I prayed, don't let me be the first guy who cracks. My prayer was answered. That dishonour fell to Raymond Dempsy, the best man. I was counting on him because of the way he had been gasping for breath since the third figure began, and sure enough, he finally folded in a pool of sweat, hands on his knees coughing up all the cigarettes he ever smoked. The rest of us gratefully stopped and started clapping, and if people thought it was for the fiddler, that was fine, but that was false: our applause, mine anyway, was for Raymond Dempsey for getting us off the floor.

Although we were leaving the floor, the music kept on, and it was only then I realized that John Ian and Catherine hadn't stopped dancing. They were facing each other now, arms on each other's shoulders, their feet weaving out reel patterns to Johnny Rosin's music. I joined the rest of the people at the wedding in watching the duel.

It was a gallant attempt, but in the end our last flag fell when John Ian MacDonald stopped, bowed to his wife, conceding that she was the better man, and walked off the floor, his wedding suit nothing but patches of perspiration. Catherine Cameron, or Catherine MacDonald now, turned to the fiddler, she and Johnny Rosin locking eyes, and whatever was holding them together was wonderful. I understood then what Mary meant when she said her sister wanted to be able to dance at her own wedding. She was beautiful to watch in that white dress slit to the knees on either side to leave her feet free. Her feet were also free of the white high heels that had carried her up the aisle because she was wearing her flat-soled black dancing shoes at the reception. The whiteness of the veil and dress framed her dark complexion, making her seem darker, more mystical, more beautiful, a mirage composed of music, as if she were someone who would exist only as long as the music played.

Every eye in the hall was riveted on Catherine's feet, trained in the Cape Breton tradition of staying close to the floor while the music swirled around them, a series of popular reels, many of which I recognized but, like Johnny Sandy Something, couldn't name a single tune. The precision of Johnny Rosin's timing grew sharper and sharper as Catherine continued to follow it, but nothing of what the effort might be costing her showed in the determined glow of her face. Once, in John Alex's barn I heard Johnny Rosin say it's not how sparsely or ornamentally a Cape Breton fiddler plays a tune that he will be judged by, but whether or not he slurs his timing. I was only now beginning to appreciate what he meant. He went on to explain that the best Cape Breton fiddlers prefer dancers to audiences. Johnny Rosin had his dancers tonight, and he had his timing. Catherine, arms relaxed and motionless by her side, standing erect, staring into the music, was dancing with little movement or motion above her feet where the energy of the dance should be focused. Her feet matched Johnny Rosin's timing, making a soft precise sound of their own under the music, and I found myself wishing Taurus were here, remembering the day in John Alex's barn when he said those things he said about Johnny Rosin's music with Johnny sitting right there.

The other fiddlers in the hall, even Johnny Sandy Something, were listening and watching like the rest of us. Everybody, of course, was hoping for the dancer because she was working so hard, but one look at Johnny Rosin and you knew he was working just as hard, the sweat spilling off his chin now and down his fiddle, dripping from there like slow tears. Nobody bothered to notice what time the last figure started, so nobody knew for sure how long they had been at it, Johnny Rosin and Catherine MacDonald, but

Catherine wasn't showing any signs of surrender, her feet weaving a vanishing tapestry of steps, still adding an occasional ornament to one of those steps, but she was clearly conserving herself now, her taps and shuffles and sweeps mostly clean and neat, and I think she had long ago stopped dancing for the audience, now dancing just for the fiddler, for Johnny Rosin, and you could tell neither one of them wanted it to end, but it did.

It ended as abruptly as the blink of an eye when the fiddler and the dancer stopped with a precision as sharp as the music itself, as if somehow Catherine and Johnny Rosin had some secret communication between them. The sudden ending silenced the wedding guests for a long moment while Catherine gave a smiling bow to the fiddler and Johnny Rosin tipped his bow to her. Then the hall exploded with appreciation.

The last set of the night was played at four o'clock, and Mary and I walked to the beach to watch the sunrise even though the beach in Shean faces the sunset. We didn't care, and we stayed there in the cool sand until it was well into the daylight morning. I walked Mary home and kept to the track to feed the horses, because I knew that once I fell asleep it might last all the way through the month of August. Calum was sitting at the kitchen table with his tea when I came in, but he asked no questions, and without offering explanations I went straight to bed.

35

F or you," Calum said, dropping an envelope on the kitchen table and continuing into his study with his own mail. At least he didn't stand around looking over my shoulder like a lot of parents would be doing tonight. I could see the return address from the sink where I was washing the supper dishes, so I decided to keep my wet hands in the water and as far away from the Department of Education envelope as possible.

Provincial examinations was a fear fed to students from primary school, with teachers all along the years waving the fact of provincials before struggling students, assuring us that even if we did manage to squeak through the lower grades, the days of judgement would catch up to us when we reached grades eleven and twelve, instilling a quiet terror of the arrival of the very envelope that lay on the kitchen table. For days now, every time Calum came back from the post office, my breath caught and my heart raced, only to be reprieved by his announcement that there was nothing for me, but I had run out of stays of execution.

Eventually, I ran out of the few dishes I had to wash, dry and save every evening, and I scoured the sink so much and so long that the enamel was in danger of peeling. With no more places to hide, I sat with the envelope and slowly slit it with a kitchen knife, withdrawing the three-folded page and, mustering as much casual indifference as possible, let my eyes give it a quick scan. Nothing jumped up to punch me in the solar plexus, so I took a closer, more interested look. There were some close calls, particularly chemistry and physics, but I was as proud of their marks, 53 and 51, as I was of my English mark, which was high enough to drag an otherwise humble average just above 60. There were two things I needed from that page of exam results, a pass for the year and an

average within the range of acceptability for a university application, and both were there. I exhaled more tension than I realized
I had, followed by a victory yelp, and took the wonderful piece
of government correspondence to Calum who scanned it with not
quite as much enthusiasm as I had, noting with grim sarcasm that
I had left myself lots of room for improvement next year.

Duncan's Oldsmobile pulled up in front of the house, and he
jumped out. Late as usual, but Calum never made much of it any
more. He just stood watching while we loaded the tools into the
trunk, then took his place in the front seat.

"Let's go," Duncan said, pulling a folded envelope from his
back pocket as he settled in behind the wheel. He threw it over his
shoulder to me, and I could see by the return address what it was.
I unfolded the torn envelope and pulled out his marks, scanning
them quickly, as I had my own, to soften any unfriendly truths
lurking inside, but I didn't scan it very far before my eyes were
snagged as if from a jig hook by a couple of Duncan's results.
"Eighty-eight in physics!" I exclaimed. "Eighty-two in chemistry?" My eyes raced back to the top of the page to be sure I was
reading Duncan's results. I caught his eyes in the rearview mirror,
and we started laughing.

"This is going to kill Mr. Steele," I said.

"Yup, and I'm going to dance on his grave," Duncan replied.

Duncan's other marks were less impressive, but they were
passes. "Maybe you should think about getting pissed off at all
your teachers," I said. "You could have a ninety average. How
did you manage this?"

"After I flunked the Easter exam, forty-nine the bastard gave
me, I made up my mind he wasn't going to have the satisfaction
of seeing me fail provincials, so I took a look at the books every
day, but I wouldn't give him an answer if he paid me. I hope this
ruins the rest of his summer."

On our way up the Highland Road, though, it wasn't his marks Duncan wanted to talk about, but the park. Mary Scotland and I told him about our conversation with Calum, and once Calum said he would talk to Mrs. MacLeod and write to some Highland societies to see if they would be interested in the idea of small park, Duncan was like a woman who gave birth.

"Know what the park would be good for?" he asked me, our eye contact taking place in the rearview mirror. "Honeymoons. Mrs. MacLeod could open an inn or something and get just-married couples to come there to walk through a living love poem. Not everybody wants to go to Niagara Falls, you know."

"But it's not a love poem, it's about Taurus's people coming here and settling in the Shean Highlands," I told him.

"Smelt, how many people do you think can read Taurus's poem in trees or words or any other way. But if they think it's a love poem Mrs. MacLeod will make more money. And those bedrooms upstairs are great for what honeymooners want to do."

"I know," I said, keeping my voice low enough to stay under the possibility that Calum's hearing aid was turned up. "You and Nicole have been practically living there all summer."

"It's a nice private place to be when my mother's watching me like a hawk, and as for getting privacy at Nicole's house, forget it. A bootlegger's open twenty-four hours a day."

At Taurus's farm, the stakes had been pulled up and thrown away. It was the third or fourth time since Calum and Duncan first found them scattered across the pasture. We had come to expect it. I said it was probably somebody who hated literature in school, and Duncan blamed it on Annie Rosary because she would be watching everything we were doing, and she was afraid that when we planted the poem, we would evoke the pagan Druids to come to the Shean Highlands. Calum never said or showed any response, just went about gathering what he could find. It was really no big deal anymore, because Calum always carried his map of where the trees went, and I was pretty familiar with the poem by now, too.

Even Duncan knew a couple of lines. But when the stakes were up, it was easy to see how far we had come with the planting and how much, how little really, was left.

Looking across the field was like looking at an orchard where all the apple trees are planted in even rows, but we all knew that in the next couple of years all the saplings would begin to grow according to their own natures, and they would grow more and more different, some taller, some shorter, some leafier, some flowered, some with berries, some, like the ivy, of which there were only three, climbing around a pole or another tree that we would have to put in. The ivy and the vine couldn't very well climb straight up like a charmed snake rising to an Indian's flute. These were still problems to be solved, but Duncan and I weren't even thinking about them because Calum would come up with something.

August is not the best time for transplanting trees, we all knew. Well, Calum knew, and now so did Duncan and I, but most of the trees we planted late in the other summers when Bartholomew was with us had taken root. Those that didn't were easily replaced the following spring, so there was nothing to lose, really, and besides, we could all sense the end of it coming. The poem was more than three-quarters in the ground, and even Calum's stern way of walking through the world was looser when he was walking like a giant through the little trees of his forest.

"You know what's been bothering me?" Duncan said, stopping his digging and looking at Calum.

"What's that?" Calum replied.

"How'd they get a tree alphabet in Scotland when they got no trees? It's all heather over there, isn't it? In pictures I've seen those hills are as bald as the tires on my car, so how do you figure they got a tree alphabet out of that?"

"There were forests in Scotland one time," Calum answered. "The Great Caledonian Forest was a mixture of every kind of tree. There were forests growing at an elevation of 1500 feet, higher than these hills. They were all cleared away for agriculture or to plant other kinds of trees, but there was a time when the Caledonian Forest covered a good part of Scotland."

"They cut it all down! A whole forest!" Duncan said, impressed. He looked out across the expanse of hills that surrounded Shean and far beyond, reaching all across Cape Breton Island, all of them dense green with a hundred kinds of trees, the density broken only occasionally by a working farm. "They'd never be able to do that here," he said, "not even with the pulp mill in Port Hawkesbury."

Calum was the foreman, and Duncan pretty well handled the shoveling now, while I scouted for saplings and carried water, and I was carrying a bucket across the field from the brook when the slamming of a car door, as sharp as a bullet shot, startled us all. I could see Duncan and even Calum raise their heads in a hurry, and we all looked toward the house where a long car was parked beside Duncan's, and a man was walking away from it toward us.

"What do you think you're doing?" the man shouted halfway across the field. "What-Do-You-Think-You-Are-Doing?" he repeated, spitting each word into the soft wind.

"Planting trees," Calum replied as the stranger approached.

"And just who gave you permission to do that?" He was standing in front of us now, a thick man, chin jutted. "Well?"

"This farm belongs to a friend. He doesn't mind."

"No! No! No! Mister! This farm belongs to me!" the man replied.

"I'm sorry," Calum answered, "but this farm belongs to a gentleman by the name of Taurus MacLeod."

"One time maybe, but this is my place now! I bought it, and I have the deed to prove it, so I'd appreciate you packing up and getting off my property. Go now! I've just come back from the dump with the garbage I had to clean up inside the house, beer cans and French safes, damn trespassers using this house for their wild parties," he said in a belligerent tone. "I've been to the RCMP to tell them that my place is being broken into all the time. They didn't seem to care very much, so it's up to me to protect my property! Now go before I have to run you off! Let's see you move, now. Move!" he said, reaching out as if he was going to take Calum by the elbow to help him along his way.

Duncan stepped between them, the shovel loose and menacing in his hands. The farm's new owner took a tiny but definite step back.

"This place is posted with No Trespassing signs," the man said. "If you'd pay attention to them there'd be no problems."

"Were those your stupid god-damned signs? They made good kindling," Duncan said, the man's eyes registering realization of who had turned his house into a party place. The man's eyes slipped from Duncan's face to the shovel in his hands and back again.

"If you don't leave, I'm going to report you to the police. They'll have to do something if I give them your licence plate number, and I have that up here," he said, finger tapping his temple.

"Look," I said, "we were just planting a few trees...."

"Plant your goddamn trees on your own goddamn property," he snapped, reaching down and pulling that day's birch from the ground, heaving it, and, as he did, Calum reached out and stayed Duncan's hands which had tightened on the shovel.

"I suppose those were your goddamn sticks that were stuck all over this field, too, were they?" the man asked, not noticing yet that they were all back up.

"They were his stakes," Duncan said, "and if you're not careful I'll drive one of them right through your fucking heart!"

"Come along," Calum said, turning away from the stranger, his face expressionless, pruning shears in his hand. I stepped up beside Duncan, neither of us wanting to just walk away, but Calum turned and beckoned us with a sharp gesture of his hand, and in that gesture I could see his anger. I followed him. Duncan was the last to leave, his eyes glaring at the owner like a double-barrelled shotgun. Finally, he turned and followed, and that was when I realized the full bucket of water was still banging against my ankles whenever I walked, so I turned and emptied it in a tidal wave over the man's feet. It felt strange to be walking out of there not knowing someone's name.

"And don't think about sneaking back here. I keep a gun handy," the owner's warning bouncing off our turned backs.

"If you can't find anything else to point it at, try your own head," Duncan hollered as we got in the car where he sat pounding his fist on the steering wheel. We sat watching as the stranger angrily stomped through Taurus's field, randomly pulling trees whose roots were not yet firmly set.

"What the hell can we do?" Duncan asked at last.

Short of walking down there and crowning him with the shovel there was nothing we could do, but our helplessness made me want to get out of the car and do just that. A moment later Duncan started the car, put it in gear and began turning on the grass to follow the wagon trail out when he slammed on the brakes. "Brace yourself," he said, throwing the Oldsmobile in reverse, then swung around to match his back bumper to the one on the stranger's car. He floored it then, the Oldsmobile charging backwards, slamming the larger car into the side of Taurus's kitchen with a cracking of old wood and a shattering of window panes, then Duncan, revving and holding it there, forced the Oldsmobile to spin against the other car while the new owner ran across the field toward us. Just as he reached the car, Duncan dropped into first gear, letting the Olds leap free with a spinning of wheels and a spray of gravel that showered the man as we fishtailed down the drive to the highlands road.

With Duncan silent behind the wheel, the car slid and skidded down the highlands road without any of us flinching over the fact that there was a steep cliff on one side of this mountain road. From the back seat I watched Calum's stony face, trying to read something that would tell me as much as his angry gesture back in the field had done, but like everything else that happened to him, it was not for public viewing.

"Thank you, Duncan," he said unexpectedly, breaking the silence as the Olds raced past Annie Rosary's house, leaving it in a cloud of angry dust, then turned as much as he could toward me in the back seat and nodded a similar appreciation.

Duncan's and my eyes met in the rear-view mirror again, neither of us able to remember the last time, if ever, Calum had called Duncan by any other name than "That Fellow" or "You."

"You're welcome, but nobody treats a friend of mine like that while I'm around," Duncan answered, his remark drawing the same surprised look from Calum as Duncan and I shared a moment before.

After another silence, Calum said, "I don't want either of you to do anything about this."

"It pisses me off that somebody could just steal Taurus's land like that for back taxes."

"He probably didn't buy it like that," Calum explained. "There are land companies that go around to tax sales all over the country buying up properties. The owner has a year to redeem the land by paying the unpaid taxes. If he doesn't then the land company owns it free and clear, and they advertise it for sale. Then people can buy the land pretty cheap, so it's not really as if that gentleman took Taurus's land. Now it's his."

"Are you his lawyer or something? This is just like the Clearances, isn't it, Calum? Other people driving our people off our land?" Duncan asked. "Still, you'd think Taurus would have paid his taxes."

"The County is supposed to notify owners when their land is going up for sale after they're three or more years in arrears, which Taurus probably was. Whether or not the County makes a real effort to inform people is something a lot of other people question. Even if they did, I don't suppose Taurus is fit to understand tax bills or much of anything any more."

"So what are we going to do now?" Duncan asked, and the car filled with silence. "My grandmother in Margaree has a lot of land she's not using. I could talk to her, or better, you could talk to her. She speaks Gaelic and everything. You'd get along great," Duncan said finally, but Calum's eyes drifted away somewhere beyond the scenery outside the car window, and he gave his head a slow definite shake. "It's done," he said sharply, then softer, said it in the Gaelic, "*Tha e criochnaichte*."

It was over.

36

It must be terrible for Calum," Mary Scotland said when Duncan and I told her what happened at Taurus's farm, and she was right. Something had seeped out of Calum. It was nothing I could actually grab hold of, and maybe nobody else would notice at all, but it was there, an almost imperceptible sag in his erectness, a longer drag to his scuffing walk. Lots of things happened to Calum over the years when I was too young or too dumb to understand, but this was something that happened to the two of us, so I could see him better than before, although there was nothing I could do about it but leave him alone.

I remembered Taurus telling me about the time Calum fell from the church roof, and they ran and got Bartholomew Fraser. Bartholomew told Taurus there was nothing he could really do for Calum's busted back, but he could tell by the way Calum was handling the pain that "this man will heal himself," and he did, the same way he had healed himself after Bartholomew died. I needed him to do it again.

The three of us were in The Turk's waiting for Nicole to get off shift, and when she did we drove down the Shore Road and walked to a sandy cove where we gathered driftwood and lit a fire. Duncan carried a case of beer he bought from Nicole's father "at cost," and when the fire was flaming pulled from his jacket pocket a package of wieners he had stolen from The Turk's fridge, no buns, no mustard, no relish, except for relishing the fact they'd been stolen from Tony.

"We have to have something in our stomachs to throw up in the morning," was Duncan's explanation. He began opening the beer by snapping the cap of one against the other and passed them around. Even Mary Scotland, who had never had a taste of beer, didn't shake her head in refusal when Duncan passed her a bottle.

We watched for shooting stars among the billions shining in the black August sky, directing each other to the vanishing tails with a pantomime of pointing fingers, forming silent wishes on each dying star. A rhythmic lapping of waves filled the ring of darkness beyond our fire, and while Duncan poked at the flames with a stick, sending up a shower of tiny, hot cinders, Nicole began to hum, the timing of the lullaby so perfectly set to the night sea it was easy to imagine it was composed along this very shore. When she moved from humming to the Gaelic itself, the words flowed from her as quietly as if she held a sleeping child in her arms, her voice sweet and soothing while the rest of us stared into the flames and listened. It was a song, she said, that her mother used to sing her to sleep with as a child. None of us had heard it before.

"I wonder how many songs there are like that all over Cape Breton?" Mary Scotland asked. "Songs that only a few people know anymore, and how many songs do you suppose have been forgotten altogether?"

"I bet my grandmother knows two hundred ghost stories just from around the Margarees alone," Duncan said. "I don't know fifty myself, but Alfred Hitchcock couldn't scare me half as much as my grandmother. And she knows songs, too, and talks Gaelic. Shit, we should have invited Calum to come with us. What do you think, Smelt?"

"Yeah, he'd enjoy this, raw wieners and beer, or maybe we could sit up in the sun porch drinking tea, all five of us, but I don't think Calum will go for that at three in the morning."

"You know what I mean," Duncan said, feeling the edge in my voice. "I know there's as much chance of Calum having a beer as there is of the Pope getting his nookie, but this is why God made booze, just for times like this. There's no sin in getting drunk over what happened today, but it happened mostly to Calum, didn't it? We were really just bystanders, so it should be Calum getting drunk and smashing things or punching people, getting it all out of his system."

"You weren't a bystander, I was," I said, remembering it had been Duncan and not me who stepped into the breach between Calum and the new owner of Taurus's farm when Calum seemed threatened. I emptied my beer and asked for another.

"What do you mean?" Duncan asked, knowing very well what I meant and answering his own question. "I know what you mean, but it doesn't mean anything. What would you have done if I wasn't there?" I shrugged and stared into the fire. "I'll tell you what you'd have done," Duncan continued, "you would have clocked the bastard with the shovel the same as I wanted to do. I was just faster, that's all."

"Look, Smelt," he said, popping and passing me the beer I asked for, "we're different, you and me, isn't that right?" he asked, looking around the fire and getting nodding confirmations from Mary Scotland and Nicole. "If it wasn't for you, I'd be in jail now for killing Ack-Ack, and if I went aboard that bastard who stole Taurus's farm, you'd have stopped me from killing him too, same as Calum when he put his hand on the shovel. I was thinking about that, that I was pissed off enough to crack that guy's skull with a shovel, but an eighty-year-old man was able to stop me with one hand. Makes you think, huh? I bet Calum never had a fight in his life, but that doesn't mean anything, and if you didn't know me, Smelt, I bet you'd never have had a fight in your life either. But when there was a war, who went? Your father and my father. When it counted they were there, same as we'd be, so don't go punching yourself in the face for being who you are." Then shifting directions, he wondered, "How do you suppose Calum's handling it? Doesn't drink. Doesn't smoke. Doesn't have a girlfriend. Hell, he doesn't even have any friends left but us, but what can we do for him? Nothing, that's what, because he doesn't drink."

"I can't help thinking how terrible it must be for him," Mary Scotland said. "That forest was like his last chance against a world that's taking away his language, and now all those little trees are lying in ruins. When you think about it, Calum learned all about the world in a language that's disappearing. Do any of us know how to say puddles and dogs and trees in Gaelic? His world is disappearing as if it was a sand castle in a rising tide. First it took his friends, and now it's taking everything else."

"You should make a song of that," Duncan said.

"I would if I knew how, but I don't speak Gaelic."

"We have songs in English, too," Duncan said. "Elvis, remember?"

"I know, but the way I feel about what happened, if I could make a song of it, it would have to be a Gaelic one. It would be cruel to sing about somebody losing their language and not even use the language they're losing."

"I feel so sorry for him. He must feel awful," Nicole said.

"You'd never know it from looking at him, though, would you, Smelt? When I picked you up this evening, he was out working in his garden as if nothing happened at all, isn't that right? Except he gave me this little wave while he was working. I think he likes me, Rod," Duncan said.

"Yeah, I think so," I said.

"But we had our times back there, me and Calum. Know what I think it was? You remember the way the old lady used to be always going on about 'Why can't you be more like Roddie?' like you're some kind of saint or something because she never had to stay up all night praying for you, did she? Used to piss me off, though, I'll tell you that, because we both knew the truth. Anyway, maybe Calum thought the same thing my old lady did, that I'd get you in a piss-pot full of trouble, that maybe you'd land in jail because of me. It's not like I'm a frigging juvenile delinquent or anything, but I can never find a halo that fits. Now, though, after all those trips to Taurus's farm we kind of got to know each other a little, me and Calum."

Duncan sipped from his beer in silence for a moment before adding, "What's bothering me is, did we do the right thing up there?"

Duncan's question was mine, too, the one that had been rumbling around in my mind ever since we left Taurus's farm. In my mind I had relived a dozen different endings, all of them ending with the new owner flat on his back, bleeding from the nose, maybe missing teeth, apologizing to Calum.

"Do you think Calum meant it when he said don't do anything about it?"

"Calum always means what he says."

"If only the guy wasn't such an arsehole. Why couldn't he just ask us what we were doing. We were really doing something, you know, planting a poem in the ground. He could've helped us finish it, and now that it's his property he could have made a fortune off people who would pay to walk around inside a poem. Instead, what does he do? Starts trying to shove an eighty-year-old man around, that's what," Duncan said in answer to his own question, his anger rising again.

"Say it, Roddie," Mary Scotland asked.

"Say what?"

"The poem, you nitwit," Duncan said. "You're the only one here who knows it."

"It doesn't make any sense to say it when the words don't mean anything," I argued.

"Did Nicole's song make any sense?" Mary asked. "Just because I don't know what the words mean doesn't mean I didn't like listening to it."

"I don't know what the words mean, either," Nicole said, "but I still like to sing it. Say it for us, Roddie."

So I said aloud the mysterious words Taurus had written, probably the last words he ever wrote, words I heard him and Calum and Bartholomew quote so often I could quote them myself like a pirate's parrot mouthing sounds without meaning.

From Taurus's poem we went on to sing songs we all knew, songs from the hit parade and from the kitchens of our homes.

The songs took us through the rest of the beer, most of that job falling to Duncan and me, and through the life of the fire which was now a dying mixture of glowing embers and grey ash. When we hit a lull in our musical repertoire, Duncan threw a rock, its arc suddenly lost in the darkness until we heard its glug in the water.

"That sounded good," Duncan said, stripping down for a skinny dip. In varying degrees of modesty we followed his lead, splashing into the ocean in a shower of joyful, half-drunken whoops until Mary Scotland pointed to the sun's red tinge at the eastern edge of the Shean Highlands. It wasn't the first time we had watched the sun come up that summer, but I found myself hurrying us along, asking Duncan to take care of feeding my horses because that was one morning I didn't want Calum to wake up alone in the house.

A few days later, something happened that shifted Duncan's attention away from what happened at Taurus's farm. His driver's licence from the United States Trotting Association arrived in the mail. Compared to this piece of paper, his licence to drive a car was nothing. Duncan had wanted a chance to race horses ever since he discovered John Alex's barn. Finally, he got John Alex and a couple of other drivers to sign affidavits swearing he had enough experience with horses to be able to handle them and wear his own colours. John Alex told him that in the first race after his licence arrived he could drive Cape Mabou. Duncan spent all summer planning how he was going to pull an upset and get the 10-year-old mare, who had never met a horse slower than herself, a maiden mark. Duncan was convinced he could win with her.

"John Alex drives a good race in the tack stall, but I'm telling you, Smelt, he doesn't drive worth a damn on the track. Scared. You watch! Every time he drives Cape Mabou, he parks on the outside. The old girl has to run about two miles out there. If I can get her to the rail and out front, the photo-finish camera will be taking a picture of my first win." The following day, though, he would be convinced that if he paced her, took her to the back end of the field and conserved her speed until the three-quarter pole, Cape Mabou would breeze by the whole card. He also raced her from the middle of the pack, and for a moment even thought about racing her loaded with some drug they couldn't pick up in the drug test. That would be a lot easier, though, he said, if only he had a friendly guy for a piss-whistler, and why didn't I try to get my old job back.

When the licence came, he carried it in the new wallet he bought the moment he left the post office. That was on a Friday, and he had to wait all the way to Sunday for the races. If the licence had come on Wednesday, he growled, he would be driving that night, not marking time all weekend waiting for his moment to arrive. He went to Mass and Communion on Sunday morning, making no bones about covering all his bases, then he spent the rest of the morning and afternoon walking around the paddock in the royal blue and silver silks his mother had sewn for him.

"How's it going?" I asked him when he came by Eric Rundle's stable.

"I can't make a spit," he said, asking the time.

Cape Mabou was going out in the first dash, the smelt race, they called it, although it wasn't a name I used myself anymore. He had jogged and turned the mare, got her loose and ready for the race. When the paddock judge called for the horses to get on the track for the first dash I went over to help Duncan hitch up the sulky, then he threw himself onto the seat, his silks billowing in the breeze as he adjusted the strap of his helmet under his chin. The previous night, remembering what his grandmother had said when we were planting the forest, that the old Scots believed the oak tree had special powers, he had me paint a green oak leaf on the front of his helmet. He tightened the strap while I ran beside Cape Mabou, snapping on her overdraw.

"You won't have any trouble winning," I told Duncan as he started through the paddock gate.

"So how much are you going to bet on me?" he called over his shoulder.

"And how much are you betting on you?" I hollered back, but he was already gone.

The starting gate paraded the horses in front of the stands where rail-birds could make their last minute assessments and the less knowledgeable fans could decide which colour horse or lucky number to bet on.

This was one race I wanted to watch from the stands. I skipped over the fence and into the crowd, finding a seat with Nicole and Mary Scotland, neither of whom had much interest in horses or the track. They were there because it was Duncan's big day. I waved to Mrs. MacFarlane who was sitting not too far away, nervously rolling her scorecard into a tight cylinder that had to be unrolled like a scroll when she wanted to look at her son's name again.

"In the number three position, Cape Mabou, a ten-year-old pacer by Mister Mist out of Jolly Mabou, owned by John Alex Rankin, driven by Duncan MacFarlane. No mark, and this is MacFarlane's first ride," the announcer told the crowd. The crowd cheered, and the tote board said Cape Mabou was thirty to one.

"You girls should split a bet," I told them. "For a dollar each you can buy a two-dollar win ticket on Duncan. If he comes in you'll make sixty-two bucks."

"Will he win?" Mary asked me.

"Think if he does and you don't have a ticket," I said.

They gave me their money and I was on my way to the pari-mutuel when Mrs. MacFarlane called out to me.

"So this is what all those days at John Alex's barn have come to," she said. "I should be grateful it wasn't some of the other awful things I imagined. Do they have many accidents?"

I assured her that accidents on the Shean track were few and far between. Then she asked me how to bet. When I told her I was on my way to the parimutuel to place a bet, she gave me two dollars to get her a ticket.

"Two wins on Cape Mabou," I said, sliding the four dollars to the ticket agent. I brought them back to Mrs. MacFarlane and to Mary and Nicole just as the starting gate called the horses and began rolling toward the turn at the eighth pole and onto the head of the stretch, the horses' hooves pounding the earth trying to keep up. The starting gate, a body-filled half-ton truck with swinging wings, sped away when it hit the wire, leaving the field behind to sort the race out on the first turn.

"It's Cape Mabou to the top," the announcer called through the settling dust. Duncan had gone with his first plan. Seven horses chased him down the back stretch, strung out one behind the other like ducklings, Bonny Lady, Ten Spot, Norvel Brook, Amtico, Ruthie's First, Lilie Clegg and Ainslie Lady, but it was Duncan's silver and blue silks showing the way at the quarter in thirty-five seconds. He was still setting the pace as they went under the wire for the first time, although Ruthie's First and Lilly Clegg pulled to the outside of the parade, making their bid to take over the lead. A glance over his shoulder told Duncan they were coming after him, and he gave the shaft of the sulky a sharp crack with the whip. They reached the half in one minute and eleven seconds, a time too slow to qualify at any other racetrack in the Maritime provinces except Shean's.

Duncan was being challenged into the first turn. He took Cape Mabou off the rail far enough so that no horse could sneak through on the inside, a move that pushed the challenging Ruthie's First further out toward the middle of the track, making its mile a few steps longer. The strategy began to falter once they reached the back stretch. Even though Mary Scotland was tearing off my arm with excitement, screaming, "He's going to win! He's going to win!" and Nicole had her eyes closed whispering encouragement across the track to Duncan, or maybe praying, Cape Mabou was fading like a forgotten dream. By the three quarters, Duncan was rocking in the sulky seat trying to push his horse through the rest of the race. He was effective enough at the reins so that when they reached the head of the stretch, Cape Mabou found a little more stamina than she usually showed for John Alex, coming up with a bit of a sprint that brought her back from eighth place to seventh to sixth, passing Ainslie Lady and Bonnie Lady. Ten Spot, finishing ahead of Cape Mabou, broke stride going under the wire and was set back, so that when the final results were announced, Cape Mabou had been moved up from a sixth place finish to fifth.

I left the stands and jumped the fence back into the paddock in time to meet Duncan coming through the gate. He had jumped off the sulky and was walking beside Cape Mabou, loosening the overdraw.

"I finished in the money," Duncan said with a smile. "Sorry you lost your money, but you got to get your licence, Smelt. I can't tell you what's its like going away behind the gate. My heart was pounding like a hundred hooves. It wasn't so great to feel my horse dying under me, though. I thought she was running in reverse on the backstretch there the way everybody started passing me. I can't wait to win, but finishing in the money's a good start," he said as John Alex and some other horsemen came by to congratulate him on a good first effort.

A little later, the race secretary came by and handed John Alex, the horse's owner, a cheque for twelve dollars. "Two bags of oats and you get the change," John Alex told him.

"What they should have here is a frigging union for the drivers. I gave that horse the best drive she's had in years, and John Alex's going to pay me in spare change," Duncan said, taking off his silks and carefully hanging them on a hook in John Alex's tack stall, hanging the helmet on top of them.

"Drivers get ten per cent of what they win," I reminded Duncan. "John Alex should be paying you a buck twenty, but there'll be more than that left over."

"Maybe," Duncan said, giving it a second thought. "Still, there should be a union."

37

The worst thing about summer was that it was too short, but what made that September interesting was Duncan getting elected president of the Student Council. I nominated him for the hell of it, and he went along with the joke, but when students from grades nine to twelve had a choice on the ballot between Daniel MacFadyen, Mother Saint Cross John's pet, and Duncan MacFarlane, who didn't really appreciate the range of his own reputation, it was, as politicians say, a landslide.

Duncan didn't want to be president, but he wouldn't give Mother Saint Cross John the satisfaction of resigning when she asked him to, telling him that it would be in the best interests of the school and the students if an honour student held that position. Being president of the student council, she said, would never do Duncan any good in his life, but someone like Daniel, who would be applying for scholarships and going on to get a good college education, would really benefit from demonstrating the student leadership qualities that come with being president of the student council.

There were lots of ways Mother Saint Cross John could have asked Duncan not to take the president's position, and he would have been glad to give it up, but by practically telling him he didn't deserve it made Duncan stick his toes in deeper than Ten Spot, the most stubborn horse at the track who would stop in the middle of a race and, no matter how hard he was beaten or whipped, wouldn't move his legs until he decided for himself it was time to go to his stall. Duncan said no, even though all he really had on his mind was winning his first race, not organizing high school dances and stuff like that.

Duncan got about twenty starts since he got his licence, and he knew from playing cards that losing streaks came to an end. It was going to happen, he said, but the horses he was getting to drive weren't helping much.

"If somebody would give me a four-legged animal instead of all these three-legged smelts, Smelt, I wouldn't be following everyone else under the wire," he said. Besides John Alex's horses, a couple of other owners asked him to drive for them when their regular drivers weren't available, but none offered a horse that could win. So on Sunday afternoons through September and into early October, Duncan went winless.

It was also in early October that there was a spill coming off the top turn, three horses, their bikes and drivers tangling in a mess of harness and panic, and when it was all sorted out the horses were fine, but two sulky shafts and one of Peter Shawl's legs was broken. Once I got his horses settled down for the night I went to see him in the hospital. He had a cast up to his hip, covering a compound fracture that would keep him in that bed for a week or longer. His horses were already entered in the last two Sunday cards of the season, so he asked me to manage his stable for him, the feeding, the bandaging, the jogging, and arrange for a driver for his horses on race days.

"Who should I get to drive the horses?" I asked Duncan later that night at The Turk's, as if seriously seeking his advice. His face filled with confusion and disbelief, and it took him a moment to gather a bunch of my shirt front in his fist and pull me across the tabletop and answer my question with one of his own.

"What the hell do you mean, who should drive those horses?"

It was a long week, having to look after the whole stable in the mornings before school and after school having to work them out, although Duncan took charge of the training, wanting to get the feel of Shawl's stable. There was also the evening feeding, the bedding changes, the bandaging, and a dozen little details I never had to worry about before. On Sunday, Duncan had six starts, two with John Alex's horses, both finishing out of the money, and four with my stable. He finished third with Epsom Salts, sixth with Jerry Dale, Jollity Roger was a fourth place finish, and his last start of the day was his first-ever start in the Shean Free-For-All. Diamond Skies, a six-year-old mare that had raced well all summer for Peter Shawl, had moved up through the classes with her consistency. In twenty-eight starts, she had six wins, and only finished out of the money, or worst than fifth place, once.

Diamond Skies' problem was that she was laying over the field in the classification below free-for-all, so she had to be moved up a couple of times through the summer to give other horses in the lower classification a chance, but she always proved too slow for the free-for-all, finishing last almost every time. Then she would be lowered back a classification and begin to dominate that field again.

Unfortunately for Duncan, Diamond Skies, instead of being in the class she dominated, was currently the free-for-all's also-ran, but he was just happy to be in the big leagues of Shean's harness racing elite. There were only five horses fast enough for the top class, where races were frequently run in times of 2:12 or fractions under that. Diamond Skies had not finished better than fourth in the free-for-all, but because there were only five horses, she couldn't finish out of the money.

"Marystien's the horse I have to beat," Duncan said, pacing back and fourth in front of Diamond Skies' stall, waiting for the seventh race, the free-for-all.

It was hard to disagree with Duncan's observation since Mary-stien had won her last six starts, but I also felt the need to point out that there were some other horses that had a pretty good history of getting between Marystien and Diamond Skies: Grey Eagle, Buddy Budlong and King Peter.

"I'm not worried about those smelts," Duncan said. "You have to figure out how to beat the winner, not the losers."

A few minutes later I was giving him a good-luck slap on the back as he lifted himself onto the sulky. He was in the free-for-all, the longshot at odds of sixty-to-one, and he had given Nicole one hundred bucks to put on Diamond Skies' nose. It must have been her big bet at a small track that dropped the odds to eighteen to one, which started other bettors wondering who knew what about Duncan MacFarlane and Diamond Skies, and by the time they paraded, Diamond Skies was five to one. By the time the horses were scored and the starting gate started to move, Diamond Skies was two to one, the race favourite, with Marystien at five to two. Duncan didn't know a thing about the dropping odds, thinking instead that he was shoring up his first win with fifty longshot tickets on himself.

If Duncan didn't know he was the favourite, Diamond Skies seemed to sense that the final odds were one to ten, odds usually reserved for Marystien. From the start Diamond Skies was in the race, tucking in on the rail behind the ghostly beauty of Grey Eagle, who was showing the way. Marystien was sitting behind Duncan, with King Peter on the outside beside Buddy Budlong. Nothing much changed at the half, which Grey Eagle cut in 1:05 and was still pacing strong into the turn onto the back stretch. Marystien came off the rail to make her move, and Duncan took Diamond Skies out at the same time, carrying Marystien out, forcing her to pace the long curve three-wide, all the while Diamond Skies was inching up on a waning Grey Eagle. On the backstretch, Diamond Skies took the lead but couldn't shake Marystien, a half length behind, froth blowing from her mouth into Duncan's face, but he held Diamond Skies there, not using his reins, not using his whip, not trying to pull away. Into the next turn it was clear why Duncan never tried to stretch that half-length lead. He continued to carry Marystien into the turn, making her work hard just to stay close. Onto the stretch, Marystien gave a burst of speed that put her ahead of Diamond Skies, but she couldn't hold it. Her strength had been used up in the turns, and Duncan went past her again and under the wire with Marystien's head practically on his shoulder. The mile was in 2:11.2, which, according to Duncan's later research, was the fourteenth-fastest mile run in Shean that summer.

When the starting gate led Duncan and Diamond Skies back to the wire to take a victory turn in front of the fans, Duncan's face was really something to see, except for a brief moment there when he glanced at the odds board and saw that his one hundred dollars was going to earn him about ten dollars.

Duncan won two more races the next Sunday, ending his first season in the sulky with three wins. Once Peter Shawl's horses had been loaded onto the box of a large truck and Peter and his crutches loaded into the passenger's seat of the same vehicle, I stood in the empty stalls, glad to see them gone, knowing for certain now that I would rather draw horses than train or drive them.

The first week back to school, I went to see if Mother Saint Margaret still wanted me as her art student, and the first thing she asked was where was my easel, so I knew. I brought it the next day after school, along with the drawings I had been working on since I already knew what I wanted to paint this time, telling her how I got the idea from painting Duncan's helmet at the racetrack, and the whole story behind it.

Still, even knowing what I wanted to do didn't make it any easier. Harder, in fact, since Mother Saint Margaret said that she knew exactly what I would need to do if the painting I planned was going to turn out at all, so instead of her going softer on my practicing, she got tougher than before.

That same September, Calum asked if I would be all right alone if he took the train to Sydney for a few days. I knew it wasn't to Sydney that he was going, though, but a place near there where Calum grew up. I had no memory of him ever going there before, but once in a while in summers past, his Cousin Archie Gillies came to Calum's house driving a huge, hump-backed car that looked like something out of the gangster movies, and Calum would entertain Archie and his wife, whose name I never knew, in the parlour instead of the sun porch where they drank tea and spoke the Gaelic. I knew that if they were cousins of Calum they were cousins of my own, although even in the same room we seemed to sit far apart, and everyone was reluctant to break away from the Gaelic to include me. The last time I had heard from Cousin Archie was when Aunt Evelyn died, and he called Calum from over by the Mira River to tell him he couldn't get to the wake because of the snow. I guessed that it was Bartholomew who told him about Aunt Evelyn. Anyway, Cousin Archie and sometimes his wife came to visit Calum, and now he wanted to visit them.

"I'll be okay," I said.

That night, Calum sat and wrote a Gaelic letter to his cousin and asked me to mail it. The name on the address was in Gaelic, although the location, Marion Bridge, was in English so the post office people wouldn't get too confused. A week later, there was a letter for him in the shaky hand of an old person, Calum's name in the Gaelic, and he began making preparation for his departure.

On Saturday morning Duncan came by, and we put Calum's Gladstone suitcase in the trunk of the Oldsmobile and drove him to the station. He had his good suit on, and when he got aboard the train he sat beside a window as erect as ever. He never once glanced out the window like the other people who were waving goodbye. Seeing him there, I guessed that the last time Calum had been on a train it was the old Judique Flyer, whose ancient steam engine started him off on his trips to Boston to look for Aunt Evelyn. The old Flyer, that people had written songs and told stories about, had laboured along the western coast of Cape Breton forever until it was retired a few years earlier, replaced by the characterless diesel engine that was pulling away from the platform.

"How long's he going for?" Duncan asked.

"A week."

"Funny he didn't take you. They're your relatives, too, right?"

"Yeah, but if I came along everybody would have to speak English. And besides, how would all those Protestants feel about having to wake a Catholic up for Mass tomorrow morning?"

"Maybe he's like those fish that swim out to sea but have this instinct to come back to die in the same river where they were born," Duncan said, the image sending a chill through me. "But you won't have to worry about waking up for Mass tomorrow because you'll probably be still awake," Duncan said. When I clearly didn't understand, he explained, "We got a house to ourselves, Dummy."

I was the last to learn that there was going to be a party at my house that night.

"Oh," Mary Scotland said apologetically when I mentioned the party to her. "I meant to tell you about that."

Duncan was taking care of the booze. Mary and Nicole were looking after the food and other arrangements, like a record player. I spent the rest of the day wandering around the house trying to hide everything breakable or valuable.

People started showing up about seven o'clock, standing around in polite groups talking about baseball or music, and for a little while I thought, and prayed, that the party might break up early due to boredom, but once Duncan went out to the Oldsmobile with its trunkload of beer, any hope for a miracle vanished. The music got louder, the furniture began to move, puddles of spilled beer appeared on the floor, and Piper fled from room to room in panic. I roamed from room to room in a less obvious but no less real panic, watching everything through Calum's eyes. I don't know who invited the Moran brothers and their station wagon full of equipment, but pretty soon they were set up in the dining room, their drum beat pulsing up and down the street, spreading the secret of the house party all through Shean.

"Great party, Smelt!" people complimented, as I moved among them, rescuing ashtrays and half-filled glasses from the arms of chairs, the top of the china cabinet and the desk in Calum's study. When I saw Farter standing on the dining room table holding one of Calum's treasured Gaelic texts in his hands, reading from it in a garbled nonsense of coughs and hacks that was supposed to pass for the Gaelic, I couldn't watch what was happening any more. I took my first bottle of beer.

The rooms were filling with increasing chatter, shy people becoming loud, loud people becoming belligerent, laughter turning to argument, argument turning to laughter, and the music pounding out the hit parade for people who wanted to dance, which seemed to be just about everybody. It took a couple of more beers for me to get the hang of the party, but eventually I found myself stepping over a turned-over ashtray, its grey, butt-laden cargo spread across the parlour floor. "You only fill 'em to spill 'em," I said to no one in particular as I kicked the evidence under the apron of the blue velvety armchair. The parlour, preserved in the past for priests, ministers, visiting cousins and wakes, was packed with dancing bodies doing The Twist, a dance that had been banned at the high school dances. Some of the dancers knocked pictures off the walls, my late family falling to the floor like a bunch of drunks.

In the kitchen I asked Farter where all the food had come from. He mumbled through a mouthful of homemade cheese, and when I didn't understand, he pointed to the fridge. I began to recognize the remnants of our week's groceries. I tried not to think about what was happening to the house. Instead, Mary and I went into the parlour to dance where she spotted, then rescued, our family photographs from the floor. It had never occurred to me, even though I had stood there watching them drop, to pick them up.

"How many beers have you had?" Mary asked, as I staggered against her again and again to the music.

"Enough to fill a horse's bladder, so don't whistle," I said, chuckling at my own wit but realizing that it was true. I excused myself, leaving her there in mid-song, making my way to the bathroom, but the door was locked with lots of loud noises coming from inside. I waited, walking restlessly up and down the upstairs hall for another few minutes until the occupants began evacuating the bathroom, Mary Jane's beehive all messed, strands of hair having escaped the hard crust of her spray-net, springing out like misshapen horns. It was not a complimentary hairdo, but it matched her make-up which was running with tears. I thought she had just broken up with her boyfriend until a very sober Daniel MacFayden said, "Sorry about that," jerking his head to indicate the flooded toilet behind him, the floor carpeted with wet towels that had been used trying to soak up the flood and wring it down the sink, a drunken and fruitless effort by Mary Jane to clean up her mess. The bowl itself, which had backed up, was still clogged with floating traces of things like Tom MacPhee's homemade cheese drifting around the rim of the bowl.

"If you find four front teeth in there," Daniel called back to me as he guided his sick girlfriend somewhere where she could lie down, "it's Mary Jane's partial." The sickness in the bathroom was making me sick, so I did the only thing I could do. I stepped back into the hall and closed the door, magically making the mess go away. Then I took my full bladder outside where I discovered a circle of similar-minded guys standing around the cairn. I joined them.

We were engaged in that relieving activity, hurting no one, when an RCMP cruiser drove slowly down Culloden Street and, hearing the music, stopped in front of the house, shining a searchlight into the yard, causing all of us to blink against the blinding light.

"When you fill your eyes, fill your pockets," someone yelled, turning away from the cairn and aiming his stream of piss at the police cruiser, a hundred feet away.

"Smelt, for Christ's sake, smarten up," Duncan said, grabbing me by the shoulder. That was when I realized who had hollered at the cops. While I was realizing that fact about myself, there was a sound of beer bottles breaking in the raspberry bushes where people heaved them like hand grenades. The searchlight went off, throwing the yard into blackness for a moment. I heard a car door slam, and then a flashlight made its way into the yard. Behind it was the shape of a uniformed policeman walking toward us.

"Stop that!" he ordered, but my bladder wouldn't empty. Hard as I was trying to bring my stupid gesture to an end, it wouldn't stop.

"You're going to get charged with indecent exposure," someone behind me with his zipper already zipped whispered. I decided then that my only chance was to run, no easy thing, I learned, when you are drunk and peeing all over yourself. A few steps into my escape a harsh hand hauled me back by the collar, drawing me off-balance. The music in the house fell silent as a church, and those people who weren't nosey enough to see what was going on decided to depart. The rest gathered in the yard to witness my arrest.

"Did you try to piss on me?" the constable asked, the beam of the flashlight igniting my face. I was trying to squint past the glare in my face, hoping it was a cop I knew, one who might understand, but I didn't recognize him.

"Not me, ossifer," I answered.

"Don't get smart with me. And put that thing away. What's your name?"

"Duncan MacFarlane," I answered, poking my now finally exhausted pecker back into my pants. A snicker ran through the crowd, and the constable shined his light on the people circled around us, trying to find the source of the joke he didn't get.

"I've heard about you, MacFarlane," he told me. "You own the Oldsmobile. I'd like to catch you behind the wheel tonight, then maybe some people in this town could get some sleep. I think it's time you boys broke it up," he said, turning the light to the gang gathered around him. "I'll be taking my regular patrol through town, and when I get back here, I think everyone should be home in bed, or I'm going to start making some arrests and calling some parents." He pulled out a notebook and began scribbling notes. "As for you," he said to me, "I'd be very careful, Mr. MacFarlane. I'll be keeping an eye out for you."

"Thanks, Smelt," Duncan said sarcastically when the patrol car pulled away. "Good thing you didn't drink four beers. I'd probably be in jail now."

"Remember the time you told Mother Saint Margaret that I volunteered to mop the art building for you? Well, I can forget it now," I replied.

The party was a lost cause. Mary Scotland and Nicole and a couple of other girls had stayed hidden in the house while the police were in the yard, but just about everyone else had disappeared. I wanted us all, Mary and Nicole and Duncan and me, to learn to play the guitar and drums and form our own band, but Mary Scotland guided me upstairs to my bedroom and laughed when I asked her to spend the night with me in my bed, leaving me instead to pass out all alone.

I woke to Sunday morning's church bells, but Mass was not going to happen. I guess Calum was a better Catholic than me, since he would never let me miss Mass. I opened the closed bathroom door and saw the disaster, remembered that somebody's teeth were stuck in the bowl, and felt my own innards heave, but with towels in the sink, there was nowhere to heave them. I was racing down the hall, trying to make it to the kitchen sink before the contents of my stomach, which were already squirting between my clamping fingers, erupted when Calum's bedroom door opened and Duncan and Nicole walked out. I had no time to think of what that meant until much later, after the heaving and the headache were gone.

Mary Scotland arrived at the house after Mass, and the four of us sat around the kitchen table drinking strong tea, carrying out an autopsy on the party, which would have been a lot more enjoyable for me if they could remember anything funnier than me pissing at the cop. Only Mary Jane's teeth, still stranded in the toilet bowl, deflected attention away from my performance. By late afternoon our stomachs were stable enough to tackle the house, Duncan and I going after the teeth in the toilet, a nasty and under-appreciated task, since Mary Jane just threw them away rather than put them back in her mouth and made an appointment with the dentist.

Mary Scotland and Nicole were attacking the downstairs, making my nightmare of Calum's return slowly disappear with an efficient return to domestic normalcy. Still, I spent just about every waking minute of the next week restoring the house to fool Calum, gathering every lingering trace of evidence of the party, which included washing his sheets and blankets, and when Calum came home, alive I was glad to see, he never noticed a thing. Not right away, anyway. A couple of days later, with a snarl on his face, he led me into the parlour and pointed to the pile of butts and ashes under the blue velvety armchair.

"Clean that up," he said.

38

"Mother Saint Cross John can veto anything she wants," Duncan was saying to Nicole, Mary Scotland and me.

At the first Student Council meeting of the year, he had declared that The Twist was no longer banned at high school dances. The rest of the council gave unanimous support, but Mother Saint Cross John said no, and that was that. "She's the faculty advisor so she gets to sit in on every word we say, and she can veto whatever she wants. The Student Council may as well be playing patty cakes in kindergarten."

The vice-president, Mary Scotland, agreed with him. Nicole and I listened to the two of them arguing, but it wasn't really an argument because they were both on the same side: the Student Council was useless if they couldn't do the things the students wanted done.

"It's not like we're talking about passing a law saying there will be no more homework or anything like that," Mary Scotland said, "but the least we should be able to do is decide what kind of dances we want to have, but Mother Saint Cross John just sits there saying no to this idea, no to that idea. The only thing we're allowed to do is put on dances to raise money for a yearbook."

"And she has to approve every word and every picture that goes in the yearbook," Duncan added. "We wanted to get you to draw everybody's cartoon instead of graduation pictures, Smelt, but she said no to that. That would have been really different."

"I still think it would be better than pictures. It would be really original," Mary said. It was the first I had heard of the yearbook plans that had also been vetoed that day. Mary Scotland, as one of those honour students Mother Saint Cross John told Duncan about, was the editor of the yearbook along with being vice-president of the student council, but she wasn't as easily handled as Daniel MacFayden by the nun's whims and wishes. She wasn't one of Mother Saint Cross John's favourites, not being afraid to wear makeup or the latest fashion, but she was never in any trouble, either.

"It makes me mad that she called the cartoons a frivolous idea," Mary said.

"Whose idea was it?" I asked.

"Mary's," Duncan answered.

I was with Mother Saint Margaret almost every day, and she was pushing me hard, insisting on details that would never be part of the painting I was planning, but over and over, she had me practicing, telling me that if I am going to do a good job of my painting, then I need to know every tiny detail about it.

"Just because it's not going to be seen by people looking at the painting, Roddie, doesn't mean that the details aren't important. What they see in the painting will depend on how well you understood and mastered every detail of what it is they are seeing. If you are painting a picture of a building, it's not enough that you know what the building looks like on the outside. You have to know why it was built, what it looks like inside, who lives there, who lived there; you should learn everything you can about the building, even if the viewer is only going to see the outside of it. If you don't know anything about the building, why would you bother painting it in the first place? But if you know your subject, then the viewer will share that knowledge. He will see the character of the building, but people can't do that unless you have control of your painting." So I was immersed in details that I had never imagined would matter, and it took more than three weeks for her to let me go to my canvas and begin.

Mother Saint Margaret had also begun to talk to me about my plans for after graduation. Going to college didn't interest me much, except that Mary Scotland was planning to apply to Saint

Francis Xavier in Antigonish, on the mainland, so I thought that I might do the same. Duncan and I talked about going away together to look for work in the factories of Toronto or the mines in Sudbury. From time to time, too, I thought about the Nova Scotia Art College in Halifax, but not in any real way, just fantasies in which I tried to convince Calum, remembering the question Duncan had asked, "What would Calum say?"

I already knew what Calum would say. I had had a taste of it after my marks arrived in August when Calum asked if I planned to go to college. I said probably not, that we couldn't afford it, and besides, I wanted to start making some money. His answer to that was that we could find the money, and I should think about a college degree. That way, Calum said, if I wanted to do other things with my life I could just stick the degree in my arse pocket and do what I wanted after college. If I ever got hurt working for a living or got tired of doing manual labour, then I would have something to fall back on. I figured he knew what he was talking about, having had nothing to fall back on after he had fallen from the church roof. Calum was nothing if not practical, and art college was hardly practical, so I never mentioned it.

On October fifteenth, Calum brought the plants inside, closed the sun porch door and turned the key in the lock, turning the place into a weaving room where spiders spun their magic, intricate webs that would be, six months from now, swept away by a single swipe of Calum's broom. He moved his activities into the house and out to the workshop, rebuilding the kitchen after having measured and dismantled the cupboards and counter. Roughing out some functional shelving and drawers so I had a place to save the dishes after washing them, Calum slowly followed the details of his own design, planing and sanding and jointing with methodical precision. It was as if he didn't care if the job ever ended.

In the evenings he began bringing the framing wood for the shelves and cupboards in from the shop, with his own sketches stencilled on them, and sat on the kitchen couch beside the stove where I had never seen him sit before. With the same razor-sharp pocketknife that he used to remove the jig hooks from my leg he carved into the face of the wood, gouging out slivers that fell into the coal scuttle at his feet. Celtic knots interlaced with wild flowers emerged from under his knife, more ornate than his other engraved work around the house, looking almost like the illustrated pages of the Bible – my Bible, not his which was awfully stark. Watching him, I saw that there was a tremble to him now, an uncertainty of the hands when he rested from carving, but no hint of it showed while carving nor in the results which were as solid as stone and as light as air.

One evening, with Mary Scotland and me sitting at the kitchen table listlessly preparing for a history test, more interested in the music from the radio than the differences between the governments of Canada and the United States, Calum took his place on the couch, took his knife from his pocket, pulled the large blade free and picked up the piece of wood he had been working on. Watching him, Mary Scotland said, "That must be where you learned to draw," the same thing Mother Saint Margaret told me years before, that my talent came from Calum. I reached over and turned the radio down.

"Calum," I called loud enough to catch his attention. "Where did you learn to do that?"

It hadn't occurred to me until that moment that there was a time when Calum had to be taught the things he knew, that he wasn't born with a knowledge of why old houses had wedge boards, or how to reveal in a piece of wood the infinity of the Celtic knot.

"Huh?" he asked, looking up, although I thought he must have heard me the first time. I repeated my question.

Calum's interest dropped back to what he was doing, and we waited in silence until that seemed to be all Calum was offering. Finally, Mary stopped waiting for an answer and looked at me. I shrugged, and turned my attention back to the uninteresting pages of my history book when Calum broke the silence.

"Donald Angus MacKinnon," Calum said, not looking up from his task. "People styled him Donald Angus the Dummy. He never learned to talk. He could hear and understand the Gaelic and English both, but he didn't have a word of either. He was an itinerant, drifting from farm to farm, spending a week here, a month there, a winter with this family, a year with another. He worked for food and board. If there was a dollar to be spared it might be slipped to him when he was leaving. No one would slip Donald Angus the Dummy a dollar while they were still trying to get work out of him. Certainly not my father. Donald had a taste for the liquor, for which my father had no tolerance. The summer I turned twelve, Donald Angus came to work on our farm.

"Donald Angus the Dummy could whistle," Calum added, seemingly out of the blue. "It was said he knew a thousand jigs and reels and was as true to the tune as a fiddle. In the evening, after supper he sat on the kitchen couch and whittled. And, of course, whistled. Even a man as firm in his faith as my father, couldn't chastise Donald Angus for his only vocal expression. So Donald Angus filled the house with music when he was there, although no one ever requested a tune.

"It wasn't the man's music that interested me. It was the way the knife in his hands carved the wood. When he saw my interest, he took a chunk of wood off the woodpile and carved it into a wooden horse. It was as well proportioned as the living beast itself, and he gave it to me.

"I spent most evenings sitting beside him. One evening, I picked up a chunk of wood myself, took out my own pocket knife, and tried to copy him. It was a failure, but Donald Angus was patient. He pointed and demonstrated until I became comfortable with the wood," Calum said, falling into a silence long enough to establish that he had finished talking about Donald Angus the Dummy.

"Was that who taught you to be a carpenter?" I asked, wanting him to go on.

"No. My father wasn't pleased with my whittling but realized I was serious about wood. He knew from hard experience that farming was a meager life, and it was getting tougher. But a farmer who could build other farmers' barns, their houses, would be able to put a decent living together. I was sixteen when he apprenticed me to a carpenter. It was a man who had been to sea as such. When he finally came to land, he began building ship-sturdy houses and barns."

Calum was talking more about himself than I ever remembered, and it occurred to me that he was looking at memories made fresh by his recent visit to cousin Archie's and the people he used to know, those who were still alive, that is.

"But you never went back to farming," I said.

"I planned to," Calum said. "There was a lot of talk back then about the coal boom in Shean. The construction boom it brought. It was an opportunity to earn some money. My father expected me to return and begin taking over the farm. I expected that, as well, and it would have turned out that way if it wasn't for the accident."

"Accident?" Mary Scotland asked. "What accident?"

Calum told her about his fall and the winter he spent in bed recovering from the injury to his back. His version wasn't nearly as full of information as Taurus's. "It was difficult enough to be a carpenter with an injured back. It would have been impossible to be a farmer back then," Calum said.

"So you didn't go back home?" Mary asked.

"Once or twice," Calum answered.

"God, you must have seen a lot of changes when you went back last September," she said to Calum, who hadn't said more than a few words about his trip since his return. I found myself gathering up the scattered clues and trying to make sense of them. Calum had lived in Shean more than fifty years. In that time his mother had died, his father had died, just about everyone, as far as I knew, had died except for his cousin Archie whom I first saw the day after my grandmother's funeral. They probably came after the funeral, Mrs. MacFarlane once said, so that they wouldn't have to go into a Catholic church.

Was that it, then? Calum hadn't travelled the hundred or so miles by train to his own home for so long because he had married a Catholic and his family would have nothing to do with him anymore? I heard of it happening before. There were plenty of examples in Shean itself of people who had been disowned by their families because they married a Catholic or Protestant. Stupid as it seemed, it could be true.

"It must have looked different," Mary Scotland said, still prodding.

Calum's head nodded in agreement with her speculation.

"I left on a dirt road. I went back on a paved one. That was different," Calum said. "It was my cousin Archie Gillies's team that took me to the station when I left, and it was Archie's car that met me at the station when I went back. That was different. Barns that were brand new when I left, some I helped build, were starting to fall down in fields nobody farms anymore. That was different. People who were once alive are now dead. That was different."

After an hour, Calum put the knife and wood away and went into his study to read. That was when I told Mary what Taurus told me about Calum marrying Belle, and about him raising everybody Catholic, even me.

"That's so romantic," Mary Scotland said. "Think how much he must have loved your grandmother."

Calum being romantic wasn't a thought I had ever had before.

"Would you do something like that for somebody you loved?"

"What? Turn Protestant?"

"Maybe not that, but get thrown out of your family because you loved somebody so much."

"There's no family left to get thrown out of," I reminded her.

"But if there was?" she continued.

"I don't know," I answered cautiously. I didn't know who Mary Scotland meant by "somebody you loved," but I suspected she meant herself since it was her I loved. Would I want Calum to never speak to me again?

"I don't know," I repeated.

39

Mrs. MacFarlane pretty nearly fainted when she saw the kitchen. At the door, when I answered her knock, she said she only a had a minute because she had more baking to do, lots of shopping to do, and a thousand other things to get ready in the few days before Christmas. She was on her way down to the Co-op, she said, and just wanted to drop off a loaf of bread for Calum and me. When she carried it into the kitchen, she gasped. Calum had put the finishing touches on his cupboards the day before, so his work was as fresh as the bread in Mrs. MacFarlane's hands, and she just sank down on my grandmother's rocking chair beside the stove and rocked and looked. The way Calum had stained his carving was the opposite of what I expected, having used a light stain in the engraving, with the rest of the wood stained dark so that it looked as if the knots and entangled flowers shone out of the wood.

"On second thought, Roddie, I think I have time for tea," she said, then got up and began looking at Calum's carving up close, tracing it with her fingers, which was what she was doing when Calum came into the kitchen and startled the daylights out of her with his Gaelic welcome. They exchanged season's greetings, and then Mrs. MacFarlane went back to English to tell him how much she admired his kitchen while I put my tea, Mrs. MacFarlane's bread and Tom MacPhee's cheese, which I was learning to like a lot myself, on the table. We sat there together in the middle of the afternoon with snowflakes melting on the window, and pretty soon Mrs. MacFarlane got to remembering, which started her telling stories.

So Mrs. MacFarlane was looking out the window at the snow capping on the cairn and holding her cup in both hands and sipping from it, and she asked Calum, "Do you remember...?" But it didn't

really matter if Calum recalled or not because it was her way of
beginning to tell us what she remembered, although most of the
time Calum nodded his head at her recollections, like the Christmas when she was twelve or thirteen and she went to midnight
Mass at Holy Family Church, and my father, who was one of the
altar boys, fell asleep holding his candle, and his soutane caught
on fire. He wasn't hurt because another altar boy, Tom MacPhee,
was standing beside the plaster angel and pulled the basin of holy
water out of her hands and threw it on my father, putting the fire
out, and Father Ranald, who was the priest at the time, scolded Tom
for using holy water when he should have run into the vestry and
gotten regular water. By the time he did that, Mrs. MacFarlane
said, my father would have been toasted like a marshmallow.

Calum clamped his lips in the tight way he had of smiling
when Mrs. MacFarlane reminded him, although he wouldn't have
remembered himself since he wouldn't have been in the church,
but I bet he heard a good version when my grandmother and my
father and my aunt all got home from church, and that was probably what Calum was recalling: all those people, all those now
dead people.

They were talking back and forth like that, Mrs. MacFarlane
talking, Calum mostly listening and confirming what she was saying about Christmases long ago compared to the way Christmas
was now, with children just interested in the Christmas catalogue
from Simpson-Sears and not interested in much else. They talked,
too, about the way Shean had changed over the years, with Mrs.
MacFarlane picking Calum's memory to reconstruct the main
street the way it was when she was young.

The streets of Shean were reassembled before me while we
sat around the table, Calum going back even further than Mrs.
MacFarlane to the beginning of time in Shean. There had been
boardwalks and brawls back then and a wildness that made me
envious. I couldn't believe they were talking about the same town.
In 1909, they sent the army in to keep the miners quiet. They didn't

need an army to do that anymore. It made me think of something Taurus said once in the sun porch, that "Shean's getting the shit kicked out of her, and we're just sitting here taking it."

Buildings went up and others came down. What Calum recalled being a grocery store was a woman's clothing store when Mrs. MacFarlane was young, and it was just a vacant building to me. I learned that there used to be a little building on the empty lot beside Bartholomew's store, a doctor's office. The property belonged to Bartholomew, but after Calum's accident he got after the town council to find a doctor and offered to build a building on the vacant lot as an incentive. If the doctor stopped using it, it came back to Bartholomew, so it wasn't like he gave the land away; Bartholomew was too good a businessman for that. The town council got busy after that, advertising in papers and everything, and that's when Dr. MacLean came. He was the town doctor until he retired, and then Dr. Proud took over, so in a way it was Calum who was responsible for getting the first doctor to come to town. It didn't say much for what the mine owners thought of miners getting hurt underground all the time, since nobody bothered getting a doctor to move to town for them. Although it was his accident that sent the town in search of a doctor, Calum had never been to see a doctor. He and Dr. Proud liked to trade ideas when they met at noon at Bartholomew's store, though.

"Do you know the biggest change I see this year?" Mrs. MacFarlane asked, then went on to say, "Bartholomew's store. Sarah Campbell has tried to do something with the window displays, but she doesn't have Bartholomew's touch. I think it would be less sad if she didn't put up a display at all."

Even I could see it was true, and she had missed Armistice Day altogether, not a poppy in the window. But the biggest change I saw about the store was that without Bartholomew in it Duncan was allowed to go back in for his cigarettes, and once a month he stole a copy of *Police Gazette* just for the hell of it.

"Do you remember the miners' memorial?" Calum asked Mrs.

MacFarlane, who said she didn't. "Probably before your time. That was what got Bartholomew started on his window displays," my grandfather remembered. There had been an accident in 1917, a roof fall that trapped four miners underground. The town was in shock. Other miners had been killed, Taurus's brother, Donald, being the first of them. Miners had been pinned between runaway coal cars over the years, and some were killed in blasts that exploded while they were being set, but it was always one miner at a time until the roof fall. Shean was luckier than most mining towns in that way. This particular roof fall closed off a section of the mine, and the draegermen took four days to reach them. They were the first miners killed who weren't brought to the surface immediately after their accidents because of the time it took to tunnel through the roof fall, shoring up the roof against further falls as they went; so the people of Shean had a long time to think about what was going on down there. There were prayer vigils in both churches because nobody knew for sure yet that the men were dead, but the faces in town were the colour of a November sky as people waited for word from underground.

While Calum was recalling the accident, Mrs. MacFarlane very softly started singing four Gaelic names, like movie music, too low to interrupt his telling of what happened. The names were from Taurus's song, "*Cumha nam Méinneadairean*."

"Bartholomew's store window was always rich with colour," Calum continued, recalling the same colours we still see in it every day, clear glass bowls of bananas and oranges and apples. They look common today, he added, something you'll see in any store window, but thirty, forty years ago oranges and bananas in a store window in the middle of a grey, grimy coal mining town evoked images of places where the sun shines forever along warm stretches of blue ocean. People used to stand and stare, especially in fall and winter, so Bartholomew always brought in fresh fruit. Even when the coal company habitually cut the miners' wages as they tended to do. Even when strikes, like the one of '32, paralyzed the town and nobody had any money, Bartholomew never stopped putting the fruit in the window, and every day he would feel it, testing the firmness and freshness of the oranges, checking for brown spotting on the bananas, and before they could turn, he took them to the schools, the Catholic school as well as the public school, for teachers to distribute among the students.

"I remember that," Mrs. MacFarlane said, "getting fresh oranges, but I thought they came from the teachers."

"With the people wandering the town's streets in a daze the day the miners' bodies were recovered, Bartholomew stripped the fruit from his store window and filled it with coal-black crepe paper and arranged four pit helmets with the name of one of the four miners beside each, and he put picks and shovels shaped like a cross under each helmet. At night, before locking up his store, he hooked freshly charged batteries up to the helmets and turned them on then turned off all the lights in the store so that those four lights shone through the night. People came and stood and looked, and some cried. The coal company itself had done nothing, so Bartholomew left the display in the window for a week after the four funerals. It was after that he began decorating the space behind his plate glass for special holidays and occasions, always returning to the fresh fruit for the rest of the year."

"So that's how it came about," Mrs. MacFarlane said. "I never heard that before. It was always so—oh, my God!" she said suddenly, staring out our kitchen window into the shortest night of the year. "It's dark! How long have I been here? I've got supper to make and shopping to do. I was just going to stay for a minute," she added, getting up and taking her coat off the back of the chair, giving the kitchen a last sweep with her eyes. "It's beautiful, Calum. I just love it."

Mary Scotland's knock on the window came through my concentration like a real telephone ringing in a dream, pulling me slowly back from the painting until I was aware I was in the studio. When

Mrs. MacFarlane jumped up from our table and raced out with so much to do, it reminded me I had things to do, too. I left shortly after her with the key to the art building that Mother Saint Margaret had given me so that I could finish the painting I was working on before Christmas. Not long after I got started, Mother Saint Margaret brought me some food from the convent, discussed the painting with me for a while, then left me to work on it.

Exams were over, school had been out for two days, and still I was going back to the art building. It was driving Duncan crazy because I clung to my superstition that I shouldn't talk about or show my paintings until they were finished. Mother Saint Margaret was the only exception to that rule, which had Duncan wondering if I was painting or if Mother Saint Margaret and I had something going on after school.

I lowered the drop cloth over the canvas and went to the door to let Mary in.

"Calum said you didn't come for supper, so I thought you might be here. How is it coming?" she asked, lifting the corner of the cloth but I caught her hand. It had become a game, Mary trying to peek, me stopping her, usually leading to our wrestling each other toward some more romantic encounter, although she was always much more reluctant than me to pursue it all the way through when it was happening in the art building, which was next door to the convent.

"Let's go for a walk instead," she said.

"Instead of what?"

"Instead of whatever you're thinking."

"I'm thinking that I'll have to go to confession tomorrow or the next day, and then we wouldn't be able to do anything to each other until after Communion at Midnight Mass, so we shouldn't waste tonight."

"Maybe I should leave you here to paint your painting and come back for you on Boxing Day," Mary said. "That way, we'll both be safe."

"Let's go for a walk." I wasn't interested in painting any

more that night.

"This is the shortest day of the year," Mary Scotland pointed out as we walked through the darkness. Not a lot of snow had fallen, so the decorated houses didn't seem as colourfully reflective as a year earlier. The stores, open late on Christmas week, were closing as we walked over Main Street, and there wasn't much else for us to do but make our way toward The Turk's. Because of Advent, there were no dances, not even bingos, so people kept busy shopping or baking like Mrs. MacFarlane. I was trying to think of somewhere we could go to be alone, when the Oldsmobile pulled up beside us.

"Get in," Duncan said.

The car leaned heavily as Duncan sped around the long curve at the top of the Big River Hill. The road had been ploughed to small, dirty banks on the shoulder, but it was cold enough outside for black ice to form in depressions on the pavement, and Mary reached across and grabbed my hand, squeezing her fear into it. Not a word had been said since we got into the back seat, Duncan behind the wheel and Farter beside him.

Outside of Shean, Duncan pulled off the pavement onto the road to St. Margaret's Cove, following it until he pulled into a popular and badly littered look-off. He killed the engine and turned off the headlights, leaving only the dash light, except for a brief moment when a match flared in front of his cigarette.

"Nicole's in the hospital," he said, the cigarette still in his mouth, exhaling as he spoke.

"God! What happened to her?" asked Mary, rising in her seat at the news.

Duncan didn't answer right away but eventually said, "She had a miscarriage."

"A miscarriage!" I said. "I didn't even know she was...."

"Neither did I," Duncan said, cutting off my words.

"She started bleeding at home, you know," Farter volunteered. "She started bleeding at home, you know, and my mother knew right away what it was, and she said she was waiting for something like this to happen to Nicole, you know, and then she made John Alex take her to the hospital, and John Alex was saying, 'I just want to buy a bottle,' you know, while my mother was pushing him out to his truck. I didn't see any blood, but that's what they said, that she was bleeding, you know. I was the one who got to tell Duncan."

"Is she all right?" Mary asked, while I tried to remember the last time I could be certain Mary wasn't pregnant. We didn't do it often enough, I decided.

"I don't know," Duncan said to her question. "I went to see her, and she was just lying in this room alone with the lights turned off, crying. Just the streetlight shining in. She didn't want to talk or anything. All she said was she had decided she was going to keep it no matter what I did."

"You know what my mother said?" Farter interrupted. "She said if Nicole was going to do it again, you know, it should be with somebody with money or at least a job, and not with somebody half her age. 'You're not going to be pretty forever, you know.' That's what my mother said to Nicole, you know."

"Farter, shut up! You're mother's a stupid pig."

"That's what she said about you, you know," Farter replied, taking one of Duncan's cigarettes from the pack on the dash and lighting it, and shutting up.

Duncan started the car, threw it in reverse, backed away from the look-off and drove to town at a normal speed, for Duncan.

"I'm going back to the hospital after I take this fellow home," he said, dropping Mary and me off at Calum's house. "I'm still going to have to tell the old lady."

Merry Christmas, Mrs. MacFarlane.

"At least she's not going to be a grandmother because of it," I said.

"Yeah, I thought of that," said Duncan. "It feels like a sin to feel so lucky."

40

It was almost three in the morning before I came into the house from Mary Scotland's, where we had gone after midnight Mass. Her family had a custom of going home to an after-Mass feast, bringing a meatball and baked potato end to the Advent fast, and opening one gift each before going to bed to wait for Santa Claus. Mary opened the gift I gave her, and, since the only gift I had at her house was the one she gave me, I opened that, an expansion strap for my Timex. While I fidgeted with changing my leather strap for the metal one, she opened mine, a large silver clasp for her long hair, an idea I got from an O. Henry story we had studied just before school let out for the holidays.

Except for the light on the front verandah that Calum had left on, the house was dark. I felt my way into the dining room, and plugged in the tree and stood in its rainbow of light, listening. What I was listening for I wasn't sure. I guess I wanted to be sure Calum was asleep, and I suppose that after the music and laughing and food at Mary's house, our own home seemed sadly silent and I walked through the silence up to my room, returning with Calum's gift which I had smuggled into the house and hidden in my room. It still had to be wrapped, which I did with a loose binding of holiday paper and placed it upright under the tree.

Finished, I went to bed weary but too anxious to sleep, dozing and waking until I heard the squeak of Calum's bedroom door opening and his shuffle to the bathroom to shave. I lay there in the near dawn waiting until he went downstairs, then I dressed and came down too.

Calum was in the kitchen setting the kettle for his tea, and placing the double-boiler over the flame to reheat the porridge he had made the night before, as if it was just another morning. Seeing me must have triggered his memory, because his expression changed – from surprise at my presence in the kitchen at that hour to something approaching a smile. "Merry Christmas," he said, turning back to the stove.

I sorted and separated our gifts under the tree for something to do while I waited for my grandfather to come back into the dining-room. He came in carrying both bowls of breakfast, setting them on the oak table and, sitting at his bowl, signalled for me to bring him one of his gifts. It wasn't as if we had as many gifts as houses with bigger families, but between Mrs. MacFarlane, who always wrapped something for him and something for me, and what we got for each other and the Santa Claus packages that mysteriously appeared with my name on them every year, it was enough, especially since most were for me. I picked up a small package for each of us, Mrs. MacFarlane's for Calum, Duncan's for me. While Calum unwrapped a nice pair of leather gloves that would wind up in the same bureau drawer where he kept the socks and scarves and gloves of other Christmases, I opened Duncan's gift, curiously reading the writing on the unfamiliar box of Sheiks, until the information on the side of the box finally bore through my thick skull to inform me that I was holding a box of French safes, which I began juggling like a hot iron in a panic to get it out of sight before Calum grew alert. I wrapped the paper back around it, then dropped the package to my lap and shoved it under my shirt as Calum slowly pulled the ribbon and tore the tape that concealed the bottle of Old Spice I wrapped for him. Then I got up, saying in a loud, explanatory voice that I had to go to the bathroom and ran upstairs and searched my room for a place to stash the condoms where Calum could never, ever stumble on them. I chose the top shelf of my closet in a box of baseball cards until I had time to think it through more thoroughly. Running back downstairs, I couldn't get mad at Duncan, because I knew that this gift was no joke. Still, the bastard could have warned me. He knew what would happen.

I walked to the tree, picked up another gift and began unwrapping the potential nitroglycerin within. Calum, by this time, had gone to the tree himself and picked up the present I had leaned against the trunk the night before, and carried it back to the table. He took his time opening the little tag that said it was to him from me, then he looked at me and nodded, thanking me in advance for whatever was inside. Calum's spotted hands began to untie the ribbon, remove it, roll it up carefully and tie it off into an untangled reusable ribbon for one of next Christmas's gifts. He started on the paper then, running his finger along the edge where the red wrapping was taped closed, carefully salvaging the same paper that had been wrapped around a pair of shin pads the Christmas before. He began folding the paper back, revealing its contents the way he opened the paper-wrapped meat I brought home from Co-op while I nervously awaited his reaction.

He stared at it curiously for a moment, and then lifted it from the bed of tissue and held it in front of him, studying the unframed painting. I studied his unflinching face, afraid of seeing that acknowledging nod again, the one that would relegate my work to the glove drawer. He was growing confused and carried the painting into his study where he took the calendar off the wall and caught the wooden back of the painting on the empty nail. He stepped back while I waited for him to ask me what it was, and I wondered what I would say when he did. Suddenly his shoulders moved like something startled him and then, without taking his eyes off the picture he took his reading glasses out of his pocket and leaned in closer. His finger, almost touching the oil, moved along the story on the canvas, a fossil forest rising out of the mine slag, coal-black trunks branching out to explosions of autumn colour, and Calum's finger guided him like a child learning to read as he sounded out each letter, "*Darach-onn-muin-uath...*," tracing its way along the oak to the furze to the vine to the hawthorn.

"*Domhnall MacLeòid*," he said. "*Domhnall MacLeòid, Fionnlagh Ceanadach...*," the separate trees faded to a blur of colour then, becoming impressions of "*Cumha nam Méinneadairean*," Taurus's lament for the miners who had been killed in the Shean mine, colours and patterns that had come to me as I hummed or sang the air to the song I had taught myself to know as well as I had come to know the words to Taurus's unplanted poem. The first miner killed in the mines was also the first miner named in the song, *Domhnall MacLeòid*, Donald MacLeod, Taurus's brother, and the second one was Finlay Kennedy, and then, if there had been more room or I knew some other way to do it, the third name would have been....

"...*Teàrlach Camshron*...," Calum continued, his eyes burning into the forest before him. "...*Coinneach Bhochanan*...," he said, reciting the names that he had typed out on his Underwood, and something leaden lifted from my body. He got it!

The names faded away from Calum's lips, but he continued to stare a while longer before straightening up, and the two of us stood there looking at the Shean forest, me seeing now all the flaws in my masterpiece, mistakes of perspective and of leaf shapes and of density of colour. They had me fooled for a while into thinking that I had recreated the perfection of Taurus's song with colour, but now I was seeing what Calum was seeing. I was becoming embarrassed, and Calum wasn't saying or doing anything to stop the flush of shame I felt creeping up from under my shirt collar.

"I should have..." Calum began to say and stopped, but when I turned to look at him his eyes were still on my painting. "I should have ... I should have taught you," he said at last, turning to look at me. He backed up then, one hand reaching behind him to guide him into his desk chair. "I should have taught you," he said again. I knew what he meant because somewhere in the summer before, amid the planting of the trees, I had come to regret that my grandfather had not taught me to speak the Gaelic.

"Taurus used to ask me all the time why you didn't," I said. "I told him I didn't know. He called me your second chance and wondered why you never took it."

"I suppose he was right," Calum said. "Your grandmother? Do you remember her?"

"A little," I answered.

"I wish you could have known her longer, better. She was made of music. That's what I first saw in her, music. Not that she played the piano much, or even sang very often. It was more of a quality, I suppose you would call it, like light filtering through stained glass to brighten dark churches. It was there in the way she laughed, in the way she would look at a person sometimes. She was a romantic, always trying to point my attention toward the stars or the sunset. We didn't have much in common, you understand, except we liked each other. People never understood it, but it doesn't matter.

"We were married a long time before the children came, Evelyn, then Roddie. They were like her. I was glad for that. The Gaelic was the language of the house, and the children took to it without shame, not even when they were old enough to realize it wasn't much use to them, that few of their friends spoke it.

"Your father had a great gift for it, making up word games as a little boy, making little boy songs, puns. When he was just this high," Calum said, holding his hand a distance from the floor, "he began pestering us for pipes. I regretted getting them for him, at first. I wasn't deaf enough then to shut out the drone of his learning. I regretted it a lot more later.

"He was a romantic like your grandmother and enjoyed wearing plaids and playing tunes made popular by Highland regiments fighting British wars. I tried to tell him there was another tradition, a truer one, but it was like trying to tell your grandmother something once her mind was made up."

Calum's eyes had not wandered from my painting all the time he spoke, and now he paused in his telling of the family story, but I knew he wasn't finished.

"He loved the language and the music with passion, and passion can be dangerous. He wasn't unlike Taurus that way, distant relatives, you know.

"When the war began, I stopped him and stalled him as much as I could, trying to teach him too late some of the hard facts of

Scottish and British history."

He stopped then, as if gazing inside himself, but I knew some of the hard facts he was referring to, had heard them from him whenever a history book of the British Empire lay open before me when I was doing homework. He was looking at a time two hundred years ago when Highland regiments were off fighting a British war, and in their absence British solders came into the Highlands and gathered up the women and children, burned their homes and herded them to the sea where boats waited to ship them off to the colonies. When the Highland soldiers returned from fighting the British war, their families were gone, and none of the men had any idea where his wife and children were, scattered as they had become from North America to Australia. I often wondered, in the controlled passion of his telling, if he knew something more, suspected something more. Our own family was so small. Did a larger family exist somewhere beyond our knowledge of them?

"When Roddie went into the mines he was exempt from military service, and I thought he was safe, but when they formed the Cape Breton Highlanders, he couldn't resist. There was no stopping him, not with his friends filling the ranks. When he wrote us that he had met and married your mother in Scotland and would be bringing her home with him and with the war clearly coming to an end, I felt he was safe, but all that came back were his pipes and not much else. Your mother and you, of course. I've kept those pipes from you because as soon as you began to move around the house I could see your grandmother, your father all through you, the same dangerous romance that could be lured to death by damned politicians and their damned wars. I forbade your grandmother, and I never forbade her before, to speak to you in the language, to protect you from it, from yourself, although I often had to pretend not to hear the Gaelic lullabies she sang you to sleep with almost every night.

"I was angry with your father for misunderstanding his people's history, and I was scared for you, but I was wrong. I should have taught you."

"But it was a war against Hitler," I said, defending my father's death while trying not to pour salt on Calum's pain.

"Back then it was a war against Germany," Calum answered. "Except for the victims, all the horror of it has already been forgiven and forgotten by the politicians and the diplomats, and now those warring countries are allies, and my son is still dead. His death never mattered one bit to anyone but those who knew him, who loved him.

"Yes, Roddie, it was a war against Hitler, and you have a right to be proud of your father, but you had a greater right to know him and be raised by him and taught by him, and that right has been taken from you. You have a right to be proud, but I will not apologize for hating the fact that my son is a name on a cross in Holland that nobody reads, least of all the people responsible for putting him there."

Calum went silent for another while.

"But I shouldn't have punished you because of it."

"You didn't punish me," I replied.

"I punished both of us. We are speaking now in a tongue that should be foreign to this house but isn't because I made a stupid decision. Whether you know it or not, whether you care or not, your life will be poorer for my failure," the sadness in Calum's voice thick with potential tears.

"You could teach me now," I suggested, but he just shook his head in the same definite way he did when Duncan said we could replant Taurus's poem on his grandmother's farm. I guess I knew when I said it that it wouldn't happen.

We sat in the silence of Calum's study, him staring at the painting, me staring at the floor, wondering how long we were going to sit there with more presents under the tree still to be opened.

"Thank you," he said finally, releasing me, not looking away from the painting.

41

My painting had hung unframed on the wall of Calum's study from Christmas until the March day I came home from school and saw it surrounded in oak. The thick frame was three inches wide at the top and around the sides, engraved with the leaves of the Gaelic alphabet. It was thicker at the bottom. It had to be because the title, "*Cumha nam Méinneadairean*," was carved into it in Celtic lettering, and under the title in five rows were carved the fifty-four Gaelic names of the miners whom Taurus had named in his song. Calum had turned my painting into a cairn.

"That's great," I said, turning when I sensed Calum standing behind me. I realized I hadn't been paying much attention to his having spent so many winter evenings sitting on the kitchen couch carving. I had become so used to it before Christmas as he was getting the kitchen ready that it never occurred to me what he might be doing now that the kitchen was finished.

"Sit down."

I moved from the doorway into the study and sat on the couch, wondering for the first time if every house had as many couches as ours with one in the kitchen, one in the study, one in the parlour and one in the sun porch.

Calum sat at his desk and looked at our work that hung over my head. I waited.

"How serious is this?"

"What?" I asked. But I knew what he meant.

"A nun came to see me today," Calum said. "It's time to begin sending out applications for university, and she has some idea that you want to apply to an art college in Halifax."

"No, I don't want to apply to an art college," I said in full retreat from my dreams. "I'm going to apply to St. FX, like Mary, or maybe St. Mary's in Halifax, or maybe..."

"How serious is this?" he asked again, lifting his square chin to the painting above my head. I didn't turn around.

"Well, pretty serious. But I don't have to go to college to learn to draw. I can just take courses."

"From a comic book?" Calum sneered. "Never mind this running away and answer the question! How serious is this?"

"It's all I really think about."

"And have you thought about how you can make a living painting pictures?"

"I sold some pictures of horses."

"Enough to pay your way through college?"

"Well, no, but...." My voice petered out, but Calum just sat there waiting. I felt trapped, pinned under his stare, and it was as if the easiest thing for me to do was just say that I wanted to go to a regular college and get a regular degree and find a regular job, but the truth of his accusation, that I was running away, formed a stubborn knot in my stomach. "Artists always starve before they get discovered," I said, "but then sometimes people pay thousands of dollars for just one of their paintings."

"The artist is usually dead by then," Calum said.

"I won't be," I answered.

"I hope not. Come with me."

Calum led me into the kitchen and, leaving me standing by the table, walked into the pantry. He came back carrying a box of oatmeal, some cans of beans and corn, a five-pound bag of flour. He went back into his study and returned with a couple of books. He tipped one of our kitchen chairs upside down, took the kettle from the stove and placed it in the middle of the table along with a cup, and a can opener.

"What do you see here?" he asked, and I shrugged, more worried about his mind than whatever meaning I was supposed to figure out.

"What do you see here?" he asked again, lifting the bag of flour.

"Robin Hood," I answered, ready to duck if the bag came flying at me.

"And what do you see here?" he asked, lifting the oatmeal box.

"A Quaker," I answered.

"And here?" he continued, pointing to the bottom of the chair.

"The bottom of the chair," I volunteered. His finger directed me closer to the print. "Bass River," I answered.

Can by kettle, stove by book cover, through the kitchen and into the dining room and the parlour Calum kept his strange game of naming things until I began to see a pattern emerge. He had directed my attention to names and images and shapes until suddenly I was leaping ahead of him, trying to find a single item in our house that had not been designed before it was created, even Calum's own work.

"Everything's got some kind of art behind it," I said.

Calum turned to me with a look that gave me a passing grade.

"Everything has some kind of art behind it," he said. "Maybe every artist doesn't want to be drawing flour bags or oatmeal boxes, but nothing can get onto the store shelf or even onto a car lot without an artist designing it in such a way that people will want it. I don't understand why that school up there would teach you about art but not tell you how many fine jobs an education in art can provide.

"I hope somebody will pay you thousands of dollars for your paintings someday, but even if they won't, you'll still have more opportunities than someone studying English or even science. That's if you understand the nature of your talent and how versatile it can be, if you let it."

"Do you think I should go to the art college?"

"If that's your preference."

The excitement bounced around inside me, but I was as unmoved as Calum on the outside because there was a more practical problem.

"Mother Saint Margaret will give a recommendation," I said, "but my marks aren't good enough to get a scholarship. Not to art college. Not anywhere."

"We'll manage," Calum said, repeating words he had said to me before about college, leaving no more to be said about the subject, although I didn't want to just let a great moment like this end on that note.

"Mother Saint Margaret really came to see you?"

"Walked into the workshop while I was framing that thing," Calum answered.

"She must have liked it," I said, turning to look at the picture and frame.

"Well, she said all the right things," Calum conceded, which meant he liked her. I wondered if she had told him what she told me, that my talent came from Calum.

"Well, she wouldn't lie, not about art," I assured him, sorry I had missed it but glad I wasn't there.

"She was concerned enough about you to come to me with what she thought you were afraid to bring up to me. Why did she have to do that?"

"I guess I thought you'd think it was a waste of time and money. I didn't know you'd think it was a good idea."

"I didn't think anything because I wasn't aware of what you wanted. You owe that nun a lot. She probably saved you a life of regret about yourself and resentment about me. I just expect you to do well when you get there."

"If I get in," I reminded him, adding that an application wasn't an acceptance.

"You'll get in."

Duncan and Nicole picked Mary and me up, and we went driving around Shean looking for something to do. In Shean, in winter, if we didn't want to sit in The Turk's on a school night, and Nicole certainly didn't, there weren't many other choices. As we drove back and forth over street, Duncan kept pulling over to pick Farter up every time we passed him on the sidewalk, only to rev the engine and pull away just as Farter reached for the door. What I noticed as we were driving back and forth was the space between Duncan and Nicole. She was against the door on her side of the car, and Duncan seemed pressed against his.

"If you two were sitting any further apart I'd say you were married," I joked, only to get Mary's elbow in my rib. At least Mary and I were still sitting close enough to touch each other – no matter how un-tender the touch, I thought, trying to figure out why I was being elbowed.

The next time over town, Farter was standing in the middle of the street flagging us.

"Stop teasing him and pick him up," Nicole told Duncan, who hit the brakes at the last minute as Farter scrambled out of the way. Nicole pushed over and made room for him in the front seat.

"Any smokes?" Farter asked, and Duncan pulled a pack from his shirt pocket and passed them across to him. Farter took one out, lit it and, exhaling the smoke, said, "You can't go to The Turk's, you know, because he went on a tear and chased everybody out, you know, and fired everybody, too. You got no job again, Nicole, you know."

"Wonderful," Nicole said, sarcastically.

Duncan drove past The Turk's. The lights were still on but a baffled customer stood on the steps jiggling the locked door handle.

"Once Tony finishes drinking whatever he has in there, I suppose he'll empty the cash register and go to your place," Duncan said.

"I don't care where he goes," Nicole answered, "but I don't want you playing cards with him."

"Why not? The guy couldn't beat my grandmother playing fish. Besides, he's an arsehole."

"So are you sometimes. I've changed my mind. Take me home."

Duncan made a sudden U-turn in the middle of the street and peeled rubber until he slowed the car enough to swing up Culloden Street and slammed on the brakes in front of my house.

"See you tomorrow," he said, as Mary and I gladly got out of the car.

"What's got into her?" I wondered aloud and immediately wished I had kept my mouth shut.

"You can be so stupid sometimes!" Mary turned on me, and I was looking at the first real fight of our lives. "Nicole lost her baby and Duncan couldn't care less. How do you think she feels about that? And he's probably happy he doesn't have to get married, but it was too close for comfort anyway. They're breaking up because of it. You'd have to be stupid not to see that, and there you were talking about how far apart they're sitting."

"Well it wasn't Duncan who moved his seat," I said.

"No, it wasn't, but it's Duncan who's pushing her all the way over to the other side of the car. He wants to get out, and you know what? Nicole's lucky, because if she married Duncan, she might as well have married her father, a bootlegger and a gambler."

"Duncan's not a bootlegger," I said. She looked at me like I was the Man in the Moon because we had stood beside Duncan on a few occasions when his trunk was open. "He just sells it to friends who can't get it anywhere else, but he's not bootlegging. Duncan might sell booze for fun, but he'd never do it for a living. He's got too much pride for that. He's not anything like Nicole's father."

"He's a bastard just like Nicole's father, Roddie. He's my friend, too, but there are times when I don't like him. He doesn't even see what he's doing to Nicole because he's too busy looking everywhere else for a way out. And neither do you, do you?"

"Do I what?"

"See what Duncan's doing to Nicole. You don't see it, do you?"

"Yeah," I said. "I, ah ... I'm not blind."

Mary shook her head as if she didn't believe what I said while I tried to find a way to say I thought she was right without actually betraying Duncan. Mary spared me by giving up any hope that I might understand.

"I don't want to talk about it anymore," she said. "I'm just going home. I'll walk myself. You don't have to come."

While I stood there wondering if "You don't have to come" meant "I want you to come," or meant "I don't want you to come," Mary walked up the road and never glanced back. I spent the whole night thinking it was over for us, but it wasn't. Still, for one night it had been real enough to know that I didn't want it to happen to us, whatever was happening to Duncan and Nicole. She caught my attention.

42

Duncan got his strike.

It was a hot school day near the end of May when a narrow, twelve-foot strip of wood fell from the ceiling and clattered to the floor in the aisle between two rows of seats, followed by a shower of dry dust from the hole it left. Mary Scotland let out a yelp. She seemed almost embarrassed at first, sitting there, holding her hand to forehead near the temple, and the rest of us laughed until we saw the blood seeping between her fingers, running down the back of her hand. The end of the tongue-and-groove board had nicked her in its fall, and both Mother Saint Cross John and I made a run to help Mary. The nun got there first, lifted Mary's hand away and examined her forehead while pulling a handkerchief from her large, black sleeve. She pressed the handkerchief against Mary's head and told Mary to keep it in place. Then she told me to get Mary's sweater from the coat hook in the lobby.

"We're going to take you over to the hospital and have this looked at," Mother Saint Cross John was telling Mary when I came back.

"I can take her," I volunteered, not knowing how I might do that, but the hospital was only a short walk from the school.

"You stay here," she ordered, and giving the class instructions to use the time for a study period she left with Mary, who seemed to be in shock as she followed Mother Saint Cross John out the door and across the road. We watched from the window as the two of them got into the convent car and drove to the hospital.

The moment the car pulled away, Duncan went over to the slender piece of hardwood, picked it up and, holding it like a claymore, said it was time for a Student Council meeting. All of the executive except for Mary was in our classroom, but Duncan sent students to each of the other classes from grades seven to eleven.

"Just say there's an important Student Council meeting going to be held. They'll think Mother Saint Cross John sent you for the class reps," Duncan reasoned, correctly as it turned out, because within minutes the whole Student Council was assembled, along with the rest of the grade twelve class, with no faculty advisor.

Duncan told them what had happened to Mary. Then breaking the brittle stick again and again over his knee he walked to the potbellied stove which hadn't been lit for a couple of weeks because of the mild spring weather. He crumpled up a couple of pages from one of his scribblers, threw it in, then threw the broken pieces on top of the paper and lit a match. Almost immediately the wood crackled, flaming as quickly as the paper itself while the members of the Student Council stood around in thoughtful confusion over Duncan's meaning.

"How much chance would anybody have if this place ever caught fire?" Duncan asked, and with that question the rest of us crowded around to see what was taking place in the stove.

"What can we do?" asked several members of the council together.

"We can strike," Duncan said. "We can walk out of here and set up a picket line. If the Student Council votes to strike, then it's a legal strike. It's not our fault the faculty advisor isn't here, is it?" he asked, anticipating the objection that seemed to be forming on Daniel MacFadyen's lips.

"My mother would kill me," Taylor Roberts, the grade seven representative on the council said. More than one head nodded in agreement.

"We would miss so much schoolwork," Doris Ainslie, the brain of grade ten, added. Not one head nodded in agreement.

"We might even get kicked out of school," John Donald MacKay said. Heads nodded in agreement.

"Listen," Duncan said, stepping up onto the low platform upon which the teacher's desk sat, giving him a nun's eye view of everyone in the room, "what have we got to lose? They can't expel everybody in the school. Mary Scotland is in the hospital right now because of that stick," Duncan pointed to the dying fire in the stove. "That stick split her head open. She's lucky it didn't knock her eye out."

He picked up Mother Saint Cross John's desk bell and threw it at the ceiling where it banged wildly, making a sharp chime in the process, and people ran from where it would fall back to the floor. Out of the long narrow gap in the ceiling came another shower of dust as old as Shean itself, and what everybody saw before they looked away and covered their eyes, was that the strip of tongue-and-groove, besides the one that already fell, was noticeably loose.

"We have a history of standing up for ourselves here in Shean," Duncan went on while the rest of us adjusted our positions to safer parts of the classroom. "In 1932, the miners in Shean went on strike for eight months," Duncan said, his version of history ignoring the fact that miners had been striking against each other over the future of the mine. "They were on strike for eight months, and they stayed on strike even though the priest was telling them from the pulpit that they had to go back to work."

"Who told you that?" Daniel MacFadyen asked.

"Taurus MacLeod told me that, and if you don't believe me, ask Smelt. He was there."

"Who?" Daniel MacFadyen asked.

"Smelt. Roddie Gillies. He's standing right there."

"I know who Smelt is," Daniel said. "But who's this Taurus guy?"

"He's the old man who's always coughing and spitting in church," Taylor Roberts explained, and some students began to giggle.

"Taurus MacLeod is the greatest man this town ever knew," Duncan said, loud enough to shout down the growing snickers.

"The strike of '32 was before he went senile, when he organized the miners against the company. Like I said, they stood up against the priest, and that's a lot harder than striking against a nun, even one as cross as Mother Saint Cross John. Taurus was the strongest man in Shean, but he never fought anybody who didn't ask for it, and he wouldn't have led the strike if he didn't believe that miners were in danger. And he was a poet, too, and he wrote songs and sang about strikes and miners and all kinds of things about Shean that we don't know about because he wrote it all in Gaelic. How many people write things about us? How many poems about us are there in the English literature books? None, that's how many. But Taurus MacLeod, the greatest man Shean ever knew, wrote about us. And that's not all he did."

Duncan then began marshalling all the knowledge he had gathered about the strike, his eyes burning intensely as he described the miners standing around a barrel fire in bitter winter weather without food or warm clothes but determined that nobody, not even the priest, was going to walk all over them. He didn't tell them that most of the miners standing around the barrel fire were Protestants, and that most of the Catholic miners backed the priest and his plan for the mine.

"Johnny Sandy MacKay was one of the leaders," Duncan said, casting one of the strikers into a leadership role, as if he didn't know that Johnny Sandy MacKay was John Donald Mac-Kay's grandfather, "and he went on strike so his children and his grandchildren would have a better life. All of them did. Arthur Ainslie got thrown in jail for disturbing the peace during the strike because he refused to get out of the way when the police tried to force their way through the picket line to let some scabs into the mines," he said, his words lassoing Doris Ainslie. As he continued I found myself standing at the back of the students who had moved closer to hear Duncan. I knew, for better or worse, that I was going to be on strike even if Duncan and I were the only two to do it. I had no choice, not with my girlfriend in the hospital and my best friend trying to do something about it, but as Duncan spoke

I got the feeling we wouldn't be alone, not the way Duncan was challenging them with stories of their own relatives.

"So do we go on strike or not?" he asked suddenly, before there could be time to reflect on the price of crossing Mother Saint Cross John.

The vote was nearly unanimous, not only from the student council but from the rest of the grade twelve class, except for two or three girls who slipped to the back of the class and Daniel who made for the door, saying, "I'm not staying here. You people are crazy."

Duncan stepped in front of him as Daniel reached for the door knob. "You don't have to strike, but you're damn well not leaving here to run to the convent like a scab and tell the nuns what's happening here. Anybody who's not going on strike, go to the back of the class," and Daniel shuffled away from Duncan's passion to join the girls. No one else left the group.

While we pulled down the bristol board with all the rules of grammar and rules of class behaviour written on them to use their blank backsides for our own posters, Duncan told the class representatives that they were to go back to their classes, and in fifteen minutes they were to stand up and tell the class there was a strike and lead them on to join the rest.

It didn't happen that way, of course. The grade twelve class walked out a quarter of an hour later and found themselves standing across the street from the school waiting for a mass of students to emerge from the buildings. Some of the student reps came out, but they weren't leading anyone, and it was clear that they had simply asked permission to leave the room to go to the toilet, but they walked across and joined us. And that's when Duncan got the whole class chanting, "New School or No School," the same words that were on the placards. The noise brought faces to the windows of the classrooms, teachers and students both. The teachers quickly disappeared, and I imagined them blocking the doorway, preventing any students from joining the strike. What the strike had going for it was that it was a warm afternoon when the last place anybody wanted to be was in school. Students began scurrying out the windows of the ground-floor classrooms, running across to join us, while others came from the upper classrooms, somehow escaping from the watchful eyes of their teachers, with the whole grade ten class getting loose of Mrs. Bruce and running out to enlist in Duncan's strike.

As we stood on strike, it became clear just how much thought Duncan had put into preparing for it, as though just waiting for something to happen like what happened to Mary Scotland. As students came across, Duncan warned them to stand in a line at the edge of the sidewalk, not to step back onto the convent property behind us, or the school property in front of us, because that would constitute trespassing, and we could be arrested. If we stayed on the sidewalk and didn't interfere with anybody walking along the sidewalk, it was a legal strike, Duncan explained.

That's where we were standing as Mother Saint Cross John turned her car into the driveway and found her students chanting and marching in front of the convent. It was hard to say who looked the most surprised, Mother Saint Cross John or her passenger, Mary Scotland, with her bandaged forehead. But as soon as the car stopped, the principal got out, slammed the door with a sound that silenced our courage and came toward us.

I can't remember if Duncan stepped to the front or if we all stepped back leaving him there alone, but it didn't take long for Mother Saint Cross John to spot the troublemaker and walk toward him with her face burning mad, Mary Scotland a step behind.

"What's going on here?"

"A strike," Duncan said.

Mother Saint Cross John's eyebrows arched at the news. She looked almost amused. "A strike," she said. "This is your idea, of course, Duncan?"

"The Student Council voted for it," Duncan said, "so it's legal."

"Nothing is legal on these school grounds unless I say it's legal."

"We aren't on school grounds," Duncan said, pointing to the sidewalk. "This is public property. We have a right to be here, and we have a right to strike."

The amusement left Mother Saint Cross John's face. "Get back to the classroom!" she ordered. Duncan didn't move. She grabbed him by the arm, and we could see her white-knuckled grip, but Duncan wrenched his arm loose and stepped back.

"We're on strike," he said. "Nobody's going back to the classroom," no fear visible in his face.

Mother Saint Cross John pushed her way past Duncan, wading into the middle of us, pushing us toward the school buildings, ordering us back to our classrooms. Most students made small motions in that direction when she was beside us, and retreated in small steps back toward the strike when she went past, not knowing whom to follow.

Mary Scotland worked her way next to me, asking for an explanation, and when she heard it took my arm and led us both back to Duncan. "New School or No School," she began to chant, linking her arms into mine and Duncan's, the three of us attracting attention away from Mother Saint Cross John's determined effort to physically throw every one of the strikers across the street and back into the classrooms. Duncan's presence loomed in front of the students again, and the fact that Mary Scotland was standing beside him with her bandaged head, two stitches under it, didn't hurt the strike's strength either. Students began moving away from Mother Saint Cross John's wrath to stand within Duncan's sphere of protection.

Seeing that she wasn't going to force us back to the classroom, the principal stormed across the street by herself. There were a few muted efforts to cheer the victory, but they were half-hearted because no one wanted to provoke Mother Saint Cross John's rage any more than had already been done. When she walked through the door into the building, though, the striking students began to chant "New School or No School! New School or No School!"

43

More than half the students had joined the strike during the walkout in the morning. At noon, Duncan made the strikers stay in place during the dinner break, refusing to give up any advantage we had gained by letting them go home to their mothers, and when classes had been dismissed by the noon bell almost all the students came across the street to stand with us. Duncan kept talking to people, mostly one by one as he walked up and down the line, because he didn't like talking to crowds. All the while Mother Saint Cross John watched him from her upstairs window, but he didn't glance up once. Mr. Steele and Mrs. Bruce and some of the other teachers came out on the step to watch us.

Duncan's face cracked open, and a faltering of his courage showed for a moment when he realized that Mrs. Bruce had come down off the steps and was walking toward us. We hadn't counted on that. Nobody wanted to say no to Mrs. Bruce, especially Duncan, and except for me, nobody knew how much more there was to the story of Mrs. Bruce and Duncan. Seeing her coming at us made Duncan and me instinctively pull closer together, knowing this was a perfect setting for her revenge.

"You've done some stupid things in your life, Duncan," Mrs. Bruce said, "but this isn't one of them. Do you mind if I stand here for awhile?"

"I thought we were dead," Duncan said to her out of the side of his mouth while I exhaled a couple of minutes of held breath, and the other students leaned and craned and tried to figure out what was going on.

"There was a time when I would have gladly killed you, but it's nobody's business but ours now. I met someone ... a doctor ... a woman ... a psychiatrist ... a head-shrinker, I guess you'd call her, and she's helped a lot. Her, and our baby. Now there's nothing left to be said about it, except I don't want my child to have to go to school in these buildings."

"You'll get fired for being here," Duncan said. "Do you belong to a good union?"

Mrs. Bruce laughed. "I'm afraid not, but that place is a firetrap, and I've been afraid to even think about it. I have to think about it now, so there's nothing else I can do but stand here. You're right about this, you know. I don't know why you're doing it, Duncan, but you're right and somebody had to have the courage to say it."

"I hope you still have your courage," I said, indicating with a nod of my head that Mother Saint Cross John had come down from her perch in the upstairs window and was now standing on the front step, evil-eyeing Mrs. Bruce until the teacher took a deep breath and left our ranks to stand on the ground in front of the steps with the principal staring down at her.

It was while Mrs. Bruce was crossing the street that Duncan had a chance to tell the people beside him, and I had a chance to tell the people beside me, that Mrs. Bruce was on our side. We watched in silence as Mother Saint Cross John and Mrs. Bruce talked, their words hissed below our hearing, but their gestures were clearly angry. Suddenly, Mrs. Bruce turned away and walked back toward us, and a huge cheer rose from the striking students as the school's favourite teacher, the one we had all had a crush on at one time or another, the guys at least, came back to stand with us, leaving Mother Saint Cross John sputtering like a spent firecracker on the school steps.

"What will you do next?" she asked Duncan.

"What do you mean?"

"You can't very well stand here for the rest of the school year."

"Why not?"

"Because it's fun for today and maybe even tomorrow because it's Friday, but your parents will send you back on Monday, especially if Mother Saint John gets Father Alex to speak from the pulpit against this."

Duncan was quiet for a moment. "What should we do?" he finally asked.

Mrs. Bruce passed him a nickel. "Go make a collect phone call," she said.

It took a moment, but Duncan seemed to finally understand, although Mary and I were baffled when he signaled for us to follow him. He led us out into the middle of the street and started toward Main, the students chanting behind him the slogan on their hurriedly made signs, "New School or No School! New School or No School!"

Our march over Main Street brought puzzled faces to store windows, cars slowed and drivers gawked as we walked along the center of the street. Duncan led his parade to Shean's only phone booth and stepped inside, Mary and I crowding halfway in, the rest of the students forming a curious circle around the booth, trying to guess what Duncan was up to.

Duncan dialed 'O' and told the operator he would like to make a collect phone call to the *Halifax Herald*. The operator was asking him questions like who it was from and who it was for, and Duncan gave his name and said it was for a reporter, he didn't have a name. It made me wish the telephone company hadn't come in last fall and changed our phones from ring-down to dial, closing Shean's telephone office. If Sally Fortune was still the operator, she wouldn't be giving Duncan the runaround like this. She would have connected him up, getting all the information on the strike from him, which would mean that when people called the operator to find out why all those kids were chanting on the street, Sally could tell them. Instead, the operator was in Sydney or someplace and didn't even introduce herself to Duncan, just asked questions.

Eventually, though, Duncan was connected with the switchboard of the *Herald*, and that was when placing the call got really difficult, the switchboard operator asked all the same questions:

Who was calling? Who was Duncan calling? Did he know who had the authority to accept the charges?

While Duncan was trying to explain, Mrs. Bruce passed me a ten dollar bill and told me to go get change in case the phone call had to be paid for. I ran the block to The Turk's where Nicole MacRory was behind the counter. Tony, having sobered up after a few weeks, had rehired his staff and reopened the restaurant.

"What's going on?" she asked, passing me a roll of quarters. She could see the milling around the phone booth from the front window of the restaurant.

"Duncan started a strike. He's calling the newspaper."

"So he finally got his strike. Congratulate him for me," she said sadly. They were no longer going together.

The quarters were unnecessary. In my absence, Duncan had talked his way into getting a reporter to accept the charges and was telling him about the strike. I guess the reporter must have asked him how many students were on strike because Duncan said, "This many," and held the phone outside the booth and everyone began chanting, "New School or No School!"

What made Duncan mad was when the reporter asked him who gave him the authority to call a strike. "I gave myself the authority!" Duncan hollered into the phone and the reporter pretty near hung up, except that Mrs. Bruce took the phone and explained that it was the Student Council that voted to strike and that the strike had the support of some of the staff. She told the reporter that the school buildings were firetraps. The reporter asked for the name of the school principal and the town clerk and told her that if he decided our strike had news value, the story would be in the next day's paper.

We cheered when Duncan told us we were going to be in the paper, but at the stroke of 3:30 when the dismissal bell rang, which we could hear all the way downtown, everybody put their signs down and went home, but not before Duncan told them that the strike would continue Friday morning.

"What was that about?" Calum asked when I got home. I knew he was asking because Duncan's parade went right down Culloden Street past Calum sitting in the sun porch, and I kept my eyes straight ahead, not giving Calum a chance to catch my eye and order me into the house.

"We're on strike," I said, explaining to him what had happened that morning, how the tongue-and-groove had fallen from the ceiling and split Mary's head open. When he heard about Mary, his interest in my story seemed to shift, as if I was no longer justifying to him, but simply explaining it.

"Is she alright?" he asked.

"She got a couple of stitches in her forehead, and she has a big headache now from all the hollering the students were doing. But this board just dropped out of the ceiling and hit her. She's lucky it didn't take her eye out," I said.

"It's an old building, and there have been thousands of coal fires in those stoves drying out the wood, and leaky roofs don't count as moisture. If the wood wasn't well-dried to begin with, then the tongue would eventually shrink out of the groove, the wood would shrink away from the headless nails holding them in place, and then something like that was inevitable. It's a good thing there wasn't a fire in a building that dry."

I told Calum about Duncan burning the wood.

"This was his idea, of course," Calum stated. There was no question in his mind. "Come have your supper."

"We're going to be still on strike tomorrow," I said across the kitchen table.

"Have you thought about the consequences?"

"Being expelled, you mean? They can't expel everybody."

"Only the ringleaders."

"Oh, I didn't have anything to do with organizing it. Duncan thought it up all by himself."

"When you marched past here, there were clearly three students who were leading this business, along with that woman."

"That's one of the teachers, Mrs. Bruce. She says the schools are firetraps, too."

"I suppose she thought about the consequences. I'm not telling you not to do what you have to do tomorrow, but you've applied for art college. So have lots of other students from all over the province. They will need to choose who gets in and who doesn't. A lot of those choices will depend on the recommendations of principals and teachers in the schools. Is it important enough to risk that?"

None of us could wait to get to Bartholomew's store at noon the next day. Most of the students remained out of school on Friday, although most had been warned by their parents not to go on strike again. Duncan, though, was on the sidewalk in front of the school at eight in the morning, having stopped by the house to wake me up and get me moving. I had been thinking a lot about what Calum had said, but face to face with Duncan, who needed someone to back him in convincing the students to stay out on strike, I knew I had no choice, although I was awfully uncomfortable in my role as his union enforcer.

"Be careful," Calum said as we left the house. "Both of you."

I assured him I would, and Duncan nodded to Calum that he had heard what he said.

Mary Scotland was already waiting for us, the bandage on her head reduced to a Band-Aid. While the three of us stood there, meeting the students who were trying to sneak into school early before we could make them stand with us, Mother Saint Cross John continued her vigil from the upper classroom window. Most of the students who stood there the previous day came back, especially when Duncan lied and told them the reporter from the *Herald* was coming to take our picture. Other students went to school, and a lot never showed up at all, not for school or the strike, home with a sudden flu, Duncan guessed. This time, though, there was no keeping us in place through the noon dinner break, not with our story going to be in the paper.

I raced to Bartholomew's to claim Calum's paper as I did every day, but never as joyfully as this time, and there it was on the front page of the second section: "Shean students strike for new school!" It was all the talk among the men who gathered there every day and I could hear them, some even arguing.

"It's things like this give the town a bad name," John Neil Kennedy growled.

"If we had the courage of these kids, we'd still be mining coal here," Sam MacPherson answered.

I walked home as fast as I could while reading and rereading the newspaper article. It was exciting and a good reason for us to stay out on strike.

"Look at this, Calum," I said loud enough to wake him where he lay on the couch.

"Calum!" I reached out and shook his foot lightly to prod him awake, then shook it harder. The salt and pepper cap fell back from his cloud of white hair but his lids didn't lift nor his hands un-join themselves from across his chest.

"Calum," I said, screaming the name in my head but it came out as barely a whisper while a great fear rose in me, and I backed out of the sun porch. I called Mrs. MacFarlane. I didn't know what else to do.

44

Mrs. MacFarlane knew exactly what to do. She arrived at the house within five minutes, hurrying out of Duncan's car which pulled away as soon as she was out of it, and Doctor Proud wasn't a minute behind her. They went into the sun porch while I waited inside, putting on the kettle for noon tea, going about the kitchen, clinging to our routine until Doctor Proud sadly told me a few moments later, "Calum's dead. Gone in his sleep. Very peaceful, it seems."

Mrs. MacFarlane put her arms around me and squeezed until I cried and she held me until I heard Mary Scotland and Duncan come into the house. When Mrs. MacFarlane released me, Mary put her arms around me for a minute and Duncan's hand more patted than slapped me on the back, but he wasn't risking a word of comfort. He just said he had to go. The strike was still on.

"Sometimes you think you know a person," Mrs. MacFarlane said when the door closed behind Duncan. "I didn't even think they were fond of each other, but when I told Duncan about Calum you'd think it was his own grandfather who died, he was so shaken."

Lost in the shock of Calum's death, I was only distantly aware of the house filling up, that people were preparing for Calum's wake, making it as easy for me as possible. By early evening the bib overalls and wine coat sweater, the salt-and-pepper cap and paint-splattered shoes had all been removed and hung up in the back porch, and Calum was washed and shaved and dressed in his best suit and laid out in a satin-lined, oak coffin. I grew conscious enough to insist that the Shean Hardware Store, which kept a rack of coffins in its warehouse, send an oak coffin, not a grey cloth-covered one, for Calum to lie in.

Sometime through that day, I changed into my own suit, one Calum had taken me to Feinstien's Clothing Store to buy. For my graduation, we thought. I sat in the parlour, Mary beside me most of the time, while a seemingly endless line of blurred faces poured condolences over me, an ointment unable to heal. Whenever I looked toward the coffin the fact of Calum's death felt like a crushed heart in my chest. At some point, Reverend Allan Smith brought me into Calum's study to discuss the arrangements, explaining that because he would not bury Calum on a Sunday, the funeral would have to be on Monday, making it a three-night wake.

After the minister left, Mrs. MacFarlane brought me into the kitchen and made me a large hot toddy and she, Mary Scotland and my confusion convinced me to try to sleep the night away.

"It's going to be a long wake," Mrs. MacFarlane said, "and you can't stay up all through it. John William and Hughie John will be here shortly, and they'll keep the vigil. I'll be here for a while longer myself and back first thing in the morning."

The toddy did the trick, and I dreamed Calum and I were in the workshop and Calum was planing the edge of a board that was gripped in the vice on his worktable. He was shaving the board with a hand plane, the pine curling off like whirls of scented smoke.

"These are for you," he said, adding the most recent board to a pile on the floor. I noticed they were planed to be narrower on one end than the other: wedge boards.

I woke just as it was getting light, drawing comfort from Piper's soft snore, and heard Mrs. MacFarlane come in. When John William and Hughie John left, she made me eat a big breakfast, sitting with me at the kitchen table. Reverend Smith had arranged for a real undertaker to come from Port Hawkesbury on Monday morning, Mrs. MacFarlane said, along with a hearse for Calum and a funeral car for the family members. There was even talk, she added, that the undertaker was thinking of opening a funeral parlour in Shean. I'm glad Calum died before that happened, I said, and she just nodded her head, saying it was the modern way of doing things, like televisions instead of radios and dial phones instead of telephone operators. Funeral homes instead of house wakes were inevitable.

We talked about what I was going to do after the funeral, Mrs. MacFarlane telling me I was welcome to come live with them, but I had already thought about it a bit and knew I would stay alone. There were just a few weeks of school left, and summer and then college, if I was accepted, which would take me away anyway. She reached across the table and squeezed my hand and it felt like a real mother's squeeze.

Some women from the Protestant church came in to help with the day, and although there were few morning mourners, the house started getting pretty busy. I left them and went to sit with Calum awhile, talking to him in my mind, sometimes cross with him because he died, sometimes crying because he died.

"Roddie, can you come into the kitchen," Mrs. MacFarlane asked, pulling me out of a lost time that had lasted a couple of hours or longer because the women had just left me alone in the parlour. Duncan and Farter were in the kitchen, dressed in their oldest clothes.

"Where's the keys to Calum's workshop?" Duncan asked. "We're going to dig the grave."

I took the keys and led them to the workshop, opening the padlocked door, catching the carpenter's scent of it as I stepped inside, standing there remembering while Duncan gathered the shovels we had used the summer before to plant the trees, and a pick.

"We'll stay after the funeral and bury him," Duncan said. "After all he taught me about planting things, who'd have thought it was him I'd be planting," he laughed. "You doing okay?"

I nodded and watched as they walked away, then sat on the cairn as the Oldsmobile pulled away, soaking up the sun, trying to let its warm light seep inside.

By the time I brought myself back into the house people were showing up, clusters of conversations going on everywhere, people breaking away from them to come to me with their condolences. It went on into the evening, a parade of people like the night before, and when I mentioned to Mrs. Bartholomew Fraser, who came to Calum's wake that night, about all the people who had come through the house that Saturday, she said, "No bingo! The wake, you know." There was nothing else to do in Shean but come look at Calum, I guess.

What was really surprising was how many people had something personal to say about Calum. I always thought with his path from the house to Bartholomew's and back, and the rest of his time in the sun porch, that he was all but invisible in Shean, but that wasn't the case at all. Some people said that he had built their house for them or built the house they were living in, and someone else told me about the time he had a shingling problem at his house, and Calum came down and solved it and wouldn't take anything for his help. Other people said he could make a rose grow out of a rock, the nice garden he had, had always had, even when the mines were still going strong and the ground around Shean seemed dead.

Calum's wake was turning into a party. More and more people were coming to pay their respects on Saturday night, but few of them seemed to be leaving, staying to visit with each other instead. It didn't get loud, but I couldn't help notice the murmur, shot through by sudden bursts of laughter, a voice rising in argument only to remember where it was and slide back down to a tense whisper, and I wondered what Calum would think of his crowded home.

When John William and Hughie John arrived for their second night's vigil, there were still lots of people in the house, so they slipped into Calum's study with a bottle to fortify themselves for the night, a bottle quickly sniffed out by some of the mourners. Mary and I were sitting with Calum in the parlour when Duncan appeared in the doorway signaling me, so we followed as his beckoning finger led us to the study.

"Sorry for your troubles there, Roddie," Angus John Rory said from his seat on Calum's couch, elbows on his knees, a glass in his hand. Johnny Rosin was sitting on one side of him and John Alex on the other, John William and Hughie John on the desk chairs.

"Yes," muttered the others, repeating the same words they had said when they visited Calum's coffin in the parlour.

"You don't come around the barn anymore," John Alex noted.

"Why should he? He's got the girlfriend now," Angus said, "prettier than yourself or your horses, too, isn't that right, Gillies?"

"Ask her yourself," Duncan said, and they noticed Mary Scotland for the first time, a blush of embarrassment reddening all their faces, ashamed of having spoken like that in mixed company.

"Sorry, Miss," they said in unison.

"It sounded like a compliment," Mary said.

"Oh, it was, Miss, it was," Angus John Rory assured her. "A compliment. It surely was, wasn't it?" he asked the others who nodded in agreement.

It was Duncan who rescued the three men from their humiliation by changing the subject.

"We were talking about your painting," he said, "the meaning behind it." Every head turned toward the wall above Calum's couch, and I could see ears growing less and less red. "I was trying to tell them about it, but I don't remember very much." Duncan was lying, of course, because he had caught onto the painting even faster than Calum when he first saw it. It was then that I told him about how when I was painting the oak leaf on his racing helmet, working out the details of a single leaf, I suddenly imagined a whole forest, the painting I eventually made for Calum. The painting wasn't as perfect as I envisioned, but it worked well enough so that when Duncan saw it he began reading the trees in it the way Calum had taught us, but I guess he thought the painting was my story to be telling.

"Do you know about the Gaelic alphabet?" I asked, knowing that all five men in the study, including John William and Hughie John, spoke the language.

"It's shorter than the English alphabet," Angus said, "easier to remember."

"Yes, there's some letters missing, I've heard, but nobody seems to know what happened to them," Johnny Rosin added.

"Correct me if I'm wrong, but I'm the only one here who can read and write in Gaelic," John William said, "and the missing letters are J, K, Q, V, W, X, Y and Z."

"If you can read Gaelic, then read this painting," Duncan interjected.

"Pardon?" John William said.

"The painting, read it. Tell them, Smelt."

And so I told the men in the study what Calum had once told Taurus and me in the sun porch what now seemed to be so many summers before.

"Well, well, well, think of that," John William said.

"Leave it to Calum to come up with something like that. Trees! Think of it," Angus John Rory added.

The others, glassy-eyed, muttered sounds of appreciation or understanding, or sounds to cover their lack of appreciation or understanding, depending on the effect the near-empty bottle on Calum's desk was having on them.

Sunday morning after both churches let out there was a huge wave of people who came to pay their respects to Calum, after which the house turned quiet as a church until I heard Mrs. MacFarlane welcoming people at the front door, directing them toward the parlour. I hurried from the kitchen table to be in the parlour when they offered their regrets and was standing solemnly beside the coffin when they entered, the man resting his hand lightly on the arm of a woman in her twenties, a frailer version of Calum. I knew immediately, either from a long ago memory or family similarity, that it was Archie Gillies, Calum's cousin, and mine.

"We heard on the radio," he said as our hands grasped, and I realized that it had never occurred to me to notify the cousin Calum had visited not a year earlier.

"I'm sorry," I said. "I should have ... I never...."

My efforts at apology were lost as Archie's eyes left mine and rested on Calum. He stood for a long, long time staring at my grandfather's remains until the woman finally eased him away to sit for a while. When Archie was seated, she asked me if she could get a cup of tea for her grandfather. I led her to the kitchen where I listened while she and Mrs. MacFarlane talked. Calum's death announcement had been on CJCB radio on Saturday afternoon, she said, and her grandfather, who did not inherit Calum's hearing problems, heard it. After services in St. Columba's Church in Marion Bridge this morning, she said, she drove him over.

"You'll be staying for the funeral, of course," Mrs. MacFarlane said.

"Is there a hotel...?" she started to ask.

"Stay here," I volunteered, offering the guest room I could never remember anybody ever staying in, yet Calum kept it as ready as if he was expecting someone every night. One of them could sleep there, and one of them could sleep in my room. I wasn't ready to give Calum's room to anyone, but I could sleep on the study couch or out in the sun porch.

"You're Roddie, right?" she said, both of us realizing that there had been no introductions. "I'm Bonnie MacRae. We're cousins, I suppose. Second? Third? I was never very good at figuring those things out."

"Me neither. This is Mrs. MacFarlane. She's ... she's my godmother," I said, surprising Mrs. MacFarlane, but it just seemed a lot easier than trying to explain why she was looking after everything. Bonnie MacRae took a cup of tea, placed a biscuit and slice of cheese on the saucer and carried it in to her grandfather.

"I'm glad. You'll have some family with you tomorrow," Mrs. MacFarlane said. "That always helps."

45

I don't remember much about Calum's funeral. On Sunday, Duncan, Mary and I stayed up all night, sitting in the sun porch for most of it, talking a little about death and the strike and the end of school, but mostly staying quiet. Except for the reason we were there, it would have been a perfect night to remember, three friends at the end of high school looking into our future. We slept sitting up with my grandmother's quilt, the one Calum had finished, stretched across us. Morning came far too soon with its hearse, its slow motion pace, Mary and me following in the funeral car along with Archie and Bonnie. Then the church, the minister, the graveyard, and the reception back at the house.

It was the reverse of the day Calum died, when the house had filled up so fast. A crowd of people came back from the cemetery, had tea, talked to each other, wished me well and vanished in a few moments, leaving just Mrs. MacFarlane and Mary and my cousins who were upstairs preparing for their trip back to the other side of the island.

Mrs. MacFarlane was the one who suggested that maybe I should go up and carry Cousin Archie's suitcase down for him. He was sitting on my bed when I got to the door, staring at something cupped in both hands.

"Is this yours?" he asked, lifting the carved wooden horse to show me.

"Yes. Calum made it for me."

Archie looked puzzled. "Did he tell you that?"

"No, but he gave it to me when I was little," I answered.

Archie remained quiet for a little while. "This horse was carved for Calum by a man we styled Donald Angus the Dummy," he said, and I realized what I should have known since autumn when Calum told Mary and me about Donald Angus the Dummy. The wooden horse that Calum had given me as a child was worn far beyond the few years I played with it. It had probably been my father's before it became mine.

"It was probably the only toy Calum ever owned," Archie said, rubbing his hand over the horse like it was a lamp that would release a genie. The comment shocked me.

"Were they poor?"

"Oh no," Archie said, "but Calum's father was what I suppose you would call severe, a man strict in his observation of the faith. They were brothers, Calum's father and mine, and we lived on the next farm. My father's faith was quite strong, as well, but not nearly as severe. There were hot summer Sundays when we spent two or three hours in church listening to the minister, and would go home to dinner and be expected to spend the afternoon in reading and reflecting on the Lord's words and works. Often my father would relent and set us free to run off to the river for a swim. I can still remember passing Calum's house and seeing his father's shape in the window, head bent over his Bible reading from it while the whole family sat and listened, chapter and verse, through the rest of the day.

"Sometimes, too, if there was an afternoon service they would return to the church. I would always wave on my way to the river because I knew where Calum sat in the room. He sat facing the window. 'I saw you,' he would say to me.

"No, no, they weren't poor, and it wasn't that Calum's father was mean. There was a lot of respect between the two of them, even when Calum was just a tot, but there was no tolerance for nonsense or papists in his father. That's why I remember this horse," he said, passing it to me, beginning to rise from the edge of the bed.

"People here say that Calum's family never forgave him for marrying my grandmother," I said.

Archie's effort to rise left him and he sagged back onto the bed. "Calum's father had absolute convictions, and mixing with papists was mixing with the Devil himself, and when Calum gave his children to them, the Catholics, I mean, that was the last straw. His mother, of course, was a mother. She used to send him messages through me. When she died, I wired Calum, and he came over to the funeral. His father never spoke one word to him, not one word, and, of course, Calum was just as stubborn."

"What was his name?" I asked. "Calum's father, my great-grandfather, what was his name?"

"Roderick," Archie said. "Roderick Gillies."

"Are you ready, Grandpa?" Bonnie asked from behind me, standing in the doorway with her own travel bag. Archie nodded his head and reached out his hand for me to help him stand, and then I took his suitcase and followed him out of the room.

"I'm glad I met you," Bonnie said from behind the wheel of her car before they pulled away. "Now that we know each other maybe we'll stay in touch, being third or fourth cousins or whatever," she added with a laugh, and I watched them pull away down Culloden Street and turn onto Main.

The sun porch had never been emptier than it was when I glanced in on my way back into the house, expecting against all reason to see Calum lying there just as I found him three days earlier with his cap and glasses on, hands crossed on his chest, thumbs slowly twirling. What diverted me away from a sudden rush of tears was the realization that Calum's plants were wilting in that hothouse of windows that was the sun porch. They had sat through all the waterless days of the wake, and their condition drew my attention to the yard itself, the flower garden with its crop of early blooms and promising buds and the inch-high growth of the vegetable garden all slightly sagging, as if their spirit had left them. They know, I thought. They know Calum is gone.

Mrs. MacFarlane was still in the kitchen cleaning up the last traces of the funeral which had already been cleaned up by the women from Calum's church.

"I'm going to have to leave, Roddie," she told me. "There's a town meeting tonight over the strike at the school. That's where Duncan went after he finished burying your grandfather, back to the school, but Mother Saint John of the Cross wouldn't let him in. He's been expelled. Anyway, the town council wants to have a public meeting to talk about the strike, and I need to be there since Duncan's father isn't here."

I could tell Mrs. MacFarlane was reluctant to leave because she knew that when she left I would be alone in the house forever.

"You go ahead," I said, picking up Calum's watering can. "I have to water Calum's plants and then I have to hose down the garden before everything around here dies." She smiled at my dark joke, hugged me and left.

I didn't go to the town meeting in the parish hall, but Mary Scotland and Duncan came right to my house after the meeting to tell me what had happened. Just about everybody in town turned out, something that usually takes a fire or a drowning. The nuns owned the school, but the town paid the teachers, including the nuns, so nobody knew who was in charge; it was just the way it had always been in Shean. Nobody ever questioned it until the strike, and there was a lot more to it than Duncan being expelled. Mrs. Bruce had been fired.

The mayor, Innis MacInnis, along with the town's councillors all thought it might be going too far, Mother Saint Cross John firing Mrs. Bruce, that is. They didn't spend a word on Duncan being expelled except to say that was the school's problem. The parents, though, were more worried about fires than somebody being fired, something almost nobody ever worried about before, but by the time the students brought home the story of Duncan burning the wood, the fire in the potbelly stove might have been started by that cow in Chicago. Parents were saying they wouldn't send their children into that firetrap.

The councillors weren't so sure that a new school could be ordered up just like that, so parents wanted Innis MacInnis to guarantee their children wouldn't be roasted alive, which made Innis MacInnis wish aloud that he weren't the mayor. Just about everybody in Shean shopped for their hardware in his store. Innis MacInnis had been the mayor for the last eleven years because he couldn't quit. Nobody else in Shean would take the job. He was stuck with it.

As gracefully as he could, the mayor steered the conversation away from fires and grieving parents and over to the subject of Mrs. Bruce. Who had the right to fire her, he asked the other councillors, the town or the convent? The councillors weren't interested in tangling with the nuns any more than the mayor wanted to talk about the school burning down.

It was Mrs. MacFarlane who stood up and said it was a crime for anybody to fire Mrs. Bruce. That teacher, she said, had more courage than anyone in the hall. "She says our children are in danger, and she believes that enough to lose her job over it," Mrs. MacFarlane said. "That's the kind of teacher we should be wanting to teach our children, not firing her."

Some other parents began to look at it from that angle, thinking maybe it wasn't such a good idea not to have Mrs. Bruce in the school looking out for their kids instead of being fired for doing just that. Once the mayor and councillors saw the way the wind was blowing they turned their backs to it and led the way.

Mrs. Bruce is not going to be fired, they said, fists hitting the table like hands stamping a seal on an oath written in blood. There was no way Mother Saint John of the Cross was going to fire the teacher, they said, and began forming a strategy for delivering that news to the convent. The councillors thought the mayor had an obligation, and the mayor thought there should be a committee formed.

That issue resolved, the attention of the crowd wandered back to the still-burning schoolhouse.

It's time for a new school, people shouted, and it's the town council's job to get it.

Innis MacInnis didn't disagree with the responsibilities of his office, but Shean would have a better chance of getting a new school if only there was an election, he said. That's when the hall broke into Liberals and Tories, and Innis MacInnis adjourned the meeting before anybody could throw a punch.

As far as Mary and Duncan and everybody else at the meeting knew, Mrs. Bruce was getting her job back, and there may or may not be a new school built in Shean.

"It doesn't matter to me if they get a new school since the only way Mother Saint Cross John would let me back into the old one is if it was on fire," Duncan said. "But they can't stop me from writing provincials."

Nothing happened to Mary or me or anyone else who was on strike, just Duncan. He would be allowed to write his provincial exams with us because Mother Saint Cross John couldn't stop him, but he couldn't graduate with us. He really didn't give a damn about that.

"I'm going to come here every day to study," he told me, brushing his hands across the dining room table as if he was clearing a place to set his books down.

While I would be in school Duncan would be sitting in my house studying for provincials and eating all my food. I was trying to think of good places to hide food when Mary said, "We can tutor you after school if you want. Sometimes the teacher is better at explaining things than the instructions in the book are." It was settled. My vote wasn't required.

Duncan drove Mary home, and as soon as they left I turned out all the lights before I had time to think about the empty house, went upstairs to my room and fell into an exhausted sleep.

46

There was nothing left to do now but leave.

The summer had slipped past in a blur of parties and races and waiting for the results of our provincial exams to turn up in post office boxes. When they did, I let out a whoop because my acceptance at the art college was conditional on passing, and I had passed with plenty to spare. Thanks to Mary Scotland's plan to tutor Duncan, the three of us had sat every day after school around my dining room table studying, but neither Mary nor I did as well as Duncan. No one in the class did.

Duncan opened his marks in the post office, not waiting like everybody else to get somewhere safe in case tears became involved. He glanced at them, passed them to me, and while I tried to absorb the numbers on the page, Duncan went to the counter and bought a stamped envelope from Lick 'n Stick, the postmaster, took his provincial results, stuck them inside, addressed the envelope to Mother Saint John of the Cross, Holy Family Convent, Shean, dropped it in the slot, turned and gave me his nod and wink and waited for me to open mine. He showed a lot more excitement over my marks than his own because, he said, "Your marks are going to take you somewhere." Duncan wasn't interested in one more day of school.

The summer had also been busy for other reasons.

Calum's death didn't end with his burial, I discovered. There was a lawyer and a banker and all sorts of government forms to fill out, not to mention selling the house.

Calum's will had left the couple of thousand dollars in his bank account to me as well as the house. I was going to be away three or four years, maybe coming home in the summers, maybe not. A couple of thousand dollars would look after me for one year, but then I would need to pay the rest of my way so it might be easier to find work in Halifax for the summers than in Shean.

I didn't know what I wanted to do until Mrs. MacFarlane came to visit me, knocking on the front door like she was a stranger, standing there until I invited her in. She didn't even help me make tea. She just sat at the kitchen table and fidgeted until the cup was in front of her, along with a plate of her own cookies.

"What are you planning to do with the house?" she asked at last, and I shrugged. I didn't know. Keeping it empty would just let it rot and fall apart like the house at Taurus's farm and so many others around Shean. Selling it seemed like a betrayal to Calum because, aside from the money, it was all of him that I had left.

"If you decide to sell it, Roddie, we would like to make you an offer."

It was almost as if Calum's ghost was standing behind me, I so clearly heard his words, the words he said in answer to my concern that we couldn't afford to send me to college. "We'll manage," he had said, and I heard him say those words again so clearly the hair stood up on the back of my neck and a shiver tingled down my spine, and I knew that this was how we would "manage."

When I told Mrs. MacFarlane I would sell her the house, she said a price that I knew, from what the lawyer told me and what the banker told me, was twice as much as they said I could expect to get if I sold it. It was enough, I knew, to carry me through my years at college. I told her yes, and Mrs. MacFarlane released a sigh that told me she must have been holding her breath ever since she came through the door, and she turned back into her usual self.

When Mr. MacFarlane came home, this time in August for two months, we visited lawyers, and I signed the house over, and they gave me a check and registered the deed in their own names but didn't come near the house again, leaving me in it until it was time to leave for Halifax.

When I was ready to go, I walked upstairs into Calum's room, going through the drawers and closets to make sure I didn't miss something I wanted to take with me. I went into my own room where Calum's Gladstone lay open on the bed, stuffed with my clothes and other belongings. I decided I would take only what could fit in it, that I would travel light if a suitcase capable of holding a hundred pounds of clothes is travelling light. I took the wooden horse down from the shelf, rubbing it the way Archie had the day of Calum's funeral. It had been Calum's toy and presumably my father's before it became mine. I wrapped it in a woolen sweater and placed it in the Gladstone. Some day it would be my son's toy, maybe, the wooden horse and the story of Donald Angus the Dummy, and of Calum, and of his father, too, and of my father, whom I never knew but worshipped in a way that had frightened Calum enough not to teach me the things he most wanted me to know.

I closed the suitcase, hefted it off the bed, picked up my easel, folded now into a case I could carry by the handle, carried them downstairs and set them on the front step, then went back into the house to explore the downstairs one last time.

The pictures were off the wall in the parlour. Mrs. MacFarlane told me she would be happy to store anything I wanted to keep but couldn't take with me, so into a streamer trunk I packed the pictures and Calum's Gaelic books, the folder filled with Taurus's poems and my father's bagpipes along with some other things I might want someday, and stored them in the workshop.

In the study, the wall above Calum's couch was bare. My painting, *Cumha nam Méinneadairean*, was gone.

A day earlier, after Mary's father picked her up at my house to drive her to Antigonish for university, I had lifted the painting off the wall, wrapped it in a blanket and carried it across town, cutting through the Co-op parking lot to make my trip with the heavily framed painting a little shorter. A truck honked its horn behind me, and I tried to step out of its way, but it pulled up beside me.

"Hello, there." It was Tom MacPhee.

"Where's the team?" I asked.

"I put them out to pasture. I'll still use them in the woods a bit, but it's time to get with the times," he said, sweeping his hand around the parking lot where there was lots of horsepower but no horses. "Where are you going?"

"Taurus's house."

"Hop in. I'm going right past."

My aching arms were glad for the ride. I could have asked Duncan, but I wanted to see Taurus alone. On our way, I told Tom about leaving the next morning.

"College, eh? You're old man'd be proud, I'll tell you that."

Mrs. MacLeod invited me into her hot kitchen that smelled of fresh bread and old people. Taurus was on a rocking chair beside the stove.

"Hello, Taurus," I said. "I brought you something," holding the painting in front of me. He stared at it but there was no recognition in his red-rimmed eyes.

"Bheil cuimhn 'agad air Ruairidh Mac'ill Ìosa, ogha Chaluim?" Mrs. MacLeod said. I understood enough Gaelic to know she was trying to prod him into remembering me. Nothing. "His English is gone," she said. "He only has the Gaelic now. That was his first language, you know, but he doesn't remember or hang on to much that I say to him in that, either, I'm afraid. It's terrible watching him shrink away inside and out, and me not being able to do anything about it. You remember him, don't you, from before?" I nodded. "Stay while I make tea."

As she fussed with the tea, a cup surrounded by buttered biscuits, cheese, molasses cookies and war cake, I stared at Taurus staring at the stove top, puffing his cigarette, flicking ashes into the coal scuttle. Mrs. MacLeod set his tea beside him, and he sipped while I answered Mrs. MacLeod's questions about school, the house, college, and then I asked her for a hammer and nail, located a stud across from what was obviously Taurus's daily perch, and hung the painting, hoping....

"*Beannachd leibh,* Taurus," I said, offering him the Gaelic goodbye. I gave my empty cup back to Mrs. MacLeod, and taking my leave, returned home.

My walk through the downstairs rooms took me into the back porch where my chest tightened to see Calum's salt-and-pepper cap, wine coat sweater and bib overalls hanging on a single hook, the paint-splattered shoes sitting under them. Pushing open the back screen door I stepped out beside the raspberries that had been ravaged by the summer birds and walked the path between them to where our shack stood, barely visible and long forgotten. I put my hand on the corner and shoved, but the shack stood as sturdy as the day Duncan and I drove the wedge boards into it. The gardens hadn't prospered as well as other years, but once Mrs. MacFarlane got her hands on them, I had a feeling they would be bursting with the same colours they were used to flying.

I walked across the yard to the front of the house, stopping by the cairn. I put my hand on top of it and suddenly recalled Calum telling me about my father asking him for a set of bagpipes. He was only this high, Calum had said, his hand sweeping a height that seemed now to be exactly the height of the cairn, the tiny height my father had been when he first marched back and forth across the lawn practising his tunes.

Not wanting to go back inside again, I walked into the sun porch to sit and wait for Duncan, pulling Calum's pocket watch from my own pocket and checking the time. There was less than a half hour before the train left when the Oldsmobile finally pulled up in front of the house. I stood up, stroking Piper goodbye lightly, barely disturbing her sleep in the heat of the sunlit ledge. The MacFarlanes promised to look after her.

"Let's just go," I said, picking up Calum's suitcase and the easel. Putting them in the trunk, we drove away, but not directly to the station, not with Duncan at the wheel, regardless of how little time I had. Instead, he steered over Main Street, and I remembered something, asking him to stop in front of Bartholomew's store. Inside, I asked Sarah Campbell to cancel my daily *Herald*. I wouldn't be coming at noon any more as I had all summer and every day since Bartholomew died. She wished me luck, telling me to get famous so my painting of the store would be worth something someday.

Then Duncan drove me up to the construction site where just a week earlier two bulldozers had begun tearing up the blueberry barrens, and carpenters were working on wooden forms to hold the cement that would be poured for the foundation of the new school. Duncan never said a word, just drove around the dump-truck-rutted road that circled the site and back onto the street and took me to the station.

We sat in the car watching the train on the turntable being rotated so that it was pointing back to the Canso Causeway and the tracks that would take me off Cape Breton Island for the first time.

"We'll be moving in today," Duncan said to break the awkward silence. "The old man and the old lady are taking Calum's room, and the old lady said your room's yours if you come for Christmas or anything like that, so I get the guest room.

"Anyway, when the old man heads back up northern Ontario in a couple of weeks, I'm going with him. Good money in the mines. I'll buy myself a horse next summer, start my own stable."

The train pulled up to the station. Duncan got out and carried my bag and easel onto the platform while I bought my ticket.

"Let's promise not to write each other," he said as I lifted the Gladstone and myself up the train steps, afraid to try to utter a word of goodbye, nodding it instead as I took the easel from him, and walked into the train's one passenger car, sandwiched between freight cars, and took the same seat Calum had sat in a year earlier when he went over Sydney way. I busied myself as the train began to move, finding distractions to keep me from turning to the window where I was aware that Duncan was still standing, receding as the engine slowly gathered its speed, and then the platform was gone.

A half mile later, I had settled back with resignation as the train reached the crossing on the highway leading into Shean, where Duncan was now standing on the hood of the Oldsmobile daring me not to wave goodbye through the window. I couldn't hear his laugh, and he couldn't hear mine, but we knew. The steeple of St. John's Church made me sit up sharply, suddenly reminded that the Protestant graveyard lay along the train's route. My eyes quickly found the side-by-side gravestones of Bartholomew Fraser and Calum Gillies, friends forever. I had noticed once that from Taurus's pasture I could see this church and cemetery, and I glanced away from the passing headstones, out the opposite window to the highlands, and knew that the two of them now gazed at a field where they once dreamed a forest. Whatever trees had been too deeply rooted to be torn up by a man's rage now waved in the September breeze like ragged flags over a lost battlefield. I glanced back at the graves, saying, "*Beannachd leibh*, Bartholomew, *beannachd leibh*, Calum," and began to sing "*Cumha nam Méinneadairean*," Taurus's lament for the lost miners of Shean. From among the scattered passengers a few voices rose to join mine.

THE END

Frank Macdonald, long-time and award-winning columnist and publisher of *The Inverness Oran*, is an accomplished writer of short stories, drama, poetry and songs. His humorous, often satirical, columns have twice been anthologized: *How to Cook Your Cat* in 2003, and *Assuming I'm Right in 1990*, which also became a stage production that has toured Nova Scotia and elsewhere in Canada. His play *Her Wake* won Best Canadian Play at the Liverpool International Theatre Festival in 2010 and, also in 2010, Frank authored *T.R.'s Adventure at Angus the Wheeler's*, a children's book, illustrated by Virginia McCoy.

He lives in Inverness, Cape Breton. *A Forest for Calum* was his first novel. His second novel, *A Possible Madness* is published by CBU Press (2011).

Praise for *A Forest for Calum*

Destined to become "a Canadian classic."

The Globe and Mail

Shortlisted for the 2006 Dartmouth Book Award
Long-listed for the 2007 International IMPAC
Dublin Literary Award
The largest and most international prize of its kind.

"*A Forest for Calum* is that rare thing—a funny, poignant book that manages to authentically replicate a time and a place in a way that any reader, regardless of their experience, can appreciate...."

Halifax Sunday Herald

"...enthralling and inspiring ... a delight and a wonder from start to finish."
"Macdonald brings a grace and a hard-edged sensitivity ... with such aplomb, such care and skill ..."

The Globe and Mail

At the centre of the narrative is literary device so stunningly imaginative and jaw-droppingly beautiful that it is unique in all of Canadian—and even perhaps most English-Language—literature."

Ron Foley MacDonald